LOOKING FOR HER

CAROLYN MARIE SOUAID

LOOKING FOR HER

Baraka
Books
Montréal

ISBN 978-1-77186-348-3 pbk; 978-1-77186-367-4 epub; 978-1-77186-368-1 pdf

Cover by Gianni Caccia
Cover illustration by Kai McCall
Book Design by Folio infographie
Editing: Blossom Thom, Elise Moser
Proofreading: Anne Marie Marko

Legal Deposit, 4th quarter 2024
Bibliothèque et Archives nationales du Québec
Library and Archives Canada

Published by Baraka Books of Montreal
Printed and bound in Quebec

TRADE DISTRIBUTION & RETURNS

Canada
UTP Distribution: UTPdistribution.com

United States
Independent Publishers Group: IPGbook.com

We acknowledge the support from the Société de développement des entreprises culturelles (SODEC) and the Government of Quebec tax credit for book publishing administered by SODEC.

Société de développement des entreprises culturelles Québec

Funded by the Government of Canada
Financé par le gouvernement du Canada | Canada

for Marcel and Pauline Souaid
my first teachers;

and for Robert Wade West
(1925–2021)

CONTENTS

Give her fish, and you feed her for a day.

Teach her to fish, and you feed her for a lifetime.

Whose fish, *which* fish? Why *fish*?

PART I

October 2019

Liam was brewing coffee when Isabel arrived.

"I got here as fast as I could." She unzipped her coat.

"You're still in your PJs?" Cate said.

"What do you expect? You call me in the middle of the night, you tell me Nuna's missing." Isabel peeled a wet leaf off the sole of her shoe. "Any idea where she went?"

Cate shook her head.

Isabel followed her to the kitchen, to her usual chair, while Liam poured them coffee. "Well, one thing's sure. She's certainly good at upsiding the apple cart."

"Upsetting," Cate corrected.

"What?"

"*Upsetting* the apple cart." She went to get the sugar bowl.

"Whatever." Isabel shrugged off her coat, unbothered about being around Liam in pyjamas. "Did she take her stuff?"

"Most of it."

"How about that notebook she's always writing in? Maybe there's a clue there."

"She didn't take it. Or any of the clothes we bought her."

Isabel stirred in two heaping teaspoonfuls of sugar, coffee sloshing over the edge of her cup.

Liam glared. He threw her a paper towel.

Cate filled her in on the details, that it had already been a couple of days, that, at first, they didn't think anything of it. "We figured she was out with what's-her-name, you know the one, who moved down here for work. The one from her village."

"Vanita." Isabel mopped her spill.

"Right. She took her knapsack, so we decided they were probably having a sleepover, maybe doing a little shopping first, getting their hair and nails done. I tried her number a few times, but nothing."

"What about her check-in calls?"

Cate sighed. "We let them slide, unfortunately. We stopped being consistent about it."

"So, why the sudden worry?"

Liam cleared his throat. "A dream."

"What dream?"

He pointed to Cate. "She woke me out of a deep sleep in a panic. Said she had a bad feeling."

Cate rarely attached much significance to her dreams. They were all just a jumble of incongruous images. But this one spooked her.

"What dream?" Isabel repeated.

Cate described everything she remembered. The packed, brightly lit arena, the electricity of the pulsing, cheering fans. Nuna facing off for the Pittsburgh Penguins.

"Boy, wouldn't that be something." Isabel slurped her coffee.

"During the pre-game skate, Nuna looks up into the crowd and sees me. She points at Sidney Crosby and smiles a big, open smile and I shoot her a thumbs-up." Cate's face clouded over. "Then the scene changes and she's in a park. Cabot Square, I think. There's a ghostly ring around the moon. She's in a grungy sweater and jeans, sitting on the steps of the marble statue. Knees hugged into her chest. A man in a slick suit and polished shoes is talking to her, harassing her, and she's shaking her head, saying, *No, no, get the fuck out*, but he won't leave her alone."

Isabel went to get the milk from the fridge. "Did you try calling Vanita?"

"We don't have her number."

"Shit, Cate. Why did you wait this long? I mean, after the last time."

"I know, I know." She bit her lip.

Liam glanced at the time. "Listen, guys, none of this is your fault."

"But we definitely need to find her," Isabel said.

Cate nodded. She stared at her fingernails, trying not to think of Nuna in a ditch somewhere, bleeding—or dead. "What if . . . ?"

"Are you afraid someone took her?"

"Or that mess of a boyfriend came back."

Isabel fiddled with the milk carton. "Hasn't she learned to handle things better now?"

Cate stared blankly at her.

"Well, ladies, if you're interested in my two cents, I think you're both overreacting." Liam rinsed his cup and put it in the dishwasher. "She's probably with Vanita smoking cigarettes and bingeing on *Game of Thrones*." He yawned into his fist. "But go look for her if it'll put your minds at rest."

PART II

Seven Months Earlier

Cate put her book down to examine her hand. It was clumsily bandaged. The blood had seeped through, but according to the reception desk her wound wasn't a priority. The wait could be well into the night. At least a dozen patients were ahead of her, some in wheelchairs, others cross-legged on the floor staring into space. And the line wasn't getting any shorter. Cate counted herself lucky to even have a seat. Except—the man beside her reeked of fish. It was his coat. Each time he shifted in his chair, she caught a whiff.

Her eyes wandered to the other patients. The woman across from her had dozed off with a whodunit in her lap. A longhaired man clutching a motorcycle helmet was gouging into his foam cup with a thumbnail, oblivious to the squeaks that were grating on Cate's nerves. Another ambulance wailed in.

Drowsy from the Tylenol they had given her, she tried to find a comfortable position. She closed her book over a pencil to mark her page, hardly able to keep her eyes open. The activity around her dissipated.

She woke to a flurry of excitement, visible through the open slats of the triage blinds. People were scurrying about. She thought it strange that the privacy blinds were open but didn't think much more about it. There were two paramedics, one of them a young female kibbitzing with the nurse, the other a clone of Al Pacino in *Dog Day Afternoon*. It looked more like a party than an emergency. Al Pacino was laughing and typing notes onto a tablet.

Cate went back to her book but couldn't concentrate. A middle-aged woman walked in with dark glasses and a fresh cut on her cheek. She took a number and stood by the elevators, an alligator-skin purse tucked under her arm. Cate wondered if she was one of those wives who made up stories about accidentally walking into a door. She checked her ticket again. With ten people still ahead of her, Cate drifted into a light sleep.

The loudspeaker calling nurses to a Code Blue jerked her awake. She sat upright. The man with the smelly coat was gone.

"No worries, it's all cool."

Cate turned to look at the person talking to her. She looked familiar. "I beg your pardon?"

The woman was leafing through *People* magazine. "It's on another floor…the Code Blue."

"Oh." Cate remembered. It was the perky paramedic she had seen earlier through the triage blinds. She had changed out of her uniform into a pair of faded jeans ripped at the knee, a hoodie, and chunky Doc Martens with yellow stitching around the sole. "Oh, it's you."

The woman looked up. "Do I know you?"

"I saw you in triage earlier. You were joking with the nurse. It caught my attention because you don't hear a lot of laughter in the ER."

"No, not usually." Her tight jeans revealed legs that were both slim and muscular. She looked as though she would be as comfortable changing a tire as sipping a margarita in a slinky cocktail dress.

"You're a paramedic, right?"

"Um, yeah." She went back to her magazine.

Cate held up her bandaged hand as though it might interest her. "Do you think I'll need stitches?"

She didn't bite.

"I mean, what's your expert opinion?"

"Huh?" She glanced over. "I don't know, possibly."

Cate nattered on, stoking the conversation, not because she was particularly interested in the woman but more as a way of passing time.

The woman closed the magazine and tossed it back onto the table. She met Cate's gaze.

Her smooth, flawless skin surprised Cate. She expected worry lines and crow's feet on the faces of medical practitioners. She couldn't remember a time when her own skin was that radiant. "So, was it a stupid accident like mine that brought your patient into the ER?"

"Pretty much. It wasn't the first time, though."

"Sounds like you know her."

She eyed Cate suspiciously. "Only as a patient."

"I see."

"A good girl who makes terrible choices."

Cate raised a brow at what seemed to be the crossing of a line. Yes, she was pumping her, but there wasn't any obligation to answer, it was just pleasantries. Cate checked her number against the monitor again. It was still gridlock. "Not to be a stickler, but is it okay for you to be divulging this kind of thing? Obviously, I don't have to tell you, that's someone's private information."

"No, you don't…and, seriously?" The paramedic glowered.

"I'm sorry." Cate pinched her thumb and finger together and brushed them across her lips to indicate the zipping of her mouth shut. "Forget I said anything."

"It's a free country. Anyway, I never mentioned anything uber-specific."

Her reaction surprised Cate. Then it occurred to her. The woman was young. Twenty-six, twenty-seven, tops. Barely older than some of her own students. Young people these days didn't live by the same protocols, they spoke their minds, they had no filters.

Slouched in her chair, the paramedic began scrolling through her messages.

Clearly, they were worlds apart. Her clothes, the casual way she sat, the way she spoke—with little forethought. They definitely didn't read the same books (if, in fact, she read at all). "To your point, though, I agree. You didn't disclose anything that could get you into trouble."

"Nope." She went on scrolling without looking up. Her left ear was ringed and studded all the way up to the cartilage.

A grizzled man talking to himself shuffled past, hospital gown sliding off his shoulder, buttocks exposed.

Cate looked away.

The paramedic called out. "Hey, buddy, your garage door is open!"

Cate chuckled. She opened her book but found herself reading the same line over and over. She slapped it shut. "The thing is..."

"Yes?" She slid the phone into the pouch of her hoodie.

"The reason I mentioned it—why I brought it up—is because you said you know her as a patient, but you seem to know a lot about her. Her choices, for example. It's touchy when you know too many details."

Isabel shrugged it off.

"A teacher, for instance, shouldn't know too much about a student, it's just not...proper. It could be misconstrued."

"But, as you already know, I'm not a teacher." She relaxed her tone, pointing to Cate's hand. "What happened, anyway?"

Cate sighed. "I was making dinner. And yes, a knife was involved." She made a slicing gesture with her good hand. "Turns out there's a name for it. 'Avocado hand.' I saw it on Facebook."

"Hmm. The old slip of the wrist."

Cate muffled a laugh.

"What? What's funny?"

"The correct expression is a *slap* on the wrist or a slip of the *tongue*. I don't think you meant either, but I appreciate the sentiment."

"Are you a teacher or something?"

Cate nodded. "Professor."

"Wait, you teach?" She perked up. "Where?"

"McGill. But I'm on sabbatical this year."

She pointed to the book on Cate's lap. "What's that you have there? Looks pretty old."

"*Lyrics of Earth.* It's by Archibald Lampman, a Canadian poet."

There was a subtle shift in energy, the woman fiddling with her hair, trying to steer the conversation toward something more meaningful than chit-chat.

It was making Cate nervous. No random stranger ever expressed any excitement about her work. Usually, their eyes glazed over until Cate changed the subject. "What is it? You obviously have something on your mind."

"Well, it just occurred to me." Her eyes widened. "Do you ever, um, teach privately...like, um, people who need tutoring at home? Is that something you do?"

"Are you interested in being tutored? Because it's not really my thing."

The paramedic sighed. "No."

Cate breathed a sigh of relief. She tilted her head sideways. "Why are you waiting around here, anyway?"

"That girl from triage."

*

Cate felt a tingling at the nape of her neck and down her back. She closed her book and tucked it into her bag. In the hours of sitting, her foot had gone to sleep. She waggled her leg to wake it up.

The ER had thinned, some treated and discharged, others, she presumed, out for a cigarette or visiting the vending machines. Or long gone, frustrated by the protracted wait.

The woman from before, the paramedic, had also vanished.

Footage from the morning's fatal plane crash in Ethiopia was looping on a wall-mounted TV. Cate watched, transfixed, lifting her feet when the janitor shuffled by, slapping his mop around. She caught sight of Liam at the intake desk in jeans and a leather jacket, clutching a takeout bag.

He thanked the receptionist and strode toward Cate, five o'clock shadow verging on scruff. "How's the patient?" He planted a kiss on her head.

"*Im*patient. And starving." Cate extended her bandaged hand for inspection.

"Wow, that's some mess you made." He glanced at the TV, dropping the takeout bag into her lap.

"Isn't that awful? Apparently, there were young people on that flight," Cate said, "on their way to some conference in Nairobi. Including Ralph Nader's grandniece, it seems."

"I can't even begin to imagine what those families must be going through." He snagged the seat across from her and whipped out his phone. "Heartbreaking."

Another good reason not to have had children, Cate thought to herself. She couldn't imagine having to bear such loss. The odds were against it, but still. Better not to have them in the first place.

Liam checked his messages without looking up. "I went to our sushi guy." Their sushi "guy" was actually a woman in a red hairnet who ran the operation while her husband slaved in the back, making the food. The pair gave new meaning to the expression "tight ship."

"Good call." Cate rifled through the bag and passed him his order with the usual extra sides of ginger and wasabi. "Here."

It took time for him to notice Cate vigorously waving the container at him. "Oops, sorry." He put away his phone.

"Truth be told, I didn't think you'd get here so soon."

"Yeah, well, the debate wrapped up sooner than I expected. And guess what?" He pumped his fist.

"You nailed it?"

"Yup! Our kids qualified for the provincials in Trois-Rivières!" He flipped up the lid and slid the chopsticks from their paper sleeve.

"Congratulations, they must be over the moon!"

"You bet they are. We *all* are!" By "we" he meant the coaches. Him and a teaching colleague, Maureen. Or Mo, as he called her, the way jocks nicknamed teammates. They'd been working all year for it.

After teaching, the high school debate team was Liam's life. The team adored him as much as his students did. Liam had a gift, a way of reaching the kids that made his compulsory history course fun. He delivered the facts without a textbook or boring lecture notes, climbing onto his desk with one or two choice props—wig, moustache, scroll—to become the famous figures he taught them about: Jacques Cartier sailing up the Saint Lawrence; Paul de Chomedey de Maisonneuve staking the first cross on Mount Royal; Jeanne Mance fighting for a hospital in the "new world"; Louis Riel leading the Métis. He was General James Wolfe, battling the French on the Plains of Abraham. Students brought stories of Liam home from school with them, elevating him to mythical status. Cate sometimes wondered about the girl-crushes he'd had to deflect over the years, blushing, doe-eyed teens tittering into their palms whenever he called on them to answer a question; the sheer number of boys who strove to be like him, smart, funny, naturally athletic. A little on the short side, he wasn't drop-dead handsome, but his charm and charisma more than made up for it. Liam had the Irish in him, like his father: the hair and skin and, if pushed, the temperament.

Cate dug out her carrot and avocado sushi rolls, flattening the paper bag into a placemat on her lap. "You watch, they'll probably call me the second I dig into this."

"Probably," Liam said, attention elsewhere.

Liam was easily distracted these days. One minute he'd be correcting papers, the next, reorganizing his office. Or responding to a phone notification. Cate turned to see who he was staring at. A child with glazed, feverish cheeks and cruddy nostrils was smiling impishly at him. Cate's first instinct was to distance herself.

Liam pulled a silly face. The child giggled. She wriggled off her mother's lap and wandered toward him, oversized colouring book flapping at her side. Her eyes were joyous constellations.

Cate sighed. *He's like a magnet, always attracting them.*

With a flourish, Liam pulled apart the chopsticks like a magician performing a trick. He rubbed them together, shaving off the splinters.

The toddler opened her mouth in awe. She dropped her book.

"And what's your name, Sunshine?"

She turned to her parents for a cue. Was the stranger safe to talk to? They nodded. She puffed out her chest. "It's Noelle!"

"Oh, my! Just like Christmas!"

She lit up.

Liam tweezed up a morsel of tuna and gobbled it down. He blotted his lips with the serviette.

"I know a secret," Noelle bragged, rocking from side to side.

Liam leaned closer. "Will you tell me?"

The little girl scooched up, cupped her hands, and whispered into his ear.

"Wow!" Liam opened his eyes wide.

She blushed and scurried back to her parents, burying her face in her mother's lap. The parents smiled.

"So," Cate said with a hint of irritation. "What was the big secret?"

"Can't tell you." Liam winked. "It's a secret."

*

Soon after the hospital visit came the phone call.

"Who is this?"

"Isabel," said the voice. "Isabel Martinez."

"Sorry, you have the wrong number." Cate hung up.

The caller rang back. "It's Cate, right? Cate Morrissey? We met in emergency the other day."

The paramedic with the holes in her jeans. Cate remembered.

"I'm sorry to disturb you."

She hardly sounded sorry. "I know I came on a bit strong, but I got a good vibe from you at the hospital."

Cate didn't remember giving off good vibes. She held her tongue.

"When you told me that you were a teacher, I got this crazy idea that you might be just the person I've been looking for."

Crazy idea indeed, Cate thought to herself. "What was your name again?"

"Isabel. Anyways, I'm pretty sure you'll come to see it's for a greater good, as they say."

Cate rolled her eyes at her invocation of "they." The generic, ubiquitous "they" that people used to lend credence to their dubious positions. As though some sacrosanct committee existed out there, endorsing or rejecting the matters of the day.

Isabel sped up, hardly taking a breath. She spoke in one continuous, run-on sentence. "That girl, you know, that I brought in by ambulance, the Inuit girl, she's damaged goods, I'm afraid to say—you know that expression, right—of course you do, you're a teacher, you would. Are you still there? Cate?"

Cate sensed a plan hatching. She hesitated. "Yes."

"I feel like as human beings we can't turn our backs on people in need, people we can help, you know what I'm saying? Like, you know, a second-chance thing. This girl should have one, don't you think?"

Cate regretted striking up that conversation in the hospital. She should have smiled once and gone back to her book. She should never have mentioned that she was a teacher. "I told you that tutoring isn't my strong suit."

Isabel waited, breathing softly.

"I mean, I really don't know how I can be of any help. How much education has she had?"

"I'm not sure, high school, I think."

"I'm a university professor. I teach *graduate* students."

"But I think you'll see she's super smart. In all sorts of ways."

"I really don't..."

"At least meet her. She once told me she wished she could go back to school."

"So what's stopping her?"

"Well, she's in a...situation."

"What kind of situation?"

"It's confidential. But if you meet her, she might tell you."

Cate rolled her eyes.

"Let's just meet and you'll see. I asked if she'd be game and she agreed."

"What? You already went and told her I'd meet with her? Behind my back?"

"She's really worth it, you'll see. I'll even pay for the coffee."

She struck Cate as someone who'd lived her whole life this way, fearlessly, impulsively, going with her gut. Hitting up complete strangers for favours. "Look, I'm not promising anything. I'm very busy with my work, but okay, I'll meet you for half an hour."

"Awesome!"

Cate could almost see Isabel pumping her fist. Wildly, with her whole body.

*

At supper, she mentioned the call to Liam, how they had arranged to meet at the Alexis Nihon food court.

"We don't even know this person."

Cate asked who he meant—Isabel, the flaky paramedic, or the young Inuit girl?

"Both. And how did she get our number, anyway?"

Cate shrugged. It was a fair question, one she hadn't considered. She hadn't shared her business card with the woman.

"Smells fishy, don't you think?

Cate made a mental note to follow up.

"So, what, exactly, are you being asked to do?"

Cate crossed her knife and fork on her plate and dabbed her lips with the serviette. "Teach this girl what she's missing to get into college, catch her up on the important works of literature."

"Hmm. Sounds like a noble idea."

Cate picked at a ragged cuticle.

"Stop!" Liam hated that habit of hers. He was always reminding her.

Cate moved her hand to her lap, out of view. "I suppose her heart's in the right place, but why me?"

"Because you're the best?"

"Even if it were true, Isabel—that's her name—has no way of knowing that. I'm used to interacting with students at a certain... level."

"Oh, don't be so snobbish, Professor Morrissey."

She raised an eyebrow.

"I've heard you bitch about your students' intellect. Usually while you're marking essays at the end of the semester."

Liam was right. Cate wondered how some of her students had ever made it into McGill. She recalled how often she and her officemate, Waleed, complained about the drop in standards.

"So, maybe the universe is calling you."

"You know as well as I do, I have a mountain of research to do. That's why I took this sabbatical in the first place. My paper's not going to write itself!"

"Excuses, excuses. That symposium's not until next year."

Cate picked her cuticle surreptitiously. She eyed Liam, wondering why the sudden about-face.

"Okay, then, maybe think about it in a different way. You say she's Indigenous. Maybe she'll have something to say that will give you a new perspective on your topic. Give you and your paper more credibility. You'd be killing two birds with one stone."

It was a crazy idea, this social work gig, but it had teeth. "You're a teacher, this is definitely your wheelhouse."

*

Clusters of Inuit were huddled outside the Alexis Nihon Plaza when Cate arrived. Two men, weather-beaten from too many winters outside, were passing a brown paper bag back and forth. Others were sprawled out on the sidewalk with a blanket over their knees, begging for money. Cate was surprised that they were smiling, given the condition of their lives. She found a loonie and dropped it into a gnarly hand.

When she arrived at the food court, Isabel and Nuna were already at a table, joking and laughing together. Isabel stood up for Cate, but Nuna remained seated, a baseball cap pulled down over her eyes. She wasn't a large person; she was rather thin and ordinary looking, and her hair looked like it needed a good wash.

Isabel jumped in with introductions. She fumbled with Cate's name, calling her Katie by mistake.

"It's Cate." She reached out to shake hands with Nuna.

"Hey."

Isabel touched Cate's bandage. "How's the hand?"

"You were right, Doctor. I needed stitches. Five altogether."

"Oh, shit." Isabel clapped a hand over her mouth, glancing at Nuna who wasn't paying attention. "I mean, yikes." She took their orders, two black teas, and went to find a concession.

It was mid-afternoon, the time in between lunch and dinner when the only people in the food court were tired shoppers laden with shopping bags and university students studying for exams. It was unusually quiet.

"You have a beautiful name," Cate finally said.

Nuna didn't react.

"Does it, uh, mean anything?"

"Does yours?"

Nuna's bluntness caught Cate off guard. Her defensiveness. "Uh, yes, actually, as a matter of fact, it does." She noticed Isabel observing them from a distance. Cate motored on. "Well...since you asked...the original Gaelic of my last name, Morrissey, is O Muirgheasa, which comes from the words 'muir' meaning sea and 'geas' meaning action. Supposedly, the Morrisseys arrived in Boston in the 19th century. I guess that's a roundabout way of telling you I'm Irish."

"Yep," said Nuna. "That's a lot of words."

Isabel returned with a cardboard tray and distributed the tea.

"Your turn," Cate said to Nuna. She jigged her teabag around.

Nuna spoke haltingly in the fewest words possible. "In Inuktitut, my language, Nuna means land."

"That's it?" Cate lifted out the teabag and set it on the tray.

"Yup."

"Simple as that?"

Nuna removed her cap, revealing a hairline cut on her forehead. "Simple as that." She turned away from Cate and tapped Isabel playfully on the arm. "Pass the sugar, Miss Booger."

Isabel giggled and tossed her a packet.

Cate felt like a third wheel. She reprimanded herself for being careless with her words, trying to put Nuna at ease. Their relationship couldn't be rushed or forced. It had to happen organically. She tried another approach, asking questions to draw Nuna out. Why did she leave the North, why was she living in Montreal, what did she want from Cate. What was her bottom line in all this.

Isabel stepped in and answered most of them, trying to keep things light. Nuna lived in Montreal with her boyfriend, who "made bank" doing shiftwork at the Raglan Mine near Deception Bay. It was a good arrangement. She came from a huge family and her house was overcrowded. She didn't even have a bed of her own. None of them did. The boyfriend went back and forth every two weeks for work while Nuna, living on a small allowance, stayed at the apartment.

Nuna finally piped up. "Maybe you can help me get into college."

Isabel slurped her coffee. She put down her cup and cleared her throat. "I think the best would be for Nuna to move in with you for a while."

Cate's eyes bugged out. She almost dropped her tea. "Pardon?"

"It would be a whole learning experience."

So this was where everything was headed. Cate sighed.

Nuna slapped her cap back on, pokerfaced. She leaned forward on her elbows. "I've always wanted a bedroom of my own."

The meeting broke up soon afterward, Cate unmoored, tea untouched. For some strange reason, she liked the girl, her name, her mystery, her piercing candour, but the decision, ultimately, would depend on Liam.

*

Things moved quickly after that. Liam went for it and Cate gave in, though she preferred to say that the stars aligned. Not that Isabel had pulled a fast one on her. She made the decision while she was listening to *The Current* on CBC Radio.

The kitchen lights flickered. Once, twice. Then the electricity went kaput. After about ten seconds, everything kicked in again, the radio, the fridge, the numbers flashing green on the stove clock.

The irony of a power outage during a show about a shortage of teachers in Indigenous communities wasn't lost on Cate. She couldn't dismiss it. It was a sign. At the same time, she could hear her father admonishing her for this sort of magical thinking. Like her, he was a scholar, and scholars, he would argue, had their reputations to uphold. Entertaining superstition or divine intervention was committing intellectual heresy.

On the other hand, literature was filled with portents, like life itself. The power went out. Then it came back. If that wasn't a sign, what was? Her father could just go and Kierkegaard himself. Cate felt good telling him off, even if it was only in her mind.

Meanwhile, Liam had agreed that Nuna could stay with them as long as she followed the house rules. They would cover the basics, room and board, the occasional outing. In his mind, it was an act of kindness. And besides, they had the means. Why shouldn't they?

Isabel and Nuna arrived after supper on a weeknight. In the hour beforehand, Cate ran around nervously, getting things ready. It was a good house, with good bones, as her father remarked when he fronted them the money for their down payment. A house like the one she grew up in on Grey Avenue by the tennis club, solidly built with decorative mouldings and woodwork, and hardy shade trees out front. She vacuumed the guest room and put a vase of freshly cut flowers on the dresser. She spelled out "Welcome Nuna" on a small word board and propped it against the vase.

Nuna came with a khaki knapsack and a fading, yellowish bruise on her cheek, which Cate had somehow missed when they went for tea. Statue still, she took everything in.

Cate tried to elicit a smile from her, but Nuna was unresponsive. Isabel, on the other hand, couldn't contain herself. She walked with a skip in her step.

As planned, Liam left for a meeting with his debate team shortly after the introductions. He and Cate didn't want to make a big deal of Nuna's arrival. They wanted to make it seem like opening up their house to a stranger was the most normal thing in the world.

Cate offered them a cup of tea. Nuna glanced at Isabel for a cue.

"Sure," Isabel said.

While they settled around the table, Cate put the kettle on and dealt out the placemats. Nuna noticed Cate's brittle copy of the *Book of Canadian Poetry* and began picking at the spine.

Cate moved it away. "It's pretty old," she said. "1957. Found it at a great bookshop called Antigone. Maybe we can go there sometime." She caught herself. She was babbling again, like at the food court. She went to get spoons.

The kettle whistled.

Cate poured the water into the blue-and-yellow teapot Liam had bought her on their honeymoon in Provence and set it on a ceramic trivet.

Nuna cleared her throat.

It startled Cate. She overfilled a cup, tea splashing over the rim and puddling in the saucer.

"The other day we were talking about names. Remember? My last name means someone who goes out on the land...like a hunter."

How perfect is that, Cate thought to herself. She poured the spilled tea back into its cup and sat down. "How old are you, Nuna?"

"Nineteen."

"So, you're a millennium baby!"

"Um, sure."

"God, I remember the Y2K scare, how everyone went crazy thinking the world was coming to an end. This is it, we all thought. The Apocalypse."

She scrunched up her nose. "Y2K?"

"December 1999. Everyone went into survival mode, stocked up on supplies—food, water, generators, candles, toilet paper. It was insane. The Millennial Bug, remember that, Isabel?"

Isabel frowned. "I was, like, eight."

Cate felt old. She felt the canyons between all their ages.

Nuna pointed to Cate's wrist. "Hey, is that a Fitbit?"

"It is. Liam got it for me. He wants me to stay in shape."

"Cool." She scanned the kitchen, noting its stainless-steel appliances, stone backsplash, quartz countertops. Its glass-fronted cabinet doors showcasing vintage dishware and Mason jars of pasta in a rainbow of colours. She whistled. "So, I'm gonna live here."

Cate nodded.

"For real?"

"Yes. How do you like that idea?" Cate followed Nuna's gaze through the doorway, past the foyer, into the living room to where the rosewood piano stood, laden with art books and family photos, the one she had inherited from the family home when her father downsized.

"You play piano?"

"Not in years," Cate said. "I took lessons when I was a kid."

"So, you're good?" Nuna lifted her cup to drink, but instantly put it down. "Eeeey, hot!"

"I'm pretty good."

"Maybe you can teach me one day."

Cate remembered all the times after school when she was stuck practicing while the late afternoon sun poured across the keys and all she could hear were the kids outside playing and laughing. "It'll take a little longer than a day."

"*Su casa es tu casa*," Isabel said. She raised her hand for a high-five. Nuna slapped it, a smile finally breaking out.

The two of them had an ease, a familiarity with each other that made Cate think there was more to their relationship than Isabel let on. She wondered whether she herself would get to a similar place with Nuna, whether their connection, now forced and unnatural, would lead to something rich, something she'd felt when she first began teaching, when her students engaged with her. When they lingered in the doorway after class, discussing Northrop Frye and Canadian modernism. "So?" Cate repeated. "What do you say?"

"I could do worse."

"Yes, you could," said Isabel, lightly punching Nuna in the arm.

"Yo, dude. I could press charges, you know."

Cate went to the pantry. "Cookies anyone?" She poured some from a bag into a dish.

"Please," said Nuna. She stuffed an Oreo into her mouth and grabbed two more.

Isabel declined.

Cate glanced at Nuna. "Why don't you go upstairs and look around?"

"Cool." Nuna backed up, chair legs screeching along the floor.

"I meant *after* you finish those cookies." Too late, Cate thought. She sounded like Liam. Liam had an aversion to crumbs and dust bunnies. Twice a week, he vacuumed the kitchen and scrubbed the counters with ammonia. It was an obsession. Before they bought the place, he had it inspected for mouse droppings, rot, cockroaches. He wanted a written report. Cate knew it was because of his childhood in The Point. "Yours is the first bedroom on the right with the flowery comforter and the small desk."

Nuna left her cookies beside the dish and flew up the stairs.

When she was out of earshot, Isabel leaned across the table. "I'm telling you, you won't regret it."

"Well...she *does* seem like a good kid." Still, Cate felt some resistance within her. If Liam was a clean freak, she was a control freak. She didn't feel like she was in the driver's seat here; she was more like a passenger along for the ride. Along for Isabel's grandstanding do-gooding. On the other hand, if she went with Liam's logic, the universe was handing her a gift: Nuna's presence, the spark of something new, could breathe fresh life into Cate's research. Her paper on settler narratives in Canadian art and poetry was still developing; having Nuna here could lead her to a road not taken.

"She just needs a solid foundation. Something to put her on the right path. I know you can do it. So do you, eh?"

Cate felt Isabel's gaze. "I'm sorry, what?"

"I know you're the right person for the job."

Her unwavering faith in Cate felt undeserved. How could she know? They had met for all of, what, ten minutes at a food court, and suddenly Cate was Mother Teresa? Sure, she would do what she could, but she was an English professor, an academic who deconstructed obscure references, fussed over poems that no one read. "What on earth can *I* teach this girl that would be of any use to her in her world?"

"I'm sure you'll figure it out."

They fell into an awkward silence. Sipping her tea, Cate took inventory of Isabel's tan complexion, her dimples, her high beautiful forehead. One of those faces you don't forget. She thought about how expressive she was with her hands, the allure it gave her. Cate imagined her at a party, chattering away with a beer in one hand and an hors d'oeuvre in the other, gesturing wildly, hardly embarrassed as she knocks over a lamp and puts it back. Still talking and carrying on as if nothing happened. She was the antithesis of what Cate expected a paramedic to be— calm, focused, professional. She probably had a hundred men after her. She was lively. She had the looks, the body, eyes that could pierce a heart.

Isabel twirled a swath of hair around her finger.

Cate wondered what she was thinking, and if she was also sizing her up.

"Yo, dude, I think I'm gonna handle this."

Cate jumped.

Nuna looked from Cate to Isabel and back to Cate again. "Did I scare you or something?"

"No, of course not," Cate said. "You just surprised me. I'm not used to having other people in the house."

"Then it's settled," Isabel said. "I'm sure you two will get along like a pair of thieves."

"Thieves? I don't get it," said Nuna.

"I think she meant that pretty soon we'll be as thick as thieves," Cate said.

"I still don't get it."

Isabel playfully tucked Nuna under her arm. "Don't worry, she'll teach you."

Nuna pulled away. For a split second, Cate thought she might back out of the whole deal.

"I'm only a bus ride away," Isabel said. "Don't be a stranger, Nuna." She snapped up her coat and planted a hasty kiss on each of Cate's cheeks, the way long-time friends do. She moved in close and whispered into Cate's ear. "*Chica*, I'm counting on you."

*

Liam was waiting up for Cate, book in hand. She grabbed her pyjamas and headed for the bathroom.

"Is she asleep yet?"

"I think she's on Facebook," Cate called out. She rinsed her face and brushed her teeth.

"It's a big change," he said.

"Not only for her." She settled in beside him.

He laid the book on the nightstand and took off his reading glasses. "Let's say we put it out of our minds for tonight. Try to relax a little." He flicked off the lamp.

But Cate couldn't relax. She couldn't get comfortable. A late-night car passed their house, bright headlights sweeping across the ceiling. "What if we made a mistake taking this on? It's a big responsibility."

Liam reached over and touched her. "You're having second thoughts?"

"And third and fourth." Cate sighed. A screaming migraine was drilling into her temple. "What the hell do I know about what this girl needs?"

"You're a teacher," he reminded her. "And a good one. It'll come to you."

"That's what Isabel said." She threw off the sheets and went to the medicine cabinet for her pills. When she returned from the bathroom, he was lying sideways, propped on an elbow.

"Headache?"

She nodded.

He stroked her hair. "You need to relax, you can't do anything about it now. Just get a good night's sleep and see how you feel about it in the morning." He caressed the side of her face.

He was right. Nothing was forcing her to do this thing, she could always change her mind. She could call Isabel tomorrow and tell her it wasn't going to work out after all. She could use her father as an excuse, say his health was failing and that he needed her help. Family had to come first. Wouldn't Isabel agree?

She detected a change in Liam's breathing, a hastening. His stroking wasn't helping her headache, it was making it worse. His hands were too eager. They were causing friction, the stirrings of a heat rash. She tensed up and pushed them away.

Liam sighed and rolled onto his back. They had been here before. Many times, in fact. Shifting uncomfortably. Breathing in the stillborn air. The first time it happened was two years into their marriage when Liam's student teacher, Beatrice, appeared on the scene. Eager to be taken under his wing. Liam began staying late at school. There was always something they had to do: review her lesson plans and classroom management, tweak a PowerPoint. Prepare for her supervisor's visit.

Cate suggested they invite her for supper.

The girl arrived holding a bouquet of flowers with an orange grocery-store sticker on the cellophane. "Hi, I'm Bea." Pixie-faced, she wore a tank top, skinny jeans, and ankle boots with a spiky heel. Liam didn't mind her walking across his floor in them. The two disappeared into the living room while Cate finished making dinner. He put on music with a techno vibe that he and Cate would never have listened to in a million years. Bea's laughter floated into the kitchen.

All through the meal, Liam teased her. She blushed and giggled. He kept filling her wine glass. They chattered about things from school that only they knew: So-and-so's stupid answer on a test. The principal's gambling problem. Liam laughed at everything she said. Cate wanted to throw up.

After she left, Cate lit into him. She accused him of treating her like she wasn't even in the room. "All night, she flirted with you—and you, you just encouraged it!"

He looked right through her, denied everything. He scoffed and went upstairs, leaving her to clean up. The next day, Cate insisted on couples therapy. He told her she was being ridiculous; they didn't need it, nothing had happened. But Cate was suspicious. Even if he hadn't broken their marriage vows, the thought was there. Reluctantly, Liam gave in.

Both said they still believed in the marriage. There was too much history to let it all unravel. The therapist advised them that if they were serious, if this little blip with Bea was really just a blip, they would have to acknowledge that something was missing in their lives. They would have to figure it out and then do what was required to rediscover each other.

They stopped going after four sessions. They got the gist and began addressing the damage. Cate took a greater interest in Liam's job, suggested activities they could do together. Spa dates, concerts, wine-tasting workshops. He attended her presentations and praised her publications. He bought her small gifts for no special reason. He said all the right things. They both tried but it seemed like work. Hard work. And despite their efforts, Cate couldn't shake her distrust. When they were in bed she wondered if he was fantasizing about Bea. Bea with her perky nose and easy laugh, her sculpted hair—glooped with product. It ruined the mood.

Eventually, with time, Bea dropped off their radar. He didn't speak of her, he spoke of a hiccup in his marriage, a momentary lapse in judgment. He spoke of a curve ball that happens to every couple.

Cate touched Liam's shoulder. She whispered his name.

He rolled on his side, away from her.

"If only my head weren't pounding..."

He sighed. "Never mind, get some sleep."

*

When Cate woke up the next morning, Liam was already gone. Her migraine, as well. She got dressed and tiptoed past Nuna's closed door, down the stairs to the kitchen. Liam had left some coffee in the carafe and a basket of bran muffins on the table. Cate promised herself she would make up for things.

She carried her coffee to the table and opened her laptop, the morning papers filled with articles about the grounding of the Boeing 737 MAX and the company's responsibility in the Ethiopian Airlines crash. Her phone rang.

"Hey girlfriend," Waleed chirped. "How goes it?"

"It goes." Cate brought him up to speed on Nuna, including her reservations. Waleed knew everything about Cate, and she about him. They were friends, confidantes, officemates. They finished each other's sentences. Liam affectionately referred to him as her gay husband. When she left on sabbatical, Waleed felt an enormous emptiness. He called twice a week, often more. "So, what's happening in your world?"

"I thought you'd never ask. For one thing, Merriam-Webster has officially welcomed *vulture capitalism* into the lexicon."

"Good God, the planet is doomed." Cate giggled.

"Laugh away, but you'll see. It's a slippery slope, my dear."

"And how's the man-cave guy?" The man-cave guy was Waleed's neighbour who had converted his tin shed in the back alley into a hangout to drink beer and watch weekend sports. "Did the garage finally detonate?"

"No such luck, *Habibti*," he whined. "It's a blight on the neighbourhood."

Cate let him vent because whenever Waleed fixated on something, there was always something more behind it. "You know as well as I do, it's not about your property values going down."

Pure Lebanese, Waleed had dark hair, long lashes, a trim beard, and the soul of a poet. He loved to sit in his favourite café on the corner of Fort and Saint Catherine, chatting with newly arrived compatriots who pontificated about the world's problems. He was a part of them but apart from them.

"I'm telling you, it must be illegal."

"What?" Cate heard stirring sounds upstairs, a bedroom door opening. "What's illegal?"

"That dump. The other day he was up on a ladder with a rag and a pail of water, trying to erase some graffiti off the door."

"So, march yourself down to city hall and ask if it's contrary to public bylaws."

Waleed sighed before changing gears. "We miss you."

"You mean *you* miss me."

He ignored her. "Our friend, Thadeus, is up to his old tricks again." Thadeus, a colleague in the English department, was a minor poet on the literary circuit. "Happily married," he always bragged, to a woman so devoted she organized his socks and underwear into different-sized Ziploc bags whenever he travelled for a book tour.

"Jesus, not that again. It's like a revolving door. How's the victim?"

"How they always are. Hysterical." Waleed lived for gossip. "For once, the higher-ups stepped in."

"Oh?"

"They're urging him to retire before the shit hits the fan like it's doing everywhere these days."

"Thank God," Cate said. "It's getting ridiculous. Remember that girl from a couple of years ago? Smart as a whip but gullible. She ended up posting on social media. Cringeworthy stuff. I never understood how his wife never found out."

"She's out to lunch, that's how. He takes her to Greece every summer and she pretends they're Leonard Cohen and Marianne."

"Spare me." Cate glanced up.

Nuna was in the doorway, barefoot in a sweatshirt and jeans, clutching her cellphone.

Cate smiled at her. "Listen, I'm going to have to let you go. Kiss, kiss."

His voice rose an octave. "Wait! I almost forgot the most important news of all. I finally got a poem accepted into the *Paris Review*! Two, actually."

"Oh, that's wonderful, I'm really proud of you." Cate waved Nuna into the kitchen. "We'll celebrate soon. Okay, I really have to go now." She tapped off her phone and smiled at Nuna. "So, you've emerged from the dead."

Nuna looked straight through her. "Is there coffee?"

"Get it yourself." Cate giggled, trying to keep things light and casual. "What do you think this is, the Ritz? This is a self-serve joint."

Nuna raided the fridge for milk. She rattled the cutlery and dropped two pieces of bread into the toaster.

"I see you're not a morning person," Cate said.

Nuna mumbled, "I guess."

Cate's cell dinged with a text from Waleed: *Life means something when you are a faithful witness to the world. When you do something small and beautiful and true.* He was always giving her advice this way, without being asked. It never bothered Cate because she knew he cared about her.

Nuna scraped butter across her toast, inhaled it the way a trucker devours a chicken-fried steak for breakfast, not saying much except, "What's the plan for today?" She croaked it with the enthusiasm of a toad.

It felt like the perfect opportunity to bow out. In her mind, Cate ran through all the ways she could make it seem like terminating the arrangement was Nuna's idea. *Look,* she could say. *You don't seem keen on doing this.* She could fold her hands on the table. Look deeply into Nuna's eyes. *Just know, there's nothing holding you here. You're a free agent. Isabel believed it was a good idea, but maybe you don't, and if that's the case, let's just call it a day.* Then she thought about Waleed's text and whether it was a sign, a wagging finger telling her she'd be heartless to turn Nuna away. Cate searched for something to say to buy more time. "You said you're planning to go to college someday. Is that true?"

Nuna lifted the hair up off her nape. "Um, yeah, maybe, I'm not sure." She released her mane.

"Well, you can't just decide to go at the last minute, you'll have some catching up to do first."

Nuna nodded. She wet her index finger and picked up the crumbs around her dish. She brought them to her tongue.

"Well, then, there's no time like the present." Cate felt a spark of excitement. "As a matter of fact, there's a new exhibit in town."

Nuna's eyes glazed over. She grabbed her cell and checked her Facebook feed.

"Have you ever heard of the Group of Seven?"

She shook her head, staring at her screen.

"There's a show of their work at the museum. And I think with your first-hand knowledge of the North, you'll enjoy it. Maybe even have some interesting observations. Some of their paintings are quite austere."

She looked up. "Austere, what's *that*?"

"It means stern. Forbidding. Of extreme simplicity." Cate stood up. "Don't forget to clear off the table."

Nuna put her dish in the dishwasher and went to get ready. "What time's Isabel coming for supper?"

"After her shift," Cate shouted from the hall closet. "If she gets off early enough." She brought out a pair of long black boots for Nuna to try, decent looking except for the fur, slightly matted from not being worn in a couple of seasons.

Nuna ran her hand along the trim as though she were trying to figure out what animal it had been. "What's wrong with mine?"

"They've got blood on them." Cate shook her head. How often had she ever said *that*?

Nuna stepped into them. "They don't fit. They're too big."

"No, they're not, now come on."

Nuna rounded her back in protest, shrugging on her parka, walking awkwardly in the boots she didn't want to wear, heels and toes not quite lining up. The entire way to the metro station, she made a point of clomping clumsily in them. Once she realized Cate wasn't biting, she stopped.

They exited at Guy-Concordia, a leaky, rundown station of exposed pipes and rust-stained concrete. A station that had been in the same state of disrepair for years, it seemed. A grey, apocalyptic eyesore. They floated up the first escalator, through a turnstile and past a sad strip of shops selling cellphones and pizza, cinnamon buns and Indian food. They followed the listless crowd up a second escalator, finally emerging into the bright sunshine.

Nuna forged ahead. She noticed the marble statue of Norman Bethune at the intersection of Guy and De Maisonneuve. "Who's *that* Qallunaaq?"

"What's a...Qallunaaq?"

"You're a Qallunaaq. Anyone who isn't Inuk is a Qallunaaq."

"You mean White?"

"I mean not Inuk. But mostly it means White people. Mostly the people who come up north to *civilize* us. My father told me that it comes from a word that means the bones behind the eyebrows. Those bones stick out more on White people than on us."

"Hmm." Cate pressed on her eyebrows. "Interesting."

"So who is he?"

"Who?"

"That Qallunaaq."

Cate explained that he was many things—teacher, army officer, author, doctor, artist. She mentioned his hero status in the eyes of the Chinese, and that he was a surgeon at the Royal

Victoria Hospital. "A lesser-known fact is that he organized painting classes for disadvantaged children in this neighbourhood."

"Disadvantaged?"

"People who are lacking. Deprived."

"I know what it means. But up north, we wouldn't say that they were lacking." Nuna gathered a mouthful of saliva and spat. "Your *disadvantaged* people still have running water, *clean* water. There's hospitals all over the city, a ton of schools, and you don't have seven people sleeping in the same bedroom."

"Actually, in the 1920s and 30s, you did. There weren't as many hospitals and schools as there are today."

"Whatever."

They continued a couple of blocks east to Bishop Street, past the brutalist architecture of Concordia University's Hall Building, where Cate's father had taught, and up to Sherbrooke Street. Cate pointed to the pillared façade of the museum with its colourful banner advertising the show.

Nuna made a visor with her hand to cut the glare. "Big place," she said with monotone enthusiasm.

Cate redirected her attention to the newer pavilion across the street. As they approached, Nuna took a cigarette from her pocket and lit it.

"Bad for you," Cate said, instantly regretting it.

Nuna shrugged and drew the smoke deeply into her lungs, consumed by the ritual of inhaling and exhaling.

They slowed their pace, other pedestrians passing them. Cate pulled out her phone and checked her text messages. One from Liam said he might or might not be home for supper and to start without him; another, from Isabel, asked how things were going. Cate shot them each a happy face emoji.

A husky shout erupted from Nuna. "Hey, you! Put it out of its misery!"

Cate nearly dropped her phone. "Why are you shouting like that?"

Nuna pointed to a nearby church, shaking her head dismissively.

Craning her neck, Cate saw a youngish woman with green hair and tatty clothes, nursing what appeared to be an injured pigeon.

Nuna cupped her hands around her mouth, cigarette poking through her fingers. She hollered again, this time loud enough for everyone around to hear. "You're not doing it any favours!"

The woman glared at them.

Cate was flustered. "It's really none of our business what she's doing."

The woman turned her back and continued stroking the bird.

Nuna puffed on her cigarette, impervious. Her voice rang out. "Even our sled dogs, which we love like part of our family, when they're injured, we shoot them." She spoke with conviction. "It's kinder," she added.

The woman ignored her.

Cate took Nuna by the elbow and guided her toward the entrance. "C'mon, the line's getting long."

Nuna pinched the tip of her cigarette and slid it back into the package. Her attention reverted to the boots she'd been made to wear. Skeptically, she touched the fur. She held her nose. They stank, they were ugly. Why did she have to wear them, anyway? The cashier processing Cate's credit card pretended not to hear Nuna's complaints. "What is this shit, anyway? Squirrel? Mouse?"

"It's factory fur, and it's infinitely better than killing animals." Cate cringed the minute it came out of her mouth.

Nuna didn't react, as though Cate's comment had flown past her, and she couldn't be bothered asking her to repeat it. "Why do they call it a museum, anyway?"

Cate was floored. What an intelligent question, she thought. It demonstrated that Nuna had promise. That she was curious. Cate's heart raced. "Well, there are two theories. One is that it comes from the Greek word 'mouseion,' which were temples dedicated to the Muses and the arts they inspired. The other is that it comes from the Latin word museum, which means place for collecting and preserving things."

Nuna flipped her hair.

Cate wasn't sure whether it had registered. But at least she had asked the question. It was enough for now. They pattered down a gently sloped staircase that always reminded Cate of piano keys.

Nuna marvelled at the *Tree of Life*, an eight-foot-tall sculpture, basking under a skylight. The artist, according to the plaque, Abraham Anghik Ruben, had intended to emulate a West Coast totem pole and suggest that the animal kingdom formed the basis of human culture. "Sick!" She ran her hands along the gleaming soapstone. "But what a funny place for a carving."

They walked to the elevator. Nuna pressed the up button. They waited. Nuna sighed loudly. "What's taking so long?" She pressed it again, twice, three times. She kept pressing until Cate told her to stop.

When the doors opened, Nuna pushed inside. Cate stood next to her, studying their mirrored reflections, Nuna at least three inches shorter, closer to Isabel's height. Their lack of conversation made Cate uneasy, but Nuna seemed perfectly content chipping at the flaking nail polish on her thumb. Adjusting her purse strap, Cate watched the consecutive floor numbers light up. She hummed with a forced nonchalance, rifling through keys and lip balms in her bag, pulling out her notebook like a showpiece. "Ta-da!"

"You have homework?" Nuna said.

"Sort of."

"I thought you were a teacher."

"Well, yes, but teachers are also students. And I'm preparing a lecture for a conference in Europe."

"You're weird."

The elevator doors slid open.

Nuna's eyes lit up. "Hey, they have headphones!"

Cate steered her away. "They're audio guides. They tell you the backstory of the paintings."

"Let's get some!"

Cate shook her head.

Nuna pleaded. "I thought you brought me here to learn something."

"I did. But I think it's better to view the work from your own perspective first. Get a personal feel for what the artist was trying to achieve." Cate directed her to the Lawren Harris collection. "You can always get the background information later."

Nuna followed, mumbling under her breath.

Cate ramped up her excitement, dragging her from one painting to the next. "What do you think of this?" she asked, and "What do you think of that?" Hoping to drum up interest.

Nuna perked up when she saw the isolated peaks, the painted canvases of ice and snow and barren shorelines. "Hey, where are the people in these?"

"Actually, I've been wondering that myself. It's partly what I'm writing my paper about."

"Well, this guy—what's his name?"

"Harris. Lawren Harris."

Nuna snapped her fingers. "Yeah, him." She didn't back down. "He got it all wrong. *People* live up there, too. It's not only land and sea and nothing else."

Cate collected her thoughts before saying she didn't think that was the point, the point was to create the impression of an unforgiving geography, a harsh landscape of startling juxtapositions. The land as something to be conquered. "It wasn't about the people when he painted it. It was about place. It was about nature." Even as she spoke, she couldn't ignore the settler colonial attitude that informed the painting.

"What's just-a-position?"

"*Juxt*. With an *x*. It's when two things are placed side by side for comparison. Like, the winter darkness and the midnight sun, for example."

"So, like you and me?" she said. "We'd be juxtapositions?"

Cate smiled, impressed with how quickly Nuna had picked up on the artist's biased lens. "Yes, I suppose you're right." Maybe their arrangement would work out after all, she thought. Maybe it would benefit them both. Cate tucked away her notebook and suggested they stop for lunch.

"Cigarette first." Nuna recycled her half-smoked butt and dangled it, unlit, from her lips.

"Not in here, you don't."

"Obviously." Nuna felt around for her silver lighter with the Penguins logo on it.

Cate noticed Nuna's torn coat pocket, made a mental note to send it to the dry cleaners to have it sewn up.

They stood by the elevator beside a tightly coiffed, elderly patron. Cate saw her sneaking sidelong glances at Nuna fiddling with her lighter, adjusting and readjusting the height of the flame. The woman's face was pinched, a leather handbag clutched to her chest.

Cate nudged Nuna to stop, glared at the snooty woman until she turned away in embarrassment. "You know, Nuna," Cate said in a voice just loud enough for the woman to hear, "some of these artists, whose works are owned by the rich, were dirt poor." She lowered her voice to a hush. "And I'm quite certain that if one of them showed up to a mansion for tea, they'd get the door slammed in their face."

Nuna stuffed the lighter in her pocket. She plucked the cigarette out of her mouth.

Cate's phone dinged with a text from Isabel. *How are things?* Cate tapped an answer with her index finger, envious of the dextrous thumbs of youth that could whip off a paragraph in ten seconds: *Surprisingly good.*

Isabel texted, *Awesome*, but she had to go, she was in the middle of something: *TTYS.*

Cate stuffed the phone back into her purse. She nudged Nuna. "On another note, why would Isabel tell me you make bad choices?"

Nuna screwed up her nose. "*Her* opinion."

*

Cate and Liam scheduled a meeting with Nuna to establish some ground rules. They held it, like a family, over supper, addressing her casually, yet firmly. Liam took the lead. There would be no smoking in the house, no overnight guests. She would have to tidy up after herself and always remember the fan after a shower, they didn't want mould growing everywhere. They explained about courtesy calls, about letting them know where she was and if she was going to be late. Nuna agreed that it sounded reasonable. Liam ended the talk with a gentle scolding: "And kindly refrain from throwing your butts on the lawn," mumbling to himself that he couldn't believe that it was still a thing in the twenty-first century.

Nuna lowered her head sheepishly. "Yes, Pops."

Liam clenched his jaw. "I'm not your pop. I'm nobody's pop."

Cate swallowed. She looked away. Liam retired to the living room.

Nuna cleared the table in silence. She made sure he was out of earshot when she whispered to Cate. "Why was Liam so pissed before? I was only joking around."

"Long story."

"And, anyways, how come you two don't have any kids? You're getting old."

"Gee, thanks."

"You know what I mean. If you were Inuk, you'd have at least five by now." She said they were seven in her family, six boys and her, plus her parents. "My mother had me when she was twenty."

Cate squirted some dish soap into the sink. "Not all women have a mother brain, you know." She filled the basin with water until the pots and pans were submerged. "Some have other ambitions and desires."

Nuna reached for a dry towel and snapped it. "Every girl I know wants kids."

Not every girl. Cate never hid the fact that she didn't want children. She could never imagine herself pregnant, bloated as a whale. She couldn't imagine a baby's lips at her nipple, pulling it out of shape, sucking it raw. She didn't know why, but she couldn't be a woman in those sorts of ways. When Liam proposed, she made it crystal clear.

They'd been painting their first apartment. Before dawn, Cate, half asleep, carried in the paint cans. The room was dark. She flicked on the light switch to "Will you marry me?" in big black Sharpie on the wall. Liam appeared from behind. He knelt on one knee and produced a velvet box. She gasped.

The diamond was exquisite, but no, this wasn't how she saw their relationship, Cate explained. Why fix what wasn't broken? He begged her to try on the ring and if, after that, she still didn't want to, he would respect that. He would be fine with living together. Cate mulled it over. She sat with him on the drop cloth and said if he really wanted the marriage thing she'd go for it, on one condition. The condition was non-negotiable. No children. Ever. And no trying to change her mind. Liam slipped the ring on her finger.

Cate didn't share this with Nuna. It was none of her business. Besides, she wouldn't have understood the nuances. The idea that childless women weren't flawed women. Cate told her the other story, instead, the more believable one, rooted in her family's thorny past.

*

Like all parents, Cate's were imperfect. They had the will, but they didn't have staying power.

Margaret was born two years before Cate, with cerebral palsy. What many had called an act of God—random, unfair. It produced a domino effect. It ruined her parents' relationship and destroyed their family.

"Don't say ruin," her father lectured her. "Remember that what lies behind and ahead of us are tiny matters compared to what lives within us. We're better people because of her."

But were they? Before Margaret, her parents were free, nothing but the wide-open road ahead of them. Her mother was a bright doctoral candidate at Concordia University. Niall, an associate professor, fell head over heels for her mind. He admired her passion for Seneca. Discreetly, they began seeing each other. Then she got pregnant. Gobsmacked by the news, Niall grew into the idea of becoming a father. He tried it on for size. "I'm up for it if you are," he said. He got cracking and published a wad of research. He passed his final tenure review. They found a place together in a nice part of town. Within days of marrying, in a complete about-face, she decided to postpone her thesis, wanting to focus on the life growing inside her.

After Margaret was born, things took a downturn. Seriously delayed, Margaret couldn't do anything a baby was supposed to: roll over, crawl, speak. Children were all different, they rationalized. She would reach the milestones when she was good and ready. Margaret missed every one of them. Soon after, the doctors diagnosed her with spastic quadriplegia, a severe form of cerebral palsy. She would never have a normal life. Cate's mother refused to accept the truth. She abandoned her doctorate and made it her life's mission to prove the medical community wrong. Niall, disheartened, desperate for a degree of normalcy in their lives, convinced her to have a second child.

In hindsight, it probably wasn't the best idea. Cate believed it was what nudged them over the edge. After seeing to Margaret's daily needs, there was little time left over for anything else, including their second-born. Not that they didn't try.

Niall picked up the slack, reducing his course load and office hours to see that Cate was properly attended to. She was a good baby, but she was work, nonetheless. They bonded. Together, Niall and Cate became the distant planets in her mother's orbit.

At seven, Cate took on chores to ease her mother's burden—loading the dishwasher, setting the table, dividing the laundry into colours and whites, always asking if there was anything more she could do. She did it without being told.

Drained of energy and patience, her mother often snapped. "Don't you see I'm busy here?" Or, "Niall, why don't you take her somewhere, do something with her." And her father would nod and say, *Come on, Cookie, get your shoes on, we're going to the Dairy Queen.*

Much later, when Cate was better able to understand, Niall confessed that one of the reasons they had her was to ensure that Margaret had family after they were gone. It never struck them as unfair. "Don't get me wrong," he said. "Now that you're here, you're way more than that." He hugged her into his chest. "You're my one and only special girl."

Once Cate figured out that she was essentially his to raise and Margaret was her mother's, she went out of her way to please him. Top grades were never enough, she had to be the best at everything. She aced her piano recitals, campaigned and got herself elected to the student council. She edited the yearbook, won every high school writing competition. In her graduating year, having discovered Allen Ginsberg and Jack Kerouac, Cate upped her game. She started a four-page underground newspaper, *Marx! Not Marks.* She published controversial editorials using information she had gleaned from Niall, things he had learned at her age about injustice and civil disobedience before leaving the States in the late sixties. She stayed after school, waiting for the janitor to finish mopping the floors, so she could leave a small pile of Xeroxed copies in the cafeteria, and in the mailboxes of every teacher and administrator. When the headmistress called Niall to say there would be no subversives at Sacred Heart, Cate saw that he was secretly pleased. Even as he was grounding her, she detected the gleam in his eye. She had used the pen as a sword. She had waged her own small war on authority. The incident strengthened her resolve: she would write and travel and be the change she wanted to see in the world. Following convocation, she announced her plans, waiting for Niall to break out the champagne. Instead, he deflated her balloon. "You'll need a stable career, Cookie. Women these days need their independence more than anything."

This, above all, was what stayed in her mind long after she graduated magna cum laude and went on to grad school. After she defended her PhD and became an assistant, then associate, then full professor. Following in his footsteps.

His intellect might have been impeccable. But it didn't save him from temptation.

*

Despite her initial misgivings, Cate warmed up to Isabel. Both recognized in the other a sincere, hardscrabble determination to help Nuna, whatever it took. Isabel trusted Cate in all matters of education. Cate let Isabel handle the social, extracurricular piece; she and Nuna shared a passion for hockey, video games, corny jokes. They were two of a kind.

Cate was surprised at how, despite their age difference, she and Isabel clicked. They riffed off each other. They criticized each other's musical tastes. Mostly, they agreed about the importance of social justice. In no time, they waded into more personal territory, trading childhood stories, hardships and heartbreaks. Revealing the skeletons in their closets. Cate vented about her damaged family; Isabel spoke of how she was raised by a fearless immigrant single mother. She confessed about her first love, a girl named Hannah, who stole and then broke her heart.

The two met in grade one, long before they had any inkling about love and the magic of attraction. Best friends forever, they played with "those huge yellow trucks with the long digging arms. The ones that look like dinosaurs."

"Excavators," Cate said.

"Yeah, those." Isabel's face brightened. "Later, when we were a bit older, we played Lord of the Rings. I pretended my mother's coat was a magic cape that protected her." The years went by like that, she said, the girls inseparable despite the changes in their world, the treachery of friends and boys, the ups and downs of puberty.

The first time they kissed, she said, in grade ten, they were in Hannah's bedroom. Hannah's mother thought they were doing trigonometry homework, but they were wrapped in a *Starry Night* comforter watching *Titanic* with Leonardo DiCaprio and Kate Winslet. After it ended, Hannah got up to lock the door. She had a weird look on her face. She smoothed back her hair and ordered Isabel to get naked so she could draw her.

Isabel thought she misheard. "What?"

"Take off your clothes."

Isabel was stunned. Her mind began racing. She knew that her next move would change everything forever. They would never be able to go back again. She squeezed her eyes shut and lifted the shirt over her head. She unclasped her bra. A shiver tickled her spine.

Cate waited patiently for the rest.

Isabel had a faraway look in her eyes. She brushed her fingers across her lips, as though the tender imprint of a kiss were still there. She told Cate about their plan to run away together after their last year of high school, about using her babysitting money to buy two one-way tickets to Saint-Joseph-de-la Rive, the most remote place in Quebec she could find. She described in detail, as though it were yesterday, the bus terminal at 6:00 a.m., too big, too still, too quiet, only a handful of people milling about. The excitement she felt. The hard bench she sat on waiting for Hannah. Going to the ticket counter at least a dozen times to see if Hannah was in line, the garbled last calls for passengers to board at the gate. Begging the driver to wait a few more minutes. "Désolé, pas possible," he said, slamming the luggage compartment, climbing into his seat, and levering the door shut. Isabel watched it pull away, staring at the space where the bus, flight to love, had just been. "It felt like a knife stabbing me." She forced a smile. "After that, I went home and cut my hair really short."

*

Isabel waited a set number of days before she began dropping in unannounced. It was Cate's idea. She wanted Nuna to have settled first, gotten comfortable around the house.

"Yo, dude!" Isabel high-fived Nuna and collapsed on the couch. "It's good to see you! Do me a favour, would ya, and get me a glass of water."

"I'll go," Cate said. "Rough day?"

"Just a lot of dumb shit. False alarms, people using our service to jump the queue, that kind of thing. Where's Liam?"

"Out with Mo and the captain of the debate team," Cate called out from the kitchen.

"Boy, he's really obsessed with that team, isn't he? Who's Mo?"

Cate returned, glass in hand. "Just another teacher, she runs the club with him."

Isabel glugged down the water, wiping her lips with the back of her sleeve. "Mo's a she?"

"Maureen…and it's not what you're thinking."

"Who says I'm thinking anything?"

Before Isabel put the glass down, Cate handed her a coaster for the table.

"So, how's the hand healing?"

Cate gave Isabel her palm to inspect. "See for yourself."

Nuna wandered over to the bookshelf, bored with their chatter. She dragged her finger along the spines of the books, pausing to read the occasional title.

Cate seized the opportunity. "If you're serious about going to college someday, you'll need to have read some of the same novels they teach high school students in the South." She got up and picked a book off the shelf. "George Orwell, for instance."

Nuna snatched it from her.

Cate winked at Isabel as she piled a few more into Nuna's hand—*Tale of Two Cities*, *Fahrenheit 451*, *Of Mice and Men*. Her own high school copies, in near perfect condition. "These are some of the classics." Cate sensed an untapped potential in Nuna, a curiosity, a willingness to venture into the unknown quite unlike the students she and Waleed had grown accustomed to, lazy, mercenary in their attitude toward learning, eager to get the diploma and get out. The new breed more interested in TikTok and texting than in a meaningful education.

"I miss country food," Nuna moaned, staring longingly at the cover of *Animal Farm*. "I want *muktuk*."

"Well, maybe we can see about it later," Isabel said, patting the space beside her on the couch.

Nuna flopped down. She offloaded the pile of books to the coffee table. "Do you know muktuk?"

They shook their heads.

"Blubber, it's so awesome, it tastes like the ocean." Her eyes had a dreamy, distant look.

"If you're still hungry, toast yourself a bagel. Or go get an apple from the fridge," Cate said.

Nuna wrinkled her nose. "Did you know that our food connects us to the earth? It connects us to the animals and the water, it connects us to each other."

Cate almost said, "You are what you eat," but it suddenly sounded trite, even to her. Instead, she smiled uncertainly.

"You might be a teacher but you have a lot to learn, Mom."

Isabel glanced at Cate, trying to read her reaction.

Mom.

It sent shockwaves through Cate. It echoed in her ears. But unlike Liam, it didn't upset her. She sat with it for a while, qualifying it, instead, as a term of endearment, a sign that Nuna might be letting her guard down.

*

The weather was warming up again, though nights were still dipping below zero. Nuna was glum. A woman from her village, homeless and in her sixties, had recently frozen to death at the construction site of a downtown luxury condo. A celebrated artist who came south to pursue her career. Her work had made it to art galleries in Paris and New York.

Nuna got word of her death on Facebook. What the mainstream media didn't report, what Nuna had told Cate and Isabel and what everyone in the Montreal urban Inuit community knew, was that she had first left her village because of an abusive husband. Nuna insisted on going to the memorial service at Cabot Square.

"Of course," Cate said, "how can you not?" She and Isabel accompanied her.

The three exited the Atwater metro and made their way to the regular meet-up spot for many of Montreal's urban Inuit who considered it their satellite home, a place to connect as a community, to laugh and cry and drink together. Cate always wondered how they came to see a small, cemented-over park in the middle of trafficky downtown as a suitable replacement for their real home of snow and ice and endless horizons. "It's so ironic," Cate blurted out.

"What?" Isabel slowed her pace so the others could keep up with her.

"A descendant of one of the First Peoples of this country, survivors of the coldest weather, unable to find a warm place to sleep."

Nuna nodded. "She was definitely homeless." She told them the woman's name meant "snow" and that she'd become one of the regulars begging for change on the metro level of the Alexis Nihon Plaza. One of the ones the cops regularly harassed or threatened to ticket for loitering.

Nuna and Isabel jaywalked through traffic while Cate waited for the light to change. They walked toward a small group of mourners in jackets and sunglasses, where an easel had been set up to honour the woman, a cardboard-mounted nine-by-twelve-inch photograph adorned with a wreath of artificial flowers.

Cate noticed a few non-Indigenous people circulating among the group. Better dressed, they wore T-shirts that said "Know History" in English and Inuktitut and went around handing out roses to everybody.

A microphone was set up near the front next to a pair of card tables pushed together for coffee and snacks. Nuna zeroed in on a pink milk crate filled with granola bars and freckled bananas. She asked if anyone wanted anything.

"Is the pope Catholic?" Isabel said.

"Huh?"

Isabel told her never mind, just get me a coffee, and don't forget the sugar. Three, just in case. "And bring me some pretzels, if they have."

Local film crews were recording clips for the six o'clock news. They interviewed someone at the foot of the John Cabot monument, a White guy from an Indigenous organization who spoke kindly about the dead woman, remembering her artwork and the things she loved, her grandchildren, sewing, her home in the North. He kept insisting that she wasn't sick or inebriated, she just lacked housing. He paused for effect and glared into the camera. "What happened to her in this day and age, in a city such as ours, is unconscionable."

Afterwards, mourners were waved to the front for the scheduled speeches. Cate huddled closer to Nuna. A leader from Kahnawake criticized the mayor for not having had the decency to show up to the ceremony. Someone from Kativik Ilisarniliriniq, the Nunavik school board, invited people to march with their roses to the site where the dead woman had been discovered.

Nuna refused to go. She didn't say why, just, "Let's take off!" She grabbed their roses and dumped them in the nearest trash bin. Cate and Isabel looked at each other in disbelief.

Nuna linked arms with them. "Come on, let's go!" She dragged them to her favourite shop in the Forum, less than two hundred metres from the square, that sold official NHL hockey sweaters and old photographs autographed by the greats.

Inside the building, Isabel pointed at the statue of Maurice Richard next to a small section of the original red tiered seats. She explained to Nuna that for seventy years, long before being converted into a multiplex movie theatre, it had been the Montreal Forum. "Home to the Canadiens, *best hockey team of all time*," she crowed.

"Seriously, dude," Nuna said. "You gotta be kidding." She looked around until she spotted an official licensed Pittsburgh Penguins trucker hat with "Crosby #87" embroidered on a side of the visor. "Oh, my God!" She put it on.

Cate noticed the price tag. "No bloody way."

"Pretty please, pretty pretty please with sugar on top?"

Isabel snatched the black and yellow cap off Nuna's head and put it on, admiring herself in the mirror. "Sold!" She took it to the cash and pulled out her debit card.

Nuna was happy as a two-year-old in a puddle. She hugged Isabel's hand into her chest with a goofy smile and her eyes squeezed shut. One crooked canine protruding like a Chiclet.

Cate glared at Isabel. She mimed her disapproval.

Whaa—? Isabel mouthed.

Isabel wrested herself from Nuna's grip, scowling at Cate. She apologized to the cashier and walked the cap back to its shelf. "I was wrong, I shouldn't have said yes, if you really want it, pay for it yourself."

"I need cash for that." Nuna pouted. "I don't have enough."

Cate stepped in. "You can always get a job." She couldn't tell if Isabel was on her side or not, but the fact that she came around and acted more or less in solidarity was good enough for Cate. There couldn't be any cracks in the armour. "Anyway, I have something else in mind for you—and I have no qualms about paying for it."

*

Having complained all the way to Papeterie Nota Bene that twenty-five bucks was a steal for the Sidney Crosby cap, Nuna chose a Moleskine called the Classic Notebook, a lined, softcover journal, hydrangea blue with rounded corners, a matching ribbon bookmark, and ivory-coloured acid-free pages.

"More like forty bucks," said Cate. "That cap was way overpriced."

"At least I'd get my money's worth."

"You mean *my* money."

Nuna shrugged.

Cate opened the book to demonstrate how its pages lay flat. "Trust me, this journal will serve you well. In no time, you'll be calling it your best friend."

"Hah! Doubtful, but whatever."

Back at home, they made a ceremony of it. Cate bought cannoli and brewed a fresh pot of coffee. She brought out a clean tablecloth and the crystal dessert plates. Everything had to be just right. She insisted on a contract; it would add gravitas to what they were about to embark on. Cate drafted and printed a short text.

"What's this?" Nuna said.

"You want to go to college someday?"

Nuna shrugged. Yes, no, maybe. Yes.

"Well, it's a contract." Cate glued it onto the first page of the notebook.

"You don't trust me?"

"A contract involves a serious commitment from both of us," Cate explained. "Learning is hard, but it affords people knowledge that's more than just a dump of information. It's about learning how to think. And a contract will make our promise real, it'll ensure accountability."

Nuna's eyes narrowed. "Like all the other contracts between my people and yours?"

Touché, Cate thought. But no, this wasn't the same thing, she would make sure of it. There would be no broken treaties, not from Cate. "Well, it's up to you. I'm not putting a gun to your head. Neither is Isabel, for that matter."

Nuna glanced from Cate to Isabel, then back to Cate again. She took her time reading through the contract, stumbling here and there on a word. She sighed and agreed to the terms and conditions, promised to read books and work hard on her assignments. The three hovered over the contract, making a tent with their bodies. She took the pen and signed her name, Nuna Maqaittik, just above Cate's. Below them, in doctor-style chicken scratch, Isabel witnessed their agreement, rendering it official.

*

Cate remembered the contract she had had with her father. It wasn't written down. It was unspoken. But it was etched in her brain. *Be the best. Let nothing get in your way.* In hindsight, Cate understood there had never really been a contract at all. There had only been her perception of one.

When her mother, barely into her forties, was diagnosed with cancer, Niall called Cate at Princeton. "Come home, your mother needs you."

"Shite," Cate barked into the phone. "Shite, shite, shite! No!"

"Not no, *now*!"

Cate squeezed her eyes shut. Tensing until they hurt.

"I didn't think I raised you to be this kind of person, that's what's shite, a festering hill of it." He breathed dramatically into the receiver.

"Come on, Dad. You, of all people, should know how important this is."

"Have you forgotten? Your mother sacrificed her life for you kids."

"For Margaret, you mean."

He didn't respond.

"I'm not saying I won't come, but it's not an emergency, it can wait a day or two."

He hung up on her.

Much as it irked her, Cate capitulated. She arranged to put her studies on hold to be her mother's caregiver. She felt guilty for her resentment, but she couldn't help it.

During the flight home, Cate thought about how her parents had met on the intoxicating grounds of academia, where older professors seduced younger women with their consummate knowledge and charm. Some of it he'd told her, the rest she'd imagined: how he wooed her mother until all she could think about was meeting him after class; how he instructed the secretary to hold his calls and cancel his appointments. She imagined him pouring them each a glass of whiskey from a bottle he hid at the back of his filing cabinet. She thought of the dimly lit office and Billie Holiday's haunting voice, crackling from his tape machine.

When Cate arrived home, Niall exploded. Growing up, she should have been more grateful, more patient. She should have tried to understand the situation they were in, the toll Margaret's handicap had taken on her mother. Cate was selfish. She was too this, not enough that. His disappointment stung.

Her mother shuffled out from the bedroom to see what all the fuss was about. Cate was shocked to see her, usually stylish and made up, wearing slippers and a track suit. Her face was ghostly pale, and her eyes were more sunken than they had ever been when Margaret lived at home. Niall scolded her for getting out of bed.

She waved her hand dismissively. "Oh, your father." Head wrapped in a paisley scarf, she led Cate to her old room, still exactly the way she'd left it with her books organized alphabetically by author, her neatly displayed medals and diplomas from elementary school to university hanging above her desk. She had forgotten about her complete set of *CIV/n* in mint condition, which Niall had given her for her high school graduation. Very few of these Montreal literary magazines from the 1950s were still in existence.

The zip came down on her mother's top. "Do you want to see my scar?"

"Not particularly."

The cut was still fresh. "The doctor did a good job, don't you think?"

Cate flinched. They'd never been the kind of mother and daughter who talked about their bodies. She fought the urge to turn away. "Glad it went well."

Visiting the rest of the house, she discovered that at some point her father's clothes, shoes, and toiletries had migrated into the guest room. Book Jenga, Cate thought, noting the precarious tower of books by his bed.

Her mother rushed to Niall's defence. "With my illness, it's for the best. And we both sleep better now."

Cate couldn't tell if her mother believed her own story. She felt like a stranger in the house.

The days crawled by, Niall locked in his study, Cate attending to her mother in the overheated bedroom, every surface cluttered with pill bottles and Kleenex boxes. Cate sat in the threadbare upholstered chair she'd lounged on as a child, sideways with her legs hanging over the arms. Mostly just reading while her mother drifted in and out of sleep or picked at the daily crossword puzzle.

"What's another word for dishevelled? Ten letters."

"Bedraggled?"

"Hm, right, how did I not think of that?"

Cate couldn't fathom why she'd been made to interrupt her studies for this. It wasn't like her mother really needed her. "That's not the point," Niall said in hushed tones. "The fact that you're here shows you care. It's important for her recovery."

Once she asked Cate to pluck her chin hairs; her eyes were failing, and Niall didn't go for lady stubble. While Cate tweezed, her mother closed her eyes and confessed how guilty she had felt when they sent Margaret off to the group home. “It was really Niall,” she said. “He wanted to lighten my load, enough was enough, I’d done my bit, we both had, no one would begrudge me a few years of doing what I wanted in life.” Tears moistened the corners of her eyes.

Cate dabbed them away.

“I was exhausted, so I gave in.”

Midweek, things came to a head. They were playing Scrabble. In the middle of the game, her mother peeled back the covers, levered herself up, and lumbered into the living room like she needed a change of scenery. She paced from the piano to the window and back again. Her lips were white, but Cate didn’t buy her excuse that it was from the chemo. Something heavy was weighing on her mind. Cate offered her a hot cup of tea.

She shook her head. “I need to share something.” She reclined on the couch and loosened her head scarf.

Cate couldn’t imagine what she wanted to say, what could possibly be worse than cancer?

Her mother spat mucus into a tissue and stuffed it under her sleeve.

Cate stared at her bald head. Did she need anything? she asked. A glass of water? Tylenol?

“Can you please just stop?”

A knot balled up inside of Cate.

Her mother inhaled with difficulty. Words tumbled out of her mouth, a secret she’d harboured for years, it seemed.

Cate grimaced. She felt like she was in a soap opera, a maudlin, implausible, meandering story about a man with a secret life. A man with another wife. Not a wife-wife, just the mother of a child who shared his DNA. Her mother rattled off the details hastily, coolly, about another family somewhere else, a family demanding—and receiving—the man’s attention. Her face was grey and dull, belying a quiet strength.

The more Cate heard, the more she wanted it to stop. She felt nauseous.

Her mother exhaled. "Your father has a child with another woman."

"I heard you the first time." Cate scratched the back of her hand. The itch was intense. When she was young, the dermatologist had prescribed a cream for it, but she hadn't needed it in years. She scratched until her skin turned red. "What the fuck!"

"Please, Cate." Her mother hated that language in the house.

Cate expected a litany of Niall's failures as a husband: liar, cheat, hypocrite. But that's not how it went. Instead, she got more information than she wanted—the woman's name, how long it had gone on for, the age of the child. All the things she had no interest in knowing. "I don't get it. How can you put up with him being in this house?" she shouted. "Why don't you just kick him out?"

Her mother shook her head. She was beyond sadness or anger. She spoke with resolve because how could she not, these were the facts, this was the reality. What could she do to change it? And what good would anger serve?

Cate thought of her father sneaking off to see his secret family, of the nights he'd been scarce, of all his lies to them about a faculty meeting or a big to-do with some visiting professor. Of his having to stay late at the office to meet an important publication deadline. She imagined their clandestine room off campus, a small two-and-a-half with mousetraps along the baseboards and food smells in the hallway. She thought of what music they would have listened to, what they ate, where they made love—on the floor or on the bed? She thought of two people going at it with such intensity they didn't give a fuck about the hurt they were causing innocent people.

She remembered a night he had made them pesto for supper, a new recipe with olives and sundried tomatoes, a recipe he said he got from a "friend." She mostly remembered the sheepish look on his face when her mother asked, What friend, who? Is it someone I know?

Her mother reached out and touched her hand.

Cate pulled away.

"We can do hard things even when we don't think we can." From the sound of it, she had already forgiven him and so should she. Her mother blamed it on circumstance, not on a lack of love for her. He was still a good man and a good father. Nothing would take away from that. Life is short, she reminded Cate, it wasn't worth letting something you can't change eat you up from the inside.

"And yet, here you are," Cate said, cruelly. "Riddled with disease." She didn't actually say it, but oh, how she wanted to. The point was, she missed Cate's point entirely. Cate was angry and hurt and disappointed in her father. She felt contempt for her mother for accepting the situation, for letting him get away with it, for turning the other cheek, for not standing up and saying, you're a bastard, I never deserved this. Cate couldn't look at her. "Why would you even consider forgiving him after all you gave up to care for Margaret?"

"Gave up?"

"Like maybe your whole fucking life." Cate knew it hurt her, but she couldn't stop herself. She attacked without remorse. "Jesus fucking Christ, what's wrong with you?"

Her mother pulled a blanket over her knees. A dreamy look came over her. "I guess…I still love him. He was a good man in a difficult position." She continued rationalizing: how could she blame him, who knows what she might have done in his shoes? Blah, blah, blah.

Cate couldn't bear to stay any longer.

Niall understood. He called her a cab. He waited outside with Cate, mumbled a weak thank you for coming. Said he appreciated her sacrifice.

Cate noticed a spot on his cheek that he had missed while shaving. "Don't appreciate *my* sacrifice, appreciate hers."

He nodded. Their roles had reversed. It was as though she was the parent and he, the child. She still loved him, of course, like any parent loves a child no matter what shit they pull. But part of her hated him too because who could ignore a deception of such magnitude?

*

Nuna kept circling back. She persisted. Why no kids? She didn't get that a person's past, good or bad, could influence their life choices, because in her world, you focused on the moment. If you were with someone, you had children. Lots. You made a family.

Cate's phone vibrated. "To be continued," she told Nuna.

Nuna went to curl up on the living room couch. She opened her novel and began reading.

Cate checked her message. Isabel texted that she was off tomorrow, and wouldn't it be fun to go shopping together, just the girls? Cate replied with a thumbs-up. She'd been meaning to splurge on a few new outfits for Nuna, skirts and blouses, accessories, decent shoes.

She didn't realize the decent shoes would be a source of conflict. Didn't realize the kind of hard bargain Nuna drove. This skirt, this pair of pants...for these. Doc Martens. Exactly like Isabel's, only in green.

After the shopping spree, wandering through the underground passage between the Bay and Place Montreal Trust, Nuna insisted they pile into a photo booth and take silly pictures. Cate told her no, it's a rip-off.

"Come on, it'll be fun," Nuna said. "A souvenir."

Isabel nudged Cate, playfully batted her lashes.

"It's two against one," Nuna said.

"Oh, what the hell." Cate pulled out her wallet. "Back in the day, it only cost a quarter for a strip of four."

"When was that, in the 1800s?" Nuna chuckled.

Cate rolled her eyes. "Hardy har har."

They crowded into the booth. Nuna slid the curtain shut.

Isabel pulled out a tube of lipstick. She ran it around Cate's lips. "Let's brighten you up, you look a little pale." She brushed some mascara on Cate's eyelashes. "Might as well go all out if we're doing this."

"Me too!" Nuna angled her head back. She had recently dyed the tips of her hair fire-engine red.

They checked themselves in the mirror. Cate was surprised at how the lipstick made her lips look full, how the mascara brought attention to her eyes. How Isabel's flourishes of makeup offset the muted earth tones of her sensible sweater, hoop earrings, and wooden beads. She quite liked herself.

"We'll probably look like a bunch of clowns," Isabel joked. "With all this makeup."

"No, we look cool, dude!"

They posed, they giggled, they hammed it up. Soon afterward, the booth spat out the photo strip.

As it turned out, the makeup was a little over the top, but they didn't, as Isabel predicted, look like clowns. The French braid that Nuna had made for Cate earlier that morning still looked impeccable, her few grey hairs, among the blond, hardly visible at all.

The first picture caught them off guard as they scrambled to arrange themselves before the flash went off. "That was shit," Isabel had snorted as they hurriedly posed for the next.

In the second picture, Nuna was making rabbit ears behind their heads; in the third, everyone was pulling silly faces. Cate's green eyes were crossed, her lips puckered like a fish. Nuna and Isabel were wagging their tongues and making Bullwinkle antlers with their fanned-out fingers.

The fourth picture was the best of all. In the lull before the final flash, Cate had called for everyone to smarten up and look nice. Nuna said, "Aww, do we have to?" and Cate said, "Come on, just do it. Let's have one nice picture of the three of us."

Cate and Isabel threw their arms around Nuna, whose hands and fingers against her chest were perfectly curled into the shape of a heart.

*

Cate watched them play street hockey from the window, Nuna in her Sidney Crosby jacket, Liam and Isabel in Habs jerseys. A month had passed since the clocks had sprung forward. The snow had melted except for a small mound, like a dirty blanket, on the edge of their lawn. The grey had lifted, and the birds were chattering again. Isabel passed to Nuna, who slipped a quick one past Liam. Isabel jumped up and high-fived Nuna.

Cate introduced Game Day after Nuna complained that all they did all week was study. On Sunday afternoons, Isabel would show up to play street hockey, while Cate, who had zero desire to run around after a ball sweating, made the meal and planned for table games that were fun but also educational.

Cate rapped on the windowpane. Supper was ready.

Liam grabbed a beer and sat at the table while the girls freshened up in the bathroom. "She's definitely got the moves, that one."

"Nuna?" Cate said.

"No, Isabel! Of course, Nuna. She's a good little player." He uncapped his beer. "Too bad she's not a boy, she could play in the NHL."

Cate had made Mexican food. She found an online recipe for fried avocado tacos, corn salad, and a side of taqueria guacamole flavoured with lime and cilantro. For dessert, rice pudding with ginger, amaranth, and mango.

"What *is* this?" Nuna asked when they were all seated.

"It's good to broaden your palate." Cate filled everyone's bowl with salad. "Learn a little something about the other cultures out there."

Isabel heaped the guacamole onto her plate. "*My* people's food. Yum." She swiped a finger through and licked it off. "So, tell us what people up north do for fun."

Nuna smiled. "Hockey, of course. Volleyball, too. Then there's radio games, like Bingo and Guess the Animal."

"Guess the Animal...what's that?" Liam chugged his beer.

"It's a radio show where people, mainly elders and hunters, call in and make animal sounds and people try to guess what it is." Nuna picked a kernel of corn out of her salad and nibbled on it.

"What a great way to pass on knowledge," Liam said. "I might use that in my history class. What's the hardest animal to imitate?"

Nuna thought for a minute. She scratched her head. "Fish."

They all looked at her, speechless.

Nuna burst out laughing. The others caught on and joined the laughter. Nuna struggled with the taco, trying to keep the chilies and cabbage from sliding out the sides. The juices splattered down her chin. She ended up wearing most of it on her face.

"I see you're enjoying that," Liam said. "How about using your napkin?"

She shrugged, talking with her mouth full. "Would be much tastier with meat."

Isabel winked at Cate.

Liam went to the fridge for another beer. Isabel asked him to bring her one, too. Cate passed, preferring not to drink around Nuna even though Liam had always argued that Nuna, like most of her people, needed to learn that it was possible to drink without getting wasted. Cate agreed that he was probably right, but still felt awkward about it. Substance abuse was rampant in northern communities and whether Nuna had a problem or not, she preferred not to open that Pandora's box. Especially in their home.

"Maybe get something for Nuna while you're there," Cate said.

He reached around and found a can of Sprite.

"No Coke?"

"Bad for you," Cate reminded her. "If a tarnished penny comes out of a glass of Coke perfectly shiny, imagine what it does to your stomach?" Her father had told her the very same thing whenever she begged for one in the grocery store.

"Not to mention your teeth," Liam said.

Nuna rolled her eyes and pulled up the tab on her can. She glugged down half of it in one go, banged the can on the table, and let out a loud *haaaaa* from the back of her throat.

Liam scowled. "How about a round of This or That?" He pointed to Nuna. "*Breaking Bad* or *Ozark*?"

"*Breaking Bad*, no contest!" Nuna turned to Isabel. "Poutine or onion rings?"

"Poutine. Cate, book or e-book?"

"Book." It was Liam's turn. "*Star Wars* or *Star Trek*?"

Liam hesitated.

"C'mon, no thinking!"

"*Star Trek*. Patrick Roy or Carey Price?"

The game had gone full circle. It was back to Nuna. "Screw the Montreal Canadiens! Pick some other team, Pops."

Cate held her breath.

Liam's jaw tightened. "I told you not to call me that."

Isabel gripped her knife and fork.

"It's Liam. Just Liam." He paused for emphasis. "Or, better yet, Mr. Connelly."

Nuna stared back stone-faced. She blinked normally.

Cate got up and collected the dishes.

"Is there dessert?" Isabel called to Cate.

Cate peeled the Saran off the pudding, racking her brain for something to lighten the mood.

Liam shouted after her to get him another beer.

Cate plopped one in front of him. "Why don't we play Bucket List?" She sat on the edge of her chair. "You first, Nuna."

"What's a bucket list?"

"It's a list of things you want to do before you die." Cate ladled the pudding into small dessert bowls and passed them around.

Nuna scratched her head. "Hmmm, well, obviously, my number one is to meet Sidney Crosby. What's on yours, Isabel?"

"I've always wanted to go to Casablanca. Cate?"

"Come on! Really?" Cate's eyes widened. "That's first on *my* list too—I just love the film. I think I've seen it a hundred times."

"Me too! I'm crazy for Ingrid Bergman." Isabel winked at her.

Liam frowned. "Casablanca? This is the first I'm hearing this."

Nuna began calling out random place names. It surprised Cate that she knew so many. And not just ordinary places that everyone knew. The Seychelles, Zanzibar, Brazil, Tibet. She rattled them off, the way balls are called in a bingo game. Like she'd memorized them for a test.

Isabel chimed in with a few more of her own while Liam stewed.

He waved at Cate. "I haven't said mine, yet." He snapped his fingers to get everyone's attention. He pointed to himself and shouted, "Hey! Over here."

Nuna turned to face him. "Yes, Pops?" She clapped a hand over her mouth and sank into her chair.

Cate's throat constricted.

"Sorry, slipped out."

He sprang to his feet and left the table without another word. Cate had no choice but damage control. She knew that if she didn't follow him, if it looked the least bit like she wasn't onside, it would fester and resurface when she least expected it. He would end up taking it out on her.

*

Cate descended the stairs, lips tight. Nuna was sitting on the bottom step, writing in her journal. Cate patted her on the shoulder. "Don't worry, he'll be fine."

Nuna slapped the book shut. She hurried up to her room and closed the door.

Isabel was loading the dishwasher.

Cate flashed her palm. "Don't ask."

"I won't then."

They sat at the table, nursing an awkward silence. Cate slipped off her wedding ring. She rubbed her finger.

Isabel reached over and took her hand.

"It's eczema," Cate said. "I've had it since childhood. It comes and goes. I have cream for it."

"That just deals with the symptom, not the cause."

"Meaning?"

"It's the body's way of telling you something's wrong." Isabel eyed her suspiciously. "You know, when I first met you, I saw death in your aura."

"Don't tell me you believe that baloney?"

"Take it or leave it," Isabel said. "But there's definitely something there."

Cate took her hand back. "Look, I'd prefer if you kept those kinds of thoughts to yourself, okay?" She put her ring back on.

Isabel shrugged. "Okay." She thought for a minute, asked how it was going with Nuna's studies and was she taking it seriously.

"Strangely, yes. We just finished *Animal Farm*."

"The one with the pigs?"

"Yes—she loved it. Especially the political aspect." Cate remembered the dishwasher. She loaded in a soap pod and pressed the start button. "And while we're on the subject of Nuna..."

"You're like a dog with a bone."

Cate sat down again. "What do you know? About her story, I mean."

Isabel leaned forward, sliding her palms across the table. "I don't know much but I know enough."

Cate wondered whether Isabel would tell all or just provide the need-to-know facts.

"There's a boyfriend named Amaruq. Nuna lives with him in his Dorval apartment. But you already know that."

"Yes."

Isabel explained that he was employed as a cook at the Raglan Mine up north, and that he spent his off weeks in the city with Nuna. "When he's in town, he spends money like there's no tomorrow. Booze, drugs, you name it. They fight a lot."

Cate couldn't imagine Nuna in a toxic relationship, not this Nuna who was now focused on books and getting her assignments done. Eager to learn. She wondered what she had told Amaruq about her whereabouts? Where did he think she had been these last weeks? Was he in town or up north? Every question sparked another. Was he the reason she was taken by ambulance to the hospital that day? Would he eventually come looking for her, and, if so, would she blow him off or cave and go back to him? Most importantly: Were she and Liam in any kind of danger?

*

It was late by the time Cate settled into bed.

Face turned toward her, Liam was asleep, hand clenched on the pillow.

"Love you," she whispered. She reached down and fondled his ear.

He stirred, eyes still closed. "Love you, too."

Liam's ears, delicate as spring petals. Sparsely freckled. His ears were what had attracted her to him when they first met. She couldn't help touching them.

Waleed had come into Cate's life by then. He was a surrogate brother to her. They had met in grad school at Queen's University and remained close, plotting their career paths together, vying for and landing jobs teaching English literature at McGill University.

They also became the official stewards of each other's love lives. In the blink of an eye, it seemed, they were celebrating five years as officemates.

Cate had had no intention of attending his annual gathering of cherry-picked students and faculty. Waleed refused to take no for an answer. "Habibti, you have to get out a little. *Yallah.*"

She didn't wear anything special, just a summer dress from Winners, leather sandals and her signature strand of wooden beads. She brought his favourite stinky cheese and a Bordeaux that had been sitting in her pantry too long.

Waleed raised his arms in a grand gesture when she walked through the door. "*Alhamdulillah!*" He cheek-kissed her Arabic style, three times, and promptly introduced her to a student in his evening class, older than the usual twentysomethings with their hair dyed every colour of the rainbow. The student had shortish auburn hair and the hint of a smile that suggested there was more to him than met the eye. Understated but mischievous. Irish, for sure, Cate thought. Complicated.

"Meet Liam Connelly, my star pupil. Liam, this is Cate." Waleed excused himself to open the wine and unwrap the cheese she had brought.

Cate and Irish Eyes hit it off. They skipped over the pleasantries and began trading friendly jabs. He teased her about her Westmount roots, tennis camps and private schools, holidays at the Cape. He called her a WASP princess; she asked if he belonged to the Balconville Catholic cell of Pointe-Saint-Charles and if they still burned old tires and broken furniture on Victoria Day. He brought her a Guinness without asking what she wanted. She swigged it straight out of the bottle. "You look familiar."

"Maybe we were married in another life."

She laughed.

He asked her to tell him a secret. She told him what she hadn't told anyone else, not even Waleed, about writing a hippie soap opera when she was eleven, about a dozen druggie teens with names like Rebecca and Faith and Gage, who lived together on a commune and hitchhiked and overdosed and made love and peace freely. "Things I knew nothing about that I thought were rebellious and romantic. Believe it or not, I filled two notebooks with that shit!" she shouted, her voice carrying across the room.

Liam politely shushed her.

She nodded and continued at a volume she mistook for a whisper. "Virginia Woolf said that no one should write anything before the age of thirty. I should've listened to her. She was fucking right."

The other guests turned to look at her.

"But you didn't know that then," he said.

"Sure I did, I had already read most of her books."

He whistled in amazement.

"So, I decided then and there that I'd only write the real book, the *book* book, when I had something worthwhile to write about."

"And? Are you writing?"

"Yes and no. I got a job." Cate finished her beer. "Now I correct the shitty papers that my students write." She clapped a hand over her mouth. "Oops, I guess I shouldn't be saying that to a student."

He touched her shoulder.

"And what I write these days are research papers. I'm very good at it." She ran her fingers along his ears. "Did you know you have the cutest ears? You even have freckles on your lobes!"

The other party guests faded away; it was only their laughter, their adrenalin in space and time. He moved so close she smelled the Guinness on his breath. Their lips brushed ever so lightly.

Cate had no idea how many drinks she'd had but it was enough to embolden her to take him by the hand and lead him into Waleed's bedroom, an oasis of dark furnishings and velvet drapery, where they collapsed on the Persian carpet and made out.

The next day when Waleed phoned to check in on her, she was still hung over, lying next to Liam who was fast asleep. She was giddy, embarrassed, trying to keep to a whisper.

"Well, young lady, this is one for the books!" He chuckled.

"What, because I drank too much?

"Because this is the first time we've both gone for the same man."

"Oh, shit." Cate couldn't think of anything intelligent to say. "Sorry, I thought you were trying to set us up."

He sighed.

"I didn't think he was your type."

"He totally was, Habibti. But I'll live."

*

Cate kissed Liam goodbye. She handed him a muffin and his coffee Thermos. He strapped his bag over his shoulder and hurried toward the yellow bus parked in front of the school, where Mo stood with a clipboard checking names off her list. From the car, Cate could hear the chorus of "Hey, Sir" as eager students accosted him with last-minute questions about the tournament. Liam had a word with Mo and got to work loading luggage onto the bus.

Cate couldn't wait for them to leave. She had a long list of activities planned with Nuna and Isabel, from sleepovers to takeout dinners to late-night movies. It was their first weekend with the house to themselves and Cate was taking full advantage of her freedom.

Her shoulders relaxed as the boisterous bus, honking goodbyes, rumbled off school property and turned the corner, en route for Trois-Rivières. By the time she got home, Isabel's Jeep was already in the driveway. "Well, that was fast," she thought to herself.

Cate cleared the kitchen table. She took out her binder of assignments and her high school copy of *Of Mice and Men*, with her youthful notes pencilled in the margins. She poured two glasses of water and went to get Nuna in the living room. "First work, then play." She clapped her hands. "Come on, chop chop, as my father used to say."

Nuna turned her nose up. "It's supposed to be relax time, Mom," she whined. "It's the weekend."

"Let me remind you, this whole thing was your idea." Cate grabbed the remote and turned off the television.

"You mean Isabel's."

"I mean yours. You agreed, you signed a contract."

"Coerced, I was coerced!"

Cate sparked with anger. "That's unfair. You know that's not true."

"Okay, I take it back then."

"So, get off your butt and get your books." They could easily have been mistaken for a bickering mother and daughter. "And get dressed while you're at it. It's ten o'clock, for heaven's sake!"

Nuna shuffled after her in protest.

"WTF?" Cate said.

"What?"

"Why the face?" Cate chortled at her own joke.

Nuna sighed and lumbered up the stairs, grumbling.

Isabel glared at Cate. She put her hands on her hips. "Seriously?"

"And you...Why don't you go...uh...read up on the latest ambulatory services in remote regions or something." Cate handed Isabel her laptop.

"Okey-dokey. You *do* know that all work and no play—"

"I'm not dull, I'm reliable. I keep my promises."

"I'll be back for lunch, you'd better be done." Isabel crossed Nuna coming down the stairs wearing Cate's grey silk blouse in a way Cate had never worn it, knotted above her jeans, at the waist, sleeves rolled up to the elbows. It looked good on her.

"Hey, dude, where are you going? I thought we were supposed to go to Ottawa to see a flower show or something."

"Tulips," Isabel said. "And that's later this afternoon." Isabel explained that she was just moving over to the living room for a couple of hours. "Anyway, you chicas are busy now."

Nuna dumped her books on the table. She dragged the chair out and plunked herself down. "*Qanuipit*?"

"*Qanuipit*," Cate repeated mindlessly, recognizing Nuna's attempt to sabotage the lesson.

"*Auka*! No! You say '*Qanuingittunga*.'"

Cate waved her hand, dismissively. "Yes, that." She tried to repeat the elusive phrase, the one Nuna had spent a week teaching her. "Uh, um, hannu…something, something, the thing you just said."

"For a teacher, you have a pretty bad memory."

Cate took it as her cue to begin. "Speaking of which: Lennie."

Nuna frowned. "Good catch!" She opened her book. "You always find a way to turn life into school."

"Tell me about Lennie," Cate said. "Lennie Small." She emphasized small.

Nuna's lightbulb went on. She tittered into her hand. "Eeeey… Small."

Cate was relieved. Irony—check. "I'm waiting."

"I'd rather talk about George." Sunlight through the window grazed her temple.

"Talking about George is talking about Lennie, too."

Nuna wrinkled her nose, opening her journal to the homework.

"So, talk to me about Lennie," Cate repeated.

"Well, besides that he's an animal?"

"A what?"

"I'm wrong?"

Cate furrowed her brow. She tried to follow Nuna's logic. Animals weren't self-reflective. They acted on instinct. They lacked empathy. They killed. Lennie fit the bill. In a final act of animal passion, he killed a human. Therefore, it followed that Lennie was an animal. "I don't know if I'd call him an animal," she countered. "He and George were best friends, they dreamed of getting a place together, they loved each other."

"Some friends," she said. "A friend doesn't shoot a friend in the back of the head."

"Actually, if you think about it, George's killing of Lennie is the ultimate act of compassion. He does it to protect Lennie. It's ironic. It's sad."

"Like me telling that girl to kill the pigeon?" said Nuna. "It's not sad at all, it just is."

Cate thought for a minute. "How is it not sad?"

Nuna reread her notes silently, mouthing the words. She picked up her pencil with its half-chewed eraser, laid her head on the table, and scrawled something into the margin.

Cate repeated herself. "How is it not sad, Nuna? George is all alone now, travelling the country in search of work. Rootless. No best buddy. No dream of home to look forward to."

"Here's how I see it," Nuna said. "Lennie is an animal."

"You said that."

"Animals act without thinking. They're all instinct. Do you agree?"

Cate imagined Nuna's brain hard at work trying to incorporate her understanding of a week's worth of literary terms. Nursing the hope that maybe if she got it right, they could cut this short and get onto the business of going to Ottawa to see the flowers.

Tulips, Cate was already correcting her. "Okay, let's assume, as you posit, that Lennie is the animal."

Nuna raised her eyebrows in agreement, Inuit-style. "And George is the human with thinking powers. He's like a hunter standing perfectly still at the breathing hole, waiting."

Cate didn't have the faintest idea where Nuna was going with this.

"Or like a hunter coming face to face with a polar bear."

"But George and Lennie are friends," Cate said, bringing fact back into the discussion.

"No!" Nuna wrinkled her nose. "One is an animal, and one is a hunter. They're face to face. There's respect but no friendship. One is saying, don't do this thing and the other is saying, I'm doing it because it's what I do."

"There's no physical fight between them," Cate reminded her. "And who's telling who not to do something?"

Nuna sighed, flushed and exasperated. "George realizes he can't stop Lennie. Lennie is big, he has control, and when an animal and a human fight each other, one wins and the other loses. One eats, the other is eaten. But they also respect each other. They respect the situation they're in. Man versus Animal. It's a sacred power struggle. In the North, nature is not our enemy. Nature just is and we're all part of it, including Lennie and George."

Cate saw that Nuna really believed this. "I've never heard of that."

"You have a lot to learn, Mom."

Cate was drained. She wondered whether to give Nuna credit for her effort or initiate a discussion about what is an acceptable interpretation and what is not. Isabel, impatient, was texting Cate. Were they done yet and was she allowed out of prison? *Sure,* Cate texted back. *I think I've hit a wall.*

Isabel reappeared with the laptop.

Nuna jumped to her feet, waving her notes at Isabel. "I think Mom is surprised that I thought of something that she didn't."

"Awesome! Hey, I like your blouse."

"*My* blouse," Cate corrected.

Isabel's eyes darted from Cate to Nuna, and back to Cate. "What's for lunch?"

"Yeah, Mom, what's for lunch?"

*

The trip to the tulip festival had been Liam's idea. "It's the country's capital and aside from being beautiful, the festival has historical significance."

Cate agreed it would be a great learning experience. On the road, she explained to both Nuna and Isabel that the festival celebrated the role of Canadian troops in the liberation of the Netherlands and commemorated the birth of Dutch Princess Margriet during World War II—the only royal ever born in Canada. "Every year the Netherlands sends Ottawa a bunch of tulips to thank them."

Nuna was braiding Isabel's hair from the back seat. "Did you know that some of our people were soldiers, too?"

Cate peered at her through the rear-view mirror. "I didn't know the Inuit fought in the war."

Nuna met her gaze. "Is that what Liam teaches?"

Cate sensed an accusatory tone.

"Our elders say that they were very good hunters."

Cate smiled, hands confidently on the wheel. "You see, we're all teachers," she said.

Nuna continued styling Isabel's hair while Cate put the car in cruise control and enjoyed the sunny panorama. It was not an uncomfortable silence.

Nuna broke it. "Hey, since we're going to Ottawa, can we visit my *sanajik*?"

"What's a sanajik?" Isabel said.

"Someone very important in my culture. Sanajik means Maker."

"Go on," Cate said.

Nuna, razor-focused on her braiding, took her time before answering. "She's the one who cut my umbilical cord when I was born."

"What's the maker part?" Isabel said.

"By cutting the cord, the sanajik sends the baby out into the world, releasing her from the mom's attachment."

"Oh, yes, I read about that somewhere," Cate said, excited to share what she knew. "It's the person you're named after, often the mother's role model. If I remember correctly, the hope is that their skills and abilities will transfer to the baby."

"Auka, no!" Nuna said. "That's the *saunik*. The sanajik is the one who blesses you at birth and foretells what kind of person you should become. We honour our sanajiks with our first accomplishments. When I killed my first goose, I gave it to my sanajik. If I ever learn to sew, I'll give her the first thing I make. Like a hat or a pair of mitts."

A rite of passage. Cate repeated the definition back to her, committing it to memory. Mostly, she wanted to express her interest.

Nuna whipped out her phone. "I'm gonna call her."

Cate shot Isabel a look. Isabel shrugged. They held their tongue while Nuna prattled away in Inuktitut. She lifted the receiver away from her mouth. "She wants to know where to meet us."

Neither had the heart to say no. Cate was almost certain they had prearranged it. But she didn't challenge her.

Nuna hung up and fastened Isabel's braid with an elastic.

Isabel reached up to touch it. She slid open the mirror on her visor and turned her head to admire it. "Pretty cool, dude," she said. "Expertly woven."

"That's gorgeous!" Through the rear-view mirror, Cate noted the sparkle in Nuna's eyes. "You've done a beautiful job there."

"Good enough to be a hairdresser?"

"Hairdressing is definitely a good skill to have," Cate said.

"But?"

"But finish your studies first. Go to college, university. You and I both know you can pick up those other...technical skills later."

Nuna's sanajik, Lizzie, was waiting for them at the designated spot when they pulled up, her kids yanking on the doorhandle, squealing, "Nuna! Nuna!"

They piled into the car, elbowing each other to sit next to Nuna. The smaller ones crouched on the floor at her feet. Lizzie leaned forward and apologized for the noise. She suggested they go to Dow's Lake for the tulips instead of Confederation Park, it would be fun to be by the water on such a nice day, would give the kids a chance to burn off some energy.

Isabel set the GPS while Cate manoeuvred back onto the road. They drove in silence while Nuna and the others joked and laughed and poked each other. Their boisterous spirit made Cate smile. She shifted into park.

The back doors flew open, everyone spilling out. Lizzie and Nuna lagged, catching up on their news, while the kids dispersed like a gaggle of geese, giggling, chasing each other down to the lake.

Cate squinted at the colourful kayaks skimming across the water. "Were you in on this?" she asked Isabel.

"In on what?" Isabel looked away sheepishly.

"You could've told me, you know." Cate felt hurt that they had left her out.

"I wasn't sure how you'd react." Isabel stared at the children turning cartwheels in the grass. "I don't think tulips are high on their bucket list, though."

They wandered among the different varieties, half-heartedly reading the information panels. "I thought this was supposed to be our quality time together," Cate said. "You, me, Nuna."

Isabel pointed toward the shoreline, sunlight dancing off the water. "Do you want to take her away from that?"

Peals of their laughter rose from the beach, where a dozen families were barbecuing and throwing Frisbees. "Hm, I guess not. This visit is probably good for her."

They found a bench and sat.

"Are you ever going to tell me about Liam?" Isabel said.

"What about him?"

"Well, for starters, why he flipped out at dinner the other night."

Cate shifted her gaze to the lake where a gull had just slapped down. She told Isabel about their pact, about her making him agree to never have children. "He so wanted them."

"And you didn't?"

Cate's face hardened. She picked at a hangnail. "No."

Nuna's shrill voice rang out from a distance. "Hey, Mom!"

Cate looked up. She shouted across the grass. "Yes?"

"This is an awesome day!" Nuna flashed a smile, canine catching the light. She hooked arms with Lizzie and ran to catch up to the children.

Isabel smirked. Her leg nudged Cate's. "So, what's next? *Mom*."

Cate rolled her eyes. "It's no different than dude."

"If you say so."

*

The debate team won the provincials. Liam texted the news to Cate on Sunday morning. He also sent photos that Mo had taken, of the final group hug, of the team hoisting Liam into the air, of them proudly holding the polished trophy. Cate imagined their celebratory dinner at some cozy restaurant with wood panelling and lanterns on the table, Liam and Mo joining the kids with sensible soft drinks fizzing in their goblets. Cate sent a triple emoji of clapping hands.

It struck her as cold that she and Liam were texting when a phone call would have been just as easy—and more personal. When had they become those people? It wasn't so long ago they'd call at the end of a day spent apart just to hear the other's voice.

He texted that he and the kids would visit the town before grabbing the bus home. The girls wanted to shop. The boys wanted to see the old prison.

"He treats that debate team like his family," Isabel had remarked on the drive back from Ottawa. "Do you ever wonder sometimes...?"

Cate shook her head. The fact that he had a pet project was comforting. It filled a void he most certainly felt. "If it makes him happy, I'm happy."

Cate decided to call and congratulate him. Then she changed her mind. *He* should've been the one to ring *her* up. It was his win to announce. She flopped onto the couch.

Isabel appeared in the doorway holding a cup of coffee. "So? What's the word on the street?"

Cate glanced up from her phone. "They won."

"You don't look thrilled," Isabel said.

Cate pasted on a smile. "Don't be silly. Of course I am."

*

Nuna wouldn't say why they were driving to the airport. At breakfast, she simply asked whether Cate had anything special planned for the day. And if not, could she do her a humongous favour and drive her out there. Nuna loved hyperbole.

"What about your essay on 'The Lottery'?"

"Done." Nuna smiled.

Cate smiled back. Nuna was becoming more proficient. Essays that used to take her two weeks were now completed within a couple of days. And with almost no complaining.

Cate shifted into park while Nuna disappeared through the revolving door on her secret mission. She switched on the radio. The wait wasn't much of a wait. Nuna emerged with a bounce in her step, arms hugging a duct-taped package. The cardboard box had an Air Inuit sticker and a red "Freezer" stamp on it. Cate popped the trunk and turned off the radio.

Nuna didn't stop talking all the way home. She announced that she wanted to do something special for them. "I was thinking you and I could make a nice dinner for Liam. To celebrate his big win."

Cate was overjoyed—and surprised. She'd always felt that Nuna was uncomfortable around Liam, that she just tolerated him. Most of the time, when she wasn't pushing his buttons, intentionally or not, her exchanges with him consisted of a curt yes, no, maybe. "Uh, that's a nice gesture. What do you have in mind?"

Nuna's eyes shone.

"And what's in that special box of yours?"

"You'll find out soon enough." She gave Cate a list of items to get from the pantry while she slit the package open and popped the contents into the freezer. She undid the rest of the box until it was laid out flat on the floor. "This'll be for later." Nuna searched for a large pot and flicked on the burner.

"What are we making?"

"Bannock." Nuna heated the canola oil on medium. "You know what that is, right?"

"Of course."

"You never know." Nuna poured four cups of flour and two teaspoons each of salt and baking powder into a bowl, mixing them well. She showed Cate how to make a hollow in the batter. "My grandma taught me how to make this."

Cate typed the instructions into her phone as she watched.

Nuna poured milk into the flour mixture and blended, avoiding lumps. She divided it into three pieces. "Now we let it sit for ten minutes so the dough can get fluffy."

Cate felt closer to Nuna than ever before—as though the divisions between them were melting away. Nuna, of her own volition, was sharing. Maybe not an ancient anthropological secret, but it was just as important. They were sharing the kitchen. They were cooking together. It was a sure sign that she was trusting Cate, letting her guard down. The connection might not have been exactly as Liam had predicted, fruitful for her research, but it was meaningful, nonetheless.

Nuna wiped her hands on a dish towel. "Going for a smoke." She put on her jacket and stepped outside. The screen door slammed behind her.

Cate followed.

Nuna lit a cigarette. She blew the smoke sideways, away from Cate. "So, what was Pops like as a child?"

Cate gazed up at the sky, feathered with clouds. She thought for a minute. Although Liam was gregarious and outgoing, he was reserved about his childhood. No one knew what Cate knew, except those he grew up with in the Point. She was hesitant to share the details but in the spirit of the give-and-take of the morning, Cate reconsidered. Perhaps disclosing something personal would prove to Nuna that she trusted her. Even if that personal thing wasn't Cate's to share.

*

As Liam told it, he didn't have an easy childhood. His father, Luke, was an angry man who worked a shitty job at a shitty company with a shitty boss and shitty pay. To boot, they lived in a shitty neighbourhood called the Point, inhabited by a shit-ton of Irish with a shitty Irish history.

During their family walks on Sundays, Liam's father always pointed to the Irish Commemorative Stone, or the Potato as he called it, stuck on the island where it divided two lanes of traffic, near the Victoria Bridge. The Potato commemorated the deaths from "ship fever" of the six thousand mostly Irish immigrants to Canada after the Great Irish Famine in the 1840s. Luke spat. "That's all they thought we were worth and that's all they think we're worth now." He was incensed that birth and circumstances had stuck him, like the Potato, into poverty.

Evenings after he punched out, he'd trudge home from his shitty job, past boarded-up buildings and crumbling tenements, to their house on Liverpool Street, with its mud-red door and flaking paint, steps from a tiny park bordered by Coleraine Street on one side and a garbage-strewn laneway on the other, a park named for his ancestors' beloved Ireland. It was the only greenery around. Luke was a big man with a booming voice that scared his children when he got angry. And he was angry most of the time. It was always sod this and sod that. He blew up for the tiniest reason. And when he did, no one was safe, not Liam's mother, not his brothers and sisters.

Liam was well on his way to following in his father's footsteps. By the time he was fourteen, he'd gained a reputation as a scrapper. There wasn't a day he didn't come home with his hair mussed up and a cut lip, or a shiner, or his knuckles crusted in blood. He called his brawls his homework from the school of hard knocks.

In his senior year, Liam's history teacher, a stodgy Brit named Mr. Broadbent, took an interest in him. One day, after a fight that nearly got him expelled, Broadbent took him aside and told him to man up and stop taking out his anger on those closest to him. "Understand the historical causes of poverty and how it leads men to turn on their own. And *do* something about it." He reminded him that he had a brain and to use it for more than a punching bag. Broadbent glowered. "And get that giant chip off your shoulder or I'll beat it off you."

Against all odds, Liam made it out, promising himself he would become the father his father could have been.

*

By the time Liam got home from work, the kitchen was tidied and the dishwasher humming with a load of soiled pots and pans. Cate, Nuna, and Isabel applauded as he entered.

"What's all this?" Liam said, setting down his briefcase.

Nuna pointed to the cardboard box slit open on the kitchen tile, a blood-red hunk of caribou at the centre. "It's supper, Inuit style."

"We're celebrating your big win," Cate said. She pecked him on the cheek.

Liam stared at the raw meat on his immaculate floor. "Oh… wow…thanks." He went to the bathroom, switched on the light, and closed the door tightly behind him.

Nuna looked disappointed.

Cate pursed her lips. After the last supper fiasco, she wanted things to go smoothly.

Isabel walked to the cardboard and dropped to the floor, cross-legged. "I don't know about you guys, but I'm starving." She slapped her thighs in anticipation.

"Me too," Cate said, settling in beside her.

Nuna knelt and distributed the serrated knives.

Liam emerged and went to the fridge. He uncapped a beer. "So, no spaghetti tonight, I'm guessing."

"Nope," said Nuna. "By the way, did you know that 'vegetarian' is an Inuit word?"

They stared at her, bewildered.

"It means 'bad hunter.'" Nuna exploded with laughter. The others joined in.

Liam brought four plates and began handing them around.

Nuna shook her head. "No. We're eating straight off the cardboard tonight. Like my people." She hacked into the meat with the steel, half-moon blade of her traditional knife. "This is called an *ulu*," she explained. "It's the woman's knife. We believe that it has memory and contains all the things it learned from long ago. When it's passed down from mother to daughter, it carries the mother's knowledge. I got mine from my grandmother, so it's really smart."

Liam blushed. "Cool." He spun around on his heel, hurrying to return the dishes to the cupboard. "So what are we having, specifically?" He sipped his beer and eased into the circle.

"This is raw caribou, *tuktuq*, my favourite." Nuna persevered with her ulu, sawing away until the last sinew finally let go. "Here." She passed Liam the first piece. "Try this."

Liam lifted the frozen morsel to his lips. He cautiously bit into it. Cate watched his face as he focused on the unfamiliar flavour and texture. "Hmm, it's actually quite delicious."

"Right?" Nuna handed Isabel a chunk on the flat side of her ulu.

Isabel grabbed it without a thought. She bared her teeth, chewed, and smiled. She put out her hand for another.

Nuna eyed Cate, uncertainly. Although Cate wasn't a proper vegetarian, she had been boycotting meat, citing climate change, the violence against animals, an awakened sense of justice. "You want to try?"

"Absolutely," Cate said, deciding that this was an ancient ritual she was partaking in and when would she get another chance. She took it from Nuna's hand, almost reverently. The still-frozen morsel burned her skin. She flinched ever so slightly, observed the thawing ice crystals as they slid in droplets from the meat down her wrist. She inserted it delicately into her mouth and let herself be surprised. It tasted like the land, sky, snow. "It's so tender it's melting in my mouth!"

Nuna nodded. "This is good on it, too." She poured some soy sauce into a bowl, dipped a piece, and opened wide. "*Mamaqtuq*, tasty. I really miss country food." Her lips shimmered.

"Since when is soya an ancient Inuit tradition?" Liam asked.

"Hey, the Japanese are our long-lost cousins." Nuna thrust her face forward. She lifted her chin. "Can't you see the resemblance?"

Nuna was having fun with them, and they all indulged her. They chomped at the carcass until everything was gone except for a kidney-shaped splatter of grease on the cardboard. Nuna got up to heat the water for tea. She brought back a pie plate with the freshly made bannock. "Look what Cate made you." She laid it down ceremonially in front of Liam and winked at Cate before Cate jumped in to confess that Nuna had made it while she only looked on. Nuna shook her head at Cate. It didn't matter who had physically rolled the dough into a thick sausage, who had spiralled it into the oil and cooked it until it was golden on one side, and then the other. They had been there, together, arms touching, as Nuna spooned the fresh bannock out of the sputtering pot and onto cardboard for the oil to soak in.

He lifted it up to sniff. A smile broke out across his face. "Is this what they call bannock?"

"Yup," said Nuna. "My family recipe."

He swept the pie plate into his chest, shielding it from the others. "Okay, so what are you women going to have?"

Cate relaxed. She filled the teapot. They ate. Liam was being good old Liam, lively, personable—he was being his old self again, the one Cate had flirted with at Waleed's party and lured into bed.

Liam yawned into his fist. One by one they stood, stretched their legs. They folded the cardboard and carried it to the garbage. Liam rested his hands on Nuna's shoulders and thanked her. He called it a night and trundled up the stairs.

"Well, I guess he isn't helping to clean up," Isabel muttered.

Nuna shrugged. "Just like the men up north."

*

Cate decided that Nuna was ready for Antigone Books & Café, a quaint, wood-floored shop with the best selection of new and used books, and the best cappuccinos in Montreal. The good thing about it, besides being down the street, was that it was a real bookstore, not a candle-and-cheeseboard shop that sold books on the side. It was run by a couple, Verity and Sloan, smart, tattooed women who knew their literature and their customers. A month or two ago, Nuna might have balked at going there. She might have called it lame and argued that she wasn't going to pretend-sip from an empty coffee cup just so she could sit there all day on her laptop like those college posers.

They walked there together the first few times, adopted a table by the window with three healthy aloe plants on the rustic sill. They spread out with their notes, opened their laptops, and worked facing each other, sipping coffee. Cate, meticulous and slow, plugged away at her paper, revising incessantly. Nuna, meanwhile, highlighted and scribbled in the margins of her book. Cate wondered what it would be like to be Nuna, jotting down whatever popped into her head, willy-nilly, without worrying too much about making sense. She did stream of consciousness like Gertrude Stein and then struggled to make it coherent. Cate needed things to be clear and precise on the first draft. She sweated over every word.

One of those afternoons, Sloan came by to ask if they were finished with their cups. Her pink hair dye looked like it needed a refresh. Nuna noticed her boots up over the knee, black, laced, asked how much.

Sloan snuck a glance at Verity, stacking new books, and told Nuna, tongue in cheek, to shush about that, it was already a sticking point with her woman. She grabbed Nuna's pen and scribbled the number on a napkin.

"For real?" Nuna said.

Sloan nodded, clearing away their cups.

"That's crazy!"

Cate could tell that Nuna felt comfortable around Sloan and hoped that, with time, the two would develop a friendship. She hoped Nuna would come to see that cool people could be interested in books, too. Cate encouraged her to begin going there on her own and she was game.

Nuna spent her mornings with Cate reading and discussing the classics that were on the high school syllabus. After lunch, she packed up her knapsack and walked to Antigone's, plunking herself down at her regular table. Nursing a cappuccino—like all the other geeks, as she called them—until closing.

One night in June, Cate, Nuna and Isabel were driving home from a Costco run to pick up supplies for Liam's fortieth birthday. Nuna wanted a copy of *The Metamorphosis* and asked if they could stop at Antigone's before closing. Cate pulled up. She dug into her purse for a twenty.

"I'll just be a few minutes."

"It's great to see Nuna doing so well," Isabel said. "And it's all thanks to you."

Cate blushed. "Well, she's pretty determined. Sometimes I think she just wants to prove us wrong."

"Whatever it is, you lit a fire under her." Her arm grazed Cate's. "The other day she told me that you've turned her into a bookworm."

Cate smiled. There were certainly worse things. She caught Isabel up on where Nuna was, what books she most enjoyed, what was next on the syllabus—light conversation to pass the time. She turned off the motor, wondering what was taking Nuna so long.

Isabel scrolled through her phone messages. "How come you never talk about your sister?"

Cate cringed. "Where's this coming from?"

She looked up. "It's Margaret, right?"

Cate nodded. Nuna's few minutes had already stretched into a half hour.

"Are you ashamed of her or something?"

"No, not at all, why would you even say such a thing?" Cate checked the time on the dashboard. "What's Nuna doing in there, anyway? She's taking forever."

Isabel shrugged and dropped the subject.

Cate stared at the bookstore, impatiently. The door opened and a customer that wasn't Nuna stepped out. She sighed. A few minutes later, Nuna appeared with Sloan and Verity, lingering by the door as they locked up. "Finally."

Nuna waved goodbye to them and strode toward the car.

"What the heck took so long?"

Nuna beamed. "I had a test to do." She pushed the twenty-dollar bill back into Cate's hand.

"Test? What test? And where's the Kafka book you wanted?"

"I got a job, I start on Monday."

*

Waleed and the man-cave guy, who now had a name—Daniel—were monopolizing the karaoke machine. It was the party Liam had wanted for his fortieth, the party of the decade with close friends, a run of booze, and non-stop music.

Liam loved music. He couldn't play a note, but he could sing. The music gene had come from his mother. Music helped her deal with her difficult life. Most nights, before Luke came home, they would sing together while she made dinner. He learned her entire repertoire—the Beatles, Motown, the Clancy Brothers. Her favourite Broadway tunes. When he and Cate were dating, he usually broke into song when he was happy about something. "Well, what do you know?" she chuckled. "I'm dating a jukebox."

Isabel and Cate were in the kitchen clanking dishes and organizing the snacks onto platters. Cate passed her a bottle of Pinot Grigio to open.

Isabel peeled off the foil cap and inserted the corkscrew with a surgeon's precision. The cork made a "plip" as it emerged intact, rouged along the bottom where it had touched the wine. "The operation was a success, the patient is ready to get drunk." She poured them each a glass.

Cate hesitated. "I feel awkward drinking with Nuna in the house."

"Come on, it's a special occasion." She drank up her wine and poured herself another. "Don't sweat it."

Cate followed suit. "We should probably join the party."

Isabel made a face. "Why?"

"Did anyone ever tell you you're intense?" Cate gulped more wine.

"Only my uptight academic friends."

Cate snorted the wine through her nose. She looked for a cloth to wipe up but couldn't find one.

Isabel pointed to the dishcloth in Cate's hand. "Don't tell me you're already a little tipsy?" She whipped off her Canadiens cap, ruffled up her hair, and put it back on. "Hey—nothing to do with anything, but if you had to go by another name, what would it be?" She cleared a space on the counter and hoisted herself up.

"It's hard keeping up with you."

"Oh, derribly, derribly tifficult." Isabel giggled, swinging her legs so they banged against the lower cupboards.

"You're something else when you're drunk."

"Who says I'm drunk?" She touched Cate's shoulder, her face playfully serious. "Anyway, what was I saying again?"

"You asked me about an alternate name. Maybe you should take notes."

"Take notes!" Isabel convulsed with laughter. "Who says that, anyway?" she hmphed. "*Alternate* name."

"*I* do," Cate said.

Isabel guzzled her wine. "Well?"

Cate could hear Waleed and Daniel at the microphone, hamming up "It's Raining Men." She smiled. "Fiona, I guess."

Isabel poured herself another glass. "Hm. Fee." Her eyes were sparkling. She rested the rim against her lower lip. "I like it."

"I have a cousin, Fiona, on my father's side. Nothing fazes her."

"Fearless Fee. Yeah, I can picture that." Isabel used her finger to wipe the glaze off her lips.

"It seems to me that Fionas aren't afraid to get their hands dirty. They're real boots-on-the-ground women." Cate signalled for Isabel to top up her wine. "And you?"

"I like my name," she said in a heartbeat. "Wouldn't change it."

"If you had to, though."

"Nope. I wouldn't. Period." Isabel was firm. It was a response that would never have occurred to Cate. She always accepted the parameters she was given.

"Okay, let's go."

They came and went from the kitchen to the living room, carrying in the hors d'oeuvres they had festively arranged on platters—lemon-herb cheese bites, pumpkin and pesto crostini, grilled apples with prosciutto and honey. Liam pulled away from Mo to make eye contact with Cate. "We're doing Ed Sheeran," he said. "You and me. So warm up those vocal cords."

“Give me a sec, I want to introduce Isabel to Waleed.” She turned but Isabel was gone. Cate scanned the room and spotted her. Isabel had already sniffed out Waleed flirting with his man at the wine bar, a cloth-covered credenza set up by the piano. Cate wandered over.

“I love-love Waleed’s outfit,” Isabel cooed, draping her arm around Cate. “Campy but sexy.”

Waleed blushed and glanced at Daniel.

The party was hopping, mainly thanks to Isabel. The snacks were varied and exotic, the music was loud, and the décor—streamers and a chocolate-filled piñata—brought the room to life. When people weren’t singing at the mic or rattling noise-makers, they were whooping it up in a wild circle, hands in the air, clapping.

“*Gracias*,” Cate said. “It’s a real fiesta.” She kissed Isabel on the cheek.

“*De nada, mi amiga*.”

Cate noticed Nuna by the front door, preparing to leave. She pushed through a wall of guests to talk to her. “Where are you going? Why don’t you stay?”

Nuna zipped up her hoodie. “It’s not my music. And anyways, I don’t know anyone except you guys.” She closed the door behind her.

The song ended and a new one began. Isabel shouted, “Hey, that’s our number!” and pulled Cate toward the karaoke machine, parting the crowd with her other hand.

Cate stumbled. “I’m too wasted. And I don’t sing. It’s not in my DNA.”

“You sing,” Isabel said. “You’re Fiona!”

Cate pleaded with her.

“You said you’d sing with Liam, what’s the diff?”

Cate shook her head no, no, she only agreed because it was his birthday, she didn’t have a choice.

Isabel took off her cap and slapped it on Cate’s head backwards. “Come on, stop being such a wuss!” She forced the mic into Cate’s hand.

Liam's burning gaze was on them.

Cate exaggerated her struggle to wrestle free. "Isabel, I hate you!"

"I hate you, too!"

The music blared, but it didn't care, it didn't fucking care about anything except being loud. Cate pushed away a memory of her mother catching her at the bathroom mirror singing into a bristled hairbrush for a pretend audience. She was barely a teenager. "You're a far better piano player than a singer," her mother had snapped, "now get cracking or you'll be late for school."

Cate cleared her throat. She raised the mic uncertainly to her lips as Isabel swayed her hips from side to side, pivoting to air-strum a guitar and batter away on an invisible drum. Cate felt everyone's eyes on her—Waleed's, Daniel's, Mo's. Liam's. Intense eyes. Isabel winked at her and kept belting it out, which drove Cate to keep going, too. A lightness came over her. She lifted her chin in the air. Woozy, she could hardly stand, but a strange confidence took hold, her voice edging toward the raspy sound of Lady Gaga. Cate sang the lines as they appeared on the screen. She glanced at Isabel and saw that she was barefoot, her toenails like glistening Smarties. She looked down. They were both barefoot. She felt warm, lightheaded. Shaky. Her vision blurred, then she saw spots.

When Cate came to, she was lying in a heap on the bathroom floor, vomit on her hands. Her lips were dry. She was sweating. The sounds from outside were muffled and indistinct but there was a pattering of feet close by. "Isabel? Is that you?"

"Shhh, take it easy." Isabel ran the water, bent down to put a towel on Cate's forehead. "Figures you'd get me working on my night off."

"How long have we been in here?" Her throat was raw.

"Only a couple of minutes. You said you were gonna puke and ran to the can."

Cate remembered. She hid her face.

"Well, you were true to your word. Now to clean you up." Isabel helped her to her feet. She sat Cate down on the toilet seat, knelt, and went to work rubbing at the vomit spots on her jeans, humming "Born This Way," the song they had just performed. Isabel wiped Cate's hands one by one, first the palms, then each finger, tenderly working around the knuckles. "You know, we killed it out there."

Cate's head felt like it was in a Vise-Grip. "Good thing Nuna's not around to see this." She grimaced. "Some role model."

"Let's just clean you up before I get you into bed," Isabel said. She reached up and swept Cate's hair off her face.

"I can't leave before the cake. I just can't." Cate rested her head on Isabel's shoulder.

"Liam will forgive you." She helped Cate to her feet. "And if he doesn't, he's a jackass." She opened the bathroom door to a din of music and chatter.

Cate felt an ocean of nausea.

People wearing tasselled hats were blowing their glitter-fringed horns and whistles, urging the birthday boy to sing: "Li-am, Li-am, Li-am." It was hot and loud. Cate saw Mo whisper into Liam's ear and touch the back of his neck. She clung to Isabel as they veered past the commotion and up the stairs toward the bedroom.

Cate fixated on the floral sheets of her marriage bed while Isabel eased her out of her soiled clothes. The window was open. Naked, she felt a tingling in her nerve endings and the hair lifting on her arms. The room smelled fresh, like an oasis.

Isabel went to the dresser and searched for Cate's pyjamas. She buttoned her top, got on her knees and guided Cate's feet, one by one, into the openings of her pyjama bottoms.

"In front of all our friends! How undignified." Cate covered her face with her hands.

"No one's passing judgment. Close your eyes and forget it." Isabel helped her into bed. She set a glass of water on the night-stand and laid a hand on Cate's cheek before flicking off the lamp.

The last thing Cate heard before drifting off to sleep was Liam's lilting voice from downstairs singing "Danny Boy."

Cate slept through until supper the next day. Her head was still throbbing. She popped a migraine tablet, got dressed, and went downstairs.

Liam glanced up from his paper. The decorations had been taken down and the dishes put away, every trace of the party eradicated. It was as though it had never even happened.

Cate sat beside him on the couch. "I'm really sorry."

He regarded her with tepid indifference. "Haven't seen you that plastered since the day we met." He buried his nose in the sports section.

Cate fondled his thigh. After a drawn-out pause, she felt him relax.

He set the newspaper aside and cupped his hand over hers. "You missed a good cake, you know." He squeezed.

Cate led him upstairs and let him undress her. She unbuttoned his shirt, breathing in his comforting smell. Most of the time their foreplay was good; there was tenderness, anticipation. Satisfaction was imminent. Then something threw a wrench into it: a distracting thought, waning desire, a subtle flinch she couldn't get past his sensitive radar.

Liam mounted her quickly.

Mo flashed through her mind. Mo with her acrylic nails. Mo with her wavy hair over one eye. Cate tried to stay focused. She imagined a tropical island, coconut trees and the sun on her face.

Liam rocked his pelvis, grunting her name.

She bit her lip and commanded that he fuck her harder. Harder, she repeated. He cried out and thrust into her with all his strength. Cate moaned, as she always did once he came, to heighten his pleasure. To express hers. He rolled off. She waited a minute and climbed on top. She ran the tip of her nose in circles on his skin where he was always ticklish and extra sensitive after sex.

Laughter rippled through him. "It's like my nerve endings are on fire!"

Cate sighed with relief.

*

Cate's cell went off. Liam rolled over and muttered, "Jesus fuck."

"Don't," Cate said.

"What the hell time is it?" Liam barked.

Cate put the phone to her ear. The voice at the other end was octaves high. "Mom!"

"Nuna?"

"Mom! Mom!" she kept repeating.

"Calm down, just calm down."

Liam rolled his eyes.

Nuna cried and spoke at the same time. It was a jumble of non sequiturs. Something about getting kicked off the bus, being stuck in Dorval, and trying to get to Saint Catherine.

"I don't understand what you're telling me."

"In downtown!" Nuna shouted.

"Street? Saint Catherine Street?"

Liam was mouthing to Cate, but she couldn't concentrate on both at once.

"Nuna, have you been drinking?" Cate waited for an answer. "Well? Have you?"

"Mmmaybe yes."

Liam kept mouthing his incomprehensible message.

Cate waved him off, dismissively. "Where are you?"

"You're screaming at me again. Stop screaming, Mom!"

"Nuna?" Cate heard muffled voices in the background. "Where are you?"

"I'm *sooo* fucked!" she wailed.

"Tell me where you are, Nuna."

Liam signalled that it was three in the bloody morning.

Cate nodded absently. The phone went dead. She called back the number. To her surprise, Nuna answered. "Nuna? Are you there? Where are you?"

"Whaaaat?"

"I said, where are you?"

"Cooch Tar."

"*Couche-Tard*? Let me speak to the guy at the cash."

"*Mom!* Help me, pleeease!"

Cate had to tell Nuna three times to put the cashier on before she understood. He came on, appropriately concerned. He gave Cate the address of the convenience store, a short distance away. Cate croaked "*Merci bien*" and asked if he could keep an eye on her until she arrived.

Liam muttered under his breath. "Not the middle of nowhere, at least." He didn't offer to go along. "You realize you're making things easy for her, right? Always coming to her rescue like this."

Cate ignored him. She saw it more as her own failure, blamed herself for not keeping her at the party, for being too drunk to pay attention.

"It's a little ironic," Liam sneered. "You never wanted kids or a family, and yet..."

"And yet what?"

Cate's phone rang again. She answered with her back to Liam. "Mom, why're you taking so long? When're you coming?"

"Hang tight, Nuna." Cate hung up, threw on some clothes. She dug through her purse, her pockets, her other purse before finding her car keys.

He flew after her downstairs.

She slammed the door while Liam was still talking.

Cate drove in silence, no radio, no music, just her own tsunami of questions. Why was Nuna drinking? Had she been with her boyfriend—what was his name again? Was Cate a bad "mom"? Was Liam right? The roads were deserted except for a feral cat crossing the road with something dead in its mouth.

Cate nabbed a spot right outside the store. The cashier pointed out Nuna slouched on a case of beer at the back of the store. She reeked of booze and cigarettes. Cate held out her hand. She spoke softly. "Come, let's get you home." She walked Nuna once around the block before getting her into the car.

"Don't tell Isabel, please don't tell!" Nuna begged. She seemed to be more afraid of Isabel than Cate. What did *that* say about their relationship? That Nuna felt she could get away with things she couldn't with Isabel? Or did Nuna trust Cate more? Did she see her as a mother figure after all?

Cate pieced together what had happened as she drove them home through the underlit neighbourhood. Nuna rambled incoherently, cryptic about where she had been. Cate hoped it was with her friend Vanita, the one with the steady job at Makivik Corporation. Drinking with someone reliable, someone who woke up at seven to get to a job every day, seemed less deadbeat than drinking with sketchy street people. Or drinking alone.

Nuna, it turned out, had gotten into a taxi without any money. She waited until halfway to her destination before telling the driver that she was broke. Livid, he dropped her somewhere in the West Island, where she got on the bus with an expired pass. "I wasn't loud," she insisted, "but the driver pulled over and told me to get the fuck off, *maudite esquimau*."

Nuna sat motionless when they pulled into the driveway. "This is a racist fuckin' town, Mom."

Cate went around and opened the door for her. "Come on, let's get you cleaned up and into bed."

Nuna dragged her legs out of the car like dead weights, one by one, and walked herself to the house. Her makeup was smeared, and her hair hung down in clumps.

"Go upstairs. I'll get the bath going. And if Liam asks you anything, just say you're fine, everything's fine." Cate sat on the edge of the tub. She twisted on the faucet, testing the water temperature with her hand.

Liam pounded on the door, opening it just enough to see Cate's face. "What's going on?" He wiped the sleep from his eyes. "Is she back?"

Cate nodded and told him to go back to bed, she'd take care of it.

"It's bloody four in the morning!"

She stiffened. "Yes. And I said I would take care of it."

Liam shook his head. "I made coffee." He closed the door and padded back to the bedroom, muttering under his breath.

A few minutes later, Nuna opened the door and poked her head in, whispering. "I didn't want to come out until he left."

Cate handed her the soap and shampoo. She unhooked her plush white robe hanging behind the door and insisted Nuna use it. "Take your time."

She nodded.

Cate waited in Nuna's bedroom. She glanced around, noting the "mess" that Liam was constantly harping on. It wasn't a pigsty, as he often complained, but it had a certain lived-in quality that Cate, to her surprise, didn't object to. The small pile of laundry in the corner was mainly underwear and socks. Except for a bra strap sticking out of the middle drawer, her dresser was neat and tidy, the top cleared of everything except for a couple of hair clips, a comb, and some roll-on deodorant. Only the desk was cluttered—with pencils, Sharpies, books, and a half-finished can of ginger ale. Cate smiled. She always appreciated the chaos associated with mental labour. It signalled industriousness, a proclivity for study.

Nuna's journal was open to a half page of blotchy writing. Cate stood up and edged closer. She squinted to make out a word here, a word there. Her chest tightened. What if there were private musings in there, unrelated to her studies? What if Cate read a comment or complaint about Liam or her or even Isabel, something she didn't want to know? She stepped back just as Nuna walked in wearing Cate's robe.

"What's up?" Her hair was in a towel twisted into a turban.

"What? Oh, nothing. Just noticing how much work you're doing." She hadn't even heard the bathwater drain.

Nuna climbed into bed, still wearing the robe.

Cate cocooned her in the comforter. She smelled of Crest and hair conditioner. "Now, don't you feel better?"

She turned on her side, facing Cate.

"You know, Nuna…things don't always go the way we want them to."

Nuna closed her eyes as if she could erase the events of the day.

"Do you trust me?"

She opened them again. "Of course I do, Mom." Her voice was hoarse with fatigue.

"I see you've been writing."

She shrugged. "Just dumb stuff. And book stuff." She stretched and yawned, her eyes moist.

"Do you want to tell me what happened tonight?" The bathroom fan was humming. "I mean, only if you want to, of course."

Nuna rearranged the pillows to prop herself up. Her eyes were bloodshot.

"You don't have to, I'm not forcing you."

Nuna looked at her with an openness and vulnerability that Cate had never seen before. She massaged the back of her neck and took a deep breath. "I don't always like to think about that shit." She swallowed hard and spoke of her culture and the struggles of her generation, their feelings of discouragement and hopelessness, the difficulty of living between two worlds, the White world and their own.

Cate listened attentively. She imagined being in Nuna's shoes, trying to navigate all those realities.

"Once, you know, I tried to break up with Amaruq."

"Your boyfriend?" Cate remained cautious. She hadn't expected Nuna to dive headlong into personal territory.

Nuna nodded. "He often trashed the apartment when he was angry or drunk. I was always the one cleaning up. Once, he tried to choke me."

Cate gasped.

"I said I've had it with your shit, I want out. A few days later, I came home and found him hanging from a door—luckily still alive. He said he did it because he was afraid I would leave him. So I stayed, maybe for longer than I should have."

"My God, I had no idea."

"It's pretty messed up," she said, before segueing into the present. "I'm really not used to living in White people's houses with all your different foods and ways. It's a big shock for me."

Cate thought of the many vegetarian meals in their household, their experiments with keto and veganism, and how hard it must have been for a full-on carnivore; how thoughtless they had been. "Why didn't you say something?"

"Inuit don't like to complain."

Cate reached her hand out but pulled back. Her voice cracked. "I'm sorry."

Nuna blinked up at the ceiling. "Most girls my age already have a kid or two."

Cate swallowed. What Nuna had discovered through literature was only the tip of the iceberg. There was still so much for her to learn. And the more she knew, the more useful she would be to her village. She was a smart girl. She could do great things for her people. "Look at me." She waited for Nuna to meet her gaze. "You have plenty of time for that. You're still young."

Nuna welled up. "My best friend, Jeannie, lives in a house up north with her baby daddy. She makes all their clothes, parkas, mitts, duffle socks." Her chin trembled. "And I can't even sew a button."

Cate nodded.

"You know it's hard to stay sober here when alcohol is so easy to get. I went through a six-pack tonight—by myself."

Cate apologized again. It seemed she had a lot to apologize for.

Nuna fiddled with the comforter. "So, what do I do when I'm craving it?" She eyed Cate with frustration.

"What can I tell you that you don't already know? Don't give in. Call me if you have to. Drink water, eat chocolate, watch TV, read. Go to bed early. Easier said than done, I know, but you can do it. You're strong when you want to be." Cate struggled to get her words right, to avoid sounding judgmental. "You're a courageous woman, Nuna."

A silence settled over them.

"You know, Mom, it's hard being nineteen, making the right decisions so my parents can be proud of me. Most of the time, I'm not sure of anything."

Cate thought of herself at that age, of her dreams of becoming a respected scholar like her father. "Well, you seem to have acquired a love for books. Why not crawl into them and save yourself? Really study them. Writers often deal with the complexities of identity and relationships. You'll learn a lot from what they have to say."

They locked eyes.

"I'm quite certain that if you work hard, you'll become a leader someday. Really make a difference."

"You're stressing me." Nuna sat upright, eyes widened in panic. "Maybe you'll realize I'm not as smart as you think."

Cate smiled. "I doubt that. Mahatma Gandhi said, 'Be the change you want to see in the world.'"

Thack, thack, thack.

They both jumped. Liam was just outside the door. "Are you coming to bed or what?"

"Yeah," Cate called out, winking at Nuna. "Give me a sec, we're almost done." They listened to his footsteps recede. Cate lowered her voice to a whisper. "I'll let you in on a little secret. I got drunk last night, too. And it wasn't pretty. Maybe we can be there for each other." She raked her fingers through Nuna's hair. "Now, get some sleep."

*

As the days warmed up, Nuna worked longer and longer hours at the bookstore. Even when she wasn't officially scheduled for a shift, she hung out there reading, researching, typing up assignments. Some nights, exhausted, she went straight to bed without dinner. Occasionally Cate had to remind her to take a break, life wasn't all work, work, work. But Nuna's enthusiasm rubbed off, and Cate rolled up her sleeves and recommitted herself to the paper she had to write for the conference in Slovenia.

One evening, Nuna came home earlier than usual. Cate was at the kitchen table watching a YouTube documentary about Emily Carr. Nuna dropped her knapsack and sat cross-legged in Liam's chair. "What's liminal space?"

Cate paused the movie. "Where did you hear that from?"

"Just a magazine article. What is it?" Her eyes were glassy and bloodshot.

"What magazine?"

"I dunno, a magazine."

Cate sensed that something was off. "What's wrong with your eyes?"

"What do you mean?"

"They're really red."

Nuna shrugged.

"You should lay off the computer for a few days, give your eyes a rest."

Nuna pressed on. "So, what is it?"

Cate closed her laptop. She liked this Nuna, filled with curiosity. Insatiable. "Physical liminal space is a kind of transition between two locations. A place you pass through on your way to somewhere else."

Nuna wrinkled her nose. "Example?"

"Think of an elevator between two floors." Cate paused. She thought she smelled alcohol on Nuna's breath. "Or a bridge between one shore and another." Cate hoped she was only imagining the booze. "It's a space in between." She folded her arms across her chest. "We cross these zones many times a day without realizing it. Unless something about them is weird. Like an empty airport terminal or a school during summer break. A mall before the stores open. An empty parking lot. We expect these areas to be a certain way and when the context changes it makes us uncomfortable."

"So, you're saying that something about the space feels off."

Cate nodded. "Exactly. We expect to see cars in a parking lot and people in an airport."

Nuna was pensive.

"And then there's liminal space as it relates to our mental state—transitional times in our life when we're on the verge of something new but we're not quite there yet. It can be emotionally unsettling and overwhelming. Sometimes the uncertainty we experience triggers anxiety. But going through it allows us to evolve and grow as people."

"Do you think that I'm in one?"

Cate's phone rang. "Well, yes, it's possible." Liam's name flashed on the screen, but she ignored it.

Nuna tossed her knapsack over her shoulder. She poured herself a tall glass of water and headed for the stairs.

"Not eating tonight?"

"No thanks."

Cate's phone pinged: *Having a quick bite with Mo to discuss strategies for next year. Won't be late. xo*

*

Liam texted again around nine to say they were grabbing beer at Hurley's with a few other colleagues but wouldn't be out past eleven. Cate carried her laptop and a cup of mint tea to bed to finish watching the documentary. She made mental notes of what might be useful to her, but her mind wandered and she found herself constantly having to rewind to where she had stopped paying attention. Nuna's question about liminal space haunted her.

Margaret was already in the home when her mother arranged a special reconciliation dinner with Niall's "other family." She insisted, knowing she didn't have much time left. The cancer had spread to her organs and although she could still manage with medication, the doctors gave her only a few short months. She took it in stride, selected the clothes for her casket—something new, all white—and chose the hymns and poems she wanted performed at the funeral service. She flat out nixed Niall's "Funeral Blues" by W.H Auden; it was excessive and far too sentimental. Why on God's good earth should they stop all the clocks and silence the pianos for her, an ordinary woman? Why should they pack up the moon and dismantle the sun? She preferred "Do not stand at my grave and weep" from Clare Harner's humbler 1934 poem, "Immortality."

She ticked off items on her to-do list until this final thing that she wanted to get right, a family dinner to quell hostility and bring everyone together under one roof. Cate's father agreed, reluctantly, "Not because I'm against the idea" but because he said it would tire her unnecessarily.

Cate's mother spent the day in the kitchen, Niall as her sous-chef doing exactly what he was told. Cate knew because she kept calling all day in the hopes that they might cancel. No, why would they cancel? Her mother was adamant that things be settled. She wanted closure, for all of them.

When Cate and Liam arrived, the others were already in the living room talking among themselves. The twentysomething son, Cate's half-brother, was tall and sullen. Fingernails painted black, he was drinking his beer straight from the bottle. Cate took a closer look. He seemed to be wearing mascara, but his eyes were definitely Niall's.

The mother, the woman her father had cheated with, was heavier than Cate expected, with long grey hair in a side ponytail and excessive nervous energy. The fact that she was nothing like the sexy homewrecker that had lived and thrived in Cate's imagination was a relief.

Liam shook the woman's hand, trying to seem casual.

"This is Glo," Niall said tentatively. "And this big guy here is Thoth."

They clasped hands.

Thoth? He named his kid after an Egyptian god? Or was that her idea? No, not likely, Cate decided. She was a secretary; secretaries wouldn't know that. Surely it was Niall's idea. Glo went to hug her, but Cate resisted, reaching to shake her hand instead.

"Apologies for my rough palms, I've been painting a lot these days and drugstore hand cream just doesn't cut it," Glo said.

Cate shrugged. Her mother piped in. "Funny, I was just about to say you have gorgeous skin. What's your secret?"

"Bananas, believe it or not." Glo giggled. "You just rub them on your face. I read somewhere that the peels are rich in antioxidants."

"How absolutely fascinating." She invited Glo to the table as though they were old college friends.

Liam whispered "Be civil" in Cate's ear.

Her jaw clenched. She offered to help in the kitchen, but Niall insisted he'd take care of everything, why didn't they all just chitchat and get to know each other. Liam and Cate took their places on one side of the table, facing the guests. Cate asked him for a double of something strong, like bourbon.

Liam served the others first—wine? Scotch and soda? another beer?—before pouring Cate a half glass of Riesling.

She gnashed her teeth.

Glo smiled. "It's so lovely to finally meet you, Cate."

"Yes," Cate said, reaching for her wine.

Liam was quick to intervene. "So, what do you do, Glo?"

Cate glared at him. "She's a secretary."

"Was." Glo corrected her with a pleasant smile.

Liam ignored the tension. "And what about now?"

"Oh, you know, this and that." She held her wineglass by the stem. "A little of this and a lot of that."

"She's a copy editor," Thoth answered.

"Was," Glo said. She looked earnestly at Cate. "It's true, for a long time, I was a secretary in the philosophy department at Concordia, then Niall said he knew a guy who knew a guy and he made some phone calls and got me an interview. Now that I'm retired, I mostly paint."

"Interesting," Liam said, keeping the conversation alive, and light. "What is it that you paint?"

Houses, was Cate's immediate thought. She paints houses. Rooms. Walls. She imagined Glo in paint-speckled overalls and a polka-dot bandana on the top rung of a rickety ladder. She imagined her falling off and severing her spinal cord.

Niall emerged from the kitchen with an oval platter of roast beef and pearl onions. "She's an abstract expressionist—and I may be biased, but she's quite good."

Glo blushed.

Cate's mother set down the scalloped potatoes and went back for the salad. "Help yourselves, everyone, before things get cold," she called out from the kitchen.

Niall swirled the wine in his glass and snuck a sip before slicing up the meat. "Hmm. Dry, crisp. Lovely notes of candied pineapple. Excellent choice, Glo."

Liam turned to Thoth. "And what's your thing?"

"Still at school."

Glo perked up. "He's very modest. He's doing his master's in English lit."

"Sounds like he's following in Cate's footsteps," Liam said.

Cate kicked him under the table.

Thoth shrugged. "I guess."

Liam rested his foot on Cate's as if to say, *Chill.* "Any thoughts on how lousy the Montreal Canadiens are these days?"

"I don't watch hockey."

Cate crossed her arms. All those years thinking she was Niall's bright star. His protégé. How could she have been so wrong? She wondered if he had spent the same long hours with her half-brother, enthusiastically discussing the *Odyssey* and Shakespearean tragedy.

When they were all seated and the food was served, Cate's mother raised her water glass in a toast. "I'd like to say something before we eat, if I may."

Cate couldn't imagine what nonsense her mother was preparing to spout, what tangled emotions they would be left sorting through, years down the road.

Her mother acknowledged each of them, in turn. She made a special point of smiling at Glo and at Thoth. "I only wish the whole family were here." She meant Margaret.

The acid rose in Cate's throat. "You don't have to do this, Mom, no one's expecting you to."

Liam elbowed her discreetly.

"My dear Cate. Now is the time for understanding, not bitterness."

Niall blew his wife a kiss and urged her to go on with her special tribute.

Cate wanted to scream. He had no right showing her affection and he especially had no right telling her what to do. He lost those rights the first time he fucked Glo. She felt a tightness in her chest.

"As you all know, I won't be getting any better."

An uncomfortable silence descended on them.

"And I don't mean for you to feel sorry for me—not at all." Light from the chandelier made her look almost translucent. "What I mean is, we all have our allotted time here. Sometimes things don't go exactly as we've planned." She paused and looked around.

"All I want to say is, find a way to make it work for you. Be good to each other."

Niall winked from across the table. "Hear, hear." He invited everyone to clink glasses.

Liam nudged Cate. She hadn't a drop of wine left and passed on replenishing. All she could think was, what a waste of a life. Be good to each other? What a joke they had become, what a shell of a family. A family in name only. She faked a smile and toasted with her empty glass, brooding in silence for the rest of the evening.

Her mother lasted another six months before the hospital took her into palliative care. Niall visited every day with magazines under his arm, mostly for him to read while she was asleep. Cate sent flowers every week and visited frequently toward the end. The last time Cate went, her mother told her that she'd always dreamt of having a daughter. "Pretty and smart, just like you," she said. "My biggest regret is that we were never close." That night, she fell asleep and never woke up.

Niall sent a limo for Margaret. In the parking lot of the funeral home, the driver struggled to get her out of the car and into her wheelchair, Margaret visibly confused and thrashing. A handful of well-meaning mourners gathered to help, calling out suggestions to move her this way or that way. *Bend her elbows. Watch her head.* A long-lost cousin handed her purse to her husband and tried pulling Margaret's arms. Cate rolled her eyes. She ordered Liam to sort it out, Niall was already in the chapel, and she had things to do.

The funeral was short. Glo and Thoth sat inconspicuously at the back of the chapel. Liam sat with Niall, their eyes focused on the bronze urn. Cate's mother had instructed them. She'd written it out in longhand, a copy for each of them. She didn't want a fuss, just that her ashes be sprinkled around the special places she and Niall had loved during their time together, before children.

PART III
Looking for Her

They sulked over Nuna's disappearance. The three of them sat in a daze, half expecting her to burst through the front door, chattering on her phone.

"The journal still feels like a good starting point," Liam said, though they were all reluctant to invade her privacy.

"Yes, but in this case," Cate argued, "it's probably warranted."

Isabel looked away. Liam ran upstairs to get it.

When it was just the two of them, Isabel reached across the table and squeezed Cate's hand. "Let's stay positive, okay?"

"Okay."

Liam returned with the journal, well worn, scruffier than when they first bought it. "Use it," Cate had said, "to write the demons out of your life, to personally connect with the books we'll be studying." Nuna loved that journal, though not at first. At first, she cursed it. She tore out pages, crumpled them up, and threw them across her room.

Liam passed it to Cate. She set it down on the table, loath to open it.

"Well, one of us has to do it," Isabel said. She slid it toward her and opened it to the first page, where she had witnessed the contract between Nuna and Cate. "Yeah, I remember this." She scanned their signatures and flipped ahead to a page with writing on it, blotchy where Nuna's hand had smeared the stray globs of ballpoint. Isabel loosened her ponytail and raked her hair with her fingers, examining the text as she would an open wound.

"Maybe read it out loud so we can all hear," Liam scoffed.

Isabel glanced up. "Okay. But you're not going to like this."

"What?" Cate's muscles tensed.

"The last entry, it's giving me goosebumps."

Cate snatched the journal from her. "To die, to drown, to be free of everything human," she read out loud. "A clean new beginning, a ghostly embryo." She drew in a sharp breath. Her mind leapt into the rabbit hole of horror stories, lowlifes preying on Indigenous women and girls, raping and assaulting them, hooking them on crack. Killing them.

"Let's not jump to conclusions just yet," Liam said.

Cate was insistent. "We can't just wait around, we have to do something. We have to find her before she turns up dead."

"Nobody's going anywhere tonight." Liam was firm. "You're not clear-headed. You wouldn't know where to start. Neither of you. Why not get a few hours of shuteye before starting out? At least in the morning you'll be fresh."

Cate pointed to the clock. "It *is* morning."

"It's three o'clock."

"He's right," Isabel said, as though it pained her to agree with him. "I'm wired. And a fresh start doesn't sound so terrible."

Liam put the cups in the sink and turned out the lights. Cate led Isabel upstairs to Nuna's room and pulled the comforter off the bed. "I'll get you a towel and some fresh sheets."

"Don't bother." Isabel pecked Cate goodnight on the cheek. "I'll sleep fine in hers."

The two sat on the bed in a stupor, staring at the walls Nuna saw every day, two wallpapered, two painted a dusty rose. All four plastered with posters of Sidney Crosby and Elisapie Isaac. When she and Liam first bought the house, Cate furnished the room with distressed pine furniture to make it look rustic: twin bed with a high headboard, dresser with porcelain knobs and matching nightstand, desk. Vintage lamp and ruffled curtains. Cate always considered it a warm, welcoming home away from home for Nuna. But now, for the first time, she saw it through Nuna's eyes—an alien place filled with stuff signifying nothing.

*

Cate woke to the sound of muffled voices in the kitchen. She rubbed the sleep from her eyes and sat up. When she heard Isabel, everything flooded back, her dream, Nuna's disappearance, Isabel staying the night. She went to the bathroom and splashed cold water on her face. She threw on some clothes and padded down the stairs.

Liam rose, barefoot, to kiss her. "Morning, kiddo."

"Is there coffee?"

"Absolutely." He gave it to her black, the way she liked it.

Cate noticed he was still in his bathrobe. "Isn't it a workday?"

"I took the morning off to help you brainstorm."

"Nice." The steaming mug warmed her hands. One of the good things about Liam was that he was dependable. He always came through in a pinch, even if it put a damper on his own plans. Waleed couldn't stop telling her how lucky she was to have him. How lucky they were to have a life together, like Gibran's oak and cypress trees, never casting a shadow over each other. Waleed was always quoting poetry to her.

Isabel twirled her hair into a bun. "So, we've got a tentative plan." She read off the notes Liam had scribbled onto his napkin. "We'll comb the neighbourhood, go to her favourite haunts, including Antigone's, find out if anyone's seen her around. We'll check the hospitals, too. See if any of my colleagues brought her in."

Cate sighed.

Liam put his hand on her shoulder. "At least this way, we're being proactive. And we get her back here as soon as possible."

"What choice do we have? We don't have much to go on." Cate glanced at the journal, still on the table.

Isabel reached for it. She held it in her hands like the royal crown. "You look like you're chomping at the bit."

Cate nodded.

"We'd be remiss not to," Liam said.

Isabel made some quick calls, one to her partner, Blanchard, to say that she'd be taking some of her overtime days. She swilled down the last drops of coffee and turned to Cate. "Give me an hour to run home and get some clothes on."

"I still can't believe you came in your pyjamas."

"I dressed for the occasion. You were in yours." Isabel grabbed her keys off the table. "I'll be back asap, so be ready."

Cate and Liam were still running around getting organized when they heard a bleating honk in the driveway.

"Jesus, could she be any louder?" Liam muttered.

"Usually, with her, it's Latino time." Cate grabbed her purse. "I think this is a first."

Liam followed her into the kitchen. "I packed you and Isabel some egg sandwiches and banana bread. Oh, and some fruit." He handed her the lunch. "Apologies for the apples, they've probably seen better days, but whatever, they're still edible."

Cate peeked into the bag. It was considerate, she thought. Liam could be that and more when he wanted to be.

"Don't forget the journal!" He ran to the table.

"Right. I'll read through while we're driving around. Maybe get some insight."

"Reading glasses?"

"Check."

He pecked her on the forehead. "Ideas for supper?"

"God, I can't think that far ahead."

"I'm assuming you'll be back well before that." His tone had a slight edge. "Right?"

"If all goes well."

"It will. You'll bring her home. And tonight, we'll all be together again." Liam opened the front door, assaulted by the thumping bass of the sound system in Isabel's Jeep. He grimaced. "Hey! Can you lower that a few thousand decibels?" He cupped his hands over his ears.

Isabel, in tinted aviator sunglasses, stuck her head out the window. "C'mon Chica, c'mon!" She clearly hadn't heard him. "We gotta get cracking."

Liam rushed Cate along. "Go, go, or she'll blame me. And don't forget to keep me posted." He nudged her out the door.

Cate walked toward the Jeep with her head down, hoping her neighbours weren't watching. "Didn't you hear Liam chewing you out?" She belted herself in. "People *are* still asleep, you know."

Isabel lowered the music. "Sorry, it's how I deal with stuff."

Cate hadn't given much thought to Isabel's work. No doubt, it was stressful, punctuated by life-and-death moments. Isabel had to keep her cool—for her sake and her patients'. All day, every day. Cate imagined the music as a kind of pressure valve.

She glanced around the Jeep, Isabel's expensive toy as she called it, a 2013 Wrangler with a gleaming red body and only 24,000 km on it, that she had bought off Kijiji. "I'll still be paying for it when I'm six feet under," she liked to joke. The dashboard was coated in dust; the cupholder filled with candy wrappers and loose change. A strip of Velcro held the glove compartment shut.

Isabel approached Cabot Square.

"This isn't one of her places," Cate said.

"We're just dotting our i's and crossing our t's. Besides, Liam put it on the list, see?" Isabel handed Cate the napkin from earlier with Liam's handwriting on it.

"I wouldn't have started here."

"Well, talk to your husband."

A police car pulled up beside them, window rolled down. "Y'a pas d'arrête ici, mesdemoiselles."

Isabel shot the officer a thumbs-up. She ordered Cate to see what she could find out while she drove around the block.

Cate hurried past the statue of John Cabot to a wooden bench where a couple of women were sharing around a brown paper bag. She kept walking, past another bench with "Fall in Love, Not in Line" scratched into the seat. She scanned the park. A familiar-looking girl about Nuna's age was there. Cate was sure Nuna had talked to her at the memorial service for the homeless woman. She went and inquired if she had seen her recently.

"I don't know no Nuna," the girl mumbled.

Cate thanked her. She checked the other faces. No, no, and no. She spotted Isabel's Jeep coming back, shook her head as if to say I told you so. She yanked the door open. "Well, that was pointless."

Isabel pulled away. "We're just getting started."

"I know, I know." Cate crossed Cabot Square off the napkin list. "Next up, the Douglas." She folded her reading glasses and tucked them away.

"I have a friend who's a caseworker there. I'm thinking to show him what she wrote, see if it means what I think it means."

Cate wrinkled her nose. "What *do* you think it means?"

Isabel accelerated as she took the ramp to the Autoroute 720 West. "I think it's kind of obvious, don't you?"

"No way. It's not her style."

"Suicide isn't about style," Isabel said. "It's about desperation, about wanting to go where the pain stops forever."

"No. Not Nuna. I'd bet my life on it."

They drove into Verdun, a borough of Montreal Cate had never been to. They passed a woman in leotards, running with a three-legged dog. Cate gestured for Isabel to slow down. "I think you underestimate Nuna."

"Everything's on the table now. At least we'll get some reassurance."

"True enough."

Isabel turned into the hospital driveway, following the signs for visitor parking.

Cate remembered what Liam and his childhood friends used to call it: The nuthouse. A bicycle ride away from the Point, they used to go there and throw crabapples at the windows "to make the crazies crazier," he once confessed. Thank goodness attitudes can change, she thought to herself. She turned to Isabel. "So, how is this going to work?"

"Carter's in emergency today. I texted him earlier." Isabel pointed to the building across from the parking lot. Cate got out to stretch her legs while Isabel got herself organized. It was bright, unseasonably warm, one of the last good days of fall. "I'll say I'm on official business, that way his boss won't go all ballistic."

Cate crossed the lawn, kicking up the scruffy leaves. She found a spot in the shade of a mature tree. The hospital reminded her of a university campus. It was situated on a big, beautiful lot dotted with old maples and willow trees and several large, brick buildings that looked like they were built in the late 1800s. Everything about the property whispered serenity—a gentle counterpoint for patients who had lost control of their turbulent lives. Cate thought about Nuna. She didn't ever want her to be here, no matter how calming it was.

Isabel was outside the building, showing Nuna's journal to someone with a mug in one hand and a cigarette in the other. Probably their guy, Carter, on break. Cate tried reviewing some notes on her phone but couldn't concentrate. She kept staring up at them, curious about their conversation. Carter checked the time and tossed the rest of his coffee into the bushes. Isabel kissed him on both cheeks. He stamped on his cigarette butt and disappeared inside.

Isabel waved Cate back. She swung her key ring with its million keys and dangling trinkets and popped open the car lock.

"So, what's the verdict?"

"I read him a bit of her text about dying and drowning." She started the motor. "The fact that Nuna took time to write all this down in a book shows a clear mind, he told me. And that we shouldn't overthink it."

Cate slapped the dashboard. "See? What did I tell you?"

"But he also said that when we find her, we should probably encourage her to get evaluated. Better she get help now before things deteriorate."

Cate was relieved that Carter had quelled Isabel's fears. It wasn't a suicide letter, it was just a girl expressing herself, as young girls did, venting, releasing stress. Documenting the emotional highs and lows of adolescence. On the other hand, Carter was no doctor. His "diagnosis," he insisted, wasn't foolproof. But Cate went with it, anyway, to keep herself from ruminating. The glass was still half empty, but at least there was water in it.

Isabel toggled her phone, looking for a playlist. She cranked the volume and pulled out of the parking lot.

Cate stared out the window. "Funny how things change."

"What?"

"Never mind."

"Liam recommended we check out some of the hospitals we took her to when me and Blanchard picked her up." Isabel turned to Cate. "Do you want me to lower this?"

"I won't say no."

Isabel drove along Lasalle Boulevard toward the Verdun Hospital, casually steering with one hand. Humming to nothing. Cate drifted. The river was almost too bright to look at. Fall had always been Cate's favourite season, saturated with deep reds and yellows, the fiery orange of overripe foliage. She loved its cool fresh mornings, its crystal-clear light. But once November arrived with its tweedy greys and sombre skies, Cate's mood shifted. She began to dwell on minutiae, on things she couldn't control, she stayed awake for hours worrying. Her migraines were always worse before Christmas.

Something flickered in her retina. Cate glanced up at the clear blue sky, just in time to see the departing geese in chevron formation. Craning her neck, she followed their ragged V, lagging birds flapping to keep up. "Amazing how they never get tired."

Isabel's fingers rifled through the cupholder. "Birds fly, it's what they do." She slowed her speed, using her free hand to unwrap a stick of Wrigley's Doublemint. "And I read somewhere that they take turns leading." She folded the gum into her mouth.

"Aren't you the ornithologist."

There was no street parking anywhere.

"Where's Doris Day when you need her?" Cate said.

"What?"

"Never mind." Cate offered to stay in the car while Isabel ran in.

"You're not coming with?"

"Makes more sense for you to go," Cate said. "This is your wheelhouse."

Isabel shrugged. Cate took the driver's seat and drove around until she found a parking spot on de l'Église. She texted Isabel her whereabouts, debating whether she should feed the meter or take a chance, Isabel wouldn't be long. In any case, she could always argue that she'd just pulled in, she couldn't be expected to get to the pay station so quickly. Cate glanced outside to where a man was purring along the sidewalk in his heart-attack chair—Liam's nickname for medical mobility scooters. It had a bright orange safety flag attached to the rear. It was the rattling six-pack of Corona in his wire basket that got her attention. And the heavy cloud of cigarette smoke engulfing him. Cate wondered what his circumstances were, was he married, did his wife have a matching scooter, how did they afford them, were they subsidized by the government. She was sure she could hear the phlegm rolling in his lungs.

Isabel yanked open the car door. "No luck."

"Nothing?"

"Nada."

Cate slid back to the passenger's side. "So, what do you think?"

Isabel turned to look at her, brows pinched together. "Do you have a year?"

Cate agreed. Nuna could be anywhere in the city. Once she understood the rules of the game, to text when she was going to be late or changed her plans, once mutual trust had been established, once she got herself a job and proved she could be reliable, they'd stopped asking about her comings and goings. Cate realized now that it had been a mistake.

Isabel had them moving again. Cate urged her to slow down, they wouldn't be any good to Nuna dead.

"Your phone," Isabel said.

"What?"

"It's ringing."

Cate reached for it.

"Who is it? No, wait, don't tell me. It's your Arab prince charming."

"Yep, it's Waleed." Cate sighed. "The man from Porlock."

"Who?"

Cate declined the call. "Long story but I'll make it short. Samuel Taylor Coleridge—a famous poet—was in the middle of writing 'Kubla Khan,' based on a wild vision he'd had after taking two grains of opium. Maybe you read it in high school?"

Isabel shrugged.

"At some point, a salesman knocks on his door and totally interrupts his flow. I must admit, Waleed has a habit of calling when I'm in the middle of something important."

Isabel gripped the steering wheel. "What's with him, anyway, always calling you at the drop of a hat?"

Cate detected a note of jealousy. Why was she making a big deal of this? She shook her head. "We're colleagues, we share an office, he's my best friend. Where are we going anyway?"

"I thought *I* was your best friend." She exaggerated a pout, checking out of the corner of her eye to see if Cate was watching.

"I'm taking this as you being melodramatic."

Isabel sighed. "He's, just, well, annoying sometimes." She edged into a parking space just outside Antigone Books & Café, beside a Hydro pole strapped with a federal election poster of Marc Garneau. It set her off on another tangent. "Hey, wasn't that guy an astronaut in another life?"

Cate was relieved. She didn't want to get into a whole thing about Waleed and having to defend their friendship. "First Canadian in outer space."

"Cool." Isabel powered the windows shut. "Didn't I hear something about an all-female spacewalk coming up?"

Cate thought for a minute. She thought so. "By the way, congrats on your Doris Day parking spot."

"What's Doris Day parking?"

Cate's phone rang again, insistently. Waleed.

Isabel tapped her fingers on the wheel, like she didn't give a hoot. She cracked her knuckles. He could call until the cows came home, and it wouldn't affect her.

"Now's not a good time," Cate said. She pictured him at his desk, cluttered with coffee cups and student papers, cursing her absence. Before she went on leave, she asked if he minded that she was taking time off, and he said, *Yes, Habibti, but what can I do about it?*

"I just can't…not now. I'll fill you in another time. Love, love." Cate ended the call before he could say a thing.

Isabel puckered up and applied a perfect ring of hot pink lipstick without a mirror. "Coming?" She collected the wrappers and bits of ephemera from the cupholder, crumpling them up for garbage.

Cate shook her head, feeling for her bag in the back seat. "You're good at this. Why don't you go? Meanwhile, I'll start going through the journal more seriously."

Isabel slammed the car door, not to make a point but because she always made noise no matter what she did. Cate was getting used to it. Isabel took up more space than anybody in the world. Except for, maybe, Waleed. And Nuna.

*

The first pages were nothing special. A line or two about Liam and her, that they seemed like alright people except for the fact that they rooted for the Montreal Canadiens, she'd have to do something about that. That Liam and Isabel played street hockey with her, that Cate was teaching her about books. A doodle caught her attention, an igloo with a penguin on top.

Cate skipped ahead to a comic strip in ballpoint pen. She didn't know who the cartoonish figures were supposed to be, but she recognized elements of the setting, the ice and rock, the vast, treeless tundra. Cate adjusted her glasses to read the text, most of it illegible. Except for the word "dream." It gave her pause.

Nuna once described a nightmare she had had when she was a child. In it, she and her family were ice fishing. Cate remembered how detailed Nuna had been. "My father looked into the distance and saw these strange creatures with bushy eyebrows and huge bellies appearing out of nowhere. They were walking toward a polar bear. Every step made a crunching sound and left a huge hole in the snow. My father's face scared me. He shouted at them to stop, keep away, don't hurt the land, but the creatures didn't listen, they kept walking in the bear's direction. Suddenly, who knows why, they understood they were in danger." Nuna looked Cate in the eye, without flinching. "In a panic, they turned and ran straight toward us—and so did the bear."

Cate followed each panel, depicting the dream as Nuna had told it. The bear morphed into a human figure with scary incisors, the ink smeared where she had sketched in the eyes. It stood on its hind legs and, in a fit of rage, tore every limb off the hairy creatures before turning on her family. It feasted on them one by one, her father, her mother, her infant brothers. Just as the bear was about to go for her, Nuna woke up in a sweat.

There was no doubt about the symbolism. What was more interesting to Cate was Nuna's intuitive understanding—at such a young age. The fact that she'd been able to predict the socio-cultural consequences of the invasion of their land. She may have woken up, but it didn't mean that the nightmare was over.

*

Isabel was back with two coffees.

"That took a while."

"I was gone, like, five minutes." She handed Cate hers, neat. "So, what did Sloan say?"

"It wasn't Sloan, it was Verity. Sloan is off getting a new tattoo, some kind of Mayan symbol, I forget what." Isabel tore the sugar packet with her teeth. She tapped some into her coffee and stirred vigorously.

"And?" Cate sighed impatiently. "What about Nuna?"

Isabel snapped the coffee lid shut. "She said Nuna hasn't come in to work since the first week of September."

"Whaaat? Where's she been going all this time?"

"The fuck if I know." Isabel flipped up the small opening in the lid and fitted her cup into the holder. "And the thing is, she was doing so well they were about to promote her to assistant manager."

Cate lowered her head. "Come to think of it, I did notice dark circles around her eyes and she certainly hasn't seemed like her old self. I just assumed she was overworked." She remembered the night she smelled alcohol on her breath.

They drank their coffees in silence, Isabel shooing away cars that pulled up beside them with their flashers, honking for the parking space. She shook her head at each of them. "Sorry, no." "Not leaving." "Nope." After a while she just ignored them.

Cate told her about the polar bear dream, excluding her analysis of Nuna as a child beyond her years. "Oh, and there was this strange drawing of an igloo with a penguin on it. Couldn't, for the life of me, see the connection."

Isabel snickered. "Don't hurt yourself, this is my wheelhouse." She popped her empty cup into the holder. "The Penguins, Professor Know-It-All, used to play their home games at an arena nicknamed the Igloo. It had a domed roof made of steel."

"Used to?"

"That place is long gone. Seven or eight years ago, they demolished it. I heard they made Christmas tree ornaments out of the roof."

"Figures. Well, the igloo thing certainly explains her love for that team."

Isabel started the car. "But it doesn't explain her current frame of mind."

Cate raised her hand in protest. "We don't even know what that is, so let's not get ahead of ourselves."

Isabel grabbed the journal from Cate. She leafed through it until she found the doodle. She studied the image for all of two seconds, then slapped the book shut. "This isn't really helping. None of it is."

Cate put her hand on Isabel's. "Not to worry, we'll find her." She was surprised that Isabel's hand was trembling—and that hers wasn't.

Another horn blared, the driver trying to make eye contact. Grey sedan, a back seat of hollering kids. The mum had a look of desperation. Isabel nodded. She pulled her hand away from Cate and shifted out of park. "I think maybe we should try that depanneur. You know the one." Isabel waved at the woman as she pulled out.

Cate rolled her eyes. "It feels like we're going from pillar to post."

"They're all on my list." Isabel waved the napkin with the crossed-off places they had already been to. "And recommended by your husband."

Cate wished she would stop mentioning Liam, it always came across as smarmy or snide or slightly sarcastic. She always unnaturally emphasized his name.

Isabel told her to check Facebook. "See if she's posted anything recent."

Cate lit up. Why hadn't they thought of it earlier? Nuna was all over social media, posting about a thousand times a day. Selfies wearing new earrings. Quotations, self-help memes, tips for detoxing your life. Three new notifications popped up from Cate's migraine support group.

"Well?"

"Hold on." Cate's fingers kept hitting the wrong keys. "All I see are public posts and nothing since last week."

Isabel grimaced. "Are you sure?"

"What the… It looks like she unfriended me."

"No way! Check mine." Isabel lifted her hip while Cate dug into her pocket, easing the phone out with her thumb and index finger.

"Sorry," Cate kept repeating. "Your jeans are so tight. How do you get into them?"

"Gawd, you're *so* Canadian."

Hers was the latest iPhone with all the bells and whistles. Cate typed in her password as Isabel dictated it, a nonsense string of letters and characters that Cate couldn't imagine having to memorize. "Nope. Looks like she's ghosted us. You and me both."

"Shit!" Isabel banged her hand on the steering wheel.

"It was a good hunch, though." Cate leaned back in her seat as they careened through a sketchy part of NDG, south of the tracks near rue Saint-Jacques, where scraggly looking men in pilled and tattered coats were going from garbage bin to garbage bin, wheeling their grandma carts past limp mattresses and broken patio chairs, rusty bedframes and old TV sets, rifling around for bottles and pop cans.

Isabel mumbled under her breath.

"What's wrong?"

She indicated the silver Audi ahead of them. "I'll bet she's wearing leggings and sequin pumps," she sneered. "I bet she's dropping her kids off at daycare so she can go shopping with all her other entitled friends." Isabel glared at the windshield and flipped her the bird. "Get a job, you parasite!"

Cate ignored it. Better she blow off steam now than save it for later when they might require a clear, cool mind.

Isabel wiggled into a parking space doors down from the depanneur with its flashing ATM sign and poster advertising

Nestle's vanilla caramel Drumsticks. The Couche-Tard, where Nuna had waited for Cate in a drunken stupor, looked more upscale in daylight with its outdoor water buckets filled with cellophane-wrapped flowers.

"Another Doris Day parking spot!" Cate unclasped her seat-belt. "You're on a roll." She swung open her door, almost hitting a kid on his skateboard. He swerved away, shouting a curse she couldn't make out.

Isabel, oblivious, went around to meet Cate on the other side. "This is the third time you've mentioned that Doris Day thing. What *is* that?"

"Before your time—mine too, actually. Doris Day was an American actress and singer. Big in the 1950s and 60s. I heard she died recently."

"What's that got to do with the price of eggs?"

"Well, in the movies, every time the character she played had to go somewhere, like to somebody's house or a restaurant, she always managed to get street parking right outside the place. And then, for no reason, she'd break into song. I always found it hilarious."

Isabel didn't laugh.

"My turn to go," Cate said, but Isabel insisted on joining her. "Suit yourself."

They headed for the store. Cate scrolled through her phone looking for pictures of Nuna, settled on one taken at her favourite restaurant. Her hair was freshly washed. She was wearing a white crewneck sweatshirt with a saying across the chest: "My mama don't—," the table with its dishes and water glasses concealing the rest. Nuna was happy that day, almost glowing. The chicken bones in her plate were scraped clean. She smiled for the camera like a satisfied hunter. Cate tried to remember what Nuna's mother "didn't" but she drew a blank.

"I should gas up while we're here," Isabel said, going back for the car.

Cate went inside. It was a different guy.

"That was my son," said the neat, clean-shaven man. He looked at the picture and shook his head. "Never seen her before." He handed the phone back. "But then again, they all look alike, eh? Frankly, I don't like them coming in here, they're loud and they're trouble. Always hitting up customers for change or cigarettes. Most of the time they only buy one bottle between them. Then they stand around outside drinking it. Right where I can see them. Why do they come to Montreal, anyways? They don't work, they take drugs. They should stay up there, I hear they have it good. They get free houses and don't pay taxes. What could be better than that?"

Cate stopped him. "Don't you think that maybe some of them have good reasons for coming here?" Her voice quavered. She couldn't get out fast enough.

"You okay? You look a little pale," Isabel said.

"Nothing here," she said, almost in a whisper. Her hands were clenched into fists.

By noon, they crossed the MUHC and the Lachine General Hospital off their list. Cate hardly spoke.

Isabel touched base with Blanchard. Nuna hadn't been on his radar. "I say we stop for lunch, take a serious peek at that journal again."

Cate agreed. She was desperate for a restroom. They found a quiet spot in Girouard Park.

"Women can hold it for up to an hour," Isabel said with authority.

"Women your age, maybe." Cate searched for a nearby Porta Potty, but imagined the state it might be in and decided she wasn't *that* desperate.

Isabel's expression changed. "What happened back there in the dep? It turned you into a ghost."

Cate took a deep breath and told her.

"Jeez, what an asshole."

"Makes me wonder how many assholes are out there." Cate remembered Nuna complaining that Montreal was racist. "I thought she was exaggerating, but now I'm not so sure." She didn't want to think about it anymore. "Let's just turn the page."

They sat near a pile of leaves and unwrapped their sandwiches. Cate opened the journal. A gust of wind sent the pages fluttering.

"Read," Isabel commanded, her mouth full of sandwich.

Cate chuckled. "Who but you manages to get egg on their cheek?" She moistened a napkin with her tongue and wiped it away, like a mother fussing over her child.

Isabel smiled a grownup smile.

The journal was heavily didactic, page after page of book summaries and analysis, character studies, rough drafts of what Cate had seen in final form on standard bond paper, typed in 12-point Times New Roman, as instructed. She opened to a puzzling entry, four double-spaced pages, dated May 15.

"What is it?"

"Hold on, I'm reading."

It was about Atlantis. She seemed to have copied quotations from a book of Plato's writings that she found in Cate's library. A second entry followed, a few days later, with additional information from Wikipedia, including citations. At the end of her notes were ruler-drawn, geometric shapes in pencil first, then bolded with a Sharpie. Mostly squares and rectangles. Underneath, a set of organic shapes, imperfect, swirly, tentative. They had once watched a Netflix documentary called *The Sinking of an Empire*, but Cate was unaware it had left an impression on her.

"What the frig?"

"She's a curious young woman. Isn't that what we've been going for?" Cate didn't know what to make of it. The entries were incoherent, random facts strung together without logic. As though by writing them down, filling up the page with quotations from books, Nuna would eventually understand. The knowledge would sink in because wasn't that what books were supposed to do, teach you things?

They sat shoulder to shoulder, reading.

The notes were punctuated with happy- and sad-face emojis, and a list of binaries: *wealth/modesty, science/spirituality, aggression/humility.* A final emphatic note, in red pen, said, *Where is Atlantis? To be continued!*

Isabel wrinkled her nose. "Lots of exclamation marks."

Cate remained pensive. She didn't know whether to consider it a clue or a red herring at this point. She laid the book down and nibbled at the crust of her sandwich, not feeling particularly hungry. In the distance, a mother was struggling to calm her child, a boy with a piercing cry—another reason why she never wanted children of her own. The battles, the constant negotiation. And, in the end, always the feeling that neither parent nor child ever got what they wanted. Not even close.

Isabel picked up the other half of her sandwich. "Hey, Cate, have you ever done anything completely crazy?"

Cate heard her the second time she said it. "Crazy, like what?"

"Totally impulsive." Isabel nudged a leaf of parsley back into her sandwich. "I mean, has a force greater than you ever caused you to do something you wouldn't have otherwise done on your own?"

What a mouthful. Cate couldn't think of anything.

The exasperated mother scolded and slapped the boy. One swift *baff* on the back of his hand. He stopped crying and backed away from her. In the ensuing silence, Cate thought of Mike. "Well..." Her voice trailed off. "One of my old boyfriends had a car with a flashing cherry light. You know, like the police. On Saturday nights, we'd go driving and pull people over on the highway. I'd say that was kind of crazy."

"Sounds illegal. But that was him, right? You just happened to be in the passenger seat. I'm talking about you, yourself. Have you ever done something completely out of character?"

"Not really." The bright sun vanished behind a cloud. "I take it *you* have, though."

"Well, there was the Hannah thing. But there was something else, too, when I was much younger."

A fork of lightning flashed overhead. The mother and son scurried past them in slightly better moods. The boy's lips were pink from a half-eaten cone of cotton candy.

Cate felt a drop on the back of her hand. She glanced up. Heavy storm clouds had gathered above them. She grabbed Nuna's journal. "Is there an abbreviated version?"

"Rude."

"You *do* realize it's about to come down, don't you?" She barely got through her warning. Huge drops of rain began to fall.

They scrambled to collect their belongings and ran toward the Jeep, thunder rumbling on the horizon. The rain came down in sheets.

Isabel aimed the fob and the doors unlocked. Closer, something caught her attention, a soaking wad of paper wedged between her wiper and the windshield. "Kill me!" she shrieked. "Are you kidding?" She peeled off the fat, wet parking ticket. "Fuck my life!" She climbed in and slammed the door.

"Didn't you check the parking sign?" Cate said.

"And what was wrong with *your* eyes?" She pulled off the Velcro holding the glove compartment shut, bumping Cate unnecessarily, without an apology. She stuffed the ticket inside and sealed it back up. She sped up the windshield wipers. They couldn't keep up with the rain.

"I say we go home, make a nice pot of tea, and think carefully about our next move."

Isabel adjusted her mirror and manoeuvred onto the road.

Cate tried to lighten the mood. "So, what was that crazy, impulsive thing you did?" She already knew the bare-bones story of Isabel's childhood, that her mother had come from Guadalajara with a man, a Quebec tourist who said he loved her and then took off after she got pregnant. "What was it?"

Isabel was attentive to the road. "Well, um, you know my mom started cleaning houses to support us."

Cate nodded.

"And that the Richardsons hired her to clean their house?"

"The family from Westmount?"

"Exactly." Isabel shoved two sticks of gum into her mouth. "They took a real liking to her—they even let her bring me to work."

The rain was starting to let up.

"My mother was thrilled; she didn't have to pay a babysitter. She couldn't have afforded one, anyway, on her salary. But she loved her job there. She sang while she cleaned. And Mrs. Richardson served us lunch and ate with us, like we were part of the family. She even bought me special baby food."

"Sounds like a great boss. Not the usual rich stereotype."

"She made my mother speak Spanish to her and gave her extra money for lessons. Such a nice lady. She didn't have kids of her own, so she sort of became my second mother."

Cate was impressed.

"Then one day, when I was about ten or eleven, I was wandering around the house and found Mrs. Richardson's purse on her dresser next to a pair of long black gloves. One of those evening clutch bags with rhinestones on it. Very fancy looking. I put on the gloves and pretended I was a rich woman getting ready to go out. When I opened the purse, I found money. I don't know why, but I took it and when we got home, I hid it under my pillow."

Cate gasped in disbelief.

"Naturally, my mother found it. When I told her where I got it from, she was furious. It was the only time she ever hit me, two whacks across my butt with a wooden spoon. And then she made me give it back. I was so ashamed."

"So, what happened?"

"The totally unexpected. My mother was sure she was going to get fired. But she didn't, and you know what? The Richardsons offered to pay my tuition to go to private school."

"That's some story," Cate said. "Restores my faith in humankind."

"Well, that's the thing." Isabel turned into Cate's driveway. "If it went another way, I wouldn't be sitting here having this conversation with you. We would've been out on the street, *point final.* My mother might've gone to jail or ended up a *puta.* For sure, social services would've taken me from her." Isabel let out a deep sigh. "Don't you get it? You're to Nuna what the Richardsons were to me."

"So, now you're paying it forward?"

"Something like that."

Cate remembered the first time she saw Nuna. Wild eyes, torn jacket. She almost looked feral.

"I really need to do this," Isabel said. "*We* need to." Isabel locked the car doors, and ran to the house ahead of Cate.

Cate stooped outside the door for a bag of junk mail and an Amazon package. Isabel's story had triggered a memory that she had long forgotten, about stealing flowers from a neighbour's garden. She joggled the house key in the lock, with its annoying faulty cylinder that Liam always promised to have replaced but never did. "Damn, I wish he would get this thing fixed."

The house still smelled of morning coffee.

"I need a shower, I feel like crap," Isabel said. She snapped off her elastic band and tossed around her hair like a pony shaking its mane. Some of the wet landed on Cate.

"Whoa, girl! Go shake that somewhere else."

"Neighhhh." She trotted up the stairs in her stocking feet.

Cate hung their jackets over the radiator. "Use the master ensuite, Liam's not here." She dug the journal out of her bag and opened it.

Upstairs, the linen closet opened and slammed. The toilet flushed and the faucet gushed on.

Cate wondered how she would have felt as a teenager, if her mother had gone through the pages of *her* journal. Not that she ever did anything wild or crazy—except for maybe the thing with Mike. She never shoplifted or dropped out of school to run away with a lover. She rarely gave her parents cause for worry. Their life with Margaret took up too much energy, it was too hard, too sad. She didn't want to add to their burden.

*

The sky began to clear. Cate decided that if the rain stopped within the hour, Nuna was safe. Her father would call it stupid. So would Liam. She set two teacups on the table and went to check on Isabel.

The bathroom door was ajar. Cate cracked it open just enough to see Isabel's discarded clothes on the floor, enough to catch her lean silhouette through the shower curtain. Cate imagined her at sixteen, hormones sending currents through her body, a girl in absolute love with a girl. In absolute, impossible love. Happy one minute, miserable the next. Cate stood dead still with her hand on the door, watching the water purl down Isabel's shoulders.

The faucet switched off.

Cate's cell rang shrilly from her pocket. She scurried to the landing as the shower curtain rings scraped across the metal rod. "Hello? What?"

"Sheesh. I just asked if there was any news," Liam said.

"No. Nothing, really." She padded down the stairs.

"What's up? You sound weird."

"I do?"

"Like you're out of breath or something."

Cate heard Isabel's approaching footsteps and scrambled to get the tea steeping.

"So, what's next?" he said, impatiently.

Isabel appeared wearing Cate's robe, her hair a glistening eel down her back. She sat at the table and rubbed cream on her feet.

"You're looking refreshed," Cate mouthed to her.

Liam's voice barked through the receiver. "What's going on?"

"Oh, sorry." Cate sped through the details of their morning, where they went, their lack of success, how they got caught in the downpour. "Isabel just got out of the shower."

"And?"

"We're regrouping, I'll let you know what the plans are once we have a clearer idea." Isabel screwed the cap back on the cream.

She rubbed her hands together, wiping off the excess, and poured the tea, sliding Cate's cup across the table.

"Talk later, bye."

"Wait," he said, as she went to hang up.

"What?"

"I just had a thought."

Cate blew on her tea.

"I was thinking that maybe we should alert the cops. Do, like, a missing person's report."

"Hm. I'll talk it over with Isabel. She has experience dealing with the police."

"It's worth a shot. At least it'll expedite things, so we can all go back to our normal lives."

Their normal lives. What he wouldn't give for that. Cate hung up quickly.

"I hope you don't mind," Isabel said, indicating the bathrobe.

Cate shook her head.

"Your bathroom's so big you can land a 747 in it."

Cate rolled her eyes.

"And did you know that your soap doesn't smell like anything?"

"It's from Aleppo," Cate said. "Waleed gets it in bulk."

"I prefer my drugstore Dove." Isabel pointed to Cate's phone. "Liam?"

"Who else?"

"I figured as much. He wants to report her missing, I take it?"

Cate nodded.

Isabel set her cup in its saucer. "I think we should hold off on that. At least for now." She didn't elaborate, but Cate's instinct was telling her the same thing.

"Anyway, I have a hunch." Cate glanced outside. The rain had stopped. Sunlight was peeking through the clouds. The sky was a silver bowl.

Isabel sprinkled more sugar into her tea. "I'm all ears."

"I have a hunch that Nuna's okay."

Isabel pinched her eyebrows together. "Why? Did you hear something?"

"I don't know, not really. I just feel it."

Isabel blew into her cup.

"You know, maybe Liam's right, maybe we need to give her a little space and time, let her do what *she* wants instead of what *we* want. That way, she can learn from her mistakes."

Isabel put down the cup and stood up. "Oh, right. Brilliant! Let's give her a way out of her shit and then step aside while she marches right back into it."

"C'mon, Isa—"

"That wasn't the original plan, and you know it. Are you trying to bail on her?"

"Of course not! You said, 'Get her ready, so she can go to college and learn to make better choices.'"

"No, I said she was a good girl who made bad choices. And she hit the jackpot with you, you taught her to think and analyze and question, you're giving her the tools she needs for a better life."

"She was already smart."

Isabel's eyes narrowed. "A smart smartass. Which isn't being smart at all."

Cate gestured for her to sit down. "Look, it isn't our responsibility to save the world."

"You sound like Liam. I'm disappointed in you."

Cate swallowed hard. Once, when Liam was wasted, he called them White Saviours. "You're too wrapped up with this girl," he said. "Every time she makes a move, and it doesn't work out, you two run to save her. Have you ever asked yourselves why? What your motives are? Are you just doing it because you'll feel guilty if she jumps into traffic or drinks herself to death?" It was harsh. The accusation never left her.

Isabel's voice was unwavering. "We need to make her understand that she's better off being as far away from that prick of a boyfriend as possible. That she's better than she thinks, and that she deserves to be the best she can be."

*

Cate showered quickly, surprised that her bathroom wasn't upside down. Given it was Isabel, she expected an inch of water on the floor, hair in the sink, a handful of towels used once and dumped into a heap. But everything was neat and tidy, fan on high, mirror and vanity buffed to a shine. There was even a white towel swan waiting for her on the bed, like the ones chambermaids left at island resorts.

Cate put on fresh clothes, blow-dried her hair, and hurried downstairs. Isabel was on her phone, Googling. "What do we do?"

"We need a new approach," Isabel said. She shredded Liam's list and threw it into the air, napkin snowflakes falling to the rug. "I've had some dealings with Ikajurtauvik, an Inuit organization that can be helpful in these types of cases. We go there next. And then on to Dorval where Nuna lived with her asshole."

Cate snatched their coats from the radiator. She ran upstairs and threw together a bag of toiletries and a change of underwear. Who knew how long any of this would take. Or where the road might lead. "Where did you learn that, by the way?"

"Learn what?"

"How to turn a towel into a swan. It reminds me of origami."

Isabel zipped up. "One of the many useless things I learned on cleaning jobs with my mother. You seem to forget that she dragged me along with her every day."

"I didn't forget."

*

Ikajurtauvik was located in a three-storey brick building under an overpass in an industrial part of town. Despite the crumbling façade, the interior was welcoming with its coat of fresh paint, new carpeting, and original paintings by Niap, a Montreal-based multidisciplinary artist from Kuujjuaq. Cate scanned the posters on the bulletin board listing resources and community organizations that dealt with addiction and mental health issues, homelessness, the sex trade, and partner violence. Others offered sewing classes, elder visits, and healing circles.

The receptionist, a middle-aged Inuk woman with an unusual cascade of white hair, said Isabel's contact person had moved back up north.

Isabel wasn't deterred. She cocked her head and smiled. "I'm Isabel and you are...? Nice to meet you, Tina. I wonder if you can help us." She took an approach that Cate hadn't seen before but one that Isabel had certainly used in her work as a paramedic, asking what protocols were in place when someone went missing, what steps were taken to locate the person, engage with the community, work with law enforcement.

A phone rang.

"One moment, please." Tina took the call, reverting to Inuktitut. She was sympathetic and took her time with the caller. After she hung up, she didn't apologize for the interruption. "You were saying? Oh, yes." She didn't provide any information that Isabel didn't already know. Her organization made sure that the police filed a report and did a proper investigation. "We offer emotional support to the families. And we've developed a welcome kit for women and girls who are new to the city." She paused. "We also encourage friends and allies to be sensitive to the cultural differences and realities of the person they think they are helping." Tina fixed her gaze on Cate.

Isabel thanked her for her time and expertise, adding that her advice was fully appreciated.

*

They were on Highway 20 headed for Dorval. "Slow down," Cate said, "you're going to get us a speeding ticket."

Liam wasn't happy. He said their plan wasn't a plan, it was just half-assed and by the seat of their pants, how rational was that? But going west made perfect sense to Cate and Isabel. It was where a certain segment of urban Inuit congregated, where they lived and shopped and hung out together. Where they met for coffee while their children played.

It was where Nuna had lived with her boyfriend, in a place of their own. Where they smoked, drank, and snorted to their hearts' content. Where they shared their country food that reminded them of home. Where they loved and hurt each other.

Isabel slammed on the brakes. A platoon of orange construction cones had narrowed the road into a single lane. It was bumper to bumper, sunlight glinting off the hoods of cars. Cate raised her hand to block the light.

They were acting on a tip from Blanchard, who'd managed to get the boyfriend's address, which Isabel had forgotten, from the hospital records.

"Fuck this," Isabel groaned. "When will this town ever get its shit together?" She fanned herself, alternating between her neck and forehead. "Jeez, it's hot in here. Help me take off my jacket." She leaned forward.

Cate struggled to wrestle off the snug jacket. It surprised her how much body heat Isabel produced, how intensely she perspired. "You're like a man after a workout. Or maybe it's just your Latino temperament."

That's better," Isabel said. "And I'll take that as a compliment." She switched on the air conditioning.

"Coming back to your story about Hannah..."

"What about it?"

"I feel like there's more." Cate pointed to the gridlock. "And it seems we have time."

Isabel hesitated; it was a wound she was unsure she wanted to open again. She stared ahead and sighed.

"Well?"

Isabel told Cate about the fantasy she had had, of the small town they would run away to, where no one would think to look for them. "I saw it had an old-fashioned bakery with a metal, rolled-up door and a striped awning." She turned up the AC. "And I pictured how it would be, rising at dawn in a new place—our place—just the two of us, Hannah still asleep, me walking along the dirt road to buy her a croissant for breakfast."

Cate pictured Isabel's bakery, wafting with the smell of fresh bread, its glass display case filled with the lightest, flakiest, tastiest pastries and sweets. She imagined sixteen-year-old Isabel pointing to the one she wanted—*Celui-ci, s'il vous plaît*—and the clerk in the flour-dusted apron lifting the croissant with her silver tongs into a cardboard box she ties with string.

"It sounds dumb now when I hear myself say it," Isabel said.

"I don't think it's dumb," Cate said. She honestly didn't think so. In fact, she was envious of their passion. Having never experienced such intense first love.

"Anyway, not long after she fucked off on me, she started dating this jock from our sister school, the captain of their football team. Sometimes I'd see them at games, necking and groping each other. At some point, when she finally came up for air, she'd notice me and say something casual like, *Hey, long time no see*. As though nothing had ever existed between us."

*

The bottleneck cleared. Isabel accelerated.

Cate's phone pinged with a text from Waleed. CALL ME. God, he never listened. She was always reminding him that caps meant you were angry, you didn't text in caps. Unless of course... "Shit. I have to call, or he won't leave me alone."

Isabel groaned. “He’s like your mother.”

“Don’t.”

He answered on the first ring. “Alhamdulillah!”

“What’s going on? I’m kind of in the middle of something.”

His tone was sarcastic. “Hello, Waleed, how are you, how are things?”

“Yeah, sorry. How goes?”

“*Mish mabsoot.* Pretty lousy, in fact.” He paused. “But, on the upside, did you hear? Atwood won the Booker.”

“That’s excellent. I haven’t been following.” Cate glanced at Isabel. “So, what’s happening? Can I have the abbreviated version?”

“I know, Habibti. Priorities.” He didn’t hide his disappointment.

“It’s just that Nuna’s missing and we’re out looking for her.”

He sighed. He empathized. He begged her for *two minutes, just two quick minutes.*

“Okay, but skip the arabesque details,” Cate said, knowing that his minutes often stretched from two to fifteen to twenty. They could stretch into an hour or two. Normally she didn’t mind.

He cleared his throat. It seemed his father, whom he hadn’t seen in over twenty years, was asking to visit him, who knew why, with Hakim, the favourite son. It was all very sudden. Waleed could have gone the rest of his life without seeing them—more specifically, without seeing his father—but it was family. You didn’t say no to family, even if they treated you like garbage. Even if they told you they couldn’t stand to look at you, that you disgusted them. Cate knew their rift had to do with Waleed being gay, his rejection of the faith, his decision not to have children and carry on the family name.

“Is Mom coming too?” Cate knew the woman could deflect, she could appease. She could dazzle and distract them with her culinary skills.

“Apparently not.”

“And now, what? After all these years. He wants to make amends?”

"I don't know, Habibti."

Cate thought for a minute. "Remember when he heard through the grapevine that you were a 'professor of the McGill University'?"

"Yeah, so?"

"Maybe deep down he's proud of you."

"Let's not go overboard. He's proud of Hakim. Hakim, the doctor, Hakim the husband and loving father. Hakim with the waterfront home. I, the fag, have tarnished the family name and reputation."

Cate wished she could hug him, shower him with love and support. If they were alone now, if she had time on her hands, she would invite him for a sleepover and a good cry the way she used to in the good old days. She would run the bath, make him soak in Epsom salts. "The fact that he wants to see you is a good sign, don't you think?"

Isabel gestured for her to hang up. "We're almost there!"

"By the way, Isabel says hi." Cate pulled a face at her. "She says she hopes that whatever your issue is, it all works out."

"You're shitting me," Waleed said. "Seriously?"

"Seriously." She smiled at Isabel. "When this is all sorted, you're coming for dinner, and that's that. It's time you met Nuna properly."

Waleed thanked Cate, said to go do what she had to do. His voice wavered. "Call me when you can."

"Could you have gone on any longer?" Isabel said, signalling for the Dorval exit.

"We're back to this again?"

"Pshaw, no way. But you must admit he *does* demand a lot of your attention."

"Look who's calling the kettle black."

Isabel stuck her tongue out at Cate. She headed along Carson Avenue past the shopping centre to Allard, slowing down to better read the numbers.

Cate waited for her to shift into park. "So, here we are."

"Here we are," Isabel repeated. She shut off the engine.

"What do we do, just sit here and wait?"

"Maybe." Isabel spat her gum into a tissue. "Or we could go ring the bell."

"Hm. Let's not. I don't want to ruffle this guy's feathers."

The building, the boyfriend's place where Nuna had lived before moving in with Cate, could have used an industrial wash. It was shabby and neglected. One of the exterior lights was broken.

Cate's thoughts drifted back to Waleed. She recalled Liam's birthday party, where Waleed and Isabel had first met. Isabel had sought him out before Cate had the chance to introduce them. She was laughing and joking and overplaying her insobriety. Maybe it had been an act, a ploy to get closer to Cate, because wasn't that the effect friends had on each other, liking all the same people and things that the other did? It had been a strange night, with Isabel cleaning her up, putting her to bed. Without criticizing her or getting mad at her for being drunk.

Cate stared at the building. Playing at being a private detective, waiting to catch Nuna's boyfriend red-handed felt a little silly all of a sudden. An enterprise she would have never suggested to Liam or Waleed because they would have said she'd lost her mind.

Isabel was nodding off. Cate plugged in her earbuds and scrolled through her favourite podcasts. Nothing called her. She launched the CBC News app. The top story was the election, followed by another about Alberta farmers and a possible teachers' strike in Ontario. She only half listened. The next one had a dire warning that the content might upset some listeners. She yanked out her earbuds and elbowed Isabel. "Wake up!"

"What, what happened?"

"Shh, listen!" Cate turned up the volume.

Montreal police are investigating the death of a twenty-year-old Indigenous woman who fell over a Laval Street balcony just before 3:00 a.m. yesterday morning. The woman had relocated from

Nunavik to Montreal three years ago to study nursing. Twelve hours after the woman's death, an unnamed source called police to report her missing. Detectives interviewed everyone who was there that night; none were aware that the woman had fallen. Montreal police say they don't have enough evidence yet to rule the case a homicide, but her family believes foul play was involved. Although exact numbers are unavailable, it is estimated that more than four thousand Indigenous women and girls have gone missing or been murdered in the country since 1980.

"It's not Nuna," Isabel said.

"Obviously. But it's unsettling."

"Unsettling, who says that? Say *worrying*, say *upsetting*." She angled her sunglasses up, resting them on the top of her head. "What do you think we should do?"

Cate took a deep breath. "Maybe Liam's right."

"About involving the cops?"

"They must have protocols for this sort of thing. I mean, who are we to think we can find her? We're just two women with no resources."

"Except..." Isabel pointed to the journal wedged in the cupholder. "We have something they don't have."

"True."

"We'd have to turn it over to them—no effing way!"

"I agree."

Isabel suggested they put off deciding and wait to see if the boyfriend showed up. "Meanwhile, I'll run to the mall and grab us something to snack on."

"Okay, but nothing too sugary." Cate pulled a ten from her wallet.

Isabel stuck it between her teeth while she tied her hair back.

Cate snatched it from Isabel's mouth. "Are you nuts? Do you know how many hands have been on that bill?"

Isabel grabbed it back. "Do you know where this mouth has been?" She disappeared down the street, ponytail swishing from side to side. She was slender and perfect, not an ounce of extra weight on her hips. Cate imagined Hannah, dark-eyed—perhaps—with an olive complexion, flirting with Isabel until it came down to the crunch, when everything was at stake. What boys used to refer to as a tease. Someone who drew you in, knowingly, who stoked your desire and your desire for more. And then left you dangling at the precipice.

Cate inserted her earbuds. She searched her music until she found an Elisapie Isaac album that Nuna had downloaded for her. She hadn't listened to it yet, but Nuna had described it as "awesome" in her usual, hyperbolic way. She pressed play and listened intently. What little Inuktitut Cate knew had consisted of glottal clicks and clucks, but this sound was tender, plaintive, haunting. Its melancholy enveloped her. The songs, in Inuktitut, French, and English, left her breathless.

Isabel returned with two drinks and a bag of potato chips under her chin.

Cate stopped the music.

"Still no sign of him?"

"Not yet. Uh, nothing for me I see?"

She handed Cate a can of iced tea. "I figured you'd prefer Liam's banana bread. And if not, I got you this." She pulled a granola bar from her pocket.

"Excellent."

Isabel pulled open the bag of chips, vinegar wafting, and fished out the biggest, saltiest one. She snapped it in two with her front teeth. "So, Amaruq, you nasty bastard, where are you?"

"Maybe he's out of town this week, maybe he's at the nickel mine." They knew it paid him a boatload of cash. Cash to party with. And partying in the city meant blowing it on whatever he could snort or drink or shoot through his veins. Sometimes Nuna got caught in the crossfire. Sometimes things got dark, very dark. Emotions flew. Cate broke off a piece of the granola bar.

"We have the apartment number, why don't we just buzz and find out for ourselves?"

"I'd rather wait and see if he comes out."

"It could be hours," Isabel groaned, licking the salt from her fingers.

"Let's give it time. If nothing happens in an hour, we'll head over to Ice on Top. Someone there is bound to have seen her. Or at least know something."

Ice on Top was what patrons, mainly Inuit, called Isotope, the dumpy bar where Isabel and Blanchard had found Nuna that night.

Cate's phone pinged with a text from Liam: *What should I take out for supper?*

"What is this, Bell Central?" Isabel capped her Gatorade. "Who is it?"

Cate raised her Stop hand.

What are we having? Liam texted again.

Cate typed: *Won't make it back in time.* She paused. The tone, she decided, was wrong. It needed a transition. She deleted it.

"Liam again?"

Cate thought a minute and tried again: *We're onto something here, why not go ahead and make yourself a sandwich, we'll catch up with you later.* Satisfied, she hit send.

He didn't answer immediately.

She crossed and uncrossed her legs, examined a new outbreak on her skin. An elderly couple walked past the Jeep, holding hands. She waited a bit longer.

The phone pinged: *Whatever.*

Isabel badgered Cate. "What's he saying?"

"This and that. Nothing important." Cate figured that calling might be better, but Isabel was already out the door. Cate slipped her cell back into her purse and joined her half-heartedly.

"Well, what did he want?" Isabel repeated.

"He said that we should take our time, do whatever we have to do to bring her home safely."

"Maybe he finally gets it."

"Maybe."

Isabel ran her finger down the apartment directory, looking for number 402. It was the only one with a pencilled-in name, which looked nothing like Amaruq whatever-his-last-name-was.

"Wait a sec!" Cate grabbed her hand. "What if he gets violent?"

"Don't worry. I'm trained to handle that."

"Have you ever had to?"

Isabel sighed. "Yeah, a few times."

"What did you do?"

"I talked them down. Calmly."

"And if it doesn't work?"

Isabel grinned. "I kick them in the nuts and run."

Cate rolled her eyes. She wasn't sure if she was serious or not. She knew Isabel was capable and willing. If cornered, she'd be ready to strike. Especially if it meant protecting someone she cared about. Cate let her guard down. She decided she was in good hands.

Isabel pressed the buzzer. No response. She waited a minute before trying again. Nothing.

"This isn't going anywhere."

"No shit, Sherlock." Isabel jingled her car keys as they walked back to the Jeep. "I've been thinking. I don't think Liam's a hundred percent on board." She popped open the locks.

Cate knit her brows together. "What do you mean?"

"I mean, no offence, but whenever you talk to him on the phone, your energy shifts. It's like you're walking on eggs around him."

"No, I'm not." Cate didn't like that she sounded defensive.

"You totally are." Isabel crooked a finger and said, "Do me a favour. Next time he calls, pay attention to how you tense up, it's kind of hard to miss."

*

With the stakeout a bust, Cate suggested they rent a motel room as a home base. They needed more time to act on their hunch. Liam would understand. Going home now only to turn around and come back tomorrow was pointless. But there was something else. Something inexplicable. The idea of sleeping out, even for one night—the change in routine, perhaps—was giving Cate a rush of adrenalin.

Isabel checked her calendar, pursed her lips, and nodded in agreement. "That way we can come and go easily. Chances are she's in this neck of the woods anyway."

It *was* logical.

They checked in to the Quality Inn & Suites, a modest, clean, two-and-a-half-star motel with Ikea art on the walls. And only an eight-minute walk to Ice on Top. Isabel chose the bed by the window, Cate, the one closer to the bathroom and door in case of emergency, something she had learned from her father who always made a point of scouting out the fire exits in public places before sitting down. Especially in movie theatres. He never stopped talking about some big fire at a downtown night club called the Blue Bird Café.

Cate made a beeline for the bathroom. She wiped down the toilet seat and doorknobs and washed out the paper-wrapped bathroom glasses while Isabel opened and closed every dresser drawer, looking for who-knew-what.

Cate re-emerged, drying her hands with a towel. "What do you think you'll find in there?"

"You never know what people leave behind." Isabel went through the last drawer. "Chargers, loose change, jewellery. My mother was always finding stuff. And what about you? Smells uber-disinfectant-y in here. You don't trust the chambermaids?" She sat on the bed to unlace her Docs. Through the window, they could hear bottles being tossed into the back of a garbage truck.

"What's the big deal if I spritz and spray a little here and there for peace of mind?"

Isabel peeled off her socks and massaged her feet. Her freshly painted toenails were an ocean turquoise. "I'm down for pizza, you?"

"Sure."

They thumbed through the stack of restaurant adverts and ordered a Domino's pizza, half vegetarian, half bacon with extra cheese. Isabel fiddled with the TV remote. She walked to the window and whistled at the view. A siren wailed past.

Cate unpacked her emergency bag of toiletries: tampons, a jar of night cream, travel-sized Crest, two toothbrushes and a rolled-up T-shirt. She laid them out on the night table.

"Wait, you packed a bag?"

"I was a Girl Guide back in the day. We were taught to always be prepared." She didn't want to admit to Isabel, or to herself, that maybe this wasn't such a spur-of-the-moment idea. Things were getting muddy in her mind; she couldn't put her finger on exactly why. Except that being here with Isabel felt like a breath of fresh air. She didn't need to explain her every move. She felt free. Cate went to the bathroom and came out with two extra-large towels, ironed and folded. "Show me how to make one of those swans."

Isabel smiled and laid them both out flat on the bed. "Easy-peasy, just copy what I do." She folded the top two corners of hers downwards and inwards so that they met in the centre. The towel resembled a sailboat.

Cate followed Isabel's lead. "So far, so good."

Isabel rolled the two outside edges of the towel inwards toward the middle, making the shape of an upward-pointing arrow. "Now, fold your arrow into a zed. See? The bottom two points of the arrow create the bottom of the zed, and the top becomes the head."

Cate's swan was lumpy and slack. It looked more like the ugly duckling. "Not as easy as all that."

Isabel propped hers on Cate's bed, squeezing the corners to set the curves. She took Cate's and positioned it to face hers. "When you put them like this, head-to-head, their necks make a heart. See?"

Cate frowned at her sloppy effort. "If you can call it that."

The delivery guy knocked on the door. The box was lukewarm. Cate paid and made Isabel fork over the tip.

Isabel ripped into it. "God, I'm starving!" She dangled a slice by its doughy crust and bit off the tip. She chewed and swallowed with relish. "Wow, it's like having an orgasm!" Flopping onto the bed, she launched a videogame, tinny and loud, on her phone.

Cate wasn't hungry after all. She tugged at her collar. "Can you lower that? I can't hear myself think." She plucked off a mushroom and stared at it, debating what to tell Liam about why they weren't coming home tonight, how to phrase it.

Isabel didn't notice Cate's reticence. She plugged in her earbuds.

Maybe Isabel was right about the tension between them. Cate ran through a few scenarios in her mind, but none seemed credible—the car broke down (he would pick them up), they were too exhausted to drive back now (he would pick them up). He'd consider the reasons fishy, and she didn't want to spark an argument.

Liam beat her to it with a text. *Sorry for before, I was being dickish.*

She couldn't believe her good fortune. The perfect entry point.

He answered on the first ring. "Hey."

"Hey." Cate sighed in a way that suggested she couldn't control what was coming, she was sorry about it, but it was what it was, there was no way around it. "Change of plan."

"Oh?"

"I'm afraid it's worse than I thought. Than *we* thought."

Isabel looked up from her game as though she'd been listening all along. Cate shrugged her shoulders.

"Jeezus, what's happened?"

Cate let a beat go by. And another. The ice machine clattered outside their room.

"Is she…? She's not…?"

"Oh, no, it's nothing like that."

Isabel pretended to resume her game, but Cate could tell by her body language that she was still eavesdropping, the volume muted.

"What, then?"

"Well, it's just that we're way further behind the eight ball than we imagined." Cate adjusted her tone to sound hopeful. "We're in Dorval but…uh…we think we finally have a lead." She glanced at Isabel, lying on her stomach, feet kicking the air behind her. The rash on Cate's hand intensified. She slapped at it to keep from scratching. "For simplicity, it's probably best if we stay the night."

There was a long silence.

"Makes sense. Really, it does." Liam said it with forced enthusiasm.

"Love you," Cate murmured, Liam disconnecting on the "you." She felt a crick in her neck and went to the bathroom for a pill. She stared at her reflection in the mirror, massaging her neck and shoulders.

"So, he's good with us staying here tonight?" Isabel called out.

"Seems so." Cate stretched out on the bed and stared at the ceiling. She made tight fists, squeezed. Slowly, she opened her fingers again. She noticed the tension leaving her hands. They felt lighter. She repeated the exercise with every muscle group, tensing and releasing. She felt like a balloon losing its shape, deflating. She closed her eyes. The drone of evening traffic settled into white noise.

Isabel revisited the pizza box. "Your whole half is still here. You should really eat something."

"I *did* eat."

"What, a couple of mushrooms? A pepper? You need carbs, girl, to put some heat in your belly."

"Okay, okay." Cate didn't mind Isabel's nagging. She felt relieved. Deliciously relieved. So relieved she could have eaten an entire extra-large pizza herself.

*

Ice on Top wasn't the sort of bar Cate would have ever gone to for drinks. The outside alone, tagged and dilapidated, would have turned her away. It advertised a dark soul. Danger. Nothing about it was inviting. Its dim, indoor lighting produced a halo effect through the drawn curtains, pale blue bedsheets stretched across a pair of windows, the only two in the place. The portico had a film of grime and soot from the constant exhaust of semi-trailers speeding down the autoroute. Ice on Top had all the markings of an abandoned warehouse. But the giant satellite dish on the roof, the blinking neon sign, the parked cars, and the front door, scuffed and battered from use, somehow infused it with life. It was a whole ecosystem unto itself.

Two women in open ski jackets were leaning against the wall, talking. Cate recognized the lilt and rhythm of their language. They could have been thirty-five or sixty-five.

"Got a smoke?" one of them asked.

Cate shook her head, no, they were sorry, they didn't smoke.

"What the fuck do people have to do around here to get a cigarette?" the other one said.

"Things definitely aren't what they used to be."

Cate smiled and asked where they were from.

"From my mother," said the one who had asked for a cigarette. The women guffawed and sauntered off, looking for others to hit up.

"I've never heard an answer quite like that," Cate said when they were inside.

Isabel giggled. She led Cate to a corner table.

Cate glanced at the dark panelled walls. The inside was as shabby as the outside with its dungeon-brown booths and worn carpet, pocked with cigarette burns. It smelled of beer and mildew, and it was packed. The music was ambient, not blaring. Most of the people looked like regulars, shift workers capping off their day, couples joking or arguing with each other. It seemed more like a community pub than a rowdy, brawling bar. "What's the story on this place?" Cate said. "Why do they call it Ice on Top?"

"Everyone these days calls it that. But the Inuit started it, I think." Isabel opened her menu, the pages sticking. "I heard that when they began hanging out here in the 90s, they thought the name Isotope sounded like Ice on Top—which, of course, reminded them of an igloo. So, they started calling it that and it kind of stuck."

"Pretty creative."

A waitress with her hair in a beehive arrived to take their order. Cate thought of the old fashion magazines from the sixties. She had on a thick layer of sparkling green eyeshadow and a leather choker with gaudy stones and an oversized Celtic cross. The cross had a metallic blue sheen. Her breasts were stuffed into a blouse two sizes too small. Tits for tips, Liam had always called it.

"What can I get you?" she asked in a hoarse voice that spoke of way too many late nights smoking cigarettes.

Isabel closed her menu. "We'll have a pitcher of your best draught." She winked at her. "Before you go, though, can you tell us if you've seen this girl around?"

Cate flashed her Nuna's picture, the one from the chicken restaurant.

The waitress squinted. "Yeah, but she hasn't been here in months. She usually comes with her boyfriend. He sometimes gets a bit loud but he's a good tipper."

While Cate and Isabel waited for their beer, they wandered from table to table asking if anyone knew Nuna.

People eyed the photo suspiciously. "Who are you, the cops?"

Others hardly looked at it before shaking their heads. Isabel asked if they knew a guy named Amaruq. No. No. No.

They tried a trio of young women in tight, low-cut tops with sparkly designs across the front. Each wearing a different shade of bright lipstick.

"So what if we do?" one said, snapping her gum. Her friend whispered something to her in Inuktitut and they burst into laughter.

"It's kind of important," Cate said. "Can you remember when and where you last saw her?"

The women ignored her, returning to their conversation.

Isabel nudged Cate to go easy. She took over, trying a gentler approach. "We're kind of worried about her."

The one with lipstick running over her lip-line flashed a venomous look. "Are you her mother or something?" She swigged her beer.

The first girl blew a pink bubble and popped it. "If not, we've got nothing to say."

Isabel persisted. "What about a guy named Amaruq, her boyfriend? Ever heard of him?"

The girls shrugged.

Their beer had arrived. Cate signalled Isabel to let things be. Isabel shook her head. She asked Cate for a pen and grabbed a napkin off their table. "Listen, ladies, if you hear anything, please let me know." She scribbled down her number. "Or if you see her boyfriend, tell him to call."

When they got back to their table, Cate groaned. "Well, that was useless."

Isabel poured them each a pint with an inch of foam on top.

"Obviously, they don't trust us."

"No shit, Sherlock." Isabel said. "Why *should* they?"

It felt like ages since Cate had had a beer. But she hadn't forgotten its cold fizz, its prickle in the throat. She tapped her hand to what was playing through the speakers.

Isabel mouthed the lyrics. "I absolutely loooooove this!"

"Catchy tune." Cate didn't know it but didn't let on.

They polished off the pitcher. Isabel held up her finger, requested another.

Cate wrinkled her nose. "What are we still doing here? Seems like a dead end."

"It's still early," Isabel said. "You never know who might walk in."

Cate didn't notice the time pass. She trusted Isabel. People came and went, including the snarky lipstick girls. Another pitcher arrived and Cate didn't say no.

By the time they staggered back to the motel, Cate was wrecked. She rifled through her purse for the key. "Hmmm, I know I had it somewhere," she slurred.

"I give you one thing to take care of and you blow it." Isabel clapped her shoulder playfully.

Cate turned her purse upside down and shook everything out—wallet, glasses, phone, key card. "Ta-da!" She raised her arms in triumph and slid the card into the slot. The red light buzzed. She pulled it out and tried again. And again. The red light kept flashing on.

Isabel grabbed the card from her. "You're going to lock us out if you keep doing that!" She turned it the other way, activating the green light. The door opened.

"Good thing we didn't drive." Cate stooped to retrieve the spilled items from her purse.

Isabel bent down to help and knocked heads with Cate. They giggled like schoolgirls, massaging their temples, pretending to feel pain but not feeling a thing. Isabel felt around in the dark for the light switch and flipped it on. "Should we order more beer? Or some tequila?"

"Tempting," Cate said. "But unwise."

"I knew you'd say that."

Waiting for Isabel to finish in the bathroom, Cate moved the swans to the overstuffed armchair, careful not to disturb them.

She stripped off her clothes except for her T-shirt. Reaching underneath, she unclasped her bra.

"I pee like a racehorse," Isabel called out. "But I pee quickly." The toilet flushed. Isabel tiptoed out of the bathroom in a matching rose camisole and underpants.

Cate looked away. "I have a spare shirt. In case you're cold, I mean."

"No thanks." She flopped into bed.

A wave of nausea hit Cate when she got to the bathroom. She felt like puking. She ran the tap and wiped her face and neck with a cold towel. She closed the toilet lid and sat, shivering, until it passed. By the time she got into bed, Isabel was asleep.

*

The motorboat travelled in circles on the lake, no one at the helm. Just boat and water and a frothing, spiralling wake. The lake went on and on. The wake went on and on. At closer range, there were people on that boat. A crew of two. Nuna in a wool hat and fur-trimmed parka, steering hand over hand. Staring down the great horizon. And Cate, frantic: "Why are we going in circles?" She shouted over the motor. Nuna: "Who says we're going in circles?" Nuna again, firmly: "We're going where we need to go."

Cate woke with a start, the room spinning. She sat up and rubbed her eyes, trying to make sense of her strange dream. She turned to tell Isabel, but Isabel was gone. An icy panic swept through her. She remembered too much beer and banging heads and laughing so hard she almost peed her pants. She remembered the girls with tight tops and too much lipstick. She remembered people's snide remarks when they asked about Nuna.

Where *was* she? And where was Isabel?

Get a grip, she thought to herself. Lightheaded, her thoughts turned to the kitschy, amateurish painting hanging above the dresser, a country scene of mountains reflected in water.

A few days after their visit to the Group of Seven exhibit at the museum, Cate had an idea for a lesson, based around Nuna's criticism of the Lawren Harris paintings. She hoped it would also lead to new insights for her research on settler narratives. Cate hauled out the *Book of Canadian Poetry* and assigned her a late-nineteenth-century poem called "The Unnamed Lake" by Frederick George Scott, which her students always referred to as "The Unbearable Bore"—until she made them analyze it carefully.

"Read it," Cate said. "Read the first stanza aloud to me."

Nuna read as most students do, racing ahead without respecting the punctuation marks.

Cate stopped her. "Start again," she said. "And when you see a comma or a line break, take a breath."

"What if I don't have to?"

"The poet wants you to."

She sighed.

"The comma is a signal to stop for a second, before going on. Partly to make you think about what you just read."

"Okay." Nuna made a show of clearing her throat. She hocked and spit into a tissue. "It sleeps among the thousand hills." She deliberately drew out each word as though she were reading to someone with no knowledge of English. "Where no man ever trod." It was taking forever. "What's trod?"

"Stepped."

She scowled. "Why didn't he just say 'stepped'?"

"Mostly for the rhyme. It was a common word back then." Cate accompanied her from memory, hoping to speed things up. They got to the last line, completely out of synch. "And only nature's music fills / The silences of God."

"Why is it called 'The Unnamed Lake'?" Nuna asked.

"Try to guess."

She looked back through the poem, squinting as though doing so would magically provide her with the answer.

"Nature is pristine," Cate reminded her.

"What's that?"

"It means untouched, unspoiled. It refers to humans messing up nature. Before humans, nature was vast and perfect."

Nuna shook her head. "Did he forget that *we* also…*trod* there? And that nature *is* perfect, even when it's ugly."

"What do you mean?"

"Like, the river and the lake and the sea, they're our grocery stores," she said. "And way cheaper. What we kill and fish from the water, we eat. It might look messy and ugly to you, but we survive this way. We've been doing it for six thousand years."

Cate took a different tack. "How about this: Why do you think the poet chose an idealized representation of nature, like the Lawren Harris paintings we saw?"

"Idealized?"

"It's when artists, including writers, create images that come close to what they believe perfection is, based on the values of their own culture and time."

Nuna shrugged. "The fuck if I know."

Cate glowered.

"Sorry, I don't know. And, by the way, we *do* have names for our bodies of water, it's just that you guys don't know them. They're *our* names."

Cate made a mental note to look them up.

"The water is also one of our churches," she continued. "It's where Sedna, the sea goddess, lives."

Cate congratulated Nuna on her ideas and told her to jot them down in her journal. "You're absolutely right. But now, let's move onto poetic techniques. How does he transmit his idea of pristine nature and God within it?"

Nuna threw her hands up. "What if I disagree?"

"You can disagree all you want, but once you're in college you can't just pout and go on strike. You have to explain the poet's intention given the context and cultural prejudices of the time. You have to write the essay you're expected to write."

*

The key card buzzed.

"Finally. You're up," Isabel said, letting in a bright wedge of daylight. "Pardon my French, but you look like shit." She set down a breakfast takeout tray and yanked open the drapes.

"God, no. That's nasty!"

"Come on, it's seven thirty! We have things to do and places to go."

Cate had forgotten what it was to be young, to have partied all night and gotten up anyway, perky as a pickle. Even though you felt like retching. Isabel handed her a coffee and a waxy envelope of lightly buttered whole wheat toast.

"I figured you wouldn't go for anything too heavy on the cholesterol." She perched on the edge of her bed, unwrapping an elaborate breakfast sandwich.

Cate's stomach churned at the greasy smell of bacon and cheese.

"FYI, I was up at six." Isabel bit into her sandwich. "Couldn't sleep, I kept picturing some piece of trash picking Nuna up on the side of a highway somewhere."

Cate peeled the lid off her coffee. She sighed. "What if...? What if Liam's right, what if she's had enough of us, what if she wanted an out and didn't know how to tell us?"

"That's not Nuna." Isabel popped a sliver of bacon into her mouth.

"Maybe she didn't want to hurt our feelings after everything we've done for her. She was the one who said she wanted to pursue higher education, we didn't force her. Maybe she changed her mind."

"But she was under our watch and now we have a responsibility to find out what happened."

"I suppose you're right."

"At least we know from the waitress that she's been around."

"Yes, but not recently." Cate suggested they take their time and really analyze the pages of her journal. "Up until now, we've been kind of wishy-washy about it."

Isabel grimaced. "I still have reservations. How would *you* like someone snooping through your stuff?"

"Let me remind you that while we dilly-dally over this, the clock is ticking." Cate picked up the journal. "I have zero qualms about it. And if Nuna gets mad, I promise to take the blame."

Isabel slapped the crumbs off her shirt and took her coffee. "Meanwhile, I'll go back and stand vigil outside Amaruq's apartment. We'll touch base with each other around lunchtime."

"We'll need to get out of here before that."

"Just ask the front desk for a late checkout, I don't see people lining up to stay here." The door closed behind her.

Cate pitched her cold toast and the scraps from Isabel's breakfast sandwich, limp lettuce and a scatter of sesame seeds. She popped a migraine pill, hung the Do Not Disturb sign over the doorknob, and hopped in the shower. Dressed, hair washed and combed, she moved the drooping swans from the armchair to her bed. She called down to negotiate a late checkout, accepting the small penalty. The minute she cracked open the journal her phone rang. She eked out a cheerful greeting. "Hey, girlfriend."

"You sound off," Waleed said.

"Still recovering from last night."

"What was last night?"

"We decided to camp out in Dorval for a while. See if Nuna turns up."

"Good call," Waleed said, but it was obvious to Cate that he was only half paying attention, because he didn't ask what she was recovering from. He repeated the story of his father coming to visit.

"You already told me." Cate put him on speaker while she flipped back to the beginning of the journal.

"You're not very sympathetic, Habibti. What am I to do? There's no way I'm abandoning my life for my father, no fucking way. I'm in love." He sounded like his usual, melodramatic self with an added spike of anxiety that his thirty mgs of Citalopram didn't seem to be suppressing.

Her phone pinged. She ignored it. "So tell him now's not a good time, just put him off. Maybe eventually he'll forget about it. Or go back to hating you and leaving you alone. This couldn't have come at a worse time—for me as well. We need to find Nuna before something happens to her."

"I know, I know. But I need your advice."

Ping.

"Okay, how about this? You once told me that we're the writers of our own stories."

"I did...and you're right. I'm right. I'll keep it in mind." He hung up quickly, as though he were suddenly aware of being an imposition.

The messages were from Liam. *Good morning, Sunshine.* And the second one: *Call me.*

Will call soon, Cate texted back.

I won't wait up.

She tossed her phone onto the bed and got busy reading.

By the time Isabel was back, Cate had read three-quarters of the journal. She circled back a couple of times to Nuna's notes and pencil sketches of Atlantis. She flagged what she felt were key words, GREEDY for wealth and power. Swept into the sea by earthquakes and floods and FOREVER GONE. She pencilled the word "disappearance?" lightly in the margin and dog-eared the page.

"Well, *I* had an interesting morning," Isabel called out from the bathroom. "I almost ran into Amaruq."

"What? Either you did, or you didn't."

Isabel tinkled into the toilet as she recapped the story.

She was so real, so unselfconscious. Cate remembered how she had looked before bed, floating across the room in her camisole and underwear.

"So, I went back to the apartment and waited. For a long time, nothing happened. Then an Inuk walks out."

"Amaruq?"

"My heart was beating fast. I jumped out of the car and started talking to him, asking questions, that sort of thing." The toilet flushed. Isabel reappeared, air-drying her hands.

"There are towels, you know." Cate threw her a swan.

"I said, 'Are you Amaruq?' and hours went by before he answered. So then I knew something was up." She wiped her hands and continued her account in fits and starts, adding details on the fly, as they occurred to her.

Cate was getting used to her. She pieced the story together without asking Isabel to slow down, start again, be more coherent.

The guy was Amaruq, Isabel swore it. He answered her questions, somewhat vaguely, until she finally figured out that he'd been putting her on the whole time. She put her hands on her hips and told him it was important. Only she said it in a threatening voice. He lit a cigarette, blew the smoke in her direction, and said, *Atsuk, I have no idea.* "I wanted to kick him in the nuts," Isabel said.

*

"So, what do I tell him?"

"Tell who?"

"Liam."

"About what?"

"Don't play dumb. About, you know, what we're doing next. He'll want to know."

"I thought maybe we could run over to the mall, see if we can find anyone who's seen her lately."

"Sounds like a long shot. Sounds like we're running out of ideas."

"We're not. It's Liam who keeps discouraging you." Isabel switched mindlessly from one channel to another. "Just call and see what he wants."

Waiting for him to answer, Cate glanced at the TV, three seconds of this and five seconds of that, musing at how everything just kept on going while somebody's life was in jeopardy. *The World's Dumbest Videos*, *The World's Dumbest People*. A Heinz commercial promising that happiness was a blob of ketchup away. Nothing stopped. The Earth just kept spinning on its axis, like nothing bad was ever going on.

Liam picked up. They exchanged pleasantries. He was low key. Cate sensed that Isabel was eavesdropping again.

Their conversation shifted.

"I really don't know, what do you mean?" Cate's muscles tightened. She lowered her voice to a whisper. "No... I don't think so... Let's wait. I'll let you know." She hung up and tossed the phone. "Jesus."

"What?"

"He said some awful things. I don't know what's gotten into him." She glanced at the TV with disbelief. "You're actually watching this shit?"

"Things like what?"

"He feels shut out. He accused the three of us of being our own little family."

"Ouch." Isabel zapped off the TV.

Cate nodded, cheeks flushed. "I never realized how sensitive he is." She reflected on whether his accusation was true. Maybe it had merit. Ever since Nuna and Isabel came along, the dynamics in her life had changed. Her focus had shifted away from him.

"Do you want to go pick him up, let him tag along with us?"

Cate shook her head. "He'll just think we invited him because of what he said. Not because we want him. Besides that, he works, he can't just take the time off."

"So, he'll have to put on his big boy pants, then. Unless you're thinking of calling off the whole thing."

"Hell, no." Cate fiddled with her swan, trying to freshen it up. She smoothed out the lumps. "But we need to decide whether it's time, and necessary, to involve the police."

"Let me talk to Blanchard first." Isabel scooped up her phone.

Cate caught snippets of their conversation. She could hear his booming voice through the receiver, hounding Isabel about when she was coming back. He hated her replacement. She paced as they spoke, agitated by the time she hung up.

"What did he say?"

"Not to involve them, if we can possibly help it."

Cate's eyes opened wide. "Really?"

"Really." Isabel sighed. "He said that notifying the cops won't do a damn thing."

Cate went to the bathroom to collect their toothbrushes. "Someone is missing for three, now four days and the cops won't look for her? Or at least put out an alert?"

"Well, they might, but think about it. She's Indigenous. They'll just say, here we go again, the way Blanchard always does. Only they're the cops. They're not supposed to do that."

Cate ran the tap, rinsing the stray hairs down the drain. "Is that true or is he just guessing?"

"Not always, but often enough. And I've seen it, too."

"We should go," Cate told her.

Isabel stooped for her knapsack. "Not only that, once they start digging into her past, they'll find out about all the times she's been picked up; to them she'll be a cliché, one of the stereotypes. And they'll treat her that way. Pardon my French, but it's pretty fucked up."

Cate zipped up her toiletries and set them by the door. "Didn't you once tell me that Nuna had a restraining order against Amaruq? Isn't that on file somewhere?"

"It is. But so's the time she got arrested for beating the hell out of him at Ice on Top. There were plenty of witnesses."

Cate pulled up her bedsheets and fluffed the pillows.

"Nuna spent the night in jail."

Cate sat on the edge of the bed. "Why have you never mentioned that?"

"I am now."

"Crap."

"And remember those Val d'Or women who accused the provincial police of physically and sexually abusing them? It was all over the news." Isabel shook her head. "We can't call them."

Cate agreed. If anything happened to Nuna because of police intervention, she would never forgive herself. "I guess you're right."

They checked out of the motel and drove a short distance to the Dorval Shopping Centre to look for some Inuit who might have news. Many of them settled in Dorval because of people they knew who had already made a go of it. They worked for Inuit organizations on the West Island. The women sewed together. They shopped at Walmart. It was a close-knit satellite community near the airport. A home away from home.

Isabel shifted into park. "What do you say we grab lunch before checking out the stores?"

"Is there a hole in your stomach? You're always hungry."

"Rude."

Cate lowered the sun visor and opened her window. "If you twist my arm I might go for some French fries."

Isabel drove to a nearby McDonald's. To save time, they ordered at the drive-thru and ate in the parking lot, in a spot of shade.

Isabel opened the other windows for air. She chuckled. "Last time I was at this McDonald's was the night we picked up Nuna. Blanchard bet me ten bucks that I couldn't drink three strawberry shakes without having to pee within the hour."

Cate squeezed ketchup on her fries.

Isabel bit into her Big Mac, sauce dribbling down her face. Cate reached over and dabbed the corner of her mouth.

Isabel took the napkin from her. "My bladder won, of course." She wiped her lips and chin. "Then the call came. We met the firefighters at Ice on Top, where Nuna was passed out cold. She had some cuts and bruises, but her life wasn't in danger."

Cate couldn't remember the last time she'd had French fries. Not like these but fresh ones, hot, golden, fried to perfection. On special occasions, or whenever her mother was in a mood, Niall would take her to Lafleur's in Lasalle for what he called the best fries in town. She closed her eyes and savoured the memory.

"We lifted her onto the stretcher, and I said to Blanchard I'd just be a second, I had to go to the washroom." Isabel spoke with her mouth full. "'You won the bet,' he said. 'But this girl, she never wins anything.'"

Isabel filled Cate in on everything that had happened before they met that night at the hospital. Nuna had become a regular pickup and Blanchard was tired of it. "*Pourquoi qu'a retourne pas dans l'nord avec son monde*?" he snapped at Isabel.

"Because maybe up north isn't such a great place for her to be right now," Isabel said.

"*Pis pourquoi qu'a persiste avec son crisse de trou de cul sale*?" He never minced words when he mentioned the boyfriend.

"*Calme-toi*," Isabel whispered. "She can probably hear you." Though they both knew she didn't speak a word of French.

At the ER, he turned on his magnetic charm to take her mind off her cuts and bruises. He pulled up his repertoire of corny jokes. "What do you get when you cross a cow and a lawnmower?"

Nuna shrugged.

"A lawnmooer!" He forced a laugh that almost sounded real.

A faint smile crossed Nuna's lips.

He ramped up his efforts. "What do you get when you cross a termite with a dinosaur? Dino-mite! Knock, knock."

Nuna bit. "Who's there?"

"Hawaii."

"Hawaii who?"

"I'm fine, Hawaii you?"

She chuckled and pleaded not to make her laugh, it hurt too much.

Isabel was concerned. After her shift, she offered Nuna a ride home. And the rest—Cate knew the rest.

"You're in la-la land," Isabel said. "Were you even listening?"

"Of course I was." Cate nibbled on a fry. "I was just thinking that if the stars hadn't lined up the way they did, we would never have met. We would never have gotten to know Nuna. We would never have lost her, either."

"We didn't lose her," Isabel said. "We've temporarily misplaced her."

Cate's phone went off.

Isabel looked at her with pleading eyes. "Don't answer. Let's just enjoy our meal in peace."

Cate ignored her.

"You have big time FOMO," Isabel muttered, munching on the last pickle from her hamburger. "Fear of missing out."

"I know what it is." Cate answered the call, listening attentively, nodding every now and again. She bit her lip. "Yeah, I'm sorry too."

Isabel glared. Of course. Who else would it be?

Cate read Isabel's body language without reacting. She sipped her coffee. She scribbled a phone number on her napkin. The conversation with Liam petered out. She hung up. Her face brightened.

"Well?"

Cate stamped her feet, she drummed on the dash with the palms of her hands. Her voice rose an octave. "I think we have a lead!" Her eyes sparkled.

"Whaaaat? OMG! Let's hear it!"

Cate repeated what Liam had told her. The details flew out of her mouth. Someone had called their land line. Liam came home and saw the number on the answering machine. Two calls. He recognized the Ottawa area code and did a reverse phone lookup but couldn't get an address.

Isabel was wide-eyed. "Are you thinking what I'm thinking?"

"Exactly! Maybe she's gone to stay with that aunt of hers we went to see the tulips with."

"The one who cut her umbilical cord?"

"Yes, her. It's not far-fetched that she would have gone there." Cate started dialling the number on her napkin. "Let's not waste a minute."

"Not so fast, Chica." Isabel pursed her lips. "We call the woman—what's her name—then she tips off Nuna, and Nuna vanishes to who-knows-where without a word to anyone. A wrong move like that could set her off."

"We can ask the aunt not to say anything, to keep her there until we arrive."

"For someone so smart, you're pretty naive."

Cate put the phone down. She crumpled her French fry bag and stuffed it into her empty cup. "I guess you're right. I mean, we're the White people. The Qallunaat. Tolerated, but regrettably the enemy."

Isabel took Cate's cup and wedged it into the takeout tray with the rest of their garbage. She opened the door. "That woman doesn't know us from a hole in the wall. She met us once. She owes us nothing." She dumped everything in a nearby wastebasket and got back into the Jeep.

"Well, then there's no question. We'll have to go." Cate balled her hand into a fist. "We have to get this one right."

"My thought exactly. But what about Liam?"

Cate said the best thing would be to go home first, run through the plan, get Liam's input. Make him feel like they were consulting him. "We can head out in the morning after dinner and a good night's sleep."

They were quiet all the way home. Isabel pulled into the driveway.

Cate turned to look at her. "Coming?" She handed Isabel her purse and toiletry kit at the front door. She fought with her key. "Jesus, I hate this thing." Inside, on the kitchen counter, she noticed a Chinese takeout menu and a couple of unopened fortune cookies. Liam didn't usually go for Chinese food—unless he was with friends and they twisted his arm.

"Your house, you first," Isabel said.

Cate picked one and cracked it open. She set down the cookie. She never ate them; she didn't know anyone who did. They tasted like cardboard.

Isabel waved impatiently. "Read."

"All things are difficult before they are easy." Cate stuffed it in her pocket. "Well, *that's* helpful. What's yours?"

"Empty, look." Isabel showed both halves to Cate. "Have you ever seen a fortune cookie with nothing inside? What a rip-off!"

"I guess you're special," Cate said. "You have enough of your own wisdom."

Isabel smirked. "Sure." She kissed Cate on both cheeks. "I'll be back in the morning to get you."

"You're not staying for dinner?"

"No, I should really go back and check in on my mother. Plus, you and Liam need to be alone tonight."

Cate realized she had a point. She walked Isabel to the hall. They lingered by the open door. Funny, Cate hadn't noticed it earlier, the entire veranda was covered with leaves. It struck her as strange for a guy like Liam who liked everything nice and tidy.

There was a chill to the air that felt like winter was on its way.

*

When Liam found Cate in the kitchen, he was taken aback. Liam was the one who usually made the meals. The one who watched popular cooking shows on TV and tried out their recipes. Cate, on the other hand, saw it as a chore. And a bore. She felt the adage that "the way to a man's heart is through his stomach" was more about manipulation than love. Or, as her feminist friends put it, a clever way to keep women in the kitchen.

She had made his favourite childhood meal, shepherd's pie. Not his mother's "world-famous recipe" that Cate never had time to learn before she died, but a relatively easy one she found online. One of the ingredients, swede, piqued her curiosity, a cross between a turnip and a cabbage. She picked it up at a specialized grocery store. For dessert she baked mint Irish cream brownies.

She laid out their finest china, and her grandmother's silver, on white linen napkins. She brought out the crystal candlesticks made in Czechoslovakia. She set the table for two the way it was in the early days of their relationship.

Liam dropped his briefcase. He gathered her up in his arms. "You sure are a sight for sore eyes."

"It's nice to be home."

He said to give him two minutes, he had to wash before supper, he'd just been in the gym playing basketball with the other teachers. "Promise, I'll be quick." He took the steps two at a time. The shower gushed on.

Cate could hear him slapping around in the water, singing. She heard the shower stop, the curtain swish open, and his bare feet on the heated tile as he towelled off and threw on some clothes. She ran a ring of Lypsyl around her lips.

Liam went straight to the living room to find the right music.

"That was fast," Cate called to him. "Are you taking requests?"

"How about John Legend?" He cranked up the volume and joined her in the kitchen, his hair still damp. He was wearing her favourite aftershave, but his T-shirt was on inside out.

She decided not to tell him. It was cute. She was touched that he had rushed.

His serving of shepherd's pie fell apart on her spatula, but Cate pieced it together and arranged it pleasingly on his plate. "Sorry about this."

"Smells amazing. What are *you* having?"

Cate lifted the foil off the quinoa salad.

They ate their first few bites in silence, enjoying the music. She remembered what had attracted her to him when they first met. His freckled ears, how he liked to call her Miss Catherine the Great before kissing her.

"This is even better than my mother's."

"Thanks."

"How about a glass of wine?" he said. "There's a bottle of white open in the fridge."

"Uh, no thanks," Cate said, still recuperating from Ice on Top.

Liam poured himself a glass, raising it to her. "Santé."

"Cheers." Cate sipped her water, savouring the pure enjoyment on Liam's face. Enjoyment of the food, of her, of the calm uninterrupted moment. The mood was exactly what she wanted. Relaxed. Free of tension and hostility. She cleared her throat. "I suppose I should tell you…"

Liam set his glass down. "Tell me what?"

Cate forked up a mouthful of salad.

"Is there news? Did the lead pay off?"

"Well, no, not yet. But we're now thinking that it might have been Nuna who called—from her aunt's phone. You remember the aunt." She reminded him of his provincials weekend in Trois-Rivières and of their Ottawa trip to see the tulips. "We're pretty hopeful."

Liam reached for his wine. "Congratulations, good detective work!"

"If it weren't for you getting that call, we'd still be going nowhere." Cate reached her hand across the table.

He squeezed it. "I didn't think of it before, but we could give the number to the police as well. Might move things along faster."

She wriggled her hand away. "Well, er, I don't think so." She poured herself more water from the pitcher. The sound of his chewing was setting her on edge. "We've actually decided that we can't call them."

The colour drained from his face. Rain from outside was pummelling the windowsill.

Cate rattled off the reasons they got from Blanchard. She told him about the Val d'Or women.

"Then what the hell are they here for, if not to help people?" He banged down his wineglass.

"You're not listening, Liam." The curtain billowed.

He pushed his plate away.

Cate got up to close the window.

Liam lowered his voice. "I'll say this again, one more time. *You* were the one who didn't want children." His neck flushed. "So what is it you're playing at now?"

"I'm not *playing* at anything."

"Well, from where I'm sitting, it looks pretty cozy, whatever it is."

Cate sat down, glaring at him. "And let *me* remind you, *you* were the one who insisted we get married. I was content just living together." Cate knew he couldn't disagree, the terms had been clear from the start.

Liam snorted. "Yes, I agreed, but maybe I shouldn't have. Love makes you do stupid things sometimes, like giving up part of yourself. I probably could have lived with it, but this business of you and Isabel co-parenting this kid makes me wonder."

"Wonder what?" Cate dropped her fork. "Oh my God, Liam, can you hear yourself? Well, can you? You're the one, if I remember correctly, who pushed me into this thing with Isabel in the first place." Cate's hand accidentally struck her glass. It tipped and shattered across the tile.

Neither of them moved.

Liam clenched his jaw. "I was only trying to help with your paper, not give you a crusade. You two, you're so tight, there's no room for anybody else."

Cate stared at her plate.

"And what if, God forbid, something bad has already happened to her? Won't you feel terrible if you didn't do all you could to get her back safely?"

Cate scraped her leftovers into his dish and stacked them. "The fact she unfriended us on Facebook is a sign she's okay." She gathered up the rest of what was on the table. "I'm pretty sure she's in Ottawa, it's the logical place. We just have to go get her."

The rain tapered off. The room breathed uneasily.

Liam touched her hand. "I want our old life back."

"Me too."

"I mean just us, you and me."

Cate looked away. She knew what he meant. "Like it or not, Isabel and I feel responsible for her disappearance. We have to make sure she's okay. For her sake and for ours."

He mumbled yeah, he got it, but he was still opposed. He mentioned the police again.

"Don't." The furrow in her brow softened. "When we get to the other side of this, we'll probably have to let her go. I mean, we can't hold her hand forever."

Liam relaxed his shoulders. "So you're going to Ottawa, I take it?" He emptied the last of the wine into his glass.

Cate sighed. "Yes, tomorrow. I'm bringing a change of clothes just in case."

"With Isabel?"

"Yes, with Isabel. What, you want to come, too?"

He moved his hand away. "Well, *that* sounds bloody inviting." He drained his glass. "Anyway, you know I have to work."

"Oh, for Christ's sake." She breathed deeply and counted to ten in her mind. "There's dessert, if you want."

He stood, scraping his chair legs back. "Maybe later." He grabbed his glass and a new bottle and went to the living room. "And by the way, do you think that someday you can clear that shit off your piano so we can at least see it?"

Cate didn't follow him to the couch, where he uncorked the bottle and poured himself a glass. She swept up the shards of her glass, scrubbed the pots and loaded the dishwasher. She covered the dessert with plastic wrap and turned everything off, except for the stove light. On her way upstairs to pack she looked in on Liam, sprawled out with his headphones on. His eyes were closed, and he was snoring lightly. She might as well have been invisible.

*

Cate's phone alarm rang. Before turning in, she had shoved it under her pillow to keep from waking Liam. But Liam wasn't in bed.

She dressed quickly and carried her duffle bag downstairs. She had given herself just enough time for a quick coffee and a banana. Liam was still asleep on the couch, where she had left him, headphones horseshoed around his neck. A plate with brownie crumbs was in the sink. Maybe Liam had cooled off before crashing for the night, she thought. Probably not, he hadn't bothered to join her in bed.

She grabbed a pen from their jar of half-working pens and wrote him a note. *Dear Liam, this won't take more than a day or two. Hang in there.* She read it over and crumpled it up. Too cool and detached. Too impersonal. She started another. *Dear Helmet of Will.* (Years ago, she looked up the meaning of his name: Helmet of Will. She used to tease him with it but hadn't in years.) *I'll be home before you know it. I promise to make things right again.*

It was 6:20 a.m., Isabel would be there soon. She finished her coffee and doodled a heart at the bottom.

"Good morning."

Cate looked up. Liam, groggy, was rubbing the sleep from his eyes.

"Well, good morning."

"I can't believe I slept through. What time is it?"

"Still early."

"Okay, good. Um, sorry about…you know." He ruffled a hand through his hair.

"There's coffee if you want. Isabel will be here any minute." She rinsed out her cup and put it in the sink next to Liam's dessert dish. She threw her banana peel in the compost pail. "I was about to leave you this note."

He skimmed it and tossed it into the recycling box. "Okay, then. Let me know when you get there. And keep me in the loop."

Cate made an extra effort to kiss him romantically. He gave into it, nudging his tongue into her mouth. Even in the early morning he had good breath.

Her phone pinged. "Isabel's here, mwah." She kissed her hand and touched his cheek with it. "See you in a couple days, Helmet."

He stood at the door with a blanket around him, waving politely at Isabel.

She tooted the horn with a light touch, leaned across the passenger seat and waved back. "We'll bring you up to speed asap! Promise!"

Liam turned and went inside.

Cate tossed her duffle bag into the back and climbed in. The light seemed different after the big rain. The branches had shed most of their leaves.

"How'd it go last night?"

"Not great, but I think we'll be okay."

Cate pointed to the roadblock at the end of the street, where a couple of construction workers were standing around a massive pothole smoking cigarettes, killing time until 7:00 a.m.

"*Maudite festival de construction*," Isabel clucked. "It's never-fucking-ending."

Cate talked her through an alternate route to the highway. "At least they're finally getting around to fixing it. It's been there since the spring."

Isabel complained it was getting bloody hard to get sick patients to a hospital these days when everywhere it was a *rue barrée* or a maze of orange cones. Montreal had become famous for it, but things were getting bad in Toronto too, from what she'd heard.

The 20 westbound was smooth sailing. It was still early, and they were going against traffic.

Cate slapped her thigh. "Dang!"

"What?" Isabel almost swerved off the road.

"Did you book a room?"

"You scared the shit out of me! Don't do that while I'm driving!"

"Sorry."

"I thought *you* would," Isabel said. "Anyway, it's Ottawa and it's a weekday. It's not like we're going to Vegas."

"True enough." Cate tuned the radio dial to CBC, even though it had begun testing her patience lately with its vapid news stories, its butchering of English grammar. She hated the new reporters who mispronounced words like nuclear and electoral. After the election update, she shut it off. "Do you want your station back?"

Isabel shook her head. She was going twenty kilometres over the speed limit.

Cate felt a tightness in her chest as they approached the exit for Rigaud. "This is where my sister lives."

"I thought she was disabled."

"She has cerebral palsy. The home my parents put her in is somewhere around here."

"You mean you never visit her?"

Cate crossed her arms. "I went once, with my father. But I can't remember exactly where it is."

Isabel slammed on the brakes. Cate's hands shot out and braced against the dashboard. The Hyundai up ahead had stopped suddenly, Isabel barely avoiding a collision. "Oh my god, kill me!"

"Maybe if you slowed down a little."

Isabel shouted a string of obscenities, shaking her fist at the driver.

Cate took a deep breath and stuck her head out the window. "Looks like an accident. No point getting upset."

Isabel was still shaking.

"Doesn't look serious, probably just drivers not paying attention."

"You mean texting and driving."

Cate nodded. She leaned back in her seat. "We'll just have to wait it out."

*

Cate was five when she snuck into Mrs. Perlman's garden and picked her tulips. She wanted to surprise her mother on Mother's Day. The Perlman yard was filled with luscious, mature tulips in every shade of pink and red; they always won prizes at the annual Spring Garden Competition. Mrs. Perlman spent her days fussing over them, watering them, picking out the weeds. Cate's mother, on the other hand, never had time for gardening with two young children, one needing round-the-clock attention. Cate decided that she wanted to put a smile on her face, at least for one day. At dawn, still in pyjamas, she crept into the garden with the kitchen scissors. She didn't think Mrs. Perlman would notice three or four tulips missing, there were so many. She wrapped the stems in a damp paper towel and brought the bouquet to her mother, chest puffed out.

Her mother stopped feeding Margaret. The colour left her face. "You didn't..." Her eyes narrowed. She glanced out the window. "Where did you get these?"

Cate's smile faded.

Her mother glared at Niall sitting in his reading chair by the fireplace. "Well?"

Niall looked up from his book.

"Do something! Say something to her!"

Cate bowed her head.

Niall removed his glasses and scratched the crown of his head. "Cookie, it was kind of you to bring these to your mother. But you can't just pick someone else's flowers like that."

"She has to go and apologize," her mother said. "Right now." She set the flowers down on the coffee table, crushing their heads, and went back to spooning food into Margaret's mouth.

They made her go alone. They made her face the shame alone. They made her ring the bell and wait at the Perlmans' mahogany door for someone to answer. They made her look up, way up, into Mrs. Perlman's eyes, and admit she had done a bad thing.

Mrs. Perlman listened solemnly to her confession. She patted her on the head. Just as she was about to send her home, Mr. Perlman appeared at the door with a disapproving look. Scowling, he bent down and whispered to Cate that she had been naughty and that she'd better be careful, naughty girls usually went to hell. Cate, shaking, ran from them in tears. When she got home, she went directly upstairs and cut the long blond hair off Margaret's favourite doll.

"Calling Cate, calling Cate." Isabel nudged her. "Do you read me? Over."

"Sorry, I was somewhere else."

"Obviously. Want to talk about it?"

"No." They had passed the scene of the accident and were about thirty minutes outside Ottawa. A weak sun was poking through the clouds.

Isabel suggested they grab a decent breakfast before resuming their search.

"Makes sense."

"You know, I've been thinking, what if the woman works, the woman who cut Nuna's umbilical cord, what's her name again? If she's at work, we'll have to wait until suppertime to go over there, and even then, we don't know where she lives. Do *you* remember? I certainly don't."

Cate rolled her eyes. "Do me a favour, let's go one step at a time."

Traffic thickened again as they approached the city.

"I feel like you're in a mood," Isabel said.

"Just thinking about my sister."

"You never talk about her."

"No."

Isabel respected the silence for as long as she could. "I don't know about you, but I'm starving."

"You're always starving." Cate admitted she could probably use another cup of coffee. She scrolled through Google's list of accommodations in Ottawa. Holiday Inn, Days Inn, the Econo Lodge. She sighed. "What would you say to a classier place this time?"

"Sure, if you're paying."

"Deal."

The GPS directed them to the Lord Elgin Hotel. Bellhops in red jackets with gold buttons stood outside the entrance like a line of guardsmen. Cate tipped the first one and requested valet parking for the Jeep.

Wandering through the lobby, Isabel whistled. "Fancy-schmancy." She took a million pictures of the old-fashioned house phones and gas fireplace.

Cate waved her over to the front desk.

The clerk, a prim and proper grey-haired employee with a prim and proper accent, informed them that there was only one room available, with one queen-sized bed.

Isabel regarded him with searing eyes. "Why are you so sure we need two beds?"

He looked away from her.

"We'll take it," Cate said. She handed him her credit card.

"By the way, what are you—a top or bottom?" Isabel asked Cate. "I forgot." She giggled.

Cate elbowed her in the ribs.

"Ouch. What was that for?"

The clerk typed in the booking information. He handed Cate an envelope with two keys and asked if they needed help with their luggage.

Isabel indicated the knapsack on her back. "No thanks, pops."

They rode the elevator up with another couple, staring at the ascending floor numbers. The door dinged open. After it closed behind them, Isabel burst out laughing. She was still laughing when they got to the room.

"Top or bottom," Cate mumbled. "I can't believe you."

"The old fart deserved it! What, we're not the governor general of Canada, so he can treat us like garbage?"

"Never mind, let's just get settled and go for breakfast."

"You're the boss."

The room, in muted tones, was stylish and elegant. It had contemporary wood furnishings, an extra-deep mattress, and a spacious bathroom with a square basin, a glassed-in granite shower, and eco-friendly skin products. Cate rinsed her face with a plush, white face cloth and rubbed the hotel hand cream into her palms. She heard the TV go on, and Isabel, on the other side of the wall, going through the dresser drawers, the mini-bar.

"Jeez, you need a ladder to get onto the bed!"

"We're paying for luxury."

"*You're* paying." Isabel flicked off the TV. "C'mon, let's get going."

Cate freshened her mascara and caught up with Isabel in the hall. They made a pit stop at the front desk for information on the nearest restaurant. It was a different front-desk clerk, a younger woman with a name tag that indicated she was in training. Isabel read her name aloud, Keren with an *e*. She asked if it was a typo. Cate rolled her eyes.

Isabel wasn't the first to ask, the clerk said. "But think about this," she added, avoiding any hint of sarcasm. "Would you wear a name tag with your name misspelled?" She pointed to the Starbucks, at the other end of the hall.

Isabel shook her head apologetically.

"We're actually looking for something that serves up breakfast with a bottomless cup of coffee, that sort of place."

"A greasy spoon," Isabel chimed in.

Keren perked up. "Well, that would be Zak's, then. Four blocks south on Elgin." She produced a glossy, illustrated map of Ottawa and used a hotel pen to mark the route, talking them through her directions. She folded it lengthwise and gave it to Isabel.

Isabel winked at her before handing the map over to Cate, as though she were the keeper of all things valuable. "Well, Keren with an e, I must say, you're a big improvement on the old geezer."

They decided to walk to stretch their legs after the long drive. Zak's was full except for a table by the bathroom. Cate vetoed it. They found a place nearby with a similar vibe. A waitress arrived with two coffees, water, menus, and paper placemats for the table. She waited, tapping her foot.

Cate glanced up. "Can you give us a few minutes?"

Isabel waited until she left. "Boy, what's the big rush?" She shook her head. "It's like, here's your hat, what's your hurry?"

Two women at a neighbouring table were playing tug of war with their bill. Cate was fascinated. Both were from a time when women wore hats and bauble necklaces, and husbands paid them an allowance to get their hair styled once a week. Except they clearly weren't from that time, they were middle-class women who bought their clothes on sale and splurged once a week on a day to themselves.

Cate noticed a trace of lipstick on the rim of her cup. She dipped her napkin in water and rubbed it.

"I've seen worse." Isabel shook the ice cubes in her glass and tipped one into her mouth.

Cate called for the waitress, requested another serviette.

"Who says serviette?" Isabel scoffed. "In this day and age."

"Can we just buckle down and decide on the plan for today?"

Isabel crunched her ice. "Where to begin? We don't have the aunt's address. Do you remember where we dropped them off that day?" Going for the sugar, she knocked over the salt shaker.

Cate set it right. “All I remember is that there were way too many of them in the back seat.”

“I think it was near a park.” Isabel poured a river of sugar into her coffee.

“That rings a bell.” The waitress slapped down a pile of napkins and took their order. “But I can’t think of her name. Can you?”

“The one who cut her umbilical cord?”

“No, the one who cut her toenails. Of course, the one who cut her umbilical cord!”

Isabel shook her head. “Beats me.” She ran through the alphabet, trying to jog her memory.

“Funny, I do that too.”

They went through the letters, a to z, before their order arrived. A shared basket of rye toast, two eggs over easy with bacon and sausage for Isabel, a poached egg and fruit for Cate. Still, they didn’t remember her name.

Cate pulled out her phone. Naturally, she thought. Two missed calls from Liam and a text message. She never even heard it ring.

Isabel dabbed at the runny egg yolk with her toast. “What’s up?”

“Liam called. I’ll call him later.” She put down the phone and forked a slice of cantaloupe into her mouth. “You know something, I was just thinking…”

“Thinking what?”

“I probably still have her contact info. I emailed her some pictures I took of the kids that day.” She wiped her hands and picked up the phone.

Isabel stirred her coffee noisily with her spoon. She watched Cate scroll through her sent mail.

“Bingo! It’s Lizzie. Lizzie Pamiurtuuq.”

“Yeah, baby!” Now they had to find out if Lizzie had a land line, and if not, they’d circle back to the park—did Cate remember where it was? Isabel rambled on. “I noticed a bunch of Inuit hanging out there, Lizzie talked to them when we dropped them off after the tulips. Once we find that park, it won't be long after that, we'll find the house, someone at the park will point it out to us, they'll say, *see that building with all the recycling bins?* Or *see that rusty bicycle locked to the streetlamp? That's where they live, that's the place.*"

For the first time, it felt like they were getting somewhere.

*

When they got back to the hotel, they were both fried. Neither felt like supper.

Cate unzipped her duffle bag. "I'm going to bed." She took out her pyjamas and went to change in the bathroom.

"It's only eight o'clock. Maybe there's something good on TV."

"You watch, I'm spent," Cate called out. "All I want to do is put this day behind me." She shook her head, remembering her mother's line that if you wanted to make God laugh, make plans. She wasn't kidding.

Things had taken a downward turn after breakfast. Cate paid the restaurant bill and popped into the ladies' room. She called Liam.

Isabel was waiting for her outside. "What's wrong?" She went back to gnawing on a toothpick.

Cate gritted her teeth. "God damn him."

"Who?"

Cate huffed. "Who else?" They walked back to the hotel, waited in silence for the valet to bring the Jeep around.

"Alright, cough it up."

"Liam called the cops." Cate hung her head. "He went and reported Nuna missing."

"After we specifically told him not to?"

"He said he was sick and tired of our bumbling strategy, this way we'll make headway faster, they have the resources. I'm pretty sure he planned to do it all along."

The Jeep arrived. Cate pushed a tip into the guy's hand. "I'm so sorry, Isa."

Isabel sighed. "Now, we really have to find her before *they* do."

Cate chastised herself for her lack of foresight, how she should have seen it coming, how she totally misread his acquiescence. Kept repeating how very, very sorry she was.

"You're overreacting," Isabel said.

"Maybe. Maybe not."

Isabel reached across and touched Cate's arm. "Never mind, let's find the park."

Cate Googled green spaces in the general area they remembered. Isabel programmed the GPS and drove to each. By mid-afternoon they zeroed in on Dundonald Park on Somerset Street West.

"This looks familiar." Isabel drove around the block a couple of times to be sure they weren't mistaken.

Cate remembered the Beer Store, the Tim Hortons, the small fenced-in kid's park. She remembered the gnarly trees and the stubby brick houses renovated into offices. While Isabel looked for parking, Cate became engrossed in a Wikipedia entry.

"What's so interesting?" Isabel said.

"Have you ever heard of the Gouzenko Affair?"

"No. What's that got to do with the price of eggs?"

"Just listen. In April 2004, the federal government put up memorial plaques in Dundonald Park commemorating the Soviet defector, Igor Gouzenko."

"Who's Igor Gouzenko?"

"Well, according to this, he was a cipher clerk for the Soviet embassy to Canada in Ottawa. On September 5, 1945, three days after the end of World War II, he defected with 109 documents on Russia's espionage activities in the West."

"What's that got to do with Nuna?"

"Absolutely nothing." Cate looked up from her phone. "But it was from this park that the RCMP monitored his apartment on the night that men from the Soviet embassy came looking for him." She pointed across the street.

"I don't see the connection."

"There's no connection, but don't you find it an interesting coincidence that we're here in this same park, tracking someone down?"

"I think you've been watching too much Netflix. Maybe you should try living in the real world for a change."

They still hadn't confirmed Lizzie's address. There was no land line associated with a Lizzie Pamiurtuuq.

They got out of the car and approached a green wooden bench where three Indigenous women sat watching their kids play on the swings.

Isabel didn't waste time. "Do any of you know a Lizzie Pamiurtuuq?"

One of them thought for a minute. "Maybe yes."

"It's really important," Isabel said. "We've come all the way from Montreal. A friend of ours is missing and we think she might be at Lizzie's place."

"I know Lizzie," said another woman. "She lives down that way. Around Bay and Gloucester." She pointed in the general direction. "Look for an apartment building with a lot of junk on the balconies and an old mattress leaning up against the hedge. She's on the third floor."

"Thanks!" Isabel grabbed Cate by the elbow. "Let's go."

"Fingers crossed," said Cate.

They headed for Lizzie's on foot, searching for a building that matched the woman's description.

Cate picked up speed. "Check out the balconies. Looks like junk to me."

"And there's the mattress," Isabel said, pointing.

Cate took out the napkin with the phone number on it and dialled, heart racing. There was no service at the number. She tried the number again. Same recording. "Fffffuck!" She shredded the napkin until it was too small to tear anymore. She threw up the pieces and stomped her feet.

"Cate, Cate," Isabel said calmly. "We're *here*. We're at her place. Lemme call 411 and see if there's a land line."

They were in luck. Isabel pumped her fist. The number was associated with an M. Pamiurtuuq on Gloucester Street, probably the husband. Cate dialled, holding her breath. It picked up after one ring. "Hello, Lizzie?"

There was a long, crackly pause. "Who is this?"

Cate nodded at Isabel. She frolicked on the spot. "I don't know if you remember. My friend Isabel and I came to Ottawa with Nuna a few months ago for the tulip festival. Does it ring a bell?"

She didn't answer.

Cate waited. *C'mon, c'mon*, she prayed to herself.

"I remember."

"Well, er, we're kind of looking for her, we're wondering if she's with you." She stuck out her tongue at Isabel, killing time. "Lizzie?"

"Yes, I'm here."

"It's really important, we haven't heard from her in quite a while, and we're really worried." After a heavy pause, she added, "We think something might have happened to her."

Lizzie sighed into the phone. "I wish I had news."

Cate remained hopeful.

"Other than social media, I haven't seen or heard from her since, well, since that day at Dow's Lake. She hasn't posted anything on Facebook for at least a month."

Cate's heart sank. After all the buildup, it was hard to take in. She promised to let Lizzie know when they found her and hung up the phone.

"I got the gist," said Isabel. "But what if… what if she's lying? To protect her."

"Now who's overthinking?"

"Like you said before, why would she trust us, we're not blood, we're not even Inuit."

Cate replayed the Lizzie conversation in her mind. "The thing is, she really sounded worried. You can't fake that." She bit her lip. "On the other hand, why not pursue it?"

"We've already paid for the room, anyway."

"Good point."

They went to get the Jeep and parked it closer to the apartment. "I'm going to give Waleed a call while you go get us some food," said Cate.

"For once, you're hungry."

"I should be. We forgot to have lunch. Plus, all this detective work has fuelled my appetite." Isabel took off down the road. Cate watched her disappear around the corner before dialling Waleed's number.

"Good to hear from you! And good timing, I don't have a student to see for another hour. How is the search going?"

She filled him in on the Ottawa lead.

"Sounds promising, Habibti."

"Well, yes and no." Her voice faltered. "Mostly no."

"You don't sound good, tell me."

Cate vented about Liam, her hurt and disappointment in him, thoughts she had never expressed out loud, to anyone.

"Hold on, hold on," Waleed said. "I'm not following." He made her start at the beginning.

"Liam called the police in to help us, after I explicitly asked him not to. He did it on purpose."

"Hard to believe, it's so unlike him."

"Not these days." She explained their mistrust of the police. "If Nuna gets a rotten apple, some scumbag with an attitude, and she happens to be drunk, he could take her god-knows-where and have his way with her. It wouldn't be the first time."

"Cate, Cate! You're going down the rabbit hole. And I, of all people, know a little something about those."

"Or they could show up in a gang and insult her or drag her through a nasty line of questioning, make her feel like everything that's happened to her is her own fault."

"First of all, why would they if they're looking for her and she's considered a missing person? She's not a criminal." He paused. "And secondly, why would Liam do that? After you instructed him not to."

"Because he's a child. Anyway, why are you defending him? You're supposed to be on my side."

"I *am* on your side. But you have to walk in someone else's shoes to understand why they do things." He paused to let it sink in. "Could it be that he's a little jealous of Isabel?"

"You're not serious?"

He didn't answer.

"You're serious?"

"Well, no offence, but you do spend an awful lot of time with her."

"That's just ludicrous." She scratched her hand. "Anyway, enough about me, how about you? How's the situation with your family?"

"My father is coming with Hakim."

"You already told me that. What about your mother?"

"He didn't ask her. I don't think she knows about their visit."

Cate sighed. "It would definitely make things easier."

"I know."

Cate ran through a list of suggestions, that they meet in a public place to keep things light, that the old hurtful stories not be regurgitated, it was time to move forward. "Does he want to make amends? Do *you*?"

"I don't want my mother to suffer over our estrangement anymore." He didn't utter a word about making it right between his father and him. Waleed had always alluded to a terrible fight between them, one he had never shared with anyone, not even Cate. And Cate never asked.

Isabel turned the corner, hands full.

"Waleed, I'm sorry to cut it short, but I have to let you go."

Suddenly he was talkative. Their meeting was happening on such and such a day, he would wear something conventional, grey pleated pants, a golf shirt with the top button undone, nothing outrageous. No earrings. No visible tattoos. He would tell them about his latest poems in the *Paris Review*, he'd inquire how Hakim's medical practice was going. They would reminisce about their childhood, their mother's unparalleled cooking, family feasts with a thousand relatives around the table. He'd refrain from talking about his private life, why did they need the details, anyway?

"Glad it's all sorted out," Cate said, "but I have to hang up now. Let me know how it goes. Big hug. Bye." She reached across to jiggle the handle open on Isabel's door. "What's all this?"

"You said you were hungry." Isabel handed Cate one of the two iced cappuccinos and slid a box of Timbits between them. "And how's the Arab prince?"

"Struggling," Cate said, uncapping her coffee. She didn't want to talk about it.

The radio was on low. Silence settled between them as Isabel polished off the Timbits and Cate zoned in and out of an author interview about a new diet book, *I Am the Big Cheat*. The idea of Lizzie lying to them popped back into her mind. It wasn't entirely implausible. What if Nuna was staying at Lizzie's and they drove back to Montreal without ever having checked it out with their own eyes? It wouldn't be unreasonable to think Lizzie would cover for her. They were family, after all. Families had your back. She glanced at Isabel. "We need to get in there and look around."

Isabel rubbed her hands together. "Great minds think alike."

"But I hate the idea of Lizzie thinking we don't trust her."

Isabel locked eyes with her. "Well, if we're being honest, we don't. So, the question is, how do we make her think that we do?"

"We can just say we need her help and advice. And that as Nuna's sanajik, we respect her supportive role in Nuna's life." The more she thought about it, the more Cate felt good about this strategy. She rang Lizzie back.

"Hello?"

"Oh, uh, hi. Me again. We were wondering if we can speak to you upstairs for a few minutes."

After some hesitation, Lizzie buzzed them in.

They took the stairs by twos to the third floor. The door was already open. One of her kids was wheeling a yellow dump truck in the hallway, making vroom, vroom noises with his mouth. Lizzie waved them inside, pushing away the clutter of toys blocking the door. She spoke firmly to the boy in Inuktitut, without raising her voice. He left his truck and followed them inside, where a strong smell of fish permeated the walls.

Isabel reached down and picked him up. She made a funny face to make him laugh, then raised him high over her head before bringing him back to the floor again. He turned to Cate with his arms in the air, waiting to be picked up. Cate tensed, reached down, and patted him awkwardly on the head. He smiled and glommed onto her leg like a koala bear to a tree.

"He likes you," Lizzie said. She shouted at the rest of her kids to come see who was visiting. They rumbled down the hall like a herd of buffalo. Lizzie disappeared into the kitchen, leaving them with the children.

Cate stood still, not knowing what to do. "He's certainly not shy."

"Move, you walking tree!" Isabel ordered.

Cate stared at her in bewilderment.

"Move, you tree-with-legs," Isabel commanded in a harsh but playful voice.

Cate took an awkward step. It was hard to move with the kid glued to her leg. She limped forward another step, lifting and dragging him along the floor. His face lit up. She made it to the couch with him giggling all the way and plopped down. "This tree is pooped," she announced in a deep tree voice.

"She said 'pooped'!" one of them cried out and the others, including Cate and Isabel, erupted into laughter.

The smallest ones jumped up and down on the couch around Cate, running their hands through her "lellow" hair. It was overwhelming, but she gave into it. Isabel winked and excused herself to use the bathroom.

The oldest girl, Susie, asked if Cate knew any card tricks. Cate shook her head, an eye on Isabel, peeking discreetly into every room off the hallway. Susie announced she'd be right back.

Isabel walked into a closet thinking it was the bathroom. She closed the door and tried the one next to it. Where was Lizzie, Cate wondered.

Susie returned with a deck of cards. She fanned them open and instructed Cate to pick a card, any card. She closed her eyes, ordering Cate not to show anyone. Cate put the card face down on her lap and told Susie she could look now. Susie shuffled the deck, half the cards falling through her fingers. The other kids scrambled after them. Susie gathered the cards into a neat pile and tapped on it, revealing that the one Cate had chosen, the one in her lap, was the queen of hearts.

Cate flipped it over with a look of surprise. "Wow! That's amazing," She raised her palm for a high-five. "You're a great magician."

Susie beamed and slapped Cate's hand.

Lizzie reappeared with a tray of bannock and tea. "Pipe down, you kids!" They zeroed in on the food, each snatching a piece and scattering. Lizzie apologized to Cate about the house being upside down, she hadn't been expecting anyone, it was a ped day and they were all just hanging out.

The toilet flushed and Isabel returned unenthusiastically. She flashed Cate a look that said there wasn't a single sign of Nuna anywhere, no Sidney Crosby jacket hanging from a hook, no Reeboks among the mountain of shoes, no cot made up in the kids' room. Her phone wasn't lying around on a table somewhere. There wasn't a smidgen of evidence that Nuna was staying there. Nada.

"We're big fans of bannock," Cate said. "Nuna made some one time when she served us country food for supper."

"Yeah, it was great," Isabel said, trying to sound excited.

Lizzie smiled with pride. "I taught her how to make it. It's my mother's recipe." She handed around their cups of tea as she haltingly explained the family connection. "Nuna's mother and I come from the same village on the Hudson coast. We're...sisters." She broke off two hunks of bannock, one for each of them.

"And you are her sajik," Cate said.

"Sanajik," Lizzie corrected. "Yes."

Cate sensed Lizzie's hesitation. The way she flinched ever so slightly when she said "sisters."

"May I ask why you, uh, moved to Ottawa?"

Lizzie waved off her question. "Oh, it's a long, boring story." She faked a laugh.

Cate and Isabel casually sipped their tea.

After a long silence, Lizzie answered. "I came down here to go to school—and met a nice man from Nunavut." Lizzie pointed to the children. "Their father. After I graduated, we got married." She glanced at the wall clock.

Cate set down her cup. "We probably should be going. Thank you for everything."

Isabel requested some bannock for the road.

Cate squirmed. "Isabel!"

Isabel shrugged her shoulders.

Lizzie smiled.

When she went to the kitchen to wrap up the leftovers, Isabel whispered to Cate. "Relax, they like it when you show appreciation for their food."

It sounded made up.

At the door, while the children surrounded them chanting "Bye, see you, bye, bye," Cate had an idea. She looked Lizzie squarely in the eye. "What if you call your sister and ask if Nuna went back up north to your village?"

Isabel's mouth fell open.

Lizzie went white. She inhaled with difficulty. "Hold on a sec." She marched the children back to the living room and popped a movie into the DVD player. She picked the remote off the floor and pressed the play button before going back to Cate and Isabel.

"Well, what do you say?" Cate said.

Lizzie lowered her voice to a whisper. "I—I really can't."

"Why not? It's your sister. She might know something."

Lizzie shrugged.

"Please!" Isabel begged. "I'll never forgive myself if something bad happens to her. *We'll* never forgive ourselves."

Lizzie shook her head. "I'm sorry." She closed the door.

They left silently, their footsteps echoing in the stairwell. Downstairs in the lobby, Cate's phone rang. She picked up. "Lizzie," she mouthed to Isabel. They stood motionless.

"Oh, God, are you kidding me?" Cate massaged her temple. "That's not good. When *was* that?"

Isabel nibbled on the bannock, pacing.

"Thanks for letting us know." Cate hung up, distraught.

"What? What happened? What did she say?"

"Lizzie remembered a phone call from Nuna about a month ago. She kind of shrugged it off as typical Nuna, one day up, the next day down. She figured Nuna would work through it, like she always did."

"That's all she said?"

"Pretty much." Cate rested her hand on Isabel's shoulder. "She didn't say it, but I get the feeling she trusts us. That's progress right there."

Outside, the light was starting to fade. Neighbourhood children on skateboards and scooters were gathered around Isabel's Jeep. As she and Cate got closer, Isabel's eyes bugged out. "Holy motherfucking Jesus!"

The kids dispersed.

Isabel shouted after them. Cate jumped when she saw the cracked windshield, a lacy spiderweb the size of a grapefruit. It wouldn't be cheap to fix.

One of the skateboarders rode back to give them a description of the guy who did it, an older kid with red hair and buck teeth. "He had a hammer. When he saw us he ran away." The skateboarder pushed off and went to join his friends.

"You can probably still see out of it. Enough to drive, anyway." Cate knew it was small consolation.

Isabel gawked at the damage, shaking her head. She ran her hand over the gaping hole. "Once again, fuck my life."

They drove straight to the hotel. Isabel asked the valet guy for a tarp to cover her windshield for the night. "Fuck my life," she kept repeating, all the way up the elevator to their floor.

Cate flopped into bed. Isabel drew the drapes, still stewing.

"You're not going to watch TV?" Cate yawned. "I don't mind if you do."

Isabel hung her clothes over the back of a chair. "Nah, it's okay." She fiddled with the switch until all the lights were off and crawled in beside Cate.

"Really, the noise won't bother me. And it'll change your mind."

"Nope, I'm done for the day."

"Me too. I'm so exhausted, I finger-brushed my teeth."

"Well, that's a first!"

"I promise not to breathe on you." Cate closed her eyes.

Shifting around, Isabel's leg grazed Cate's. Cate didn't move away. She could feel Isabel's eyes on her, intense but comforting. She let herself drift toward sleep, imagined a field of lavender swathed in sunlight. She thought of the shapely clouds on a spring evening, long ago, when her whole life was still ahead of her.

*

With the drapes drawn, Cate couldn't tell if it was morning yet, or just later the same day. Although they hadn't located

Nuna, Cate felt strangely serene. She didn't have the knot in her stomach that she'd had for the past few days. She remembered falling, exhausted, into bed. And Isabel's leg touching hers under the covers.

The volume was on low, blue TV light flickering. Isabel was sitting up in bed in her pink camisole, eating Doritos out of a bag. "Snore much?"

Cate rubbed her eyes.

"That must've been some dream."

"Yeah. I'm sure it means something, but God knows what."

Isabel shrugged. She brushed the Dorito crumbs off her chest. "I never remember mine."

Cate closed her eyes, struggling to recall it. She sighed. Waited. Concentrated on the wafting shapes behind her eyelids. The image that finally came to her was of an old, homeless woman with a ruddy complexion, huddled under a pile of blankets. She was wearing an orange knitted hat with a dangling tassel, but no mitts. Her hands were chapped. In the dream, Cate was walking past. She stopped, felt around for some change, and gave her a toonie. The woman smiled with a prominent canine tooth, wrinkles sprouting from the corners of her eyes. She crooked an arthritic finger—come closer, she had something to say. Something important, something that could save Cate's life. Cate's heart skipped a beat. The woman whispered into her ear. "Be careful, your boots are untied."

Isabel passed her the bag of Doritos. "Maybe you should eat something. Here."

Cate pushed it away, still trying to make sense of the dream. She stared blankly into space. "Loose ends."

"What?" Isabel clicked off the remote. "Listen, Cate, don't go overanalyzing everything."

"I'm not overanalyzing." Cate touched the bedsheet to her cheek. "Anyway, the dream has nothing to do with Nuna, it's about me."

Isabel yawned.

"I think I have some loose ends I need to tie up."

"Sounds more like you're looking for drama. I mean, more drama than we already have."

"This might come as a shock, but not everything revolves around you and Nuna. I have a life too, you know."

Isabel raised her eyebrows. "I hadn't noticed."

"Things were going along fine and dandy before all this shit started." Cate felt her heart race.

Isabel crumpled up the bag. "Oh, they were, were they?"

"Yeah, before you showed up and turned everything upside-fucking-down."

"So, now it's *my* fault." Isabel flung off the covers and leapt out of bed. She grabbed her jeans from the back of the chair, keys and loose coins scattering on the floor. "It's *my* fault you don't know what you want out of life, it's *my* fault you have a controlling husband." She pulled on her T-shirt.

Cate watched in disbelief as Isabel ran around the room collecting her things, phone, wallet, sunglasses, Swiss Army knife. Where did she get off criticizing Cate's life? She had a good job, a career, a home.

"Funny, I had this crazy idea that we were in this together. That we both believed in the cause."

Cate shook her head. "Nuna isn't a cause, she's a person."

"Oh my god." Isabel stuffed her brush and nail clippers into her knapsack.

"Isabel, stop."

She marched into the bathroom for the rest of her things.

"Come on."

Isabel glared at Cate.

"I'm just saying I need to work out my own shit, too. It's nothing against you." Cate beckoned her over.

Isabel stood firm.

"It's late. Come back to bed."

"You're not the only one, it's getting to me, too." Isabel rubbed her eyes. "This trip started out so promising and now, I have no idea what to do anymore." She sighed.

Cate put an arm around her. "Let's just get some sleep." Isabel rested her head against Cate's shoulder. "Maybe in the morning, something will come to us."

Isabel slid off her jeans and slipped under the covers.

Cate moved closer.

"Just hold me," Isabel said. Her feet were ice cold. "At least until I fall asleep."

*

The next morning, they stood at the sink together brushing their teeth, Isabel in her bare feet and T-shirt, Cate fully dressed, still pondering her dream. She fetched the remote and went to sit on the end of the bed, looking for a news channel. It was all election news, parties promising the moon to everyone. Especially to Indigenous people. Support had grown for the NDP, they were serious about implementing all the recommendations from the inquiry into the missing and murdered Indigenous women and girls. In two years, all drinking water advisories would be lifted. The Conservatives were vowing to review the Indian Act. The Bloc Québécois was calling itself an ally of the First Peoples. Lies, Cate thought. All lies. She zapped off the TV.

Isabel emerged from the bathroom. She read the guest card on the back of the door. "Checkout's at 11:00 a.m. What's the time?"

"We're good."

Isabel pulled on her jeans. She dropped to the floor to pick up the coins that had fallen there while they were arguing.

Cate's phone rang. "Hello? Lizzie?"

Isabel glanced up.

Lizzie cleared her throat. "I didn't sleep at all last night. You girls really got me worried."

"I'm sorry, but we didn't know who to turn to. And we were under the impression you might have been able to help us."

Lizzie sighed.

"Did you reconsider calling your sister?"

There was a long pause. Lizzie sighed again. She explained that her kids were in school, and her husband was at work. "I'm free today, if you want to come over."

Cate's eyes widened. She celebrated with a fist pump.

Keren, without the typo, was on duty at the front desk. She instantly recognized Isabel and smiled. "How was your stay?"

"Three stars, Ker." Isabel winked. "Room service was decent, but it took forever. I could've had a bath and done my nails in the time it took for them to bring up the stuff. If you know what I mean."

Cate smiled at Keren and reassured her that everything was just fine, thank you. Keren printed the bill, folded it, and returned it to Cate with two cellophane-wrapped mints.

The valet brought the Jeep around.

"Still cracked," Isabel said, as though a part of her had hoped for the magic sprinkle of fairy dust while they slept.

"Appears so."

"You're going to want to have that looked at," the valet said to Isabel. "Do you need the number of a good garage?"

"Nope, we're good."

Cate gave him a ten-dollar bill and climbed in.

Isabel plugged in her phone, scrolling for a playlist that suited the moment. She smiled at Cate. "This one's for you."

"I doubt it."

Isabel screeched away from the hotel, the wind blowing leaves and litter across the road.

Cate groaned. "What *is* this crap?"

"Nicki Minaj, 'Starships.'" Isabel tapped the beat on the steering wheel. "I can't believe you don't know this."

"Just focus, would you." Cate noticed a proliferation of election signs—red, blue, orange, green. Many more than the day before. They were everywhere. "Do you remember the way?"

Isabel offered a two-finger salute. "Do you forget what I do for a living?"

"Right." Cate leaned back in her seat, leaving Isabel to navigate, the way she navigated her ambulance, with acumen, with prudence, belting her lungs out.

Isabel cleared her throat. "So, here's a question for you. Nothing to do with anything. Let's say we're Thelma and Louise. Who, would you say, is who?"

"That's an oldie, I'm surprised you know it."

"Who doesn't know *Thelma and Louise*?"

"What?"

"I said, 'Who doesn't know *Thelma and Louise*?'"

"Sorry, I can't hear anything with that music blasting in my ears!"

"All right, all right." Isabel lowered it, waited a half second, then shut it off altogether. "Actually, come to think of it, you're definitely Thelma, five minutes into the movie."

Cate rolled her eyes. She reached over and put the song back on. She cranked it up louder than before. "Think again."

*

A pot of Red Rose tea was on the table when they arrived. Lizzie fetched three clean mugs from the dishwasher and brought out the bannock, bandaged in tin foil. "You ladies aren't the only ones who are concerned. I hardly slept a wink."

"More than concerned, we're downright scared," Cate said. "The longer she's out there without a word, the worse it is."

Lizzie nodded. She broke off a hunk of bannock, avoiding their eyes, and dunked it in her tea, slow to get the words out. "I'm embarrassed to say, I left my village in shame. To avoid gossip."

Cate was certain it had to do with sex. It usually did. She resisted the temptation to jump in with reassurances that it was okay, she could trust them.

The kitchen was small, counters cluttered with the provisions required to feed a large family. An open bag of flour had left a fine film over everything, toaster, coffee maker, catch-all utensil holder filled with ladles and spatulas. The fridge was a bulletin board of coupons and knick-knacks, magnetic letters of the alphabet, children's art projects. But not a single photo of the place she came from, only school pictures of the kids that came in strips that you cut up and sent in Christmas cards. She thought of how spotless Liam kept their kitchen and how bare the face of their fridge, a perfect mirror, nothing on it, not even a thumbprint.

"You know that Nuna's mother, Lucy, is my older sister, right?" Lizzie stuffed the morsel into her mouth.

Cate and Isabel nodded.

"We haven't spoken in years."

"We just thought if you called, checked in with her, we could at least have some peace of mind."

Lizzie's face drained of colour. She twirled her wedding ring nervously. "I don't know why…"

"Don't know why what?" Isabel said.

"I don't know why I'm telling you this, except that I want to do what's right. Nuna might be in danger, like you said."

Cate reached over and put her hand on Lizzie's. "You're doing the right thing."

The women looked across the table at each other, away from each other. They stared into their tea, touched their cups, drank.

"I remember the last time I spoke to her." Lizzie tilted her head. "She was in a pretty bad place."

"That time she phoned, a month ago?"

Lizzie nodded.

"What do you mean by a 'bad place'?" Cate asked.

"Nuna was pretty upset. I could have sworn I heard her boyfriend's voice in the background, but she denied it. She said she was alone."

"Amaruq?"

Lizzie scowled. She shook her head. "I never liked that boy. Always up to no good."

"One thing we can tell you that may give you hope is that she unfriended us on Facebook," Isabel said. "If there was foul play, she couldn't have told her assailant, 'Hold on a sec, I need to unfriend these people.'"

"That's good to know."

"And she took most of her clothes with her, things she had before she came to live with us." Cate shifted in her chair. "Can you just tell us why you can't call your sister?"

"It's not that I can't, it's that she won't pick up. Let's just say we parted on bad terms."

Cate's phone vibrated. She ignored it, refusing to break eye contact with Lizzie.

Lizzie sighed. "I haven't talked about it in years." She lifted her cup. "My sister refuses to forgive me."

Cate nodded empathetically.

"It never should've happened, but we let it. We were both drunk, we weren't thinking straight."

Sex. Cate was right. She retained a poker face, giving Isabel the eye to do likewise. They had to let Lizzie work through it herself. They didn't want to force her to make the call.

"Did I say we were drunk?"

"You did." Cate smiled with compassion.

Lizzie stared into her cup. "Nuna's father was my boyfriend before he married my sister. About a year after I broke up with him, he took up with Lucy. Nobody minded by then, we were all friends. They even asked me to be Nuna's sanajik."

Isabel stood up. She spun her chair around and sat as though she were riding a horse, with her legs on either side and her hands gripping the backrest.

Lizzie hurried through the rest of her story. "A few years later, after the Christmas party at the community centre, a bunch of us ended up at their place. We were all pretty drunk. At one point, Joanasi went out for a smoke. I put on my coat and joined him. We started flirting. There were so many people partying inside I didn't think anyone would notice if we left for a half hour."

"I get the picture," Cate said. "Lucy found out."

"Yes. I knew right away I had to get out of there. So, I came down here to go to school and get a job. I told myself I'd never go back." Her eyes were distant. "And him...I don't know if I could ever face him again." Her expression hardened. "I'm guessing they stayed together because of Nuna and the others." She fiddled with the tag on the end of the tea bag. "And as for me, I've moved on. I have a wonderful husband and bright, beautiful kids."

Cate nodded. "Your kids are definitely sweet." She ran her finger around the rim of the cup. "What would happen now if you casually messaged her about Nuna's whereabouts?"

Isabel chimed in on cue. "Maybe say you haven't heard from her in a while."

"You could say it isn't like her and you're worried," Cate added.

Lizzie got up to look for her iPad. She searched the whole kitchen until she finally found it near the toaster under a pie tin.

Isabel glanced expectantly at Cate.

Lizzie carried it to the table. She typed a message and hit the send button. They waited in silence. Voices and garbled TV sounds were coming through the walls of the next-door apartment.

Lizzie pulled the collar away from her neck. She spotted a bit of food stuck to the table and scraped it off with her fingernail. Her eyes flickered. "Okay. She saw my message." She fanned herself with her hand.

Everyone stared at the iPad. Isabel tapped her fingers on the table.

"She isn't answering." Lizzie frowned. "Oh, wait, no, I see the moving dots. It looks like she's typing something!"

Isabel raised her eyebrows. "What's she saying?"

"Damn, she stopped." Lizzie hesitated. She reached for her phone. "It's taking too long, I'm just gonna call." She let it ring for a while and hung up. Then she tried again.

Isabel crossed her fingers on both hands. She flashed them at Lizzie. Lizzie nodded, waiting for Lucy to pick up.

Cate hummed softly.

A voice came on. Lizzie's eyes lit up. She spoke calmly, evenly, almost businesslike. Her voice trembled ever so slightly when she named Nuna.

Isabel stood, sat, then stood again. She paced to the sink and back.

Cate wondered what the women were saying to each other, what the nuances were. Whatever else, it would be strained. And intense. The short conversation ended abruptly. Lizzie pitched the phone. It clattered on the floor. She rubbed her hands on her pant legs. "Nuna's not there."

Isabel sat down. "That's it?"

"What else did you expect?" Cate said. "At least she talked to her. It's a step in the right direction."

Lizzie drifted into silence.

Isabel sulked. Then she exploded. "I don't buy that she isn't there! This is the first time Lucy answers Lizzie's call in, what, forever, and now she's cooperating just like that? If I were her, I wouldn't give Lizzie the time of day, let alone the satisfaction of telling her that Nuna's safe and sound. I'd lie like crazy. I'd want her to suffer."

"Isabel!" Cate snapped.

Lizzie's head was downcast, her hands in her lap.

"I'm sorry," Isabel said softly. "We all do things, especially when we're young."

Lizzie nodded without looking up.

Cate reached her hand across the table. "Lizzie, is there even a slim possibility that Isabel might be right? You know Lucy better than anyone. Could she be lying out of revenge?"

Lizzie brushed away a tear. "She could be, I don't know. She never got over the fact that Nuna and I stayed close after all that... Joanasi business."

Cate sighed. "I guess we'll never know for sure, then. Unless of course..."

"...one of us actually hops on a plane and finds out." Isabel emptied her cup in the sink.

Lizzie agreed. "You're probably right. But no way in hell I'm going back."

Isabel filled her cup with tap water. "Yeah, it's a bloody fortune to fly there, I don't blame you." She drank the water in one go.

Cate stood up. "I'm sorry we put you through this. And I'm sorry it led to a dead end."

They hugged her by turn, Isabel first, then Cate, reminding her to call if she heard anything, even if it didn't seem like anything. You never knew.

Lizzie bid them a stolid, lacklustre goodbye.

"Don't forget," Cate said. "You have our number."

*

Isabel got them back on the highway for Montreal, clutching the steering wheel like she wanted a fight. Everything was a huff and a puff. This pothole, that lousy driver. "I could murder a beer right about now."

"Take it easy, you'll give yourself an aneurysm."

"We gave up too quickly, don't you think?" Isabel shot Cate a glance.

"What are we supposed to do, fly up to Saqijuvik? We don't even know for sure that she's there."

"I get it now." Isabel swerved to avoid a dead animal. "Is it that you think *your* hunches are better than mine? Because maybe I have better ones, more in tune with what's right in front of me."

Cate scoffed. "You said it yourself, it costs the moon to go there."

"That's for sure," Isabel said. "Do me a favour, check Nuna's Facebook again. Maybe she's posted something public that could give us a clue."

Cate searched through Nuna's feed. "Nothing new since the last time we looked."

"This is fucking insane!"

Cate decided not to rein her in. Or encourage her. Instead, she changed the subject entirely. "Funny, I didn't think Lizzie was the type."

"What type?"

"The type to go after her sister's husband. She seems more, uh, principled than that."

"What does principle have to do with sex? They were drunk. He was her old boyfriend, they fucked because they felt like it!"

"Why are you getting so upset?"

"I'm not upset, I'm just saying, you can never be too sure about anybody. One minute you think they're a certain way, good, honest, you think you can really trust them, and the next, they're lying through their teeth."

Cate's phone vibrated. It was Waleed: *Can you talk?*

Not really, she texted back. He ignored her message.

Turns out only Hakim is coming.

Cate typed. *Coming home soon, hang in there.* She slid the phone back into her purse.

Isabel relaxed her grip on the wheel, scanning the road. "You know, I was just thinking, Nuna's probably with that friend of hers, Vanita. Like we said earlier."

"Then why would she have unfriended us? B doesn't follow logically from A."

"That, Chica, is the million-dollar question."

"I can't believe we don't even know Vanita's last name." Cate shook her head. "How could we never have asked for it?" She thought about a time she overheard the girls talking on the phone. She had almost forgotten about it. It was after dinner. Cate was carrying the laundry upstairs when she heard Nuna's voice through her bedroom door. The door was closed but she could make out the words. Nuna didn't sound like her usual monotone self. She sounded different, full of hope. Her voice was rich, and it carried. She was saying something like *I know more than I think I know.* Cate stood outside the door listening for what seemed like a long time. It might have only been a minute, though. But in that minute...she struggled to remember. Nuna was telling Vanita that this was what it was like to be Inuk and to stand up for yourself. She was telling Vanita a story. "I was so bored," she was saying. "Cate was bored too. I could tell by her face. The way she looked at me with her I'm-going-to-fix-you-up eyes... What did you say? No, she gave me a book instead... I didn't like it. The author was boring and repetitive. I told her. I said Cate, the author is boring and repetitive. I underlined all the bad parts. She said, Let's talk about it. I said, What more is there to say, I know it's bad."

Isabel snapped her fingers at Cate. "Where are you, Chica?"

Cate blinked. "Actually, I've been thinking about what you said. What if it's true, what if Lucy's lying? Maybe Nuna just went home and told her mother *if anyone asks, I'm not here.*" She rubbed a hand through her hair. "God, we seem to be going in circles."

Isabel fell in with the flow of traffic. "But why would Nuna do that, why would she go back to a village where people live ten to a house? Where there's mould growing in the walls? Where there aren't enough beds for everyone? Where everyone and their dog knows your private business? It doesn't compute."

Cate knew the argument. She remembered a tiff she and Nuna had had. It was about perspective. Cate argued that the North would be better off once the elders had embraced both traditional and western education, once they learned how to take the best from both worlds and discarded the rest. Nuna disagreed. She said it was someone's agenda to push that, maybe even the government's.

The sky clouded over.

Isabel threw her sunglasses in the cupholder. "Agenda?"

"There's always an agenda. You can't say we didn't have one."

"What agenda?"

"The agenda where we put Nuna under *our* microscope and tell her what she's doing right, what she's doing wrong, what's good for her."

"It's for her own good to be educated!" Isabel waved her hand. "Where would I be now if my mother went back to Mexico after my father left us? Cleaning hotel rooms, like her." She swerved at the last minute to take the exit.

The car behind blared its horn.

"Are you nuts? What the hell are you doing?"

"I can't drive right now, I'm too pissed." She drove into the parking lot of a Tim Hortons and switched off the motor. Neither of them moved or said anything.

Cate watched the customers coming and going, coffee in hand, children tagging along, their faces smeared with frosting. Cate's phone vibrated through her purse, but she ignored it. "Do you want me to drive?"

Isabel mumbled something in Spanish.

"In case you've forgotten, we're on the same side."

"Then why do I feel like you're always looking for a fight?"

Cate shook her head that she wasn't, she definitely wasn't, she was just trying to look at things from every angle.

"I think you'd love it if she were back up north running the school or the mayor's office." Isabel slapped the side of the steering wheel. "Well, I wouldn't. I want her here, in the big city, where she can get a job and support herself and, yes, maybe find love. Real love. Not with an asshole who gets drunk and beats the crap out of her."

Cate pushed her face into Isabel's. "See what I mean? That's *your* agenda." The garish sun returned.

Neither spoke for a while. A bickering couple stepped out of the restaurant, the man, hands in his pockets, striding past his wife.

"You know, I've been thinking about her weird interest in Atlantis. The whole idea of a submerged landmass."

Isabel looked at her. "And?"

"I don't exactly know. But I do find it interesting that Nuna means 'land' in Inuktitut. Maybe we've just been getting in her way."

"I don't know what you mean."

"I could use a coffee. You?"

Isabel nodded. She disappeared into to the restroom while Cate stood in line, checking Liam's latest text message. *Cops have a lead. Call me asap.*

She called but it went straight to voicemail. Given the time, he was probably teaching. *Sorry I missed you*, she texted. *Waiting for your call back.* She felt a jab and spun around, dropping her phone.

Isabel. Less gloomy, more like herself again. "What's up?"

Cate bent down to pick up her phone. "Text from Liam. Cops may have something."

"I don't know if that's good or bad," Isabel said. "Given it's the cops."

"I know, but at least it's something."

Outside, a stocky man with a sunburn on his neck and a case of beer under his arm was inspecting the damage on their windshield. The crack glinted like a diamond bracelet under the bright sky. "That's some hole you got there." His T-shirt bulged over his gut. All black except for the slogan: *Drink up, pussies.* The shirt had a white stain under "Drink."

Isabel scowled at Cate. "Ew, cringe." They climbed into the Jeep.

"Never mind. I once saw one that said 'Tell Your Boobs to Quit Staring at My Eyes.' I'm always surprised at how low men can go."

Isabel handed Cate her coffee so she could belt herself in. Cate rolled down her window and shouted to the guy. "You should see the other car!"

He lifted his hunting cap, wiping the sweat off his forehead with the back of his hand. "You gals take care now, it's an ugly world out there."

Isabel started the motor.

"Are you good to drive, or should I?"

"I'm fine." She lowered the visor and shifted into reverse. "Anyways, you know I'm right."

"Right about what?" Cate set Isabel's coffee in the cupholder. "What were we arguing about again?"

Isabel shifted. The car lurched forward.

Scalding drops of Isabel's coffee splashed Cate's wrist. "Slow down, woman!"

"Well, we gotta get the show on the road if we're going to stop to visit Margaret." Isabel retraced their route back to the highway.

"What? Who said anything about that?"

"Neither of us. But I put two and two together after you told me about that weird dream of yours, about your laces being untied."

"Now you're a shrink?"

"We should be getting close. Rigaud, right?"

"Yes. But this isn't the right time."

"You said you had some loose ends to tie up. If not now, when? Plus, we're inches away."

"What about Nuna?"

"A half hour isn't going to change anything."

Before Cate could object any further, Isabel took the exit. She made Cate Google the quickest route there. ETA: five minutes.

Cate couldn't remember the last time she saw her sister. Whether it was months or years. Probably years. A couple at least. It had been easier to send flowers than sit around in a stuffy room trying to connect with someone so cut off from the world.

Isabel rolled up to the residence, a red-shuttered, Cape Cod style house with Adirondack chairs on the porch, a corn-husk wreath on the door, and an unnaturally green lawn. She drove into the parking lot. "Smaller than I thought."

"My mother made my father promise. Nothing institutional."

Isabel offered to go with her for support, but Cate said no, if this was something she was going to do, she needed to do it alone.

"Sure, I get it."

Cate hesitated before going inside. She didn't know what she was doing there. Or what possessed her to listen to Isabel, who knew next to nothing about her life. Who knew only superficially what it was like for Cate to carry the weight of her past, to be two daughters in one. She floated past the receptionist, a prissy fiftyish woman behind a Plexiglas divider, her nose in a book.

"Excuse me," the receptionist called after her. "Are you here to see a resident?"

"Yes, I've come to see Margaret, Margaret Morrissey. I'm her sister."

The woman slid the register through the slot, a clipboard with a pen hanging from a string. "Funny, I've never seen you before." It sounded accusatory.

Cate signed and slid it back. "You must be new, then."

The woman set her book down, spoke through tight lips. "Please indicate the date and time." She pushed the register back.

"Listen, can't you just do it for me? I'm in a bit of a rush."

"I'm sorry, you're who again?"

"Cate. I'm her sister."

"Well, I don't see your name on her list of visitors. I see a Niall Morrissey, I see a Gloria Morrissey, but I don't see a Cate Morrissey."

Cate gnashed her teeth. "Yes, that's my father and his wife. And I'm her sister, now would you please open this door!"

The woman shook her head disapprovingly. "I'll add you to the list, then." A shrill buzzer unlocked the door.

Cate stepped into a large, cheerful sitting room with potted azaleas and walls painted the colours of nature. A resident in a wheelchair was laughing at a television cartoon. An attendant in a pink track suit, leafing through a magazine, asked if she could help Cate. Her sunny mood was a relief after the receptionist. The girl put down what she was doing and escorted Cate to Margaret's room. Back in the day, her parents had paid a little more for something bright, overlooking the rose garden. The people had never moved her.

The door was ajar. Cate knocked uncertainly. She nudged it open and peered in, eyes coming to rest on a familiar family photo taken at Sears when Cate was six. It was in the same brass frame it had always been in, her mother looking tired, her father with a smile that suddenly struck Cate as phoney. It was one of the rare photos where Margaret didn't look handicapped. It pleased her to see the vase of cut flowers on the dresser, the usual assortment of carnations, greenery, and baby's breath that Cate sent weekly to brighten up the room—and assuage her guilt.

Margaret was belted in her wheelchair, neatly dressed in a loose hoodie and pleated slacks. She was by the window, staring outside at the sparrows perched on a bird feeder. Cate recognized the deep curvature of her spine.

Another attendant in the same pink track suit was making up the bed, her blond hair in a tidy bun. A tag with her picture on it was clipped to her belt loop. She looked up, sensing a presence in the room. "Visitor for Maggie?"

"Margaret." Cate stepped inside. "Yes, I'm her sister."

The attendant's face brightened. "Your timing's perfect. She has a whole hour before physical therapy." She finished fluffing the pillow and crossed the room to turn the wheelchair so that it was facing Cate. She leaned down with her hands on her knees and a pleasant smile. "Look who's here, Maggie. You have a visitor!"

Margaret flailed with excitement at seeing Cate, manoeuvring in the way she did, limited by her muscle tightness and spasticity.

It was like no time had passed in her world. She reacted to Cate as though she had seen her just the day before, and the day before that. She beamed, squealed, her eyes glittered like pools of water in the noonday sun. Cate bent down and kissed her on both cheeks. They were softer than she remembered.

Margaret's condition had been explained to her when Cate was old enough to understand. Her parents said that something had happened during her birth to cause serious brain damage. They didn't sugar-coat it. She'll never be like you, they said. She won't talk, she won't walk, she'll just sit in her chair and have everything done for her. For the rest of her life. The professional diagnosis was that she wouldn't live past forty.

And yet, against all odds, here she was.

Cate wheeled Margaret closer to the bed so that, sitting, they would be at eye level. She didn't recall what a beautiful hazel Margaret's eyes were. The attendant excused herself, telling Cate to buzz if they needed anything, she'd be back in an hour or so to take her to physio. With a hand on Margaret's shoulder she said, "You ladies have fun catching up."

Cate smiled. She recalled an early morning years ago when she had stood precariously on a rocking chair trying to do the right thing. Maybe four, Cate worried about Margaret's strange gurgling sounds. Keeping her balance, she lifted Margaret out of the crib, and carried her down the long hall to her mother. She felt useful. Protective of her sister. But instead of thanking Cate, her mother, frightened and angry, mouth set in a hard line, snatched the child from her. Niall hung his head and went to put on his robe. He took Cate's hand and led her downstairs for blueberry waffles and ice cream. Cate never forgot the expression on her mother's face. Her cold eyes, her lips of ice. She blinked the memory away.

Margaret had always made what Cate felt were hideous, unrestrained noises—wild, unintelligible, erratic. She "spoke" in a braying baritone. Despite what the doctors had said, that

Margaret was locked in a sort of developmental prison, her mother always behaved as though she understood everything. She believed that if someone inflected in a particular way or made a certain type of eye contact, Margaret would somehow grasp the essence of what they were saying. This put her mother on permanent high alert, scolding or shushing anyone who said anything hurtful in Margaret's presence.

Cate didn't know who to believe. Did Margaret understand? Did she not understand? As Cate got older, she leaned toward the latter, toward the cold hard facts of science and medicine. There was no way on earth that someone with such a truncated mind could apprehend the complex world.

Cate looked Margaret in the eye, still wondering why she had come. "I see you got the flowers. They're lovely, aren't they?"

Margaret's muscles spasmed.

"Listen, Margaret, I don't know why I'm talking to you, you probably won't understand anything of what I'm saying." She looked deeply into her sister's eyes. "However..." Cate's phone rang through her purse, startling her. It was probably Liam, returning her call. The ringing persisted.

Margaret cocked her head forward and back and side to side. Her movements were jerky and uncontrolled.

"Just a sec, Margaret." Cate signed that she needed to answer the call, this one was important. By the time she got to it, the ringing had stopped.

Margaret stopped flapping her arms. She looked almost pensive.

Cate put down the phone. After a long silence she said, "I don't think you know how much I hated you growing up. How many nights I stayed awake wishing you would just die." She nervously fiddled with her purse strap, recalling the bitterness and guilt she had endured as a child. And had repressed. "I blamed you for ruining our family, you and your fucking handicap." She remembered the night of her high school graduation, when her parents stayed home with Margaret, who was in a terrible state, hitting herself, shrieking wildly. Niall stood by his wife. He winked at Cate, he knew she would be a trooper about this, she was smart, resilient, she could handle it. Because when the going got tough, as Niall often reminded her, the Morrisseys got going.

Margaret was uncharacteristically still. A leaf from the weekly bouquet fell to the floor like a scrap of paper.

"That night, you know, I was getting the gold medal for English. They knew and they didn't come."

Margaret's eyes were locked on Cate.

Cate shifted uncomfortably. Her temples throbbed. "And now, after all this time, I've finally come to the realization that *you* didn't ruin our family, our father did." The blood rushed to her cheeks. "Turns out he was a weak man. He had none of the loyalty I thought he had." She apologized for being a bad sister, for shearing Margaret's doll, for hiding her toys, for blaming her for their mother's cancer and untimely death. She didn't harp on her resentment over Niall's part in it, those were her own issues to deal with.

Cate's phone vibrated. "Listen, Margaret, I want you to know I'm exhausted. I'm done with this. I don't know how to fix it, but I won't hold you responsible anymore. I'll just have to work through it somehow and learn to be a better sister, a better human being."

Margaret's body jerked forward. Her face lit up. She squealed. For a moment, there was no infirmity, there was only an unencumbered purity of heart.

Cate checked her phone, ignoring the notifications. She smiled. "I want you to hear a song before I go." She found "The Whole of the Moon" in her library and hit play. "I think you'll love it." She took Margaret's hand and belted out the lyrics as Margaret thrashed about in her chair, inhabiting her immense pleasure, the two moving as one.

Margaret laughed and brayed and shrieked until she was out of breath.

The song ended. An ear-piercing whistle came from the blond-haired attendant standing in the doorway. "That was awesome, ladies!"

"I hope we weren't too loud," Cate said.

"Not in the least." She padded toward them in her cushioned shoes, checking her watch. "I hate to break up the party, but she's due in physio."

"Of course." Cate put her arms around Margaret's bony shoulders and gently squeezed. "I'm glad I came." She smiled at the attendant. "By the way, what's your name?"

"Maggie—which may be why the two of us get on so well." She put a hand on Margaret's shoulder. "Not the same sign as your sister, mind you. I'm a Taurus, stubborn as all get-out."

"I highly doubt that. But thank you, Maggie, for your dedication and hard work."

Maggie spun Margaret's wheelchair around so they could follow Cate back to the lobby. Cate promised Margaret that she'd be back. Sooner rather than later. Margaret stiffened in her chair and squealed. Maggie pressed the exit buzzer.

Cate turned and waved before the door locked behind her.

The snarky receptionist looked up from her book. "Um, excuse me, you have to sign out."

Cate sneered at her before slamming the door.

Outside, Isabel was leaning against the Jeep, talking on her cell. As soon as she saw Cate, she wrapped things up and blew a kiss into the phone. "*Si, jefa, mañana.*"

"Is your mother, okay?"

"Yeah, yeah, I was just checking in, catching up on her news. She wanted to know who she should vote for."

"What did you tell her?"

"The Rhinoceros Party. But she's gonna vote Liberal, she always votes Liberal. They could run a dog in her riding and he'd still win. Jeez, you were in there forever."

Cate hugged her, squeezing tight. Isabel stood there, flabbergasted, until Cate let go.

"Did Liam call you? He rang while I was inside, but I was in the middle of something."

"Nope, nothing. Maybe call him?"

"I was just about to." She checked the time. "I think he might be teaching, though."

He picked up on the first ring. "Connelly secretary, how may I help you?" The voice was Mo's. "Cate?"

Cate felt a niggle of annoyance.

"Sorry, Liam told me to answer, he's busy setting up. We're doing a presentation on the debate club."

"Well, can you get him on the phone? It's important." Cate knew from their muffled voices that Mo's hand was covering the receiver.

She came back on. "He told me to tell you to give him a minute."

Cate sighed. The sound got muffled again. Her voice, his voice. Their voices speaking over each other. Laughter.

Liam answered out of breath. "I don't have time. I'm teaching in five."

"Well, this won't take long."

"I left a message telling you it was urgent."

"Yeah, I know. Sorry."

"What have you two been doing, anyway? I thought you were desperate to find her."

"Things aren't going as smoothly as we thought they would."

"Big surprise."

Isabel gestured for Cate to make it snappy.

Cate nodded, she was doing her best. "So, did the cops find anything?" Liam's voice was drowned out by the five-minute warning bell and an echoey intercom message about volleyball tryouts after school. "Whaaat? I can hardly hear you."

He balked at having to repeat himself, barking into the phone. "I said their lead was a bust."

"How so?"

"The police tracked Amaruq down and warned him to come clean. What? Hold on a sec." Liam whispered inaudibly to Mo. Mo's laughter filled the receiver.

Cate rolled her eyes at Isabel.

Liam came back on. "Anyway, Amaruq claimed that the last time he saw Nuna was sometime in May. They met at some bar for a few drinks and went back to the apartment and had sex. According to Amaruq, Nuna woke up and went through his cell while he was still sleeping. She found a bunch of texts he sent to another girl, some friend of hers, who, as it turned out, he was also sleeping with."

Cate lifted the phone away from her ears like the news was too much.

"Nuna lost it and punched him out. Okay, okay, I'm coming!"

"You're putting me on, right?"

"That's what I was told. Anyway, I really have to go." Liam hung up.

"What? What happened?" Isabel crossed her arms. She tapped her foot. "Are you gonna tell me or what?"

"I'll tell you in the car." Cate massaged her temples. Back on the highway, she repeated the story.

Isabel listened, for once, without interrupting. "I don't blame her, I would've done the same. Maybe worse."

"Never mind that, what I want to know is what got into her? Why on earth would she have slept with him? After everything."

"What everything?"

"After all the talks we had, after her telling me she wanted to start her life again from scratch."

Isabel agreed. "I hate that prick and I've never even met him." She sounded like an overprotective father.

"Anyway, that lead is dead now. Cross it off the list."

"What list? I think we're at the end of the line." Isabel pounded the dashboard. She plugged in her phone.

"Uh, can we listen to my music for a change?"

Isabel shrugged. "Whatever." She handed Cate the cable wire.

Cate found her mellow playlist, Folk Rock Café, a gentle mix of Bob Dylan, Joni Mitchell, Leonard Cohen. "You'll like this, I promise. And if you don't, tough."

Isabel fake-snored through "Dance Me to the End of Love."

They passed an army of orange pylons, indicating detours and roadwork ahead, but no one was on the job.

"Quelle surprise," Isabel muttered.

Cate felt a weight on her chest, a crushing need to figure out their next move. Her lids drooped. Before dozing off, something occurred to her.

*

Cate jerked awake, suddenly, seconds before the exit to her place.

Isabel signalled and cut across the lane.

"No! Keep going!" Cate commanded.

Isabel swerved back into the centre lane. "Shit, woman!"

"Sorry."

"What are we doing?"

Cate dithered. "Uh, I dunno, maybe we, maybe I…"

"Just spit it out, Cate."

"To be honest, I'd rather not face Liam right now. Plus, I feel a headache coming on." She searched for her pills, but the bottle was empty. She reached for the Evian that had been rolling around in the back seat since they left Ottawa. It was warm but she drank it anyway.

Isabel sat upright. "No problem." She gave Cate her jacket to use as a pillow.

Cate reclined. She rested her head against the door and closed her eyes. It was like being at sea in the middle of a storm. "Whoa, girl! Easy on the gas pedal," she groaned. Next thing she knew, Isabel was nudging her awake. She squinted into the light. "Where are we?"

"My place."

"How long was I asleep?"

"Not long, twenty minutes or so. How's your head?"

"I think I warded it off."

"Still, you look a little pale." Isabel carried their bags in and got Cate a glass of water. She dampened a face cloth and pressed it to Cate's neck. "Now that's better, isn't it?"

They sat. Cate gulped down the water, searching for something to set the glass on.

"Don't bother. It's not like your place. Every surface is a coaster here."

Cate kicked her shoes off and curled up on the couch.

Isabel covered her with a blanket.

"I've been thinking a lot about her journal entry, the one about Atlantis. Do you remember what she wrote?"

"I remember a lot of exclamation marks."

"She mainly copied out a bunch of facts. But at the very end, most importantly, she wrote in red pen. *Come back to this.*"

Isabel stared blankly at her.

"Atlantis disappears," said Cate.

"So?"

"One thing I learned about Nuna is that she enjoys making connections. But sometimes she gets things wrong, latches onto an idea that isn't on point."

"I'm not following."

"Let's call Lizzie back."

"Say what?"

"Never mind, just leave it to me." Cate called Lizzie's land line and got the husband. She introduced herself and after a brief exchange, said she'd call back later. She smiled at Isabel. "Lizzie's running an errand."

Isabel shrugged. "Okay, so?"

"So, I've been thinking." Cate went to the sink to fill up her glass. She removed the face cloth from around her neck and hung it next to a dish towel. "As Nuna's sanajik, Lizzie must have some sort of insight into Nuna as a person."

"So, why wouldn't she have shared it with us while we were there?"

"Because we never asked her."

Isabel scoffed.

"Nuna told us that parents up north typically choose a sanajik who will help the child reach their full potential." Cate spoke with the same enthusiasm she felt when she tracked down an obscure poem in a literary archive. "It's the Inuit version of a godparent."

"I have no idea where you're going with this. Anyways, how about we talk over dinner? Feel like eating?"

Cate nodded. Whenever she nipped a headache in the bud or experienced a full day without the insufferable throb, she was always ready to conquer the world. "Why don't you start cooking something. I'll pick up some wine and dessert."

Isabel threw Cate the keys and directed her to the nearest SAQ and bakery. She babbled with the same excitement she had when they first met.

*

A strobing red light engulfed the rear-view mirror. Cate pulled over. The police car pulled up behind her. Cate's stomach churned. She stared straight ahead.

The officer signalled for her to roll down her window. He asked if it was her vehicle.

"It's a friend's," Cate said, in her accented but proficient French.

"Is better in English?"

She batted her lashes. "Oui...mais je parle français aussi."

He asked for her driver's license.

Hands trembling, Cate opened her wallet. She slid her license from its plastic protector and handed it to him.

"Registration?"

She peeled the Velcro off the glove compartment, gas receipts, concert stubs, and parking tickets, including the latest from Girouard Park, spilling out onto the floor. She casually tossed her purse over the mess and began searching. "I know it's in here somewhere."

"It's okay, madame."

"Aha!" Cate verified that the registration hadn't expired before handing it over.

He said it wouldn't be long.

She stared into the windshield. The crack made her think of Nuna's drawing of Atlantis, an island submerged, overgrown with algae. Silent, deserted, void of human activity.

The officer returned.

"Did I do something wrong, Officer?"

"Your stop back there." He pointed at the intersection in question. "It was an illegal stop."

Cate stuck her head out the window. No way in hell had she made an American stop. "I beg your pardon, Officer, but I definitely stopped there. I'm certain of it."

He shook his head.

"I'm 110 percent sure." Sweat trickled down the back of her neck.

He handed her the ticket, instructing her in a monotone on how to contest the infraction. "And please get your windshield repaired immediately. It's probably why you didn't see the stop sign."

"I beg your pardon?" Her anger surged. "The windshield thing just happened yesterday. Some asshole smashed it with a hammer. My friend will take care of it as soon as she can." He looked like some high school student who needed to be put in his place. "This isn't a quota thing, is it?" Her eyes bored into him.

"Listen, madame," he consulted her driver's license, "Madame Morrissey...would you like I increase the amount of the contravention?"

"Ticket," Cate muttered under her breath.

The officer's eyes narrowed. "I don't like your attitude."

"What attitude? I'm just telling you." Cate glowered. "We'll fix it when we get around to it."

He shifted his weight to the other foot. He lingered at her window while she tore open the fine.

"Two hundred bucks and three demerit points? Are you kidding me? For something I didn't do?"

He smirked. "Et voilà! Une belle admission."

"What?"

"You just admitted you went through the stop."

Cate stiffened. She gnashed her teeth.

"I see here you got a parking contravention, as well."

Cate's lips curved into a smile. "Don't you have some donuts to eat?" The words were hers, but they sounded like Isabel's.

He ordered her out of the car.

"What the fucking fuck?" She thrust the door open, nearly hitting him with it. "Don't you have some real crimes to solve? Like people who've gone missing?"

"Stand there, and don't move!"

The street lights flickered on. Cate's face flushed. She noticed a few passersby eyeing her, wondering what a nice girl like Cate could have possibly done wrong. She thought of a sketch in Nuna's journal, of a sea goddess exploding from the ocean in a myriad of colours. Everything shimmering with light.

The cop strode back like a cocky cowboy, thumb tucked into his gun belt. He ordered her back into the car and slapped another ticket into her palm. "For obstruction of justice," he grunted. "And if I ever stop you again, you will be very sorry, madame." He sauntered back to the idling police car, turned off the flasher, and cruised slowly past her.

Cate flipped him the bird. "Have a shitty night, tabarnac!" She pulled out, tires screeching, hitting every green light on her way back to Isabel's. Singing made-up songs until her throat was raw.

She slid into a vacant parking spot right outside the apartment building. "Yeah, baby! Doris Day!"

The front door was unlocked. Isabel was in the kitchen, fussing with a salad. Something in the oven smelled delicious.

"Holy fucking fuck!" Cate shouted.

Isabel gasped. "Jeez, you scared me!" She caught her breath. "Did someone slip you some Molly or something?"

Cate still couldn't believe it. She had gone apeshit, yielded to her baser instincts. "Holy cow," she marvelled. She'd never done anything like it before. It went against everything she'd been taught about decorum and respect. Her father would have admonished her: tantrums were the fruit of a child's logic. Liam would've advised her to shut up and take it to court. But, no. She lashed out at an officer of the law. She crowed, mockingly, and swaggered into the living room.

Isabel dropped her peeling knife. "You're kidding, right?" She followed Cate.

"You know that Edvard Munch painting of the *Scream*?"

"You mean that guy with his mouth in an O, holding the sides of his head?"

"Yeah, that's the one." Cate threw Isabel her car keys. "I'm surprised you know that."

"What do you take me for? I went to college."

"Well, if you can imagine, that was me a few minutes ago." She parodied the painting.

Isabel clapped a hand over her mouth. "Seriously?"

"You should've seen me, Isa, you would've been proud!"

"You finally grew a pair!"

"A pair of balls?"

"Boobs," Isabel said. "You finally grew a pair of boobs!"

Cate laughed. "Just call me Fiona." She dug the tickets out of her purse and waved them at Isabel. "Here. Check out the damage."

"Holy shit! Three hundred bucks, plus demerit points..."

Cate shrugged as if to say, what's next on the bucket list? "It was worth it!"

"I see that."

Cate noticed the music. "Who is this?"

"Alicia Keys."

"I like it," Cate said. "Pump it up!" She put her hands on Isabel's hips and led her around the floor. "Let's have some more of that." Falling into step, they belted their girlish lungs out. As the song went, the pair were on fire. They clapped and twirled, they boogied and box stepped. Their thumping feet made the wineglasses vibrate. They danced non-stop, through Beyoncé and Christina Aguilera and Katy Perry's "Firework," until they fell breathlessly on the couch.

Cawwww. Smoke was pouring out of the oven. Cawwww. Isabel ran toward it, shouting at Cate to grab a magazine and wave it under the smoke detector. She grabbed the oven mitts and pulled out the blackened casserole dish. Dinner was ruined. Shrunken, charred, it was hard to tell what it had been.

Cate didn't ask. She didn't really care. "Do you know it's the first time?" The alarm stopped screeching.

"First time for what?" Isabel said, fanning the air.

"First fine."

"Can't say I'm surprised." Isabel added some tomatoes to the salad. "Why don't you go freshen up while I salvage what I can here." She invited Cate to use her room, she'd left a towel on the bed.

In all this time, Cate had never been to Isabel's apartment. The room was tidy-ish, but cluttered, clothes hanging from hooks on the back of the door. A couple of books were on her nightstand, one called *Women* by an author she'd never heard of, with a Georgia O'Keeffe painting on the cover. It was bookmarked with a sheet of toilet paper. Cate smiled. The fact that Isabel read things other than celebrity magazines surprised her. Near the closet, there were pictures arranged on a beige corkboard, including the photobooth strip of the three of them that belonged to Nuna. She unpinned it, remembering how they had crowded into the booth, how silly and lighthearted they had been that day. She held the picture at arm's length. There was something in Nuna's expression that she had never noticed before, a hint of resignation. Had it always been there, she wondered, and if so, how had they missed it?

Isabel called out to her. "Need anything?"

"No, I'll be right out." Cate returned the photo to its place. She put on a clean pair of underwear and changed her shirt. She rolled on some deodorant and pulled her hair forward over her shoulders. Examining herself in the mirror, she made sure that nothing embarrassing was sticking out of her nose. She checked her phone for messages before powering down. Nothing from Liam. Nothing, either, from Waleed. She decided not to ask why Isabel had taken the picture from Nuna's room.

Dinner was everything that hadn't burned: the leafy salad, a shrunken block of cheese and some ciabatta buns she found in her freezer. It was the first time they were having a meal that wasn't at Cate's place or in some diner or fast-food joint. Isabel tonged some salad into Cate's dish. "Don't worry, it's vegetarian." She laughed.

"Looks amazing." Cate said.

"No need to be polite." Isabel uncorked the wine.

"What were we going to have anyway? Before the oven killed it."

"Black bean tamale pie, my mother's recipe. Full of black beans, onion, garlic, and zucchini. You would've loved it."

"Salad's fine."

Isabel poured. "So, what should we toast to?"

"Well, to Nuna, of course."

"Of course. To Nuna. May the gods align so that we find her soon."

Cate muffled a giggle. "And the stars, as well."

They clinked glasses.

"This wine is dope! What is it?" Isabel examined the label and nodded. "I'm impressed."

"Lovely, isn't it?"

After dinner, they sat on the floor on either side of the coffee table, bare feet stretched out underneath. It reminded Cate of her university days when she and her friends held potluck suppers with cheap wine, and "deep" thoughts pervaded the apartments of the student ghetto.

"You didn't tell me about your visit with Margaret."

Cate paused for a moment. "I'm glad I went. I don't really know what it accomplished, except I feel a hundred pounds lighter. And I don't resent her anymore."

"That's huge."

Cate described the neglect she had felt from her mother, the constant but futile efforts to please her. "It's too bad I never found a way to connect with her, especially after she got sick. Things were always so complicated."

"I'm lucky, I guess. As an only child, I didn't have that issue." Isabel rubbed her foot. "Mine never pressured me to be anything but myself." She stretched out again, legs between Cate's.

What was happening under the coffee table was unclear to Cate. Unclear, but not unwelcome. She emptied her glass and poured herself some more.

"Me, too," Isabel said, finishing off the last of it. "The first dead soldier."

Cate went to get another bottle from the kitchen. "You know why they call it a dead soldier?" She sat again, legs back on either side of Isabel's, grazing her hips.

"Something to do with war, I'm guessing."

"It's military slang from the late nineteenth century. Because empty bottles lying around after a drinking spree resemble corpses on the battlefield."

"Are we killing soldiers tonight?"

Cate smiled at her, relieved she wasn't at home. She went to open the new bottle.

"Well? Are we?"

Cate struggled to insert the corkscrew.

"I guess not, if that's how you screw. Hand it over." Isabel popped the cork off with minimal effort.

"They don't make 'em like they used to, eh?"

"Yeah, right." Isabel stood up. "I see you've finally gotten rid of that stick up your ass."

Cate turned up the music, looped her hands around Isabel's waist, and danced with her to the song that was playing, heavily percussive. When it ended, she asked Isabel to search Spotify for Blossom Dearie.

"Blossom who?"

"My favourite. American jazz singer and pianist. Girlish voice."

"Never heard of her." Isabel scrolled until she landed on "Someone to Watch Over Me."

"And I don't have a stick up my ass," Cate said. "It's more like a pen." She liked the feeling of Isabel's head against her shoulder, heavy but not too heavy, her hair smelling of vanilla.

When the song ended, Isabel went to get the pastries. Cate patted the space beside her on the sofa. Isabel sat and slid the ribbon off the box. She opened it carefully and peeked inside. "Ooh-la-la!"

Cate was pleased that Isabel approved of her choice, two chocolate éclairs and what the baker touted as the fattiest pastry in the world, Kouign-amann. Your husband will love it, he promised, praising its flaky dough, its lavish quantities of sugar and butter. He even threw a complimentary macaroon into the box.

Isabel nibbled the tip of an éclair. "It's probably a million calories but fuck it." She licked the chocolate fondant and gingerly bit into it, soft custard squishing out the sides. There wasn't a thing Isabel could eat that would make her gain weight or put a pimple on her face. "God, Nuna was crazy for these. She couldn't get enough." Isabel swiped her finger through the custard and held it at Cate's mouth.

Cate licked it with relish. She spoke through a mouthful. "Remember that time you brought us some for dessert and Nuna thought they were all for her?"

Isabel grinned. "Much to Liam's dismay."

"And how royally bummed he was when he discovered she had polished them all off before supper?"

They laughed.

Isabel's cell rang. "It's Blanchard. He wouldn't call unless it was important."

Cate sipped her wine, listening but not listening to Isabel's half-a-logue. Half-a-logues were irritating because your brain worked overtime to decipher what the person on the other end was saying, even if you weren't interested. It drew you in. It held you hostage. Once Cate was at a Second Cup trying to read while the guy at the next table was on his phone conducting a business meeting. He wasn't being particularly loud, but the constant drone was annoying. "This isn't an office," she snapped. "It's not a library, either," he retorted, turning his back on her.

Cate got up and disappeared into the bedroom with Nuna's journal.

*

"Hurry! Your wine's getting cold," Isabel shouted through the closed door.

Cate snapped the journal shut. Getting off the bed, she lost her balance and bumped into the dresser. "Ouch!"

"Need help?"

"Nope!" Cate paused to catch her breath. She smoothed down her clothes and opened the door.

"What've you been doing in there?" Isabel held a glass for Cate to drink from. "Or don't you want to say?" She snickered.

"I needed some privacy."

Isabel leered. "What kind of privacy?"

Cate waved the journal. "I wanted to probe the depths," she leered back.

Isabel looked disappointed.

They moved back to the couch. Cate flipped open the journal. "I found something."

Isabel moved closer.

"Remember that entry of hers that freaked you out, 'To die, to drown, to be free of everything human?'" She thumbed through the pages. "Well, there was always something about it that sounded vaguely familiar. And, then I remembered that it came from a book-length poem by Louis Dudek. A Montreal poet. To make sure, I checked online. Guess what the title is?"

Isabel shrugged.

"Atlantis."

Isabel's eyes widened.

"Don't you see? Those words were copied directly from his book. They weren't a cry for help or a suicide note."

She sat up. "You mean all this time we've been running around like chickens with our heads cut off and the answer's been right under our nose?"

"I don't know, maybe." Cate stared at Isabel's glass. "I'm waiting for another sip of inspiration." She cracked open her mouth and tilted back her head while Isabel poured. She used her sleeve to wipe her lips. "So, get this. One of the last times we talked seriously, Nuna told me about this book she'd been reading by Richard Wagamese, an Anishinaabe writer. This must've been, like, late September. A few weeks before we, uh, lost her."

"Yeah, so? She was always reading, you accomplished your mission." Isabel brushed a strand of hair away from Cate's face.

"Nuna read me a passage. The book was called *Embers*."

"Go on."

"Listen." Cate cleared her throat. "When there's a crack in my mirror I can't see myself as I am—all I see is the crack. The crack tells me that there is something wrong with me, that I'm not enough and that this is how others see me, too. It's not a question of finding a better mirror. It's about seeing beyond the crack." Cate waited for Isabel process it.

"Okay, so?"

"It made me think. All these months, I've been teaching her Dickens, Steinbeck, Orwell, but why didn't it ever occur to me to use Indigenous texts that might have made more sense to her? That she could relate to? What was I thinking?"

"What do you mean?"

"I mean the so-called expert has years of study behind her, a sense of the broader context, an aptitude for judging what betterment might look like theoretically. And so she does whatever it takes to move the student closer to that ocean of freedom that comes with education and knowledge."

"I'm not following."

"I mean, as her teacher I was thinking White. The more I think about it, the more I think she just had enough and went home."

Isabel set down her glass. "Why wouldn't she have said something to us, like 'Goodbye, thanks for the memories, I'm going home now'? As it is, there was nothing, no thank you, no kiss my ass, nothing." Isabel stood up.

"Don't say it."

"After all we've done for her."

Cate remembered an essay Nuna had written, a few days before she went missing. It was nothing Cate had assigned. She wrote it because she wanted to. The paper was mature, insightful, well beyond her years. It was about liminal spaces, how they intrigued and terrified her at the same time. She described twilight after everyone's left the playground and the squeaky swing swaying gently in the breeze. She wrote about empty, fluorescent-lit waiting rooms, abandoned parking lots, endless beige corridors without a single window. She wrote about glaring human absence and how Western artists like Lawren Harris painted the North as an unsettling space, void of living beings. Liminal spaces are deeply relatable, she wrote. She was obsessed with them. They were ordinary and familiar, but eerily uncomfortable. They were transitional, unlivable. The essay grappled, it asked questions. It was brilliant in its own way.

Cate flashed her palm. "Listen, Isabel, after our lives intersected—you, me, her—did we consult her even once? Or did we just take over and make her do what *we* wanted?" Glass in hand, Cate stood up, steadying herself against Isabel's shoulder. "Don't get me wrong. Our hearts were definitely in the right place. But we never really gave her any agency."

Isabel took the glass away. She put it down and steadied Cate. "What do you mean, agency?"

"The capacity of people to make their own free choices, act independently."

"Okay, okay. I get your point."

Cate stared up at the ceiling. "Listen, we'll never know for sure, but I think it's time to trust the universe that sent her to us and stop looking for her."

Isabel nodded without conviction.

"I'll let Lizzie know in the morning. Not that I'm thrilled, but at least the cops are on it. They can't all be bad apples." She rolled her eyes. "Well, except for, maybe, that smarmy, pimple-faced dick who stopped me for nothing tonight!"

Isabel didn't laugh, she didn't crack a smile. A mischievous look didn't cross her face.

They both felt it. They both knew the end was in sight. The end was in sight, and they hadn't brought Nuna home. They were ending things without an ending—something they would have to live with. And without Nuna, the glue, the reason for their friendship, they would go their separate ways. Maybe not right away, but eventually. The phone calls would taper off. Reasons to meet would disappear. One day, months down the road, they might run into each other, on the street or in a restaurant, but not likely. They didn't live in the same neighbourhood.

Cate slid her hand from Isabel's grip. "Well, what are you thinking?" She sat down again and grabbed her wine.

"Do you think she'll ever find Atlantis? Or whatever it is she's looking for?"

"I dunno. But you want to know something? I think Nuna finally realized that Montreal isn't the paradise she thought it was." Cate fumbled with her glass, wine splashing. "Oh God, I think I ruined your sofa, Isa. I'm such a klutz sometimes." She went to wipe it with the corner of her shirt, but Isabel beat her to it, dabbing at the spill with her fingers. Their hands collided. They locked eyes. "I'll, uh, pay for the cleaning."

Isabel leaned forward. Her lips brushed Cate's.

Cate pulled back, blushing.

Isabel pretended that everything was normal. She sighed and cracked her knuckles. "If, um, you weren't thinking about Nuna now, who would you be thinking about?"

Cate was still reeling from the kiss. "Uh, I dunno. I'm not thinking about anything, really. You?"

"My father, surprisingly. The absent dad."

"I thought you didn't know anything about him."

"I told my high school friends he died choking on a peanut."

Cate frowned. "A peanut?"

"It was the most embarrassing death I could think of."

Cate touched Isabel's cheek. Her feet rooted to the floor. "I'm sorry you had to go through that."

"No biggie. I'm over it now." Isabel squeezed an eye shut and stared down the shaft of the bottle. "Another dead soldier. What do you know?"

Cate suggested they pause on the wine. "You know where I end up when I've had too much."

Isabel nodded. She spread out on the sofa, head in Cate's lap. "Okay, the story of my father. It's crazy, um, but whatever." She closed her eyes. "Every birthday from about twelve on I'd wander the streets searching for him." She pressed her toes into the armrest. "Whenever I saw a man who matched my description of what I thought he looked like, I'd follow him, trying to guess what sort of life he led. Did he have a wife and kids, or was he still making empty promises to vulnerable women?" She breathed deeply. "All I ever knew was that he was a computer guy with some kind of tribal tattoo on his arm. There wasn't a picture of him anywhere in the house, so I was really going on nothing."

Isabel got so involved with her story, she forgot their plan to lay off the drinking. She got up and went to get a bottle of tequila. "Once while I was stealing a cigarette from Mama's purse, I found a picture of her. She was young. Her legs were up on a table, and she was in her underwear. The note on the back said, *Chu fou de toi.* I figured it was from him." Isabel poured them each a shot. "By the time I got to college, I was tired of looking for him. I hated that he was just some random dude who got my mom pregnant, it was lame. I wanted a larger-than-life father with fire in his belly. I wanted a man with *cojones.* So I invented one, a famous Chilean painter named Jorge Ruiz Cortés who escaped the Pinochet regime and went to Nicaragua to fight in their army. I bragged to everyone that he died a martyr."

Goosebumps tickled the back of Cate's neck.

"It made his leaving us more bearable." She tapped her glass against Cate's. "Cheers. Drink up, Chica."

Cate swallowed the tequila. A little voice inside told her she shouldn't be drinking but a louder voice drowned it out and encouraged her to live a little, have fun for once. The tequila burned her throat. "I wonder what's better, a seriously flawed father or none at all?"

"Beats the hell out of me." Isabel dipped a thumb into her drink and smeared it across Cate's lips. She nudged closer.

Isabel's outbreaths felt warm on her neck. "I think I'm drunk," Cate said.

"Maybe, but so what if you are?" Isabel licked the tequila from her lips.

Cate trembled. Her tongue found Isabel's, then she stopped cold. "I'm sorry. I can't do this." She pushed Isabel away.

"You're not doing anything wrong."

Cate stammered. "I have a husband. I have a life. And I don't know...how any of this, er, fits ..."

"How *what* fits?" Isabel combed her fingers through Cate's hair.

Cate's eyelids drooped. Her scalp prickled with excitement. She felt ephemeral, her boundaries dissolving. "How this...fits into my life."

"Shhh. This is now," Isabel said. "It's only us, it's got nothing to do with anyone else." She pulled Cate off the sofa and blew out the candle.

Cate gathered the empty bottles.

"Leave it," Isabel insisted. "Leave everything." She took the bottles from Cate and set them back down on the coffee table. She turned out the lights.

Cate could hear the ringing darkness, the blood rushing in her ears. She had trouble walking in a straight line.

Isabel led Cate to her room and sat her on the bed. Her face glowed in the light of her phone as she scrolled for ambient music.

"Maybe we don't need that," Cate said. "Maybe let's just be us." Now that she'd said it, she couldn't take it back. The air was still. Street light bathed the walls in a warm buff.

Isabel put down her phone.

Cate's eyes adjusted to night, things edging into focus, dresser, table, bed. Isabel's cast-off shirt on the floor. A voice whispered in her ear. "Do you want to smoke? It'll relax you."

"Smoke what?"

Isabel smiled.

"Oh...uh, I don't know, should we?"

"Should, what's should?" Isabel flopped on the bed in her camisole and prepared the space beside her. "Come." She pulled out a bag of weed from the drawer of her nightstand. "You know you want to."

Cate watched her roll, quickly, expertly. She could hear a siren outside, a car being jumpstarted.

Isabel slid the joint into her mouth and twirled it in her saliva. "This is smooth stuff, don't worry." She lit the joint, her face flickering in the orange flame. She took a long haul and passed it to Cate.

"My god, I haven't smoked pot since university." Cate held in the smoke for as long as she could without coughing, but she coughed anyway. She wheezed and sputtered and had trouble catching her breath.

Isabel got her some water. "Don't take such deep tokes. Slow and easy does it."

Cate nodded.

They smoked it down to the embers, one flaking off onto the rug. It seethed and flickered.

"Jeez, are you trying to start a fire in here?" Isabel went to stomp on it, but remembered she was barefoot. She grabbed her book with the Georgia O'Keeffe image on the cover and smothered it.

Cate fell backwards on the bed. The headlights from a passing car swept across the ceiling. "I haven't felt this fucking light in…well, since I got that ticket before supper." She giggled. "But seriously…"

Isabel grinned. "What, seriously?"

"Just that, I don't know. I feel good. Period. Good times a thousand, times ten thousand."

"Me, too." Isabel fell alongside Cate. Their fingers interlaced.

Cate couldn't remember what day it was or whether she had shaved her underarms. She couldn't remember when she had crossed the line from being Isabel's friend to being her…her what? She couldn't find the word.

Isabel propped herself up on an elbow, pushed her hair back, and kissed Cate, holding her in a possessive grip. Cate yielded to the deepening kiss, to the slow-moving hands under her shirt. She heard herself make sounds she had never made before, an animal kind. They startled her. Cate pulled back and opened her eyes just as Isabel pulled the camisole over her head. "Hey, this is going a little fast for me." Isabel's moist print was still on her lips.

Isabel fumbled with Cate's zipper. "Let's just chill. Make room for what's good." Her whisper carried Cate like a raft. Isabel released the buttons on Cate's shirt. She undid Cate's jeans and then her own. When they were fully naked, Isabel arched her back. She touched her bush to Cate's.

Cate parted her thighs and thrust out her chest. Everything was moving quickly and not quickly enough. She was hungry.

Isabel snaked along Cate like a wave, exploring with her tongue, teeth, fingernails. She lapped and pinched, nipped and squeezed until her lover responded with a moan, a cry, a plea to stop…to keep going.

Cate's pulse quickened, the hairs rising along her nape. She stroked Isabel's back and opened wider. She felt weightless. And like a piece of the sky. She felt the immensity of the ocean.

The room was still vibrating when Isabel came up for air. Through the window, they saw snowflakes falling, the first of the season. Cate felt a chill and pulled the sheet over them.

Isabel stretched like a cat. Her eyelids dipped. Breathing softly, she kissed Cate and spooned in.

Cate wondered why Liam had never been able to make her feel this way. Gratified. Invigorated. Like she could do anything. Sex had always been about him—had he come? Was he satisfied? This was the first time it had been about *her* pleasure. Cate touched herself in all the places Isabel had. She felt a surge of energy, the way she did all those years ago when her fingers travelled the piano keys with abandon.

*

Cate woke, surprised she didn't have a headache. Her mouth was dry as a sweater.

Isabel was in the armchair with her feet up, staring at her phone. "Hey, sleepyhead." She was wearing Cate's shirt.

Cate sat up. She rubbed her eyes. "What time is it?" The light through the window was soft and dreamy.

"Why do we care?" Isabel levered herself off the chair, walked to the bed, and planted a long, wet kiss on Cate's mouth.

Cate tightened up. The roach smelled foul in the ashtray.

"What's wrong?"

"God, nothing. Nothing at all. Last night was fan-fucking-tastic!"

"Wasn't it?"

Cate swallowed. "You weren't watching me sleep, were you?"

"Maybe for a bit."

Cate didn't know what to say. All through their lovemaking she had been there in the moment. There was no conference, there was no paper. There were no nagging thoughts about her mother, her father, her sister, Liam.

Liam. He wasn't even on her radar.

Even Nuna was a distant thought. Cate had surrendered, she had given in to pleasure, freedom, her own begging erotic desire. Her body had been totally and absolutely with another body, face to belly and belly to face, and she had liked it.

But now, in the light of morning, things looked different, felt different. The real world was crashing in. Obligations. Expectations. It was no longer just the two of them. "Last night was amazing. Truly it was. It was probably the best night of my life."

"But?"

Cate looked away.

Isabel leapt onto the bed and snuggled in beside her. "Check this out!" She flashed her phone at Cate. "I found dirt-cheap flights to Morocco."

Cate smelled Isabel's fear. She took a deep breath. She squinted at the screen, at the images of zithers and mosques, camels and snake charmers. She knew that what was coming would hurt, would probably kill everything that was between them. But she couldn't help it. She couldn't pretend. "Like I said, last night was...I don't even have words. It was like dessert. It was *better* than dessert."

Isabel motored on. "I was thinking, I can probably sublet this place, in fact I know I can, the apartments in this building go really fast, and then we can move in together, and I can save up and maybe next year I'll quit my job and we can go there for good, just the two of us. Start a different life together." Her eyes sparkled. "What's so great about being here, anyway?"

Cate's voice trembled. "That's a beautiful idea."

"It's not just an idea if we make it happen." Isabel locked eyes with her. "I'm in love with you, Cate."

"I know," Cate whispered. "I've kind of suspected it for a while."

Isabel moved away from her. "You're making me nervous."

Cate licked her lips.

"Don't you feel the same way about me?"

"Isabel." Cate took a deep, distant, bottomless breath. "We need to talk."

"What's to say? I know you feel it, it was so obvious last night, how you gave yourself over like that." Isabel got off the bed. "How you came alive maybe for the first time in your life."

"And I don't regret a single minute."

"Regret?" Isabel ran out.

"Isabel, please." Cate wrapped herself in the sheet and followed her into the living room, where the dead soldiers lay and the pastries still sat in their box, barely touched.

"I can't go through this again. It hurts too much."

"Come on, Isabel." Cate took a step toward her. "I'm not Hannah."

"No—you're worse. Because you're better than her and you're free to choose."

"Isabel, you have to hear this." Cate begged her to sit down.

Isabel moved to the far side of the room.

"I'll never forget last night." Cate swallowed. "I love you. Maybe not in the way you want, but I do!"

"Yeah, sure. Whatever."

"You opened my eyes the way no one ever has. Everything feels possible now." Cate moved closer. She put her arm around Isabel. "Look at me."

Isabel fought back tears.

"It's not over. I want us to still be friends," Cate said. "And I think you should go to Morocco, if that's what you want to do."

An iridescent tear slid down Isabel's cheek. She brushed it away with the back of her hand. "How could I have been so wrong? I feel stupid."

Cate whispered into Isabel's ear. "Love is never stupid."

Isabel wrestled herself away from Cate.

Cate stayed strong. She kept her composure. "Look, go have an adventure, have the best adventure of your life! And then come home and tell me about it."

Isabel lowered her head. "Come on. You and I both know..." Her voice trailed off. "This is the nail in the coffin."

*

Isabel told her to go. Now. She gave Cate back her shirt. She didn't care that her sock had a hole in the toe or that her hair was a mess. She called for a cab. She went to get the spare key to Cate's house. And the photo strip she had taken from Nuna's room. Cate shook her head, no, we're not done yet, keep that stuff. But Isabel dropped them at Cate's feet. Half-heartedly Cate reached down and stuffed them into her pocket.

The air was suffocating. Their talk was broken. Cate did all the asking: When are you going back to work? Do you get time off for Christmas? I don't know. I don't know. Isabel was a shell of herself.

Cate remembered what Isabel had said while they were lying naked in the tender moments after making love. Talking though a lens of fog. She said that Cate was probably always attracted to girls but suppressed it because of her Catholic guilt. "You may be forty-three, but you're only fourteen in lesbian years. You have a lot of growing up to do." She was certainly right about the growing up part, Cate thought to herself.

The driver buzzed the apartment. Isabel opened the door and stepped aside.

Cate knew there was no repairing this. She had to walk away without looking back. She had to do it quickly—like ripping off a Band-Aid. She had to be calm and detached. It was the only way to lessen the hurt. "Is there anything I can do for you?"

"Just go."

Cate went to kiss her on the cheek, the way she would a friend, but Isabel turned away. "Don't." She meant for it to sting.

"This isn't goodbye, Isabel." Cate stooped for her things. "It's not."

The driver took her bag. Cate climbed into the back seat and slammed the door. She looked up to see if Isabel was watching from the bedroom window where everything between them had bloomed and died. The curtain was drawn. There was no sign of her.

"Where to, madame?"

Cate gave him her address. She tried not to think of Isabel. Isabel crying, Isabel throwing things. Isabel on the phone to her mother, heartbroken. If only it had been the tarmac scene in *Casablanca*, where everyone kind of got what they wanted.

The driver's eyes peered at her through the rear-view mirror. "It's quite something, eh?"

"I'm sorry. What?"

"You didn't see it on the news? The first all-female walk in space."

"Oh, yeah," she lied. "It's something, all right."

He changed the subject to the election. What did she think of Trudeau, did she think it was going to be another Liberal win? A majority or minority government? Who's going to be the official opposition, not the Green Party, I hope? They're good to have around, but they're not a party.

"Listen, I don't mean to be rude, but I don't feel like talking, if you don't mind." She stared out the window.

The ride home was smooth. No potholes, no detours, no traffic. She interpreted it as a good sign. She knew she was fooling herself.

Liam was uppermost in her mind. She wondered how she would ever look him in the eye again. She remembered his sheepish behaviour after the Bea incident, how ardent his denial that anything had happened between them. He blamed Cate instead, accused her of making him look outside their marriage.

But Cate had more than looked. She had acted. She'd been a willing participant. More than willing. And because of it, she couldn't shift the blame onto Liam even though, she could argue, she had good cause. They had always had a strained power dynamic. Deep down he was insecure. He never said it in words but Liam was constantly jealous of her successes. She had a PhD and taught in a university. Her published papers were praised around the world. He, on the other hand, was a high school teacher who ran a club and organized field trips. And though he always claimed that it was her decision to turn down an invitation to be a visiting scholar at Oxford, she only did it because of his fragile ego. She didn't want to pay for it for the rest of her life.

It surprised her that after all these years, she still harboured resentment.

The cab pulled up to the house. Liam's car was gone. There was no sign of him anywhere.

Cate struggled with the key. She forced the door open and dropped her duffle bag by the stairs. She strode to the living room and threw open the curtains. She cleared the piano of the heavy art books, the scraggly philodendron, and the bulging shoebox of classical CDs. She moved their thirty-five-dollar wedding portrait, taken at city hall, to the coffee table. She wiped down the piano with what was at hand—a white doily—before opening the fallboard.

She opened the wooden bench and dug out Prokofiev's *Piano Concerto No. 2 in G minor*, a difficult piece that she had aced in her final recital. She hadn't looked at it in more than two decades. She sat. She studied the keys, yellow with age, remembering what it felt like to play, the tension in a piece mounting, drama building, the music carrying her to faraway places. She clenched and unclenched her fists, stretching her fingers. She rotated her wrists, played a C scale with her right hand, then her left. The piano needed a serious tuning, but she ignored it.

She sat upright, back straight, shoulders relaxed, feet on the floor. Fingers lightly touching the keys. Wrists soft, she played the way she'd been taught, fingers rusty at first, then easing into it as though no time at all had passed. She played fluidly. After she finished, she closed the fallboard and went to the window, noticing that she was still wearing her coat.

The neighbours were outside stringing their Christmas lights, testing that the bulbs were still working. She remembered the time she and Isabel stood in the flashing neon of a shop advertising piercings and tattoos. Isabel wanted them to get their belly buttons pierced but Cate said, "Not in a million years."

Cate left her coat on. She dug out the bottle of Murphy's Oil, squirted some into a pail of warm water and cleaned the piano with a rag. After it dried, she buffed it up with Lemon Pledge. She wiped the keys down with vinegar and water and sat again.

She interlocked fingers, bent them back and cracked her knuckles, wanting to play everything she knew, starting with the popular songs of her youth, songs her piano teacher never wanted to teach her—"Let it Be," "Your Song," "Total Eclipse of the Heart." Body tipped forward, she pounded out every song that came to mind until finally launching into "Love is Everything" by k.d. lang. She sang with feeling.

By the time Cate heard Liam's key forcing the lock, she was onto "Fix You" by Coldplay. Her voice didn't crack as she sang plaintively about losses and letting go, and of the lights from somewhere guiding people back. Exhausted, she ended her recital there. She slammed the piano shut, final chord hanging in the air.

Cate spun around, half expecting to find Liam listening behind her. He wasn't. She walked past his briefcase, into the kitchen.

Liam was sitting on the counter chugging milk out of the carton. "It's nice to hear you play that thing again."

"Thanks." She spoke unblinkingly. "About the piano..."

"How come you're still wearing your coat?"

She shrugged. "I hope you don't mind, but, uh..." She didn't overthink it. "I'll be taking it with me when I go."

Liam did a double take. "I'm sorry?"

Cate pulled out a chair to sit. "I think you heard me." She waited for her words to register. "Aren't you going to say something?"

His mouth fell open. "Like what? Like I'm a jerk and I deserve it? Damn, I should've seen this coming from a thousand miles a—." He banged the carton down.

"Don't blame yourself. It's not you, Liam, it's me."

"Blah-blah-blah. With all your degrees, I'm surprised you can't come up with a better cliché."

Cate zoned out. She thought of the first day they moved into their house, how happy they were. How, slowly, over the years, they were going to fix it up, add an extension for a luxury bedroom with floor-to-ceiling windows and built-in cupboards. How the first night, before the movers brought their furniture, they slept on an inflatable mattress and made love on the kitchen floor, in the exact spot where they were sitting now.

He kicked his heels against the bottom cupboards. "What did I do?"

"You didn't do anything."

"Then why are we having this conversation? I don't get it." His hair hadn't been cut in a while, the curls growing down over the tops of his ears. It looked good on him.

"Believe it or not, I'm doing it for both of us."

He glared at her like she had hit him with a rock. "Don't give me that bullshit, something else is going on here."

"Like what?"

"I think it's Isabel."

Cate froze.

"I think she brainwashed you. Royally fucked you up."

"She's made me see things differently, but that's not the point."

"To be honest, she's been a pain in my ass since the beginning."

"Really? Why?"

"Isn't it obvious?" He shook his head. "She comes and goes as if she lives here. She takes you out of my life to go on a wild goose chase." He folded his arms over his chest. "I only tolerated her for your sake—and the kid's."

"Nuna."

He grunted.

"I'm sorry, I don't buy that."

"Whatever, it's the truth." He leapt off the counter and poked his head in the fridge, knocking over bottles and Tupperware containers to look for a beer. "You made promises, Cate, you didn't say you'd be gone with her for days on end. Christ, where's the fucking beer in this house?" He slammed the door.

Cate raised her eyebrows. "Oh my God, Liam. Promises? Days on end? Listen to yourself. We were in Ottawa, not Siberia!" She thought of throwing Mo in his face, of all the time he spent with her in the name of the debate team, the cozy meet-ups and trips out of town. But this wasn't about that.

Liam slumped into a chair.

She toned it down. "I forget where, but I heard an interesting story."

He waved his hand dismissively.

"For once can you just listen?"

He groaned.

"It might clarify things." She ran through it in her mind to get the details right. "It's a legend often attributed to the Cherokee people. It involves two characters, a grandfather and his grandson." She waited for him to look at her. "One day the old man tells the grandson that everyone has two wolves inside them, one good, one evil. The evil one is filled with emotions like anger, envy, regret, self-pity, guilt, and resentment. But the good one's filled with joy, love, empathy, kindness, et cetera. And the two are at war with each other."

Liam huffed impatiently. "What the hell does this have to do with us?"

"It has everything to do with us," Cate said. "When the kid asks his grandfather which wolf is going to win, guess what the old man answers?

"I don't give a shit."

"The one you feed."

"Is this about Oxford again? Or Bea?"

"No, Liam. It's not about either of them—though, I won't deny, they both hurt." She paused to let it sink in. "What I'm saying is that we've both been feeding the wrong wolf. And now, I need to feed my good one."

He refused to look at her. "You want to know something? You were more of a family with Isabel and that kid than you ever were with me! How's that supposed to make me feel?" The colour rose in his cheeks.

"Why don't you just admit that you never wanted to be a part of it. Not really."

There was a prickly silence. He didn't disagree.

"Another thing. I finally realized my father was an a-hole."

Liam knit his brows together. "And what does *that* have to do with *us*?"

"Well, I've begun to realize that in some ways I'm exactly like him. And I don't like it."

"What are you talking about?" Liam screwed up his face. "You *love* your dad."

"Maybe, but it doesn't change the facts." Cate remembered Isabel's light touch. She brought a hand to her lips. "He was a liar and a cheater, and I don't want to be like that, I don't want to stay in a situation that I don't want to be in—out of duty, out of obligation. My whole life's been that."

He scratched his head. "You're saying you married me out of duty?"

"No, no, not at all. I loved you."

"Loved?"

Cate scrambled for words. "Look, I don't want to put you in the same boat my mother was in, tied to someone who has other needs. It's unfair."

He blinked away a tear. "Other needs? Like what?"

"I'm not sure, but it's not this."

He lowered his head. "Jesus, you can't even say it."

"Say what?"

"That you don't love me anymore." He stood and scuffled to the back door. "I need some air." The door slammed behind him.

Cate watched him through the window, holding on to the railing. He stared up at the sky. In the old days, he would have lit a cigarette.

Cate brought his coat out to him. "Here, you'll catch your death." She draped it over his shoulders.

He regarded her with wet, dull eyes. "Remember when there were stars in the sky?"

She glanced up. "There still are, Liam. You just have to look harder."

"I haven't seen them in a long time."

"Neither have I."

*

Cate boarded the plane with knots in her stomach. It was smaller than what she was used to, with seating for about forty or so. The passengers, Inuit and White, all looked as though they had done this trip a hundred times—for work, for family, for medical appointments. They knew the drill. Sitting upright, seatbelts locked, they tended to children and typed on laptops. They leafed through the *Nunatsiaq News*, sipping the rest of an airport coffee. Almost everyone talked through the safety announcements.

The man in the seat beside her cleared his throat. "Are you a teacher?"

She remained polite, straining to hear what to do if the plane went down. "Yeah, McGill."

"Oh, so you don't teach on the ground."

Cate looked puzzled.

"In one of the villages, I meant."

The engine roared. The speaker crackled and popped. "Welcome aboard. This is your captain speaking." The pilot announced the speed of the aircraft, the weather, flying time to the various communities.

"Why did you think I was a teacher?"

"I just assumed. Most of the women on these flights are teachers or nurses. Or social workers. Where are you flying to?"

She glanced out the window as the plane gathered speed and lifted upward. Even now, even after many trips to Europe and South America, she couldn't help but marvel that such colossal machines managed to keep themselves aloft. She curled her fingers around the armrests and inhaled deeply. "A village called Saqijuvik."

"Oh, yeah. Nice place. Small but nice. A little rock-and-roll sometimes, though. Like all the communities."

She didn't ask what he meant by rock-and-roll. She had a pretty good idea. "And you?"

“This time, Puvirnituq. Next week Kuujjuaq. I’m going up to train some of the locals in furnace repair.”

Cate watched Montreal get smaller and smaller. She craned her neck and squinted until it was no longer visible. They flew into a patch of fog. “I take it you come up often?”

“I make the rounds. There’s always something somewhere that needs fixing.” He offered her half of his sandwich.

“No, thanks.” Cate reached for the airline magazine behind the vomit bag. She thumbed through, still surprised she was on her way to the Arctic. The cold, ice-covered Arctic.

Cate had been about to text Lizzie to say she and Isabel were giving up on the search when she got a surprising phone call from Lizzie herself, voice a whisper. She hemmed and hawed before getting around to the subject of her call. “I contacted Nuna’s father.”

“Are you serious?” Cate heard the sound of Lizzie’s breathing. “You’re serious.”

“I had to do something, I just had to. Even if it meant going over my sister’s head.”

“So what did he say?”

“That he was sorry for what happened between us that night, that he’s been five years sober.”

“That’s good news. But what did he say about Nuna? Is she there? What’s happened?”

“He wouldn’t say,” Lizzie said. “But I’m almost positive I heard her voice in the background.”

Cate closed her eyes.

“I’d go, but money’s tight right now.”

“I don’t know what to tell you.”

Her voice cracked. “I just want to know she’s safe.”

Cate slid the airline magazine back into the pocket. The next time she looked out the window, the view had morphed into patches of black rock and waning vegetation. It looked unforgiving.

“First time in the Arctic?” the man asked.

"First time north of the Laurentians." Cate chuckled.

"Once you get used to these planes, it's clear sailing. You should've been here in the '80s when it was just the Twin Otter." He bit into his sandwich. Crumbs fell into his lap without him noticing. "Only eighteen seats."

Cate's ear was starting to block. She yawned to try popping it.

"You be staying at the hotel?"

"Yeah. Surprising that a place of only six hundred people even has one."

He nodded. "Things sure have changed over the years. Back in the day, there weren't even flush toilets up here, let alone hotels. Everyone squatted over honey buckets to do their business."

Cate pulled out her water bottle. "What's a honey bucket?"

"It's, hm, how do I explain this? Picture a big, plastic-lined metal bucket with a toilet seat on top and liquid chemical poured into the bottom." He snickered. "When it stank too much, after about a week, you'd tie up the bag and toss it outside where it would harden into ice and thaw again in spring."

Cate grimaced. She wouldn't have handled it well. And she knew it would finish Liam, having to shit in a pail. Never mind letting it sit in green garbage bags outside your house all winter, an accumulating graveyard of poop.

"I know what you're thinking. But it wasn't that bad according to the older guys, everyone just got used to it." He brushed away the crumbs in his lap. "So, what's your story, if you don't mind me asking?"

Cate didn't know where to start, or whether she even felt like sharing. The story was too big. It was complicated. And where did it really start? With Liam? Her family? Or had everything unravelled because of Isabel and Nuna?

"Sorry, that was, well, I guess a little too personal." He took the last bite of his sandwich. "You'll find that up north, boundaries get a little blurred. You connect with people fast, not the locals, I mean the other Whites. The regulars. We keep crossing paths, so we get to know each other pretty well." He folded his crusts into the plastic wrap.

Cate screwed the cap back on her bottle. "I'm actually looking for someone."

He put out his hand. "I'm Jamie," by the way."

"I'm…I'm Fiona."

"Irish?" He waited for her to nod, treating their exchange of names as a lifting of the barrier between them. He jabbered away with friendly advice, tips for hot-button situations, things to avoid. Walking alone at night. Drinking with the locals. "Oh, some of them are alright," Jamie said. "They've got their heads screwed on right. They know how to drink like the rest of us. But some of them…" His voice trailed off. He glanced out the window and pointed.

Cate held her breath. The world outside was minimal, yet majestic. She gawked at the sprawling terrain. Repeated, uncurated nothingness. Ice, rock, snow, ice, rock, snow. Cate remembered Nuna's complaint that people were missing from Harris's art. That he had painted a holding pattern. Cate couldn't imagine a whit of life surviving down there. Let alone living and thriving.

The pilot announced they'd be landing soon. Cate opened her eyes and sat up. She couldn't remember nodding off.

In the distance, a dot appeared next to a grey expanse of water. She watched it grow into a larger speck, then a clot of earth, then a constellation of houses loosely organized around a tangle of roads. Quickly, it went from diorama to full-blown town. The bay shimmered under the setting sun. The droning plane approached its destination. It flew low, over life-sized houses and buildings, touching down onto the runway. Back pinned to her seat, a blur of landscape zooming past, Cate breathed deeply until friction and the pilot broke speed. The plane came to a stop. It turned a half circle and taxied back.

Workers with glowing X's on their backs waved fluorescent flags to guide the plane. The sky was darkening. The pilot welcomed them to Saqijuvik, "place where the wind changes and travels in many directions." The weather, he announced in too loud a voice, was cloudy and minus twenty degrees Celsius.

Jamie was continuing up the coast. He shook Cate's hand. "Best of luck, Fiona. Until we meet again."

Cate was surprised at his civility. She had expected Whites in the North to be rough and gruff. Probably there were plenty of those too. There strictly for the money. Enduring the many inconveniences for a final, sumptuous payoff and a debt-free future.

Things thumped against the fuselage as the door opened and the staircase was lowered. Men in caps and reflective vests were on the runway by a pickup truck, loading and unloading luggage.

Cate deplaned with a wizened Inuit woman wearing a factory-made ski jacket too big for her. The woman walked with a cane, clutching a Dollarama bag with the other hand. Cate followed her along a gravel path marked out with orange cones, to a flight of metal stairs leading to the terminal, which, from the plane, had looked more like a flimsy warehouse of corrugated tin. A handful of people waved at them from the brightly lit window.

Cate scurried ahead and held the door open for the woman, who was swarmed by family members removing their gloves to shake hands and welcome her home. Moving on, they welcomed Cate. She followed the custom, took off a mitt, and shook their hands.

The truck left the tarmac. The crowd dispersed. The plane groaned and disappeared into the night. Outside, a single phosphorescent light shone down on a squashed Coke can lying in the snow.

The guys at the ticket counter began packing up. They turned off the overhead lights. A straggler tapped her on the shoulder and pointed to her solitary duffle bag sitting outside.

Cate went out and dragged it into the terminal, shaking the snow off. She called out to the ticket agents. "Excuse me, how do I get to the hotel?"

"*Atsuk*," said one with a cigarette behind his ear. He shrugged.

The other told her to wait. He dialled a number and spoke quickly, in Inuktitut, to someone Cate assumed was the hotel manager. "Jimmy was supposed to be here to get you," he said when he hung up. "But I can take you." He told his pal to lock up and grabbed Cate's duffle bag. "Follow me." He threw her bag into the back of his truck next to some wooden crates and a red plastic fuel container.

Cate struggled with the frozen door handle. He reached over to jiggle it open and she climbed into the passenger seat. The truck looked relatively new, but the fender was dented and the windshield had a crack in it. She smiled. "That'll cost you a lot to fix," she said. She wondered if Isabel had replaced hers, and how she was doing. She thought how surprised she'd be if she knew where Cate was. "Same thing happened to my friend, but luckily her insurance is covering it."

He blasted the heat and cracked open his window. He lit a cigarette. "Are you a teacher?"

Her eyes widened. What, did she have a big T stamped to her forehead? "No, I'm visiting a friend."

"*Qina*?" he said. "Who?"

"Someone named Nuna. Maybe you know her?"

He puffed on his cigarette, razor-focused on the road ahead, awash in headlights and whirling snow. "Everyone here knows everybody. There are a lot of Nunas. You got a last name to go with that?"

"Maqaittik."

He corrected her pronunciation. "Ma-HAY-tik."

"Um, yeah."

"Joanasi's daughter?"

"I guess."

They arrived into town, streetlights casting their dim glow. He pointed out the school, the fire department, the police station, the FM radio station. To Cate, there was no discernible organization, buildings growing helter-skelter from the land. He accelerated up a hill that ended at the hotel, a modern bunker-like cube, green as broccoli. It reminded her of something from a sci-fi novel.

"This is it." He tossed his butt out the window. "Just be careful of the polar bears."

Her heart skipped a beat. "You're joking, right?"

"No. They sometimes like to sleep here. Under the hotel. Just pay attention."

*

Cate hardly slept. She tossed and turned in the lumpy bed. She ruminated over what the guy in the plane, Jamie, had told her about polar bears and how to defend yourself in case of attack. "Put a mitt on the end of a long stick," he had said. "Then ram that fucker down the bear's throat. Because it's either you or him." Cate wondered where she'd find a stick when there wasn't a single tree around. And if, for the sake of argument, there *was* a tree somewhere, one tree, a single tree, what would she cut the branches down with? How would she make sticks out of those branches quickly—before she became bear food? And being that there was only one tree, wouldn't branches be scarce? Wouldn't people hoard them and guard them with their life?

Cate woke early, got dressed, and headed to the lobby with its matching leatherette loveseats. It was still dark outside. Reception was closed, a metal, padlocked gate pulled across the desk. A wall-mounted TV was running the news from Quebec City, though no one was sitting there, watching.

She examined the items for sale in a glass display case, ivory earrings like the ones Nuna wore, a few thickly knitted hats with tassels and geometric designs, a couple of small, expensive carvings. She made a note of the earrings she would buy for Waleed when it opened later.

She went to investigate the communal kitchen. To her surprise, it was fully equipped. It had a fridge, two stoves, two upright freezers, a Black and Decker toaster oven, various kettles and coffee machines, and a Brita water pitcher. She noticed an assortment of complimentary breakfast items in baskets on the counter—bread loaves, jam packets, flavoured coffee pods—and a faded "boil water" advisory above the sink. She could tell from the drying rack, overloaded with pots and inverted wine glasses, that she wasn't the only guest in town.

She glanced at the laminate tables, a dozen or so, arranged cafeteria style in rows. Each with its own napkin dispenser and sugar caddy, a pair of glass salt and pepper shakers. A White man in a flannel work shirt was sitting alone, gnawing on a toothpick. One of the transitory guys, Cate assumed, like Jamie, there to build or fix something and be gone. He looked up from his phone.

Cate nodded hello. She selected a pod, French vanilla, and loaded it into the Keurig machine, a technology she mostly avoided for environmental reasons but embraced in the moment, enthusiastically, because what else was there. "Bon matin."

"Bonjour," he said, dropping the toothpick in his dish.

Cate carried her cup to a table by the window, where silhouettes of things were beginning to peek through the velvet darkness. She powered on her phone and checked the weather. Nothing had changed since the previous day; it was still minus twenty. For fun, she compared the forecast in Montreal: above zero, unusually warm for November. She fought with the spotty Wi-Fi connection, the little, annoying spinning wheel that made everything take forever. Couldn't understand how the toothpick guy seemed to have no trouble connecting. Maybe there was a trick.

She sipped her coffee, clicked on her Notes app, and reviewed what she had copied and pasted from Wikipedia before leaving: Saqijuvik: *First trading post, Hudson Bay Company, 1933. Catholic mission, 1956. Population, 642. Inaccessible by road. Polar climate. Abundance of Arctic char and lake trout. Small clinic staffed by one nurse for non-critical care. Air ambulance for emergencies.* She imagined Isabel on one, cool as a cucumber. Caring for the critically ill in a dedicated aircraft equipped with stretchers, ventilators, monitoring devices, defibrillators.

Hands curled around her mug, Cate stared out the window, watching the deep indigo of sky become pinkish dawn. A grey stretch of water drifted into view, not yet frozen over. In the distance, ancient mountains capped with snow.

The man in the work shirt got up, scraping his chair legs across the floor. He shrugged on his parka, rinsed his cup and plate at the sink, and loaded them into the dishwasher. Cate trained her eyes on him as he walked to the door and stepped into his unlaced work boots. He took a cigarette from his pack, ducked outside, and lit up.

Cate swallowed. She had an urge to smoke. Her last cigarette had been with Liam in Hawaii while they were both trying to quit. They'd shared it on their balcony, with cocktails, in the setting sun. She rinsed her mug in the sink. She got the man's attention through the window and signed to ask if he would give her one. He scowled and shook his head, then smiled to say *ben, non*, he was only kidding, come on out.

Cate ran to her room for her coat and hat. She pulled on her boots and joined him outside, where his Dodge Ram, parked by the steps, was running its cold engine. The whole porch smelled like gasoline.

He picked out a cigarette for her and flicked his lighter. His hands were dry and cracked; his fingernails had black crud under them. She bent in against the wind and sucked until the tip was a bright orange coal.

"You can speak English," he said with a Québécois accent. "Most people in north talk English. If they talk French, c'est un cadeau."

Cate struggled to smoke with her bulky mitt. She pulled it off and wedged it between her knees. "On gèle ici."

"Just wait until February. Brrr. Ça pince dur." He did an impression of being cold, arms crossed over his chest, body trembling. "C'est rien, ça, this is the Bahamas."

"I'm not staying long." The nicotine was giving her a head rush. "I'm only here to see someone. Then I'm gone."

He screwed up his face as if to say, why would you pay all that money when you can easily pick up the phone.

Not wanting to get into it, Cate changed the subject. "Aren't you afraid standing out here? I mean, with all the polar bears."

He chuckled. In all the years he'd been up north, he'd never once seen one. And no, he didn't walk around with the proverbial stick. He checked his phone and took a long haul on his cigarette, exhaling through his nose like the pack-a-day handymen she and Liam hired for odd jobs around the house. "Time to go work."

Cate saw that it was only 7:30.

"I'll probably be the first one there, comme d'habitude." He tossed his butt and stamped it out.

Cate pinched out her cigarette for later, the way Nuna always did when she was short on supply. She put her mitt back on, wiggling her fingers to get the blood circulating again.

"Maybe we can eat together supper," he said. "I have some good T-bones in the freezer. And a bottle of Cabernet Sauvignon from Québec."

Cate thought it might be nice to have company, even though she didn't know his name and didn't necessarily care to. It wasn't like they were going to keep in touch once they went home to the life they knew.

*

Cate made herself a second cup of coffee and three pieces of toast with peanut butter before hitting the road. She was sweating in her long johns and polar fleece, but she knew that once she was outside, she would appreciate the extra layers.

Cate tiptoed down the metal grille staircase, fearful of polar bears lurking under the building. Hoping, if there was one, it was hibernating. With climate change, she had heard there were more and more incidents of hungry bears wandering into communities like this. The hotel, like most structures, stood on footers off the frozen ground, making it a good shelter from the cold. Once she made it down the steps, she peeked under the building, breathed a sigh of relief, and took off down the winding road, past a dumping ground of shipping containers and an abandoned shack nailed together with mismatched plywood. She didn't notice how fast she'd been walking until she lost her footing on a rock jutting up from the ground and fell on her behind. She got up and brushed herself off. She glanced around to see if anyone saw. The town, for the most part, was still asleep except for a pair of fenced-in dogs, growling and sniffing each other's butts.

Now that she had distanced herself from the hotel and its polar bears, she slowed her pace. She donned her amateur sociologist's hat and took a good hard look around. What first caught her attention were the duplexes along the road, in the primary colours of Lego blocks. It seemed a creative way to brighten up a town that lived ten months of the year buried under snow and ice. On the other hand, she thought, the decision may have been arbitrary, approved by government bureaucrats with little to no interest in urban design north of the treeline, in a town they would never visit let alone reside in.

She kept walking, mindful not to trip again. In the distance, on higher ground, a handful of vehicles, including her cigarette pal's, were idling outside a cluster of warehouses. It appeared to be a hub, the central nervous system of the village, a place of buzzing machinery where things got built and fixed and transported to other areas of town. She wondered whether the Inuit built their own schools from scratch or if prefabricated, modular sections came up by ship, like puzzle pieces that were later fitted together. Another thing she never bothered to ask Nuna.

A yellow school bus filled with children passed her on the road. She never pictured school buses in the Arctic. She noticed some older teens making their way on foot, boys with open jackets smoking cigarettes. Like boys everywhere, they were jostling and bugging each other, trying to make the girls laugh. Some girls had babies on their backs. Cate wondered how anyone could concentrate on schoolwork with a kid in tow. Never mind a mom so young.

After the children got delivered and the school bell rang, things quieted down again, except for the occasional vehicle rumbling past, a sewage truck, a water truck, a pickup headed to the airport.

Across from the school was a tubular silver building of corrugated siding, which Cate inferred was the Co-op. Two Skidoos with their engines running were parked outside. She felt around for the half-smoked cigarette in her pocket, remembering she didn't have a lighter.

Inside, the store was a mishmash of groceries, clothes, hunting gear and household items, just as Nuna had described. Tools, toasters, drapes, shower curtain rods, toilet seats, everything double or more what it cost in Montreal. A 2.63 litre jug of Tropicana orange juice was going for $18.99, a block of cheddar almost forty dollars. She couldn't in a million years ever imagine having to fork over ten dollars for a limp head of broccoli.

The cashier was wiping down the conveyor belt when Cate got to the checkout counter.

"*Ullaakut*," Cate said in her rudimentary Inuktitut. She put down a lighter, a pack of no-name chewing gum, Schweppes ginger ale, and a Mars bar.

The girl glanced up without looking Cate directly in the eye. "Good morning."

"And some Du Maurier Light, please." Cate promised herself she would ditch them before leaving town. Waleed would shoot her if he knew she had relapsed.

The girl rang up the cigarettes. Cate did the math in her head. A pack-a-day smoker would be out $6,000 by the end of the year. How obscene, she thought. Forced to pay so much to an industry that packages death. And so many of them now smoked. So many were getting lung cancer. Not to mention heart disease and diabetes. It was shameful what Canada had done to them. Cate ignored the other items being scanned and pushed to the end of the counter and took advantage of the fact that no one was in line behind her. "Excuse me, do you know someone by the name of Nuna?"

The girl took the cash from Cate's hand. "Nuna who?" She emptied a roll of quarters in her till and counted out the change.

"Nuna Maqaittik."

The girl nodded. She started bagging the groceries.

Cate's heart raced. She tried to stay measured, questioned her, casually. Where is she? Is she working? If so, where? Is she still with that asshole of a boyfriend? She didn't say asshole. "Do you know where she lives?"

The girl wrinkled her nose. "I know her, but we aren't friends or anything. Are you a teacher?"

"I just want to talk to her."

She called out to a woman wheeling her cart down an aisle, an infant resting in the hood of her coat. Cate glanced at the woman's groceries: three frozen pizzas, a case of pop, a family-sized bag of Lay's chips, the salty ones. The fruit of White progress, she sighed, knowing that Nuna would've called her out: "Look at the crap you've given us." But, then again, maybe not. She did love her Coke.

She and the cashier chattered convivially. It was a longish conversation for what Cate had asked. She checked the time on her phone. They looked at her and laughed, but not unkindly.

The cashier switched back to English. "Roda says she lives with her father and mother, three houses past the fire department."

"Three houses?"

Her eyebrows lifted in a yes.

"Nakurmiik." Outside, Cate lit her recycled cigarette, enjoying it the way she used to, after coffee or a glass of red wine. It scared her to think of how easy it would be to get hooked again.

A morning recess bell rang. Across the road, kids poured out of the school into the playground, climbing the monkey bars, swinging on swings as though the cold didn't exist. The older ones, barely twelve, walked off school property and down to the road to light up. Cate waved. They looked away, whispering behind their hands.

Roda exited the Co-op and climbed onto her Skidoo with her groceries. She smiled and pointed into the distance and Cate realized that she was indicating the direction to Nuna's house. Cate smiled back and repeated "Nakurmiik" before stamping out her cigarette and getting back on the road.

The wind had picked up with a force that slowed her pace. She pushed on, pulling the scarf up over her nose. The sky was patchy with clouds. All evidence of the sun had disappeared. Cate rehearsed what she would say to Nuna when she saw her. In one version, she would hug her and say how happy she was to see her again. In another, Cate, standoffish, would explain how hurt they had been after she took off without a word and scared the hell out of them. Or, she would just casually say "I get it" and leave it at that.

Cate approached a small square building with a red garage door wide enough for a fire truck. She counted off three houses. Nuna's was much smaller than what Cate had imagined would be suitable for such a large family. Nuna had said that houses were at a premium and that the bigger ones, like the duplexes, were next to impossible to get unless you had a connection. A newish pickup truck was parked out front near an overturned tricycle, half buried in the snow.

The house was an imitation wood bungalow, like the others on her road, with two front windows and a side staircase leading to a cold porch, like a mudroom, that protected the main entrance from harsh weather. Green paint on the front door was scaly and peeling off. Cate took out her phone and snapped a picture of a polar bear hide hanging over the railing. She remembered reading about a woman from one of these villages who ended up at the Montreal General Hospital after being savagely mauled. The bear nearly tore her head off before a hunter came out of his house with a rifle and shot it dead.

Cate went to knock but lost her nerve. Had she overstepped by coming here? Was she trespassing on land she had no business being on? How much of her decision to fly to Nunavik had been driven by White guilt? She began to have second and third and fourth thoughts. She had to get out of there before someone saw her. In her hurry to leave, she slipped and fell.

She heard Isabel's voice accusing her of overthinking again. She brushed off the snow and marched back up the steps. Pressing an ear to the door, she heard noises inside, a man, a baby crying. The lilting voice of a woman. Cate knocked. The voices stopped.

She remembered Nuna saying that nobody knocked up north, people just walked into each other's houses. They sat. They watched TV. If they were hungry, they helped themselves to bannock or tea or whatever else was in the kitchen, and when it was time to leave, they just put on their coats and took off.

Just as her hand gripped the knob, the door opened unexpectedly. It pulled her off balance. Cate caught herself before falling forward into the house.

The man standing there, the father, she presumed, Joanasi Ma-HAY-tik with a face full of grizzled stubble, was dressed for work. Coat. Hat. Tool kit and Thermos. He regarded her with suspicious eyes. "Yes? What do you want?" he mumbled.

"Does Nuna live here?"

"Who are *you*?"

"Just a friend."

Joanasi gave her a dismissive once-over before summoning his wife. Lucy came to the door with a sleeping baby in her arms. She looked markedly younger than her husband and bore a strong resemblance to her sister, Lizzie. The two spoke without looking at Cate. A kid in a diaper and nothing else stuck his head out from behind the door. Lucy shooed him inside, without raising her voice.

"I just want to talk to her," Cate said to Lucy. "Please."

"She's not here."

Joanasi brushed past Cate, jangling the keys to his truck.

"I know you. You're that friend of my sister who made her call me. You're wasting your time coming here."

Joanasi revved the engine and drove off.

Cate refused to back down. "Well, have you heard from her, at least?"

Lucy looked right through her. "No."

It was a punch to the gut. Lizzie had managed to convince Cate that Nuna was there, that she had gone home to be with her people. She even said she heard Nuna's voice during her call to Joanasi. These were the things that had given Cate hope when she left Montreal on this wild goose chase. They had given her the incentive to go. Now she was crushed. "Do you know if any of her friends have heard from her?"

She shook her head.

"Well, do you have any idea, even the slightest, where she might be?"

Lucy shifted the baby to her other side. "Nuna is where she has to be."

"What do you mean?"

"I mean, she has to be where she is." Lucy closed the door.

Cate knew that Lucy was stonewalling her. It hurt but didn't surprise her.

Cate stood there for a while, reflecting. Her concern for Nuna was genuine. She knew it, Isabel knew it, and even Lizzie knew it. But Lucy? She was a whole other story. Cate was fresh off the plane, she was one of those Whites who knew what was best for everyone. Lucy was skeptical of those people, it was clear to Cate the minute she set eyes on her. Lucy barely spoke to her own sister, why would she even consider helping Cate, a complete stranger? And White.

She trudged past the fire station and the prefab bungalows. There wasn't a soul on the road. Halfway back to the hotel, she saw a wheelchair-accessible building with a Quebec flag out front that she hadn't noticed before. It was the Nursing Station. Cate had an idea.

The receptionist looked up. She set down her sewing. Cate lied that she was a paramedic from Montreal. "I'd like to see the doctor, please."

"You missed him by a day. He won't be here again until next month. Do you want to speak to the nurse?"

Cate nodded, admiring the colourful hats and mittens for sale on the counter, prices pinned to them on scraps of looseleaf. Nothing under seventy-five dollars. She picked up some foil-wrapped bannock. "How much?"

"Fifteen." The receptionist smiled. "That's Eva's bannock, best in the village."

Cate handed her a twenty and told her to keep the rest. On her way to the crowded waiting room, she passed a man holding an ice pack over his eye. Nearby a baby wailed, face covered in welts. The mother rocked him, stood up, paced the hall, and sat down again, trying to pacify him. The screaming was relentless. Cate found a seat across from a teenage girl, lids darkened with eye shadow. She wondered if the girl was there to get birth control. Probably not, she thought. Nuna had often mentioned how many adolescent girls lived, contentedly, with their baby daddies.

The nurse emerged with a clipboard. She invited the mother into the examining room with her thrashing infant. The mother gestured for the teenager to bring her coat and diaper bag and they all clomped down the hall to the examining room.

Cate approached the nurse. She asked to see her privately—just for a minute. "I'm a paramedic. From Montreal."

She nodded and they stepped into her office. The nurse introduced herself as Liette Rochon, from Moncton, a short, solid woman with wire glasses and permed hair. Cate was surprised that she wasn't wearing a lab coat with a name tag. She could have been anyone in her brown corduroys, plaid shirt, and yellow Crocs.

"I'm not here for a job," Cate said. "I'm looking for a girl." She gave Liette a bare-bones account, using what little medical jargon she had picked up from Isabel. "I'd like to know if she's been in here lately—or any time for that matter."

"I'm sorry, I can't tell you anything. Medical records, as you know, are confidential. Even in the North." She was firm but polite.

"Of course, I understand, but…well, the girl went missing in Montreal and I came all this way because—"

"They come and go," Liette said. "Sometimes I help them."

"Well, do you know this girl?"

Liette nodded. "Yes, the Maqaittik girl. Do you think she might be in trouble?"

"I'm worried she might have mental health issues."

There was an urgent knock on the door. The receptionist poked her head in to ask where the sterile pads had been moved to. "Zebedee just came in with a cut on his hand that won't stop bleeding."

"I'll be right out!" Liette opened a drawer and pulled out a pair of surgical gloves. "Listen, um…"

"Fiona."

"Listen, Fiona, I can't really talk now, but one thing I can tell you is that suicide is one of our biggest challenges here."

Cate read between the lines. Suicide wasn't a *problem*, it was something they needed to address—and would, in due course. It had a hopeful ring to it.

"Many of our youth are at risk. But many are resilient. It's a question of finding their strength and channelling it." Lingering at the door, she told Cate that if she was free she was welcome to come by for supper, she had Arctic char on the menu. "The cops are coming, they might have some info. And they're always good for a story or two."

A story or two. Cate hesitated. Her suspicions and prejudices about the relationship between law enforcement and the Indigenous made her uneasy about accepting the invitation. Also, she had lied about being a paramedic, so things could go south. "I'm sorry but I've already accepted an invitation. Some guy at the hotel has offered me his steak."

Liette giggled. "Sounds promising."

Cate thanked her for her time. Retracing her steps back to the hotel, it dawned on her that her steak remark had alluded to something more...illicit with Monsieur Cigarette, a man with whom she had nothing in common. Zero. She chuckled to herself. And, yet, Waleed had managed to make things work with his man-cave guy, Daniel, someone clearly on a lower intellectual rung. Waleed rationalized: some were bookish friends, others, carnal friends. Why did one person have to be everything to another?

The wind died down and there were more people outside again, women carrying groceries, toddlers playing hockey with sticks that were too big for them. The sewage truck was outside the hotel, pumping out the communal shit. Cate caught a whiff and gagged.

She punched in the door code. On the third try, it worked. She left her boots puddling on a rubber mat in the entrance next to an enormous pair of grotty, once-white Sorels. Still shivering from the outside cold, she kept her coat on. It surprised her to see that the registration desk was still closed. She headed for the kitchen. It smelled like disinfectant. The counters were wiped down and the dishes in the rack had been put away. A tinny radio on one of the tables was playing country and western but the place was deserted.

An unusual sound startled her—a growl followed by a forceful grunt. She tried to scream but couldn't find her voice. As she prepared to run, a large shape backed out from under the kitchen sink on all fours. It lumbered slowly. The figure stood up and Cate saw that it was Nuna's father, Joanasi. She took a step back and giggled.

He eyed her intensely before shutting off his soldering torch. He tested the faucet. Water from the tap gushed into the sink.

He packed up his tool case, reached over, and selected a pod from the basket. He made himself a coffee. He went to the fridge for a carton of milk and poured too much. He mopped the counter with his sleeve and carried his cup over to the table where the radio was playing.

Cate ran a hand through her hair. She took a calming breath and decided to make herself coffee as well. She tossed Joanasi's pod into the garbage and replaced it with one that had Rainforest in its name. Cate felt his eyes on her. She set her mug on the tray under the dispenser and selected the smallest brew size.

Nuna once told her that people up north can sit for hours together without saying a single word. "What's the point of talking if you have nothing to say?" she said. Nuna hated small talk, especially in cities where people used the weather as filler, a throwaway. "Weather is important to us. It can mean life or death."

The machine pumped the water for a few seconds before hot, fresh coffee piddled into her cup.

Joanasi studied her with a stern expression. "Why did you come here?"

She thought hard about what to answer, but nothing came to her that she hadn't already said. The coffee maker stopped. Cate removed her cup, careful not to spill, and took a sip.

A baritone radio voice broke into the music, announcing a bingo game at 8:00 p.m., right after *Identify the Animal.*

Cate snorted the coffee through her nose. She exploded into uncontrollable laughter.

Joanasi stared, perplexed.

"I'm sorry," she kept repeating, lapsing into laughter each time she tried to explain. She wiped her nose and cleaned up the spill.

Joanasi stiffened.

She apologized again and explained what was comical. She told him about Nuna's description of the show and how she had pulled their leg, telling them that the fish sound was the hardest to imitate.

He didn't join her laughter. "Are you a teacher?"

"Why's that always the first question around here?"

"Because most White women who come up here are." His voice had an edge. "They come up, with their pure White hearts, to make a difference. But they don't know the first thing about us." He sighed. "And they don't have a clue what we need."

Cate tried to read him, choosing her words carefully. Trying to make the case for herself. "I doubt they're all like that."

He raised his voice. "I tell you—they find us exotic, like animals in a zoo. They come for a year, sometimes less, they make friendships, win people's trust, and then they leave." His eyes were leery slits. "A good teacher should also be a good student."

"And they aren't?"

He shook his head. "Most of them, no."

Cate took a measured step toward him. He was definitely Nuna's father; they had the same nose, the same guarded look. She took her chances and joined him at the table. "Nuna and I were friends." She smiled. "She jokingly called me Mom."

He cleared his throat. "Nuna *has* a mother. Her name is Lucy."

"Of course she does. I meant no disrespect." Cate got up to get a glass of water. "I'm just saying we were close."

Joanasi mumbled inaudibly. He took a cigarette pack from his shirt pocket and scratched his head. "Are those the only clothes you brought?"

Cate inspected her coat. "The man at the army surplus store said it would be enough for what I needed."

He stuck a cigarette into his mouth. "Come."

Cate didn't know what to do. There were no witnesses around, there was no one to say *Yeah, he was the last person she was with before she disappeared*. She hesitated.

"Come, I said."

Cate decided that she was being ridiculous. Here was a nice man trying to help her out. Not like his spiteful wife. Joanasi drove her back to his place, speeding over bumps that made the seat springs squeak. He clouded up the truck with cigarette smoke and nodded to the drivers of the vehicles they passed on the way. He pulled up onto their property and shifted into park. Cate noticed the skid mark where she had fallen earlier. "By the way, I'm Cate," she said.

Inside the house, the vacuum was going. Something strong and gamey was boiling on the stove. A kid with crusty mucus under his nose ran to see who his father had brought home. "*Qinauvit*?"

Cate pointed to herself. "Me? *Cate-uvunga*."

He giggled and tugged on her coat sleeve.

Joanasi picked out a parka and a pair of snow pants from the jumble of outerwear hanging in the entranceway. "Here, put these on."

Cate accepted them without a word.

"And use these instead of yours." He passed her some bulky animal-hide mitts trimmed with fur. She wondered if they were Nuna's; they looked about her size.

Lucy appeared wrapping the cord around the vacuum cleaner. She glared at Cate, then at Joanasi. She chided him in Inuktitut. Joanasi cut her off. He lowered his voice. Cate fingered the stitching on the parka he had told her to wear, pretending not to hear. She put on the snow pants. Lucy turned on her heel and stomped into the kitchen.

Joanasi bent down to pick up a different child, the diapered one from earlier. He sniffed his neck and face. He blew a raspberry on his stomach. The child giggled. Joanasi put him down and asked Cate if she had kids.

"No." It was the first time she felt funny saying it.

Joanasi led her outside.

"Where are we going, anyway?"

"Be patient." Joanasi unhooked the wooden sled from his Skidoo. He mounted and started the engine, gesturing for Cate to hop on behind him. He turned his head slightly and shouted over the motor. "You okay back there?"

"I think so!"

"Then hold on tight."

She put a hand on his shoulder, the other wrapped around his waist.

Joanasi sped up past a mangy dog, scrounging around for animal scraps. He turned onto the airport road and accelerated against the wind, past the police station and the last of the houses, past the tarmac and all signs of life. He drove past a moraine of broken furniture and appliances, dead Skidoos and rusted engines, the village dump Nuna fondly called their Canadian Tire, where they could go and forage for the parts they needed to make old things work again.

Cate turned to look behind them as the village went from a blur to a speck, to nothing at all. She was thankful for Joanasi, her human shield against the elements. "Where are we going?" she asked again. She pulled the scarf over her nose.

It was a Harris painting, all snow and ice and outcrops of rock. It was what everyday people who didn't know better imagined the North to be, a fearsome land that needed to be conquered. A place of hungry creatures that peered out from the crevices of nature, eyes darting nervously. Caribou. Geese. Polar bears and their arsenal of teeth.

Joanasi cut the engine and pointed into the distance. "Do you see that?"

"You mean that rock over there?"

"It's a caribou."

Cate struggled to make it out.

He turned to face her. "When you're out on the land, you have to look for the movement, not the thing."

Cate squinted. She still saw a rock. "Are you going to shoot it?"

"Do you see a gun here?" He yanked the pull-cord to power up the engine again. The motor startled Cate after the piercing silence. "There's an Inukshuk over there." He pointed in a different direction. "That's where we're going."

They sped toward the last streak of daylight. The closer they got, the more impressive the Inukshuk became, an almost-human presence against the stark landscape.

In no time, they were there. An unfamiliar energy rushed through Cate. Like a shiver but protracted. The Inukshuk was about seven feet high.

He found them a comfortable spot at the base and invited her to sit. "I bet you thought it was just a pile of rocks balancing on each other," he said. "Right?"

"Pretty much." Cate played along, even though she, like many Canadians, knew what an Inukshuk was. The stone marker had become a cultural icon. It was on the flag of Nunavut. It was the official logo for the 2010 Vancouver Winter Olympic Games. Likenesses, of every material and size, were sold in every gift shop across the country. Glass ones, plastic ones, quilted ones. Ones in cheap metal you could hang around your neck. She knew darn well what they were. She didn't know why she was being disingenuous except that this was his turf and she decided that he should have the upper hand.

He lit a cigarette.

She desperately wanted one but remembered that the pack she had bought was in her other coat. "I've seen them around. Inukshuks, I mean."

He studied the figure as though he were looking at it for the first time. "Inuksuit. Plural. Means pretend people. You've probably seen them in museums and government buildings."

She nodded. She wanted to smoke. Maybe smoking together, she thought, would establish a bond of trust. Smoking had a certain cachet. It united people who couldn't or wouldn't kick the habit, puffing outside their workplaces in every kind of weather. It gave strangers with nothing in common a common ritual. Something to do with their hands while they shot the breeze. When you're smoking together, you're not killing each other, Liam once remarked. Cate touched Joanasi's arm. "Can I steal a cigarette?"

He gave her one, along with his lighter. The sky was a deep magenta.

She tried for a flame, but the wind kept blowing it out. She tried again, and again.

He handed her his cigarette. "Here. Use this."

She held the fiery tip to hers, sucking until it finally ignited and burned on its own. She inhaled deeply the way she did in the old days. Together, smoking, they admired the Inukshuk.

She was conscious of silence. She thought of the chattering soundtrack of her life, texts and Tweets, traffic and small talk. Television. She thought of the incessant buzz of electricity in the atmosphere.

He cleared his throat and spat an orbit of phlegm. "In our culture it's forbidden to destroy them."

She heard the silences between his words, the lilting air. The wind brushed her face. "What are they for?" The cigarette was helping her act more naturally around him.

"There are different kinds and they're called different things. Some show where the hunting or fishing is good, some are warnings to travellers. Some provide food for those in need. Sometimes hunters hide behind them so they can sneak up on their prey." He scanned the land with humble respect. "I brought you here because I wanted you to experience what we experience. Big land, big sky. The smell of rock and rain and snow. You people in Montreal don't understand that." He tossed his cigarette sideways into the snow. "You don't accept the fact that you're only stardust."

Cate nodded.

"Sure, the city is fun for a while. You have movie theatres and bars and shopping centres, and everything costs less than it costs here, but Nuna was lost there. This is her place, we are her people. She belongs here."

Cate didn't know what was true anymore. Isabel had convinced her that Nuna would be a goner unless they stepped in, that she'd eventually end up in a gutter somewhere, dead. Cate accepted it without question. She had clung to the idea that without their intervention, Nuna would have a more difficult life. That she needed Cate to be her teacher. Someone who knew better than Nuna did what betterment might look like. With her support, Nuna would become a "better" version of herself.

But Cate was beginning to see that perhaps she had had an incomplete understanding. Her role as a teacher should not have been to impart knowledge but to accompany Nuna on her inner journey—toward her own questions and answers. "I don't know what to say."

"Just listen, then." He reached for another cigarette but changed his mind. "Do you know how it feels to wake up at the crack of dawn and head out of town on a Skidoo or boat to go fishing or hunting? How it feels to stand at the breathing hole, sometimes for hours, until a seal tugs at the line? Or what it feels like to cut up a freshly killed goose or caribou? Down south, time is so precious, but here, time is only day and night. If Monday comes along and the hunting is good, the job at the municipal office or the school or the Co-op has to wait." His eyes sparkled. "We know what our priorities are."

Cate smoked her cigarette down to the filter before chucking it. She pictured Nuna on the ice, wearing the same snow pants Cate was wearing. She imagined her slitting and cleaning a boatload of fish, the sun reflecting off her shiny black hair. She thought of her wide smile—and her mischievous canine tooth that stuck out when she was happy. Cate contemplated the giant slabs of the Inukshuk, behind which the earliest hunters hid with bows and arrows while women and children chased their prey into the crosshairs. She didn't say it, but she was embarrassed. Here she was, a respected scholar, and never had she learned anything about the cultural infrastructure here. Not really. She had read things, certainly, but none of the books ever accurately expressed how the land had its own heartbeat, its own inherent validity. It didn't need people like Cate to give it meaning.

Joanasi stood up and brushed the snow off his pants. It was dark. "We should probably get going."

Cate didn't want to leave. Stars lit the sky, thousands with their hot white light, a fraction, Cate knew, of the tens of billions of trillions of stars visible to the human eye. They made her feel safe. Protected.

The ride home was colder and something about the air had sharpened Cate's senses. She remembered an afternoon she found Nuna seated with her elbow propped on the kitchen table, head resting in her hand. It reminded her of Rodin's bronze statue. "What are you thinking about?" Cate asked.

"Nothing," Nuna said. "Why do I have to be thinking about something?"

"Because that's what the mind does," Cate said. "You always have thoughts running around in the background without being aware of them, there's no way of turning them off. The brain is always active." Nuna shrugged. Cate persisted. "Just try meditating one day and you'll see how almost impossible it is to think of nothing for more than a few seconds. Slowly, thoughts flood back, first one and then another until your mind is filled to bursting: what groceries do I need today, do I need to do laundry, is there enough gas in the car, and on and on ad infinitum." Nuna gawked at her as though she'd never had a such a pointless conversation in her life.

The village reappeared over the airport road, porch lights winking yellow and orange. Cate thought of the people in their houses making dinner, watching TV, rocking children to sleep. So many families living their lives. Like yet unlike the people back home. She remembered the night when she let go and surrendered to Isabel. When her rational mind dissolved, and she became matter and energy. When she got closer to truth than she had ever been.

She remembered her supper date with Monsieur Cigarette.

Before dropping her back at the hotel, Joanasi stopped at his place so that Cate could change back into her clothes. Her coat, the one from the army surplus store, felt tight across her chest. It didn't protect her from the cold the way the other one had.

Joanasi pulled up to the hotel.

Cate tried one last time. "Tell me honestly. Do you have any idea where Nuna is?"

Joanasi smiled. "I think it's time you went home. Nuna is where she's supposed to be."

On some level, Cate understood. She removed her mitt, shook Joanasi's hand, and walked up the steps, without checking for polar bears.

He revved his engine.

Cate stopped cold, remembering Nuna's journal. She shouted and waved her hands at Joanasi. "Hey! Wait! Don't go yet!"

He nodded.

Cate scrambled up the steps and unlocked the door on her first try. She clomped past the hotel clerk in her wet boots, promising to clean up her mess. She burst into her room and rummaged through her luggage until she found the blue Moleskine journal. The photobooth strip slipped out and fell to the floor. She stooped and examined it, carefully tearing off the last picture, the one with Nuna making a heart with her hands, the best of the four images. She tucked the rest back inside the book. Joanasi was waiting. She hugged it to her chest. As she flew past the reception desk, the clerk blurted something out, but Cate didn't hear her. She didn't even know if it was directed at her. She bounded down the steps and put the notebook in Joanasi's hands. "Would you please give this to Nuna when you see her?"

She didn't know if Nuna would even want it. She hoped so. She hoped it still meant something special to her.

*

Fat Jimmy, the hotel driver, arrived five minutes late to pick up Cate and take her to the airport. A pinecone air freshener, dangling from the mirror, hardly masked the smell of smoke and animal fur.

Jimmy had shoulder-length hair, a face full of acne, and a pleasant demeanor. He was more of a gabber than Joanasi. "Hopefully you'll get out today. Crosswinds are a big problem in this village. If the plane overshoots, you'll be stuck here."

She glanced up at the sky. The snow was coming down in needles. "I hope not."

"I hear you. But Negafook might have other plans." He pulled over to let a dump truck pass, then muscled back onto the road. The wipers made loud rubbery noises.

"Who's Negafook?"

"He's what the Inuit from Alaska call the North Wind. Negafook loves cold, stormy weather."

"Well, I really have to get home, I'm in the middle of some… Well… I'm dealing with a complicated situation."

Jimmy coughed, opened and shut the door to spit before lighting a cigarette. "Then you better pray to him, eh? Weather is the great equalizer."

Cate could hear the wheeze in his chest.

"It doesn't care if you're a bear, a caribou, or if you're a Qallunaaq."

She laughed politely. "Hey, not to change the subject, but I've been meaning to ask someone. I've seen a lot of women around town with tattoos on their faces, especially V-shaped ones."

"Hey, they used to tell us in school never to say hey, hay is for horses. But since we don't have horses up here, it's okay, eh?" He chuckled. "Just kidding." He puffed on his cigarette. "Face tattoos are called *tunnitt* in our language."

"Are they just decorative or do they mean something?"

"The one with a V is for Sedna, the sea goddess. Women get that tattoo so that Sedna will recognize them in the afterlife."

Cate wished she had planned a longer stay; there was so much to learn here, so much history.

"It's a big thing these days, tattoos. It's a way of reconnecting with our ancestors."

Something off the road caught her attention, a presence in the landscape. It flickered in her peripheral vision. She turned to look, remembering what Joanasi had told her. In the North, you focused on the movement, not the object. The break in the pattern, the moving vector. That was how you spotted your prey. How you tipped the scales in favour of eating that night. Your survival depended on it. She pointed. "Is that a fox out there?"

"Good eye. But no. It's a dog."

Cate smiled. She might have gotten it wrong, but she understood the lesson.

Jimmy pulled into the parking lot. He opened the back of the truck and lifted out her bag. She followed him inside, where people with carry-on luggage drank from Styrofoam coffee cups, waiting for the plane to arrive. A giggling toddler was running around like a wind-up toy. Cate stared. She didn't mind the disturbance.

She checked the screen for departures. The plane was on time. She thanked Jimmy and offered him a twenty. He refused. "At least take my cigarettes then. You'll be doing me a favour."

"I won't say no."

Soon, the plane they were all waiting for landed. It taxied along the runway and came to a stop. Workers in fluorescent vests scurried out to unload the aircraft. The ticket agent called the passengers to the exit. Cate joined the line. It felt like she'd been there for a hundred years. It felt like a minute. She handed the agent her ticket.

"Montreal?"

Cate nodded. And just like that, she was headed home, walking along the tarmac with a handful of strangers, all with their own struggles and successes, following the same orange cones she'd followed when she arrived. She felt strangely free. Free from Nuna's grip on her, free from her grip on Nuna. Free to admit that there had always been an unequal power dynamic even though she told herself that theirs was a relationship of equals. Free to accept that she couldn't solve other people's problems. The world was rife with uncertainty. It was filled with stories. Some of them intersected and some never did. And each story had its own author, its own beginning and sort-of ending—and a litany of detours in between. Headed home, Cate understood. She finally understood that Nuna's story wasn't hers—or Isabel's—to finish.

*

Waleed was cooking. Something from the Old Country, as he liked to say, one of his mother's recipes, a favourite of his, chickpea stew with tabouleh and a side of hummus. For dessert, *ghraybeh*, a Lebanese shortbread and a bowl of Medjool dates. He'd been at it all day now that classes had ended for the Christmas break.

A week ago, he greeted Cate at the airport, having done what she had asked him to do: move some of the essentials out of her house—her winter clothes, books, her laptop. He told her she could stay indefinitely now that they were both single and feeling their way forward.

Waleed insisted that Cate take his room. He made up a bed for himself on the living room couch. He opened the closet and indicated the space he had made for her clothes. It felt strange sleeping in the room where she and Liam had first made out.

Waleed refused to tell her why he and Daniel had broken up. He didn't want to talk about it. A guest in his home, she waited. She gave him his space. When enough time had passed, according to her way of thinking, she told him enough was enough, he knew her story, she deserved to know his.

Cate rustled up a bottle of wine. He said no, not that, bring the arak.

"That moonshine?" Cate joked. She filled two tumblers with ice.

"Yallah," he said. "Pour."

Waleed had introduced her to arak in grad school. He promised that the licorice flavour was an acquired taste that she would eventually come to appreciate and enjoy. He was right and it soon became a December tradition, their go-to drink to toast the end of a semester, another cohort come and gone.

They sat on opposite ends of the couch, feet touching.

"You go first," Cate said.

"Tsk, tsk. Why me?"

"Because you already know my story. What are you hiding from me?"

"I'm not hiding anything. Just delaying telling you." They shot back their drinks in unison the way they always did, draining their glasses. Waleed jiggled his ice cubes around. He picked one out, sucked on it and spat it back. "I see your eczema's clearing up."

"Nice try, but no changing the subject."

"Okay." He poured them another.

"Well?"

It turned out that it wasn't his father, after all, who had come to visit but his brother, Hakim, the doctor. He came bearing news, news that deserved to be told in person, about their father who had lost his will to live, who had grown gaunt and stopped taking care of himself, who had decided, one night, to leave the house and walk out onto the metro tracks. Waleed gulped his arak. He dabbed the corner of his eye.

"Holy shit!"

"Luckily, he wasn't electrocuted. They shut down the power immediately. The fire department and first responders came to remove him and take him in for a psychiatric evaluation."

"Why didn't you tell me this before?"

"I wanted to leave you be until you were sorted out."

"But this is huge." Cate gasped. "I'm sorry you had to go through it alone."

Waleed shrugged. "You had your own stuff to deal with." He summarized the rest, that Hakim had come on behalf of their mother, who'd always known there was something unresolved between her husband and son, something huge and life-altering. Hakim explained that these days their mother spent all her mornings by his father's side in the hospital and all her evenings at home cursing God for doing this to them.

"You've never told her that you're gay?"

"Not in so many words." He tossed back his drink. "I think she might have suspected, though."

"I can't imagine a mother not knowing a thing so fundamental about her child."

He sighed. "The thing is, my father found out. He saw it with his own eyes."

"How? When?"

He waved her to the table. "I was doing my shift at the store." He shook his head. "It was the day after my eighteenth birthday. My father showed up unexpectedly and caught me with the Serbian guy who usually brought our deliveries in. We were in the stockroom."

"Ouch. But what does any of this have to do with you and Daniel?"

Waleed sneered. "Family."

"I get it, but..."

"No, you don't. My parents aren't assimilated. They're the Muslims who pray to Allah five times a day, not the cultural ones who drink and intermarry. And tolerate their children's *deviant* behaviour."

"Okay, but you're the one always pushing me to go for the moon and everything else be damned. Even when you were hesitant, you always chose the road not taken. It's the reason I'm here now, in a mess, trying to figure things out."

"I know, I'm sorry, Habibti."

"So what happened exactly?"

"I came up with a plan." His breathing sped up. "Before Hakim arrived, I asked Daniel to hide his personal things, I told him to go someplace and have a coffee, wait it out, and that I'd call him, *Insha'allah*, once the coast was clear."

"I can't believe you did that."

He nodded with a look of shame. "Daniel lost it. And I don't blame him. He said if I was that ashamed of him, then he couldn't be with me anymore. So, he packed his things. I begged him to understand. I told him I come from a complicated culture." Waleed frowned. "But I didn't lift a finger to stop him." His eyes glistened with tears.

Cate sighed. Sitting at the table where both men had once sat sharing meals, dreams, life, she wondered whether Waleed regretted the decision that cost him his relationship. Whether he wanted Daniel back or was just doing his best to move on. And if he moved on, wouldn't the same scenario just repeat itself, the hurt compounding until something in his brain convinced him to abandon love forever because he wasn't worthy?

"I shook hands with my brother and agreed to visit my father in the hospital—the next day. He was conscious but heavily sedated. My mother and I sat quietly, the light from the window shining on his face. My father and I exchanged knowing looks. We didn't speak, but I sensed that maybe with time there could be forgiveness. But I've been wrong before." Waleed spooned some tabouleh into Cate's dish. "And what about your missing girl?" He tore her a piece of pita. "Nuna."

Cate put a hand on her chin. "You know, I've been thinking a lot about it lately. I mean, who the hell was I to stick my nose into someone else's life when I was barely muddling through my own?" Her phone dinged. Automatically, she reached for it.

"You aren't the prime minister, it can wait."

"You're right." She put her hand in her lap and tried to come up with something nice to say about the meal, a compliment that would redirect the conversation away from Liam's and her divorce. Everything always seemed to link back to that. She remembered an Arabic phrase he had taught her, about blessing the hands of the one who made the food. She forced herself to get the pronunciation right. "Uh, *Yesallem … edeiki kelshi tayyeb*."

Waleed smiled. "Thank you, I'm honoured."

They ate heartily, chatting about work-related things, what her plans were after the sabbatical, where she intended to live. She had no answers except to see where the road took her. "I guess I'll go where I have to go." Her phone went off again.

"Leave it." He forked some tabouleh into his mouth. "How's your paper for the symposium coming along? What's the title again?"

"'Settler Narratives in Early Canadian Art and Poetry.' And, well, to be perfectly honest, it isn't."

"Do tell."

"The other night I dreamt about it."

He leaned forward on his elbows. "Now you've piqued my curiosity."

Cate clasped her hands. "So, uh, everything starts off normally—in the dream, I mean—I'm about to give my talk." She accelerated, building up the drama. "I'm at the lectern, nervous as hell. My throat is dry, so I pour myself some water from the pitcher. For some weird reason, Isabel is offstage, behind a curtain. I can sense her presence."

"Go on."

"I'm looking through my briefcase for my notes, but I can't find them. Anywhere. I start to freak out. I cover the mic and ask Isabel to bring them to me."

Waleed put a hand over his mouth.

"But Isabel isn't Isabel anymore, she's Nuna. I look out at the audience but there's no one there. The auditorium is dark. Every seat is empty. Then Nuna steps out from behind the curtain and hands me my notes. I put on my glasses but can't read anything. Not a single thing that's written. So I take them off, breathe on the lenses, and wipe the fog away with my thumb. And guess what? I still can't see. It's like when the font is so big on your cell phone that the text runs off the screen." Cate sipped her water.

"Help me read this, Nuna, I tell her, but she shakes her head, and says no, you can do it, you don't need me. Next thing I know, she's gone." Cate snapped her fingers. "She vanishes into thin air, just like that."

"Y'a Allah."

"So now I'm alone on the stage. A giant spotlight is on me. Suddenly, the place is packed. I toss my notes into the air and improvise something right on the spot. And it's filled with brilliant insights. I'm coherent, the words flow without my having to think about them. When I'm done, the place goes wild. I get a standing ovation."

"Bravo, Habibti."

"Yeah. It was a great dream. Funny thing is, I can't recall a single one of those brilliant insights."

"What are you saying?"

"I'm saying that maybe there won't be a symposium, at least not this one. Maybe I don't even want to teach anymore. Who knows? I don't know."

"Yesterday I was clever, so I wanted to change the world. Today I am wise, so I'm changing myself," Waleed said. "Rumi."

"Could be...but for now, let's have dessert." She got up to clear the dishes off the table, asked him to bring the *habeeb* from the fridge.

He chuckled.

"What?"

"You just told me to take your lover out of the fridge. Milk is *haleeb*."

"Oops, slip of the tongue." Cate smiled, remembering when Isabel called it a slip of the wrist. They had just met in the hospital.

Cate sat at the table while Waleed brewed coffee on the stove the way his mother did, Arabic-style, in a long-handled copper pot. She thought some more about Isabel, her plucky determination, how short their time together had been. She prayed that Isabel would find someone who wouldn't hurt her again, the way she had. The way Hannah had. She closed her eyes and imagined her own new beginnings: the winding roads, the stories waiting to unfold. Her mind expanded and contracted, making room for infinite possibility. She was keenly aware of her own heartbeat, the blood humming in her ears.

Her phone dinged again. Insistent.

She glanced down. It was from the same number that had previously texted, one she didn't recognize. The message, sent to Isabel as well, had an attachment. She clicked on it, squinting. She put on her glasses. The hazy, grey-and-white image resembled hoarfrost. Something afloat, small and nebulous. Cell-like. She enlarged it with her thumb and forefinger. Her pulse quickened.

If she didn't know better, she'd have said it was a sonogram.

It *was* a sonogram.

Her hands shook. She laughed, she wept. She clutched the phone to her bosom. She looked again. Her knees weakened.

The message was short, a single word carefully chosen. Curated, she might say.

Atlantis.

ACKNOWLEDGMENTS

I was on my way to work in 2019 when an ambulance wailed past. I'd just finished reading Elizabeth Gilbert's book on creativity, *Big Magic*, in which she argues that the planet is buzzing with ideas and if one of them senses your openness, "it will start to do its work on you." It will tease you in the middle of the night. It will ask you to collaborate. You can either nurture it, or it will find somebody else. It's fair to say, the ambulance kept me awake; however, I couldn't have completed this novel without the generous contributions of a small village.

Thank you, April Bosshard, "story whisperer," for helping me turn three characters and a vague idea into a novel.

Thanks to my beta readers, Joan Fiedler Mele and Kassandra Churcher for providing helpful feedback on an earlier version; and to Judy Seaman, Joan Boxall, and Candy Haskell for writerly friendship, advice, and support.

To the generous team at Baraka Books, especially Robin Philpot and the late Blossom Thom—thank you for this opportunity. Gratitude to Elise Moser for brilliant insights and editing and for pushing me to get it right.

While some locations in this novel exist, others are fictional. Still others are imagined but loosely based on real places. I am grateful to Joanne Souaid and Pierre Leveillé for all things Ottawa. And to Brock Cummings, for museum research. Thanks to Jeffery Brown and the late Richard King for sharing your expertise and/or first-hand knowledge about emergency room procedures; gracias, Beatriz Meza, for the Spanish translations. All errors are my own.

Nakurmiik iluunnasi: Lizzie Tukai, Suzanne Naluiyuk, Mary Nassak, Julie Katsuak Lussier, Nancy Etok, Thomassie Mangiok, and Jimmy Uquittuk for sharing various details about your culture with me. And to three decades of Nunavik students who have taught me a great deal about Inuit customs and traditions.

Love and gratitude to my family for your unwavering support, encouragement, and a lifetime of laughter; especially to my son, who continues to be curious about the world and its crazy workings. And, fearless. Writing is mostly a solitary pursuit with a steep learning curve. Thank you, Alex, for your vital reminder to follow the thread wherever it leads.

Finally, to Endre Farkas, partner in life and Art—thanks for your insights, editing, sensitivity, and vision. And for always being there for me. Life wouldn't be the same without you.

CREDITS

Excerpt from *Atlantis* by Louis Dudek published in 1967 by Delta Canada. Used with permission from Gregory Dudek.

"The Unnamed Lake" (1897) by Frederick George Scott. Public domain.

Excerpt found in the book *Embers*, by Richard Wagamese published in 2016 by Douglas and McIntyre (2013) Ltd. Reprinted with permission from the publisher.

MIX
Paper
FSC
www.fsc.org FSC® C100212

Printed by Imprimerie Gauvin
Gatineau, Québec